DEC 1 1 2019

D1300381

A Dream Come True

THE COLLECTED STORIES OF JUAN CARLOS ONETTI

Translated from the Spanish by Katherine Silver

archipelago books

First Archipelago Books Edition, 2019

Archipelago Books
232 3rd Street #A111
Brooklyn, NY 11215
www.archipelagobooks.org

Library of Congress Cataloging-in-Publication Data available upon request

Distributed by Penguin Random House
www.penguinrandomhouse.com

Cover art: Jean Dubuffet
Book design: Zoe Guttenplan

This book was made possible by the New York State Council on the Arts
with the support of Governor Andrew M. Cuomo and the New York State Legislature.

Archipelago Books also gratefully acknowledges the generous support of the New York City
Department of Cultural Affairs, the National Endowment for the Arts, Lannan Foundation,
the Carl Lesnor Family Foundation, and the Nimick Forbesway Foundation.

PRINTED IN THE UNITED STATES

Contents

Translator's Note

Many of the stories in this volume take place in Santa María.

Santa María, like Buenos Aires and Montevideo, is a town on a navigable river in the Southern Hemisphere, and most of its inhabitants are immigrants from Europe. Unlike Buenos Aires and Montevideo, however, Santa María exists on the map of Juan Carlos Onetti's imagination and that of his devoted readers. One could say Santa María is Onetti's Macando.

The characters from Santa María – Our Lord Brausen, Dr. Diaz Grey, Jorge Malabia and family, Jeremías "Old Man" Petrus, the Bergner family, among others, are, like their creator, living in exile in Madrid or Paris. They do not have traditionally coherent life trajectories, their ages are often static, and their back stories are sometimes hinted at but never affirmed. "It is demonstrably true that time doesn't exist on its own," Onetti says, seemingly apropos of nothing, in "Death and the Girl," "It is the child of movement, and if things stopped moving we would have neither time nor erosion nor beginnings nor endings. In literature, Time is always written with a capital letter." In literature. In Santa María.

Onetti once wrote "A poet is someone who writes things – not necessarily in verse – that arouse in me mysterious sensations, which I call poetic, for lack of a better word. Full stop."

I can only hope that my rendering in English of this poet's work arouses a host of mysterious sensations in the reader. Full stop.

Katherine Silver

A Dream Come True

Avenida de Mayo – Diagonal – Avenida de Mayo

He crossed the avenue during a pause in the traffic and started walking down Calle Florida. A cold shiver shook his shoulders, and his resolve to be stronger than the adventuring air immediately removed his hands from the shelter of his pockets, increased the curve of his chest, and lifted his head – a divine search through the monotonous sky. He could withstand any temperature; he could live way down south, farther even than Ushuaia.

His lips were sharpening with the same intent that contracted his eyes and squared his jaw.

First, he acquired an extravagant vision of the poles, without huts or penguins; below, white with two patches of yellow; and the sky above, a sky of fifteen minutes before rain.

Then: Alaska – Jack London – thick furs obliterating the anatomies of bearded men, high boots transforming them into toy soldiers that could not be felled in spite of the blue smoke from the long handguns of the chief of the mounted police; instinctively they crouched down, the steam from their breath imitating a halo over their fur hats and filthy brown beards; Tongass bared its teeth along the shores of the Yukon; his gaze like a strong arm swept out to grab the trunks coursing down the river – foam again: Tongass is in Sitka – beautiful Sitka, like the name of a courtesan.

On Rivadavia a car tried to stop him, but a spirited maneuver left it in the dust, along with its accomplice on a bicycle. He carried the car's two headlights, like easily won trophies, toward the desolate Alaskan horizon. In the middle of the block, he effortlessly avoided the warm air in the poster that was resting on Clark Gable's powerful shoulders and Crawford's hips; though he did have the urge to raise to his brow the roses that the star with the big eyes held up in the middle of her chest. Three nights or three months ago he had dreamed about a woman with white roses instead of eyes. But the memory of the dream was merely a flash of lightning to his reason; the memory quickly slipped away, with a flutter, like a sheet of paper just released from a printing press, which settles quietly under the other images that continue to fall.

He installed the stolen headlights on the car in the sky that was copied from the Yukon, and the car's English brand made the dry air of the Nordic night resound with energetic *What*'s, not shuttered away in a muffled room but exploding like gunshots into the cold blue between the giant pine trees, only to rise like rockets into the starry whiteness of the Great Craggy Mountains.

When Brughtton knelt down, shielding the enormous bonfire with his body, and he, Víctor Suaid, stood up next to the Coroner, ready to fire, a woman made her eyes as well as a cross under the fur of her coat shimmer, so close that their elbows touched.

On his mysterious back, Suaid's vest rose and fell like two to the pulse of the breathing, as he sought to embed in his brain the perfume of the woman and the woman herself, mixed with the dry cold of the street.

Between the two opposing currents of pedestrians, the woman soon became a spot that rose and fell, from the shadows into the shop lights then back into the shadows. But the perfume remained with Suaid, gently and decisively expelling the landscape and the men; and from the shores of the Yukon only the snow remained, a strip of snow the width of the roadway.

"The United States bought Alaska from Russia for seven million dollars."

Years before, that fact would have softened the fountain pen of the oldest Astin boy in geography class. Now it was nothing but a pretext for a new reverie.

He made rise lines of mounted soldiers along both sides of the strips of snow. He, the Grand Duke Alexander Ivanovich, marched between them alongside Nicolas II, cleaning the snow off his boots after every step with the edge of his fur-lined ulster.

The emperor swayed as he walked, like that Englishman, the assistant traffic manager at Central Station. His small boots shimmered to a martial beat, which was by now the only possible expression of his mobility.

"Stalin ended the drought in the Volga."

"Congratulations to the boatmen, Your Majesty!"

The tsar's gold eyetooth reassured him. Nothing mattered at all – energy, energy – and his pectoral muscles tensed under the curve of the cordons and the large cross, the ancient beard of Verchenko, the conspirator.

He stopped at Diagonal, where the Boston Building slumbered under the grey sky across the street from the parking lot.

Naturally, María Eugenia came to the foreground with the swirl of her white skirts.

Only once, years ago, had he seen her in white. So well disguised as a schoolgirl that the two simultaneous punches of her breasts against the fabric, colliding with the purity of the large black ribbon, turned the little girl into a mature, skeptical, and weary adult woman.

He was afraid. Anxiety began to rise in short bursts into his chest till it almost reached his throat. He lit a cigarette and leaned against a wall.

His legs were shackled with indifference and his attention drew down, like the sails on an anchored ship.

With the silence of the moviemakers of his childhood, the neon letters sailed along the tracks of the sign: YESTERDAY IN BASEL, MORE THAN TWO THOUSAND VICTIMS.

He turned his head in anger.

"Let them all blow up!"

He knew that María Eugenia was coming. He knew that he'd have to do something and his heart totally lost its rhythm. It annoyed him to have to lean into that thought; to know that, no matter how much his brain would stumble through labyrinths before stopping to rest, he would meet María Eugenia at a crossroads.

Nevertheless, he automatically made an attempt to escape: "For a cigarette . . . I would go to the ends of the earth . . ."

Twenty thousand posters proclaimed their plague upon the city. The man with perfect teeth and hair offered his red hand, the pack showing two cigarettes – ¼ and ¾ – like cannons on a destroyer taking aim at the boredom of the passersby.

" . . . to the ends of the earth."

María Eugenia was coming in her white dress. Before the surfaces of her face became features, between the slopes of black hair, he tried to stop the attack. Fear rumbled at the level of his tonsils.

"Woman!"

Desperate, he climbed up to the neon letters that were popping, one by one, as gently as bubbles off the black wall: RACER MCCORMICK BREAKS WORLD LAND SPEED RECORD.

Hope gave him the strength to expel the smoke in one blow, joining the *o* of his mouth to the landscape.

EED RECORD — TODAY IN MIAMI

The trail of smoke conveniently camouflaged the profile that had begun to take shape. Forming a triangle with the wall's rough skin and the square-checkered ground, his body stayed put. The cigarette between his fingers announced a suicide with the slow thread of smoke.

TODAY IN MIAMI REACHING AN AVERAGE SPEED

On the gold sand, between loud shouts, Jack Ligett, the "manager," polished and repolished the shiny parts of the engine. The car, named after a bird of prey, looked like a gigantic black lobster, tirelessly holding the razorblade of the prow with its two extra legs.

The twisted organ pipes, port and starboard, each emitted twenty simultaneous blasts, which rose in slow billows. With the edge of the wheels at the same level as his ears, the race began. Each blast resonated triumphantly inside his skull and velocity was the space between two footprints, transformed into a viper dancing in his belly.

He looked at McCormick's face, dark skin stretched over thin bones. Under his leather helmet, behind his grotesque goggles, his eyes were hard with courage, and, out of the smile thirsty for kilometers that just barely stretched his mouth, there filtered a brief order, condensed into a verb in the infinitive.

Suaid leaned over the pump and hit the car to push it forward. He hit it till the wind became a bellow and the wheels gently touched the ground, which quickly repelled them, as a roulette wheel does the marble ball. He hit until the viper in his belly ached, as thin and rigid as a needle.

But the image was forced, and the futility of this effort became evident, certain, without any possible subterfuge.

Escape was thwarted as if under a blast of water, and Suaid was left with his face half buried in the ground, his arms waving with the same movements as a semaphore.

"To hide myself..."

But he slid under himself, as if the ground were a mirror and his last *I* the reflected image.

He looked at his veiled eyes and the damp earth in his left socket. The tip of his nose was squished, like those of children looking through shop windows, and his jaws champed at the hard, smooth sheet of anguish. His thin blond hair edged onto his forehead, and the patch of beard on his neck was turning violet.

He squeezed his eyes tightly shut and tried to submerge himself; but his nails slipped on the mirror. Vanquished, his body slackened, surrendered, alone, on the corner of Diagonal.

He was the center of a circle of serenity that continued to expand, wiping out buildings and people.

Then he saw himself, small and alone, in the middle of that infinite quietude that kept spreading. Gently, he remembered Franck, the last of the clay soldiers he would smash; in his memory, the doll, when viewed from afar, had only one leg and the blackened U of its mustache.

He looked at himself from many meters above, tenderly observing the familiar shape of his shoulders, the hollow of his neck, and his left ear flattened by his hat.

Slowly he unbuttoned his coat, pulled on the bottom of his vest, and again slipped the buttons into the slits of the buttonholes. Once he'd concluded this deliberate act, he became sad and serene, with María Eugenia stuck in his chest.

Now the scabs of indifference that protected his own disquietude dropped away and the outside world began to reach him.

Without needing to think about it, he started back down Calle Florida. The street, devoid of reveries, had lost Tongass's teeth and the blond beard of His Imperial Majesty.

The brightness of the shop windows and the large lamps hanging from the street corners lent the narrow sidewalk an intimate atmosphere. He felt a yearning for a nineteenth-century salon, so refined that the men did not need to remove their hats.

He quickened his step, wanting to erase an indefinite feeling with touches of weakness and tenderness, which began to work its way in.

A machine gun on every side street could do away with all this riffraff.

It was nightfall everywhere in the world.

In Puerta del Sol, on Regent Street, on Boulevard Montmartre, on Broadway, on Unter den Linden, in all the most crowded places in all the cities, the throngs pressing together, just like yesterday's and tomorrow's. Tomorrow! Suaid smiled with an air of mystery.

The machine guns were hidden on balconies, in newspaper stands, in flowerpots, on rooftops. They were all different sizes and all of them were clean, a ray of cold and joyous light on the polished barrels.

Owen was sprawled in an armchair, smoking. The window, under the angle formed by his legs, let in the blinking of the first neon signs, the muffled sounds of the city, growing dimmer, and the pallor of the sky.

Suaid, sitting next to his telegraph machine, stalked the passing of the seconds with a malignant smile. He awaited, more than the blasts of the machine guns, the decisive moment when Owen's facial muscles would tremble, revealing emotions through the corneas of his light eyes.

The Englishman kept smoking until a click of the clock announced that the small hammer was rising to strike the first blow in that series of seven, which would then be reproduced, unexpectedly and multitudinously, under the bells of all the skies in the Western World.

Owen rose and threw away his cigarette.

"*Ya.*"

Suaid started walking, trembling with nervous happiness. Nobody on Calle Florida knew how oddly literary his feeling was. The tall women and the doorman at the Grand were equally oblivious to the polyfurcation Owen's *ya* took on in his brain. Because *ya*, or *ja*, could be either Spanish or German; and from here there arose unforeseen paths, paths where Owen's incomprehensible figure split into a thousand different shapes, many of them antagonistic.

Facing the traffic on the avenue, he wanted the machine guns to rapidly entone, amid balls of smoke, their rosary of drawn-out stories.

But he couldn't make it happen, and he returned to his contemplation of Calle Florida.

He felt tired and calm, as if he had cried for a long time. Tamely, with a grateful smile for María Eugenia, he approached the window glass and the multicolored lights, which sheltered the street with their rhythmic pulse.

1933

The Obstacle

He stopped gradually, fearing that the abrupt cessation of his footsteps would violently destabilize the ensemble of sounds mixed with the silence. Silence and shadows along a swath that ran from the muffled roar of the brightly lit factory to the four windows of the club, closed to no avail against the laughter and the clinking of glasses, and, at moments, the billiards shots. Silence and shadows peppered with the quivering of crickets on the ground and of stars in the lofty black sky.

It must have already been ten o'clock, so there was no danger. He turned right and entered the woods, treading carefully on the crunching leaves and carrying his pack on his back, his arms crossed over his chest. Dark and cold; but he knew the way by heart, and his half-open mouth warmed his chest, long warm brushstrokes slipping under his striped grey shirt.

He stopped again in front of the whitewashed gate. There, under the dangerous light of the streetlamps, began the sidewalk made of square bricks outlined in white that led to the administration building. If they see me, I'll say I couldn't sleep. They won't say anything. I just went out for a bit of fresh air. He lobbed one leg over the mesh, but had a thought that calmed him, mounted on top of the barbed wire. How changed everything was! Ten years ago . . . He stopped thinking, but a quick sequence of memories came to him, clear and familiar by virtue of being always the same . . . That summer morning they brought him to school . . . The principal's office, the fat man looking at him affectionately from behind his glasses and patting him on the back.

"You look like a good boy, Brownie." He laughed because Brownie was so weak and small. "You're not going to run away, are you?"

He swung over his other leg and sat there. And I didn't run away. But when that one retired and the German came . . . He smiled.

When they brought the German . . . He balanced on the barbed wire, watching the evening flee, the shelter of the reeds, the men bending over him, taking turns beating him.

Sons of –

He shuddered at the sound of his own voice and started walking quickly through the trees. Sons of bitches. And they were all the same. He tripped on a tree trunk and looked around, opening his eyes wide. The trench, the trunk of the eucalyptus tree, the lance on the old stockade . . . No, it was farther on. He kept going. He was trying to remember when they'd installed the brick sidewalk and the streetlamps and the barbed wire. He was sure it was when they built the new administration building, but now he thought he'd seen the gym teacher watching them as they worked on the sidewalk. And since the teacher arrived long after they'd inaugurated the new building . . . He smelled tobacco and stopped, his back pressed against a tree . . . Yes, there they were. He saw their faces redden slightly next to the cigarettes. He gave two soft whistles, two short and one long. They answered, and he went straight to where the others were waiting.

"Hi, Brownie."

"Hey."

"You're just getting here?"

Barreiro was sitting on the ground, his hands clutching his knees. Slim was lying on his back on the grass, smoking, a cigarette planted between his lips. He glanced at them and then at the windows of the club. No way to know what time they'll tire of playing. Already on the ground, he kept thinking with delight about the room in the club and the voices rising through the floating blue smoke, the soft leather armchairs, and the enormous portrait over the fireplace. And the brick sidewalk and the string of lights hanging over the street weren't there when they built the director's house. That's for sure; it doesn't matter, he kept seeing the gym teacher, with his white canvas hat and his hands in his pockets, talking to the men building the sidewalk. He shrugged his shoulders and pulled his cap down over his eyes.

"Give me a cigarette."

Laboriously, Slim dug his hand into his pants pocket, held out the pack, then returned to his former position, the cigarette hanging out of one side of his mouth, his half-closed eyes looking straight up. Barreiro handed him a light.

"So, tonight's the night, eh?"

He lit it and took a strong drag, warming himself with the harsh smoke.

"Yeah. As soon as they turn off the lights in the club, we're off."

"Wouldn't it be better to go straight through the farm to the road?"

"No, we'll go along the stream."

The other again crossed his hands over his lap . . . Carefully, Slim took the cigarette and threw it far away. He lifted his head to watch the ember go out. Then he spit, crossed his hands behind his neck, and laughed softly.

"Hey, Brownie . . . What if tonight the director decides to make you factory foreman? And you out there, hungry . . ."

He laughed again as he crossed his legs.

"Don't worry . . . They're going to pick that ass-licker Fernández. The engineer told me this afternoon."

Barreiro looked at him with a friendly smile:

"So . . . you're coming with us?"

"You bet . . . they've jerked me around long enough."

Slim laughed again, and, not knowing why, Brownie felt like pissing on his face; but he said nothing and kept smoking, observing through the blur of smoke the yellow squares on the club's façade. It would be lovely to be inside, sitting in an armchair with his feet up on the table and ordering something strong to drink. Taking billiards shots again and again, never missing one, until he'd had enough. Playing cards, he and the director against the doctor and the engineer. A game of *truco* in which his hand would fill with flowers and thirty-eights. But even better would be to start bashing the employees, the lights, and the bottles. Sons of bitches . . .

Sinking into his sudden hatred, he felt Slim's laughter tinged with personal insult. He waited, clenching his teeth.

"You know Forchela's sick?" He turned his head quickly to look at Slim's pale, wicked face.

"He can piss off!"

Slim laughed again, now for a long time, his chest heaving and shaking. He muttered:

"What a way you have of treating your —" he said, and Brownie leaped up, his eyes locked on the face he was about to smash with his boot.

"My *what* did you say?"

He didn't care what they said to him; he didn't care about saying it himself. But he knew that Slim made fun of him behind his back, and he sensed it was driven by bitter malice.

"Come on, cut it out. . . . You're not going to fight now," Barreiro intervened, afraid that their dispute would doom their escape. "I was at the hospital this afternoon. Forchela's delirious."

He bit down on his cigarette with rage and glued his eyes on the windows. They wouldn't leave before twelve. If the nurse let him in . . .

Barreiro stretched out his arms and yawned. Then he lay down.

"Why don't you go around to the hospital?"

"Yeah. You gotta say goodbye to your friends," the other said in a hoarse voice.

Brownie took a few steps, hesitated, tried to guess the others' thoughts. Then he said loudly:

"Me? What do I care . . ." He put on his jacket, adding between clenched teeth:

"I'm going to take a walk. Anyhow, before midnight . . ."

He was still expecting something: a movement, an expression of protest or suspicion that would help him to assert himself from within, to understand why he was now weak and restless. But they didn't help him, and he had to go back through the trees, looking with furrowed brow at the motionless leaves that the light of a lantern slipping through the branches made softly shine every so often.

Ten years earlier. Everything had changed, and the gym teacher spent the bright morning calmly chatting with the bricklayers. Behind the windowpane the kind eyes of the director shine as he pats him on the shoulder. "You're not going to run away . . ."

He shook his head to sink it into other thoughts. Within two hours they will be running across the wet earth, slipping between the sheathed stalks of the reeds. Buenos Aires. He thought of the city and felt uneasy as he scratched the rough surface of the gate.

Because behind that city's name was the neighborhood of Bajo Flores, the newspapers sold in the plaza, the corner of the Banco Español, his first cigarette, and the first time he stole from the grocery store. There was his childhood, neither sad nor happy, but with the unmistakable features of a strange and different life, one he could not now fully understand. But there was also the Buenos Aires created by the stories of the other boys and the employees, the photographs in the heavy Sunday newspapers. The soccer fields, the music of the shooting galleries of Leandro Alem.

Brooding, he kicked his heels into the fence and a vibration ran rapidly through the shadows. He was unable to reconcile the images, comprehend that the city contained both things. Sometimes, Buenos Aires was the people surrounding the red pavilion they put up on Saturday afternoons in San José de Flores; at others, a street flanked by colorful signs with blinking lights, past which people walked, laughing and talking in loud voices. And there was always, next to the welcoming entrance to the shooting range, a blond and drunken sailor, with a rose held captive between his teeth.

He was snapped out of it by the sound of footsteps, and Barreiro, already next to him, didn't give him time to get scared.

"Look, Brownie."

He was talking quickly, a cigarette in his mouth, his fists digging into his waist, a vague translation of a jot of resolve and challenge.

"Just warning you, if you stay, we'll go all the same."

"Of course we'll go. The three of us. What's this about?"

Barreiro shook his head and looked away.

"No, nothing. Just wanted to tell you, that's all. That we'll go all the same."

Brownie shrugged his shoulders. He was choking on a pile of words and fierce, incomprehensible hatred. While Barreiro peered over the gate to get a look at the club, he breathed uneasily and narrowed his eyes.

"When will those people leave . . ."

Barreiro tightened his belt and walked away noiselessly, disappearing slowly into the darkness.

Brownie watched the white line of his shirt collar as it slipped away beneath the trees, until it was gone. He swung his legs over the barbed wire and continued walking through the night.

He stopped, undecided, inhaling the indistinct smell of disinfectant. Like a skeleton in a museum, the trellis of Pavilion A. He knew that he would have to pass through the main ward, and the boys who were still awake would see him. Shame that they would know that he had come at that hour to see Forchela. Mocking looks and dirty jokes would tie up his legs. He leaned against the posts entwined by roses. A flower, the last one, was hiding its yellowish petals against the white slat. Since they were going to laugh anyway, he would beat them to it. He would walk through the hall with a cynical smile, the rose held high.

He picked it and climbed the three steps. In the hall, the nurse was sitting and reading on a bench, noisily sucking maté through his straw.

"Hi Brownie. What are you doing here at this time of night?"

"Nothing. . . They sent me to see if the tools were put away, and I thought . . ."

The nurse took off his glasses and looked at him for a moment, focusing on the hand that held the hat and the flower. In spite of the open invitation on the boy's face, he didn't smile. Maybe he didn't know how. He put down the newspaper and rose with a tired air.

"Did they tell you about Forchela? If you want to see him . . . He might not make it through the night."

He followed him past rows of beds, without seeing anything, his face now hanging in an idiotic expression as he mechanically hid the rose in his pants pocket. Words leaped out at him from among the grey blankets on the beds; but they all fell without touching him, as if vanquished in midair by their lack of weight.

Alone in the small room, at the foot of the bed, he tried to fight off the drowsiness that enveloped him. He leaned on the bedpost and smiled at the head on the pillow. The nurse straightened the blankets, took the patient's pulse, and stood up, saying:

"If you've got nothing else to do, stay for a while. I'm going to the pharmacy to prepare some medicine."

Brownie nodded, but he didn't understand anything, looking with terror at Forchela's thin, red face that moved rhythmically as he struggled to breathe. Something of the boy remained in the fair hair, in the teeth where the light became a streak, maybe in the round forehead. But everything else was the face of an old man, a disgusting old man ravaged by sin.

He stared at him, hypnotized by a strange fear, afraid to talk or move, waiting with the idea that the other would wake up, smile at him with his burning, wilted mouth, and even look at him with his glass eyes.

He made an effort and managed to pull himself away from the bed, taking several silent steps across the flagstone floor. In vain he searched for something to stare at on the clean tiled walls. He stood next to the partially open window, where the night air helped him cling to the idea of escape. Before morning, they would be passing the stables, two blocks from the road. At dawn, on the corner of the grocery store . . . But immediately he turned, afraid to give him his back, certain that if he didn't pay attention, the dying man would smile, lift his head, his eyelids, his thin crumpled hands. Cold and terrible things because death had already entered his body, and the slightest movement could spill it into the room.

He approached the bed, took the clipboard off its hook. Name: Pedro Panón. Argentinean. Diagnosis. He didn't understand the strange words written in round letters or the zigzagging black line that plotted the fever. Then he sighed and knitted his brow, comforted in the cowardice of pretending that he was engrossed in the hesitant broken line, that he was carefully analyzing the patient's condition. For no more than a moment; because at once he intuited a new and harrowing meaning in the name written on the clipboard; the name that designated that motionless body in the bed and that nonetheless was no longer Pedro Panón or anybody else. He hung the clipboard back on the hook and filled his chest with implacable disquietude, his eyes darting back and forth like those of a cornered animal. He sighed and drew closer to the head.

Yes. He needed to be brave in order to keep going until that head was under his eyes and to look at it carefully, with cold curiosity. There it was, in its mystery, the face making an invisible grimace, calling to him in the silent room. He had to see it.

He felt more confident when he recognized him more fully: his forehead and also his eyes. He even managed to smile at him, hinting at a caress with his hand. But suddenly he felt that it was preferable to not see anything of the young man's face, which the sheet cut off at the chin. It was monstrous to ascertain that the features that still held out against the illness, those that continued to belong to his friend, were joined in that face with those strange and repulsive features. And they would never be able to separate, these and those melded together forever in the heat of the fever. He pulled away, about to leave, but then the old-man face on the pillow moved slightly to one side, freezing him in place. He heard him breathe more easily through his quivering nose, while two lines of spit stretched from the corners of his mouth. Now he couldn't leave. He bent his knees until he was sitting in the iron chair, his hands folded over his belly, and looked quietly at the thin profile, the shaved head pitched forward.

"How's he doing? Is he still resting peacefully? I'll be back shortly."

The nurse's white coat disappeared from the door. He settled into the chair, once again alone with the angular face on the pillow, suddenly understanding the futility of struggling against it, that he was a prisoner in the dying man's room and would not leave that night or ever. Barreiro and Slim would slip through the night toward the scrubland along the river, they would reach the open fields before dawn, and the sun would find them far away, walking quickly along the road. By night they would be in the city of the drunken sailor, wandering through the streets with frolicsome lights. He couldn't leave; he had to stay till the end of this mysterious ritual of death.

He sat up straight, still looking at the patient's red nose, the drool from his twisted mouth. He slowly gnawed on the filthiest possible insult, and one idea swept over his face like the shadow of a smile. The image of the others, free, running hunched over through the dusky fields, burned stubbornly in his chest.

"No, not me, they're not going to . . ."

In the hall he crossed paths with the nurse. He mumbled something and skipped down the stairs. He started to jog down the dirt path, staring at the club windows that were still yellow with light.

He was still looking at the head when the morning light spread its canvas over the bluish glass. It was paler, and the air entered and exited slowly, accompanied by a faint whistle but causing no other disturbance. It had also grown heavier and was now sunk up to the ears in a hollow of the fabric, as if the neck had spent the whole night stubbornly digging away. The retreating illness revealed to him the familiar face, which the intense light of morning was cleansing of the last stains of fever.

"Good morning. How's the patient?"

The grey suit and gold eyeglasses of the director. How strange that he hadn't heard the car. Behind him, the faces of many employees. Someone turned off the now useless light. The nurse: for a moment at the door. In and among the clouds of drowsiness, now almost unbearable, he watched them surround the bed and lean over it while speaking in low voices. Through the window entered a strip of breeze, which shook the clipboard with the broken black line, as well as the sound of rapid footsteps. The doctor entered, buttoning up his coat, large drops of water shining on his hair. He took in his hand the thin wrist fallen over the blanket. Then he lifted one eyelid, which was growing whiter and whiter. He couldn't remember if the doctor had said "What a pity" or "He's ready" to the director, who was stroking his mouth with his fingers, his chin resting on his chest. He lifted it and turned to him, placing a hand on his shoulder.

"I want to thank you; you have behaved like a grown man. We found them an hour ago in the reeds along the river."

He paused. Brownie took the opportunity to delight in the thought of the beating the others would have received, and the other beatings that awaited them, for several nights, in the cells of the correctional wing.

"Moreover, you have acted with nobility – not going to sleep so you could watch over your poor friend. I imposed iron discipline because it was necessary. But I also know how to reward those who deserve it. I've just spoken to the engineer. The job of factory foreman is yours. You'll begin your new job on Monday. And now you must get some sleep, you need it."

Brownie said thank you and smiled in confusion. The employees didn't know if they should direct their hardened expressions of solemnity toward the body in the bed, the escape they had prevented, or the generosity of the director. He left thinking that the director spoke like a priest and, once at the door, he greeted the day with a furious:

"What a son of a bitch!"

What a son of a bitch! he mumbled, without knowing whom for, as he rose and pressed on his aching back. The others were ahead of him, for moments blending into the night, which was rapidly falling. Against the blackened sky, the bodies, made longer by their work tools, drew strange dark shapes. The guard kept watch over the returning formation, riding up and down its length on horseback, lifting the thick riding crop that hung from his wrist.

Brownie bent down again between the wheels, trying to figure out why the tractor wasn't working. His greasy hands groped the cold metal. I think . . . It's already dark and we don't have a flashlight. He saw himself again, on the way to the cemetery, half his body taut under the weight of the coffin. It's not as if it were full of lead. All day with no sleep. Remembering it, he felt the stabbing pain in his back. He swung his hips around and laboriously loosened a bolt with the pliers. And then the speeches, standing in the cold, dead tired, stupefied by exhaustion. His arm reached out and returned with the crowbar. He used leverage, pushing with all his might. Futile. Then he closed his eyes in despair, motionless on all fours next to the metal blade of the engine. And the worst part wasn't the exhaustion or the heaviness of sleep but rather that muted anguish that had been churning slowly in his chest since yesterday. The thing that smothered him constantly and was impossible for him to know.

The horse's warm breath stroked his neck and the harsh voice fell on him like a ton of bricks.

"What're you doing there? Haven't you fixed it?"

He answered without moving:

"I don't know. Without any light . . ."

He heard the other dismount. Only then did he open his eyes and stand up.

"I don't think it's the bolt. We'll have to remove the blade."

The other squatted down, bending his head to get a better look. Brownie glanced with sleepy eyes into the depths of the landscape, where his comrades were nothing more than a long black cloud. Then he looked down. That was when the stubborn anguish in his chest let go, and an enormous peace violently entered his soul. Now everything was clear and simple, and although he would never have been able to explain the reason for his sudden joy, not even to himself, he finally knew what he had to do. As if someone, invisible in the quiet icy edge of night, had poured truth into his ears.

The man grumbled between the black spokes of the wheels. The hand that held the silver-handled whip approached him.

"Do you have a match?"

It was simple joy that strengthened his legs, contracted the muscles in his arm.

"Yes. Here."

The crowbar flashed through its quick circular journey and hit the man's lowered head near the dark curve of his temple. There was no need for more because the body lay still under the engine, curled up in a ball as if to make sure its heat departed slowly, stingily. He opened his hand and the tool disappeared on the ground. Slowly he wiped the back of his hand on his trousers because something had splashed onto it. He lifted his head toward the swelling sky, and then the night plunged irrepressibly into the landscape, vibrating mysteriously in the stars, in the distant dogs, and in the rustling sounds of the puddles.

Night was coming. He moved quickly away from the tractor and toward his assignation. He ran in a straight line, agile and happy, certain that the anguish would stay back there, growing cold on top of the round black earth. The enormous night, incomprehensible and secretive, swiftly came to find him and slipped under his tireless body. He scrambled through the barbed wire and kept running. He jumped over the ditch with its broken mirror at the bottom and kept running. Now his feet were pounding madly on the damp grass, dizzyingly drawing the ombú tree next to the well toward them. He ran several meters in an arc then veered to the right, dragging with him the long shadow the moon had just given birth to. His chest shook fiercely from fatigue, his lips parted over his clenched teeth; but he kept running, running, accumulating minutes and meters, as if the wild happiness that had appeared so suddenly would pull him swiftly along by the hand, slicing through the icy night. He reached the cornfield running; then he tripped, disappearing face down in the shadows.

He twisted, his arms splayed. A burning pain in his cheek roused him, and he opened his eyes onto a small round moon, high in the sky. He rose cautiously and listened. Nothing. On his knees, he lifted his head and looked around. Nobody. He stood up and kept walking, limping slightly, the small round shadow trembling behind him. A cockcrow followed him along the barbed wire bordering the road, clambering intermittently into the night. Then, cheerfully, he pushed off from the wire and crossed over the ditch. He pulled his hand out of his pocket holding the dry, ragged rose and threw it far away, then rubbed his fingers together to get rid of its traces. He quickened his footsteps and took off down the road, in search of the coming night, which had been waiting for him for ten years on the street bedecked with lights, with the clatter of shots from the shooting range, the laughter of the women, the blond and staggering sailor.

1935

The Possible Baldi

Baldi stopped on the concrete island the speeding vehicles were circum-
venting and waited for the final whistle from the traffic cop, a dark blot
against the tall white booth. He smiled, thinking about himself, bearded,
his hat pushed back on his head, his hands in his pants pockets, the fingers
of one curled around the fee paid for Antonio Vergara v. Samuel Freider.
He told himself that he had a jovial and relaxed air, his body balanced
over his open legs as he looked calmly at the sky, the trees in front of the
Congress, the colors of the buses. Certain that he'd resolved the issues of
that night with his visit to the barber, dinner, the movies with Nené. And
full of confidence in his own powers – his hand squeezing the banknotes
– because the pale eyes of a blond and unknown woman, standing beside
him, grazed him from time to time. And if he wanted to . . .

The cars stopped, and he crossed over to the plaza. He kept walking
listlessly. A basket of flowers reminded him of the sidewalk in Palermo, the
kiss among the jasmine their last night together. The woman's head with

its tousled hair dropped into his arms. Then the quick kiss on the corner, the tenderness of her mouth, the everlasting sparkle in her eyes. And tonight, also tonight. Without warning, he felt that he was happy, so clearly that he almost stopped in his tracks, as if his happiness were walking past him, and he could see it – agile and refined – as it crossed the plaza with rapid steps.

He smiled at the quivering water in the fountain. Next to the large sleeping stone child, he handed a coin to a man in rags who had not yet asked for one. Now he would have liked to come across a child's head that he could pat. But the children were playing farther away, running around the rectangle of red gravel. He could only lean over, clenching his chest muscles as he stepped down firmly on the grating that filtered the warm air blowing from under ground.

He kept walking, thinking about Nené's fingers gratefully caressing his arm as he tells her about this blast of joy, which came from her, and how a certain amount of training is needed to be able to bottle happiness. They were about to found the Academy of Bliss – a project that would prove magnificent, with a bold glass edifice rising out of a garden city, full of bars, metal colonnades, orchestras playing next to golden beaches, and thousands of pink billboards, where women with drunken eyes were smiling – when he noticed that the blond and unknown woman from a moment before was now walking beside him, just a few meters to his right. He turned to look at her.

Small, wearing a long olive-green raincoat tied at her waist as if breaking her in half, her hands in her pockets, a polo shirt collar, a red bow tie over her chest. She was walking slowly, her knees hitting the fabric of her coat with the feeble sound of an awning blowing in the wind. Two handfuls of red hair spilled out of her brimless hat. Her profile sharp and all the lights glinting in her eyes. But the secret of her tiny figure was in her too-high heels, which forced her to walk with slow majesty, to strike the pavement with the invariable rhythm of clockwork. And quickly, as if shaking off sad thoughts, her head turned to the left, poured out a glance at Baldi, then turned forward again. Two, four, six times, a fleeting glimpse.

Suddenly, a short, fat man with a long, black mustache. Hewing with his twisted mouth fastened to the woman's half-concealed ear, following her insistently and muttering on the diagonal tacks she took to get away from him.

Baldi smiled and lifted his eyes to the top of the building. It was already eight fifteen. The silky brush at the barbershop, the blue suit on the bed, the restaurant lounge. No matter what, he could be in Palermo by nine thirty. He quickly buttoned up his jacket and kept walking until he was flush with the couple. With his face darkened by his beard and his chest puffed up with air, he pitched slightly forward as if the weight of his fists had altered his balance. The man with the long mustache turned his eyes to quickly size him up, then brought them to rest, as if with deep interest, on the farthest corner of the plaza. He walked away silently, taking small steps, and went to sit down on a stone bench, letting out a sigh of gratified relief. Baldi heard him whistle a children's ditty, cheerful and absentminded.

But there was the woman, her large blue eyes fastened onto his face, her nervous and restless smile, a vague thank you, thank you, sir . . . She exposed something subjugated and seduced, which drove him to not remove his hat, to seal his lips, while his hand brushed the rim.

"It was nothing," and he shrugged, as if he were accustomed to making vexing and mustachioed men take flight.

"Why did you do it, sir? The moment I saw you . . ."

She stopped, flustered; but they were already walking together. Only until we reach the other side of the plaza, Baldi told himself.

"Please, don't call me sir. What were you saying? The moment you saw me . . ."

He noticed that the woman's hands, moving through the air as if squeezing lemons, were white and delicate. The hands of a lady in such clothes, with that raincoat on a moonlit night.

"Oh, you'll just laugh at me."

But she was the one laughing, falteringly, her head shaking. He understood, from her soft *r*'s and hissing *s*'s, that she was a foreigner. Maybe German. Without knowing why, this annoyed him, and he wanted to cut it short.

"I'm happy, miss, that I was able to . . ."

"No, it doesn't matter if you laugh. The moment I saw you waiting to cross the street, I knew that you were not like other men. There's something unusual about you, so much strength, something fiery . . . And that beard, which makes you look so proud . . ."

Hysterical and literary, Baldi sighed. I should have shaved this afternoon. But he felt the woman's intense admiration; he looked at her askance, with cold, probing eyes.

"Why do you think that? Do you think you know me?"

"I don't know, it's just a feeling. Men, the way they wear their hats . . . I don't know. Something. I asked God to make you talk to me."

They kept walking through a pause during which Baldi thought about all the stages he still had to go through in order to arrive in Palermo on time. Pedestrian and vehicular traffic had thinned out. The sounds of the avenue reached him, the isolated shouts – now lacking conviction – of the newspaper vendors.

They stopped at the corner. Baldi searched in the street signs, the streetlights, and the new-moon sky for to the words to say goodbye. She ended the pause with short spurts of laughter that filtered through her nose. A tender laugh, almost a cry, as if she were pressing a child against herself. Then she lifted a timorous gaze.

"So different from the others . . . Clerks, gentlemen, office managers . . ." Her hands pressed together quickly as she added, "If you would be so kind as to stop for a few minutes. If you want to tell me about your life . . . I'm certain it's extraordinary!"

Baldi again stroked the banknotes from Antonio Vergara v. Samuel Freider. Not knowing if out of vanity or pity, he made up his mind. He took the woman's arm and, without looking at her, indifferent to the awestruck and grateful blue eyes resting on his face, gruffly led her over to the corner of Victoria, where the night was more powerful.

A few red streetlights nailed into the darkened air. They were repairing the street. A wooden railing surrounding machinery, bricks, piles of bags. He leaned against the stockade. The woman stopped hesitantly, then took a few short steps, her hands in the pockets of her raincoat, looking attentively at Baldi's hardened face bent over the broken pavement. Then she approached, leaning toward him, looking with forced interest at the equipment under the canvas tarp.

Clearly, the stockade surrounded Fort Colonel Rich, on the Colorado River, at x miles from the Nevada border. But what about him, was he Wenonga, he of the solitary feather over the greased skull, or Bloody Hand, or White Horse, chief of the Sioux? Because if he were on the other side of the banners decorated with fleurs-de-lis — what would the woman think if he leaped over the posts, because if the guardrail surrounded him, he would be a white defender of the fort, a Buffalo Bill in high boots, musketeer gloves, and a defiant mustache. There was no point, he didn't want to frighten the woman with children's stories. But he had embarked, and he pressed his lips together with confidence and strength.

He abruptly pulled away. Once again, without looking at her, his gaze fixed on the end of the block as if it were the other end of the world:

"Let's go."

Then, when he saw that the woman, docile and attentive, obeyed him:

"Have you ever been to South Africa?"

"Africa . . . ?"

"Yes, South Africa. Cape Colony. Transvaal Province."

"No. It's . . . far away, isn't it?"

"Far away . . . ! Oh, yes, several days from here!"

"English, there?"

"Yes, mostly English. But there's a little of everything."

"You were there?"

"Yes, I was!" His face bobbed as he pondered his memories. "Transvaal . . . Yes, for almost two years."

Then, in English:

"So, do you know English?"

"Very little and very bad. I pretty much forgot all of it."

"What were you doing there?"

"A strange job. Really, I didn't need to know any languages."

She kept walking, her head turning toward Baldi then back, like someone about to say something then hesitating; but she didn't say anything, only nervously moving her olive-green shoulders. Baldi looked at her sideways, smiling at his South African profession. It must have already been eight thirty. He felt the pressure of time so strongly that it was as if he were already stretched out in the chair at the barbershop smelling the perfumed air, eyes closed as the warm lather thickened around his face. But the solution had arrived; now the woman would have to leave. Her frightened eyes opened wide as she walked quickly, wordlessly away. What was that about extraordinary men, eh . . .?

He stopped in front of her and leaned over, bringing his face close to hers.

"I didn't need to know English because bullets speak a universal language. In Transvaal, South Africa, I hunted blacks."

She hadn't understood because she kept smiling and blinking:

"Hunted blacks? Black men?"

He felt as if the boot treading across the Transvaal was sinking into ridicule. But her dilated blue eyes remained expectant with so much humble longing that he wanted to continue the descent.

"Yes, a position of great responsibility. A guard at the diamond mines. In a very remote place. They send replacements every six months. But it's a good job; they pay in sterling. And, despite the loneliness, not always boring. Sometimes there are blacks who try to make off with diamonds, dirty stones, bags with dust. There were electric fences. But there was also me, who felt like having a little fun taking shots at those thieving blacks. A lot of fun, I can assure you. Bam, bam, and that blackie's race ends right there, face down."

Now the woman was furrowing her brow, moving her eyes over Baldi's chest without touching him.

"You killed blacks? Just like that? With a rifle?"

"A rifle? Oh, no. Black thieves are hunted with machine guns. Schneiders. Two hundred and fifty shots per minute."

"And you . . . ?"

"Of course me! And I enjoyed it immensely!"

Now, finally. The woman had stepped back and was looking around, her mouth half open, breathing with agitation. It would be funny if she called over a cop. But she turned shyly to the hunter of black men, to make a suggestion:

"If you'd like . . . we could sit for a moment in the plaza."

"Let's."

As they walked across the plaza he made one last attempt:

"Don't you feel disgusted? By me, by what I've told you?" he said in a mocking tone that must have sounded irritated.

She shook her head energetically.

"Oh, no! I think you must have suffered so much."

"You don't know me. Why would I suffer for the blacks?"

"Before, I mean. In order to be capable of doing that, of taking that job."

She was still able to stretch her hand over his head, mumbling an absolution. Let's see how far this German governess attitude can go.

"In my house I had a little telegraph machine so I could report when a black died due to his own carelessness. But sometimes I was so bored I wouldn't report it. I'd take apart the machine so I'd have an excuse for the delay, in case there was an inspection, and then I'd make friends with the corpse. For two or three days I'd watch it rot, turn grey, swell up. I'd bring a book and my pipe over to it, and I'd sit there and read; sometimes when I found an interesting paragraph, I'd read it out loud. Until my friend would start to stink in a rather inappropriate way. Then I'd fix the machine, report the incident, and hang out on the other side of the house."

She didn't suffer and sigh for the poor black man rotting in the sun. She shook her sad, bent head to say:

"My poor friend. What a life you've led! Always so lonely . . ."

Until he, now sitting on a bench in the plaza, gave up the night and began to enjoy the game. Quickly, in an intense and nervous style, he continued to create the Baldi of a thousand ferocious faces made possible by the woman's admiration. From her meek attention, trembling against his body, he extracted the Baldi who spent the money of his skinny and heavily made-up lovers on hard liquor in a tavern full of sailors wearing thick sweaters in Marseilles or Le Havre. From the storm surge feigned by the clouds in the grey sky came the Baldi who one day at noon boarded the *Santa Cecilia* with ten dollars and a pistol; from the quick gust of wind that kicked up the dust of a house under construction – a great sandstorm in the desert – came the Baldi who enlisted in the Foreign Legion, returning to a village with the tragic head of a Moor skewered on his bayonet.

Just like that, until the other Baldi was so alive that he was able to think of him as an acquaintance. And then, suddenly, an idea clung tenaciously to him. A thought rendered him disconsolate next to the raincoat of the already forgotten woman.

He compared the supposed Baldi with himself, with this calm and inoffensive man who told stories to the Madame Bovarys of the Plaza Congreso. With the Baldi who had a fiancée, a law office, the doorman's respectful smile, the roll of bills from Antonio Vergara v. Samuel Freider, paid in pesos. A slow idiotic life, like everybody else. Filled with bitterness, he puffed quickly on his cigarette, staring at the squareness of a flowerbed. Deaf to the hesitant words of the woman, who had finally grown silent, hunching over to make herself smaller.

Because Mr. Baldi, Esq., was incapable of leaping onto the deck of a barge loaded with sacks and lumber. Because he had not had the urge to admit that life is something else, that life is what you cannot live in the company of faithful women or sensible men. Because he had closed his eyes and given up, like everybody else. Clerks, gentlemen, office managers.

He tossed away his cigarette and stood up. He took the money out of his pocket and placed a bill on the woman's lap.

"Here. Do you want more?"

He added another one, of higher denomination, feeling that he hated her, that he would have given anything to not have met her. She held the bills in her hand to protect them from the wind.

"But . . . I didn't tell you . . . I don't know . . ." she said, her big eyes bluer than ever, her disillusioned mouth leaning toward him. "Are you leaving?"

"Yes, I have things to do. Ciao."

He waved again, with the quick gesture the possible Baldi would have used, and he left. But after a few steps he turned back and brought his bearded face up to the woman's hopeful charade, as she held up the bills, turning her wrist. He spoke, his face clouded, spitting his words out like curses.

"That money I gave you, I made it selling cocaine. Up north."

1936

The Tragic End of Alfredo Plumet

Alfredo Plumet looks at his watch; it is one forty. He finishes his glass of cognac, wipes his short mustache with his fingers, and rises from his chair.

"Please excuse me, my friends. It's time for me to go."

"Come on," Adela says, "you still have a minute."

"Maybe even two," Luciano Dirán, Alfredo's former classmate and to-day's lunch guest, says. "So you'll be late for once . . ."

Plumet shakes his bony head.

"No, my old friend, you know my principles. For the twenty years I've worked at Salustín Stationers, I've always been at my desk when the clock strikes two . . . Never tardy, never absent. I've always been like that, in spite of my migraines. But that doesn't mean you have to leave," he rushes to add when he sees his friend stand up. "Not when you have the good fortune to hold a higher position! Here, ask Adela to pour you another glass."

He kisses the woman on her forehead, shakes Luciano's hand, walks to the coat rack, and removes his fedora, the only headpiece that, according to him, any accountant worthy of the title should wear. As he walks past the glass door of the dining room, he drums his fingers on the pane and directs a long wave at Adela and his friend, who respond by lifting their glasses.

Alfredo Plumet belonged to that very small group of individuals – alas! – who are careful to avoid inconveniencing others. Therefore, according to his custom, he does not slam the door, and he uses his key to lock it after he has gone out.

Then, with a light step, he descends the three stairs. But when he reaches the sidewalk, a violent storm erupts, one that could not have been predicted.

Nobody will ever again see the poor man alive.

Toward evening, several vagrants find Alfredo Plumet's body on the rocks along Rambla Sur, behind the Central Cemetery, about five blocks from the incinerator at the corner of Curuguatí and Rambla. The autopsy reveals that the cause of death was a fractured skull.

The investigation

"So, what now?" I asked, after Detective Luponi had finished his account.

The policeman was leaning back in his armchair, his thumbs in the pockets of his vest, the eternal English cigarette between his lips.

"So now, it's all quite recent. The autopsy determined that it was not suicide and says the body had not been moved; but it's impossible to determine if it was murder or accident. The blow might have been delivered with a blunt object, but equally plausible, caused by a fatal fall. You know the place. The shore is right next to Rambla, the promenade, only part of which is protected by the new sea wall. There's no adequate protection at the spot where the vagrants made their gruesome find. Alfredo Plumet could have fallen and broken his skull on a rock. The rain has washed away all footprints, but the fact that his wallet and his gold watch were found in his pockets eliminates robbery as a motive. I might add that his death must have occurred somewhere around three in the afternoon . . . Now you know as much as I do."

I look at Luponi in astonishment.

"Have you discovered the truth? . . . But, how could you have? . . ."

Luponi points to the folder, on top of which are several sheets of paper – three photographs and a partially folded map of Montevideo.

"Here you have the layout of Plumet's apartment. Here's a map of Sector 4, which includes the suburbs of Palermo. I've already told you that Plumet lived on Calle Cuareim, number . . . May I point out, in case you don't know, that the uneven numbers are on the right side of the street when going from the Casa de Gobierno toward the sea."

"What difference does that make?" I ask, even more amazed.

"A difference of the utmost importance. It's very possible that if his address had been an even number, Alfredo Plumet would still be alive."

He was a low-level clerk

I look through the documents. One of the photographs shows a small, neatly dressed man wearing a fedora and a starched collar. His face is anonymous, his features soft.

"A humble, diffident, and tidy man, living in a state of perpetual diffidence in order to avoid being a nuisance to anyone; fearful in the extreme and very thrifty. Obviously a model employee: serious, honest, and punctual. He had been working for twenty years at Salustín Hermanos Stationers on Calle Juan Carlos Gómez."

"On Calle Juan Carlos Gómez!" I shout.

"Yes, in the Barrio Sur neighborhood."

The detective whistles sarcastically.

"Aha! You are making progress."

"What's this piece of paper?" I ask irritably.

"A report from the National Meteorological Observatory regarding the storm that broke out yesterday over Montevideo at one forty-five, including several technical details of no interest to our investigation. As for the two photographs – the house on Calle Cuareim and the spot where the body was found – they also hold no practical interest."

"But with this – ?"

"With this I have been able to reconstruct the drama, and you will also reconstruct it if you have even a bit of a knack for observation."

"Come on, be serious! If we accept that it's a case of revenge, how can you expect me to reach – ?"

He slams his fist down on the desk.

"Damn! I see why you're confused. I forgot the main clue: I should tell you that I found the deceased's umbrella on the coat rack. Now do you understand?"

And you, dear reader, do you understand?

Case solved

"Let's try, together, to shed light on this affair. I have just told you that I found Plumet's umbrella on the coat rack. He had forgotten to take it, for there was no warning of the storm. But it begins to rain. So I ask you, what would this methodical and cautious man have done under the circumstances and in keeping with his habits? We know that Plumet was horrified of making noise. Obviously, he would have returned to his house as quietly as he had left and gone straight to the coat rack. And to do this, he would have had to walk past the glass door of the dining room, where he had left his wife and his best friend. It is clear that at that moment, they were a thousand leagues away from Mr. Plumet."

"What?" I cry out. "Adela and Luciano . . ."

"But, of course . . . ! The eternal story."

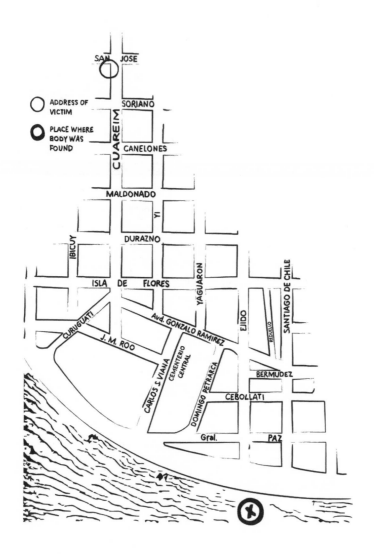

Like a sleepwalker

He leaves as he came, silently, and starts walking in the rain, straight ahead without thinking. Now look at the map of Montevideo. Our man has continued down Cuareim, crossing Soriano, Canelones . . . Straight, always straight, and without crossing over to the other side of the street. Remember my comment about the uneven numbers. If he had lived across the street, there is no doubt that, upon reaching Gonzalo Ramírez, he would have continued along that avenue and not along Curuguatí. We can assume, in that case, that the tragedy would have turned out quite differently. But let us leave our speculations and return to the facts. Upon reaching the promenade, the cuckolded husband changes direction. He turns left. Why? Because he cannot resist the pull a body of water always exerts upon us. The poor man will not continue far along the promenade. He is, it seems, a kind of sleepwalker, who continues along the rocky path, without the protection of a sea wall. The slightest obstacle – a hole, a rock, any irregularity along the way – leads to the fatal fall . . .

1939

The Perfect Crime

A DETECTIVE STORY

With his hands clasped behind his back, his pipe between his teeth, Julián Chapars stood next to the pond, its waters reflecting the grey sky and the melancholy branches of the willow trees, where the sounds of birds were coming from. Chapars's wristwatch showed six o'clock. He had committed his crime the night before, at around eight, Chapars figured, telling himself that he'd been a murderer for ten hours.

He heard himself say to himself, almost out loud:

"Fernando has been a corpse for ten hours . . ."

He glanced around. Nobody. He shrugged. His thoughts went into reverse. Again he saw himself the night before, when he ran into poor Fernando on an almost deserted street.

"Hey, cuz. How's it going?"

Fernando was on foot, and he was driving his luxury automobile. Fernando approached the car.

"What luck to run into you, Julián. You've been playing me for a fool for a long time, with all your promises to pay me back... I guess you think it's alright for a working man like me to be exploited by a lazy pig like you. Well, you're wrong. I've decided to have a lien placed on your assets. Right here I have your bounced checks, take a look. Your signed invoices, your letters of credit, all of it... And I took them all out of my safe to give them to my lawyer first thing tomorrow."

Julián was so upset that he was unable to speak, his hands gripping the steering wheel. Finally, he pulled himself together.

"You're not going to do that, Fernando. You're not going to do that because within ten hours I am going to pay you every last cent I owe. I've got the money at home. I rented a place for the summer, in Atlántida; I've got the money there. Let's go have dinner together and then I'll pay you all of it. Anyway... you're on your own, your wife's out of town... Let's go."

"You sure you have the money? All of it?"

"If I didn't... Let's go, get in."

"That's remarkable. Just like you, always full of surprises."

Fernando got in the car. The trip along the coast was uneventful. Finally the car stopped on a secluded road, surrounded by vegetation. A private road, undoubtedly.

"It's a charming place," Fernando said, cheerful at the prospect of collecting his money.

"Yes, you'd be hard pressed to find anything better. I brought you here to show you a property I'm thinking of buying."

Julián talked without knowing what he was saying. He was trying to gain time. From the very first moment he had only one concern: How would he kill his creditor, his cousin?

It was Fernando himself who resolved his dilemma, unwittingly.

"Look at that pond. If you buy this land you should make sure you have access to this pond."

"It's already mine, or almost. Half the pond belongs to me."

He stopped the car and suggested to Fernando that they get out.

"Just for a minute. You like to fish; here you can see magnificent fish, just two meters down."

Suspecting nothing, Fernando followed his cousin. He walked up to the pond and received a fierce blow to the back of his neck, which knocked him out.

Five minutes later, the creditor cousin was sleeping forever at the bottom of the pond, weighed down by enormous rocks, more than thirty kilos, tied onto him with thick wire stolen from a nearby fence.

Having finished his macabre task, Julián went to his rented house, about a kilometer from the pond. The bounced checks, the signed bills, the letters: they were all reduced to ash.

But he slept poorly, and at dawn he got up to check his car and examine the pond. He wasn't really worried. He'd done it without a weapon; he'd left no traces. His crime had been a perfect crime. Nobody could know that he had run into his cousin Fernando. Before hitting him, he had looked around carefully. Nobody. No, he wasn't afraid of anything. He was relaxed. But he felt like taking a walk on that beautiful morning. Why not go to the pond? He wasn't going to let himself be dissuaded by the theory that the criminal is drawn back to the scene of the crime. Anyway, he wasn't some common murderer.

Of course, Fernando's disappearance would not pass in silence. They would notice at the factory, they would tell his wife, they would publish a photo of him in the newspapers. And then what? Nobody would think to look at the bottom of this abandoned pond.

That idea made the murderer laugh.

Common criminals really had to be idiots to let themselves get caught, in most cases anyway. They spent a long time planning their crimes, weighing their options, trying to foresee everything. . . And the result? They allowed the corpse to be found and ended up under the blade of the guillotine. Whereas he, Julián Chapars, was not in any danger, none at all.

He laughed gaily again. But his laughter was abruptly cut off.

"How are you, Mr. Chapars? Quite cheerful this morning, I see?"

The murderer turned and found himself face-to-face with Fermín, the forest warden working for Mr. Sandoval, the owner of the pond.

"Lovely day, isn't it?" the warden said.

"Yes, quite . . ."

With great effort, Julián managed to control his nerves. His fear was nonsense. He wasn't in any danger. This exchange was completely normal. He asked:

"How much does it cost, Don Fermín, to get a fishing license for this pond?"

"Five pesos. Do you like to fish, Mr. Chapars?"

"Yes . . . I'd like to start . . ."

"Unfortunately, this year you won't catch very much in this pond."

"Why not?"

Fermín laughed.

"Because there won't be any."

"I don't understand what you're trying to tell me . . ."

Fermín raised his stick and pointed to the road. Julián saw a truck driving toward the pond.

"That truck," said the warden, "it's bringing the workers and the equipment we need to empty the pond . . ."

"Huh?"

"That's right. Every three years, Mr. Sandoval has us empty the pond. It doesn't take long. The water drains into that stream. The wells are emptied with a vacuum pump. You'll see how much fish we take out. Baskets and baskets full of them. This afternoon everybody from town will be here; you should come, too. It's quite interesting.

The murderer saw the truck stop. The workers got off, carrying their equipment. Chapars broke out in a cold sweat. He stammered:

"Do you think the police are already in the office at this time of day?"

After hearing an affirmative from the forest warden, who didn't understand the reason for the question, the murderer set off toward his punishment.

1940

Convalescence

It was almost midday when the man sprinkled me with sand, pushing with his bare foot. I turned, half asleep, spread out in the shadow of the smiling face hovering over me. The man frequently changed or slightly altered his bathing suits. But his sharp face remained the same and incomprehensible, smiling at me. His face reminded me intensely of an unfamiliar animal. At the same time, by effortlessly following the lines of his face, I saw there an expression of human and malicious intelligence.

Only at the end of April, far away and during a harsh autumn, was I able to understand how much his face resembled that of a small and cheerful faun.

Stretched out in the grassy hollow, I was unable to see the far side of the hotel and the rocks. The beach was reduced to a triangle whose points were firmly nailed into the horizon.

One morning the sea was blue, rough, hoisting sudden waves against the sand. Three girls walked slowly along the seashore. I could hear only their laughter, unsynchronized, light liquid laughter, the same melody the water played at daybreak on the distant rocky point.

Only at one particular hour, at dawn, could that melody be heard. No matter where I was, I felt it approach, oblique, fretful, sidestepping like the purebred horses who walked along the sand at dawn.

The colors the three girls wore appeared cold and strange under the blazing sun. The ones on either side had on dark blue bathing suits, while the tallest one wore blue pants and a white blouse and took long strides between her two friends, creating a gap that was quickly closed.

I would have liked to dress those girls in oranges and yellows, in violent reds. But then I discovered that the dark blue of their bathing suits and the white of the blouse matched the sea, a friendly response that only girls in the morning could offer. I saw them, upon their return, walking along the shoreline of small and docile waves, accompanied by the sound of their laughter, patches of water and light on their bare feet, which they pushed and shaped with the colors of their garments.

From the pavilion of the German club, close and invisible, came a masculine voice. A woman's laugh, happy and mysterious, cooed. Then, between giggles:

"No peeking where the sun doesn't shine . . . !"

Until ten o'clock I could imagine I was alone. Along the twisting path between the tamarisks came footsteps and an Anglo-Saxon voice. They turned off to my right and took possession of a stretch of beach, setting up an enormous, colorful umbrella. The man was blond and greying, athletic, with a smile that meant: *The air and the sun, they're so lovely in the morning at the beach, aren't they?* His laughter always ended in a question, gently. The woman didn't answer. She undressed the boy and then encouraged him to chase her, crawling. She was wearing white shorts over her bathing suit, and dark glasses. She made a beeline to the sea, her hands behind her. Her faith in the soul of the water was evident. She continued to the shore, still in a straight line, to greet the sea and render tribute to it.

Once, the man called out to the woman in white shorts: *Tuca*. It was almost noon and at the sound of the name, the seagulls took off in a reconnaissance flight, squalling over the deserted stretch of beach.

When it came time to tan my back, I tried to say goodbye to the beach with a quick glance. A new and powerful wisdom now held sway in my body, and obedience to it was obligatory. I settled with my face nestled between my elbows, immediately passing into the world of sharp yellow grass and ants. But I never managed to comprehend the insects' activity, their indecisive dashing about, forever searching. I smiled at them, blowing a few grains of sand to cover them then watch them rise, on their third try, from the dead.

Behind and above me the sea huffed and puffed, strong now, tossing and burying the insignificant human voices that tried to reconstruct the lost beach for me. And just when I could no longer tolerate the sun on my shoulders and back, a shadow appeared from somewhere.

"Were you sleeping?"

I lifted my sandy cheek to greet him. Each day by evening I had forgotten the face of my beach neighbor. Now, in the morning, I came to know it again. His laugh, stretching out his eyes, promised to reveal the key to his face, the clue that would allow me to remember it forever.

"How do you feel today, ma'am?"

I always felt fine, but a little less fine whenever he approached. I saw him as a messenger of a thousand things that were a nuisance to remember. The moment would always arrive when, stretched out, his elbows supporting his body, the man would smile at his own moving foot and mumble:

"You know what he says in today's letter?"

"Eduardo? A letter a day! Sometimes I think you are inventing them."

"If you want to see them . . . From a certain distance, of course. They're not only about you."

"No. Not even from a distance. But, can he possibly understand what it means to have no relationships with anybody, not man or woman, not anywhere in the world? There is nothing but the beach and me."

"Thanks."

"Bah. You don't exist, not as an individual. You're just at the beach."

"Okay. So you don't plan to write him back?"

"I can't. Look: I'm happy. What can I say to Eduardo?"

He made a mocking face and didn't speak. Before leaving, he insisted:

"Of course, Eduardo is intelligent, and he can understand. But you're better. You will have to go back. If you invent complications ahead of time . . ."

I dismissed him with a wave of my hand and lay back down.

It wasn't until one morning when the colorful umbrella was set up earlier than usual that I was able to learn the secret of the woman with the white shorts. She walked to the water, as usual, her hands clasped behind her back. Confident in her solitude at that hour, she betrayed herself: I saw her offer her legs to the sea, the movement of her walking legs. On all fours, the infant had stopped and stared, with a tiny and confused fright, at his mother's footsteps. I understood the marine nature of those steps, slightly faltering, suddenly rapid, like the mad dash of crustaceans. Steps suspended in air, gentle movements involving her entire legs, like fish curves in the light. Calmly caressing the air, until nothing remained but pure contact. And then the sea surrounded her legs, scaling them, then broke against them more powerfully, with the snort of an animal finally recognizing the scent it had been sniffing around for.

I remember that since then I have felt great affection for those slender legs in motion.

Previously, I'd had an inkling of that freedom, the feeling of freedom that the beach filled me with on bright mornings. It was as if someone were skillfully loosening all my bonds. I felt settled into a long-lost time, certain of my unpopulated earth, before the tribe and the first gods.

A boat made its way between the island and the horizon. I heard a bird picking at the trunk of a tree. That morning, the last one, the man said to me:

"Hey. You were asleep, weren't you? Well, my esteemed young lady . . . It so happens . . . Today's letter . . . An ultimatum, my damsel. Final deadline. You have been given till one o'clock to call. It's up to you. Did you notice the clouds to the left? A storm. So says an old sea dog. You probably have about a half hour. I'm sure you'll regret it. Anyway, you're fully cured. One day, sooner or later, you'll have to return. And then what? Lightning is already striking next to the hotel. It wouldn't be a good idea for you to catch a cold."

He stood up, laughing, eyeing the approaching clouds. Before he left, he smiled at me again. The expression on his face, at that moment, showed nothing but peevish mockery, aggressive scorn. I was certain he would call Eduardo.

I stood up a while later and wrapped myself in my robe. I remember looking at the dark sky and then at the beach. My gaze was held and returned by the sea, by the smooth damp shore, by the woman with the white shorts, the child, the long humble grass. All of it, so old and so stubbornly pure, all of it that had nurtured me with its substance, day after day.

While waiting in the telephone booth at the hotel for the call to go through, I heard the thunderclaps and the first raindrops hitting the windows. Eduardo's distant voice began to repeat, "Hello, hello . . . Who is it? Hello . . ." Behind the voice, beyond the face the voice shaped, I imagined I could hear the buzz of the city, the past, passion, the absurdity of the life of man.

From the car on my way to the station, collapsed between suitcases, I searched for the stretch of beach where I had lived. The sand, the friendly colors, bliss, everything was buried under dirty, foamy water. I remember I had the sensation that my face was quickly aging while the pain of my disease – muffled and cautious – was returning to gnaw at my body.

1940

A Dream Come True

Blanes invented the joke. He'd come by my office – in the days when I had one – and the café – when things started going badly and I no longer had an office – and, standing on the rug, one fist leaning on the desk, his tie of pretty colors fastened to his shirt with a gold pin, and that head – square and shaved, his dark eyes unable to stay focused for more than a minute and promptly sagging, as if Blanes were on the verge of falling asleep or had remembered some pristine and sentimental moment in his life that he never could have had – that head devoid of a single superfluous particle, silhouetted against the wall covered with portraits and posters, he would let me talk and then begin to form a circle with his lips: "Because you, of course, were ruined by *Hamlet*." Or, also: "Yes, we know. You've always sacrificed yourself for art, and if it hadn't been for your passionate love for *Hamlet*..."

And I spent all those many years putting up with so many wretched people, authors and actors and actresses and theater owners and newspaper critics, and their families, friends, and lovers, and all that time losing and making money that God and I both knew I would necessarily lose again the following season, and that bead of water on that shaved head, that low blow to my ribs, that bittersweet draft, that taunt from Blanes I never fully understood:

"Damn right. Those insane lengths you went to out of your excessive love for *Hamlet* . . ."

If I'd asked him what he meant the first time, if I'd confessed to him that I knew as much about *Hamlet* as I knew how much money a farce would bring in after first reading it, the joke would have ended there. But I was afraid of the host of unborn jokes my question would evoke, so I only made a face and told him to get lost. And this is how I managed to live for twenty years without knowing what *Hamlet* was, without having read it, but knowing, from the intention I could see in Blanes's face and the nodding of his head, that *Hamlet* was art, pure art, great art, and also knowing, because I had become imbued with it without realizing, that it was also an actor or an actress, in this case always an actress with ridiculous hips dressed in tight black garments, a skull, a cemetery, a duel, an act of revenge, a girl who drowns. And also William Shakespeare.

That's why now, only now, with my blond wig parted down the middle that I prefer not to remove when I sleep, with dentures that never managed to fit quite right and that make me hiss and speak very carefully, when I found in the library of this asylum for destitute people of the theater – though it is known by a more respectable name – that very small book with a dark-blue cover and gold embossed letters spelling *Hamlet*, I sat down in the armchair without opening the book, resolved to never open the book or read a single line, and I thought about Blanes, how this was my revenge against his taunt, and about the night Blanes came to see me in a hotel in a provincial capital, and, after letting me talk, smoking and looking up at the ceiling and at people entering the lounge, he puckered his lips to tell me, in front of that poor crazy woman:

"And just think . . . someone like you, who was ruined by *Hamlet*."

I had arranged to meet him at the hotel so that he would play the role of a character in something quick and silly that was called, I think, *A Dream Come True*. One character in the cast of that madness was an unnamed leading man, and Blanes was the only one who could do it, because by the time the woman came to see me, he and I were the only ones left; the rest of the company had managed to flee to Buenos Aires.

The woman had come to the hotel at noon and, having found me still asleep, she returned at the hour of the day that was for her and everybody else in that hot provincial town the end of the siesta, when I was sitting in the coolest spot in the dining room, eating a round veal cutlet and drinking white wine, the only decent thing to drink around there. I'm not going to claim that at the first glance – when she stopped under the halo of heat in front of the curtained door, her eyes dilating in the shadowy dining room, and the waiter pointed to my table, and she promptly started making a beeline toward me, her skirts swirling around her – I intuited what was inside that woman, or that thing like a soft and supple strip of madness that was unwinding, tearing off with gentle tugs as if it were a bandage over a wound of her years past, her solitary years, so she could swaddle me in it, like a mummy, me and a few of those days spent in that boring place, so full of fat and poorly dressed people. But there was, it's true, something in the woman's smile that made me nervous, and it was impossible for me to keep my eyes on her small crooked teeth, exposed like those of a sleeping child breathing with her mouth half open. Her almost grey hair was coiled in braids, and her clothes were old-fashioned, clothes a teenager rather than a grown woman would have worn in a past era. Her skirt reached down to her shoes, the kind that are called boots or high shoes, it was long and dark and kept opening out as she walked and curling back in and trembling again with each step. Her blouse had lace and fit very tightly, she wore a large cameo between her sharp girlish breasts, and her blouse and skirt were joined and separated by a rose at her waist, perhaps artificial now that I think about it, a flower with a large corolla and a bowed head, its thorny stem threatening her belly.

The woman must have been around fifty, and the one thing that was unforgettable about her, that I feel again now as I remember her walking toward me through the hotel dining room, was her demeanor of a young girl from a past century who had just woken up after a long sleep with her hair slightly mussed and having barely aged, but who was about to reach her own age at any moment and in one fell swoop, and then silently fall to pieces, eroded by the stealthy work of time. And her smile was hard to look at because one could not help thinking that, considering the woman's apparent ignorance of the dangers of aging and sudden death, on the brink of which she stood, that wise smile, or at least the defenseless little teeth, sensed the revolting failure that threatened them.

All of that was now standing in the gloom of the dining room, and I clumsily placed my cutlery down next to my plate and stood up.

"Are you Mr. Langman, the theater impresario?"

I nodded, smiling, and invited her to sit down. She didn't want to eat or drink anything; with the table between us, I glanced at her mouth with its shape intact and only a touch of lipstick, right there in the middle where her voice, tinged with a peninsular accent, had hummed as it slipped through the uneven edges of her teeth. I couldn't derive anything from her eyes – small and serene, straining to grow bigger. I would have to wait for her to talk, and, I thought, whatever shape of woman or existence her words would evoke, they would fit her strange appearance well, and then her strange appearance would vanish.

"I wanted to see you about a performance. I mean, I have a play..."

Everything indicated that she was going to keep talking, but she stopped and waited for me to respond; she gave me the floor with her irresistible silence, her smile. She was relaxed, her hands folded on her lap. I pushed aside my plate with its half-eaten cutlet and ordered a coffee. I offered her a cigarette, and she shook her head and briefly prolonged her smile, which meant that she didn't smoke. I lit mine and began to talk, trying to get rid of her peacefully, but rid of her soon and forever, though I used a cautious style that was somehow forced upon me, I don't know why.

"Alas, ma'am... You've never been staged, have you? Naturally. What's the title of the play?"

"No, it doesn't have a title," she answered. "It's so difficult to describe... It's not what you think. Of course, I could give it a title. It could be called *The Dream, The Dream Come True, A Dream Come True.*"

I understood now, without any doubt, that she was crazy, and I felt more comfortable.

"Great. *A Dream Come True.* Not a bad name. I've always had an interest, that is, a personal interest, disinterested in the other sense, in helping people get started. Setting new standards for our national theater. Though I don't need to tell you, ma'am, that gratitude is not what one receives in return. Many owe me for their first break, many who now earn exorbitant royalties on Calle Corrientes and win annual prizes. They no longer remember when they first came to me, almost begging..."

Even the dining-room waiter, from the corner next to the refrigerator where he was shooing away flies and heat with his napkin, could see that this

strange creature didn't care in the least about a single syllable I was uttering. I gave her a last glance with one eye, out of the warmth of my coffee
cup, and said:

"Anyway, ma'am. You must have heard that the season here has been
a complete failure. We've had to cut it short, and I've stayed on alone for
personal reasons. But I, too, will be returning to Buenos Aires next week.
I've gotten it wrong again, there's nothing for it. This milieu, it simply isn't
ready, and in spite of having resigned myself to a season of comedies and
farces . . . well, you see how it's gone. Which means . . . Now, here's what
we can do. If you'd like, you can give me a copy of your play, and I'll see if
maybe in Buenos Aires . . . Does it have three acts?"

She had to answer, but only because I, taking a cue from her, had
stopped talking and remained leaning toward her, scraping the bottom of
the ashtray with the burning tip of my cigarette. She blinked.

"What?"

"Your play, ma'am. *A Dream Come True*. Three acts?"

"No, they're not acts."

"Oh, tableaux. It's common practice now . . ."

"I don't have copies. It's not something I've written down," she
continued.

This was my moment to escape.

"I'll leave you my address in Buenos Aires and when you've written
it . . ."

I saw her recoil, her body hunching over; but she lifted her head, her
smile steady. I waited, certain she was going to get up and leave, but a moment later she moved her hand in front of her face and continued talking.

"No, it's completely different from what you think. It's a moment, a
scene, one could say, where nothing happens, as if we were staging this scene

here in this dining room and I left and nothing else happened. No," she continued, "it has no plot. There are some people on a street and some houses and two cars drive by. I'm there with a man, and a woman steps out of a shop across the street and hands him a glass of beer. There's nobody else, just the three of us. The man crosses the street to where the woman comes out the door with the mug of beer, and then he crosses the street again and sits down at the same table, near mine, where he was at the beginning."

She stopped talking for a moment and now her smile wasn't for me or the cupboard filled with table linens opening slightly out of the dining-room wall. Then, in conclusion:

"Do you understand?"

I found a way out because I thought of Intimate Theater, and I started telling her about it and the impossibility of creating pure art in this milieu, how nobody would go to the theater to see that, and how I was perhaps the only one in the entire province who could understand the value of such a piece and the meaning of the movements and the symbol of the cars and the woman who hands a *bock* of beer to the man crossing the street and then returns to her side, to your side, ma'am.

She looked at me, and there was something in her face that reminded me of Blanes whenever he found himself in the position of asking me for money and mentioned *Hamlet*: a dash of pity and all the rest pure mockery and antipathy.

"No, Mr. Langman, that's not it at all," she said. "It's something I alone want to see, nobody else, no audience. Me and the actors, that's all. I want to see it once, but that once has to be exactly as I'm going to tell you, and you have to do what I tell you to do and nothing else. Understand? Please, tell me how much money we'll need to do it, and I'll give it to you."

There was no longer any point in talking about Intimate Theater or anything else, not there, face-to-face with a crazy woman who opened her purse and took out two fifty-peso bills.

"This is to hire the actors and pay for the preliminary expenses, and then you'll tell me how much more you need."

I was keen for the money, stuck as I was in that damn pit until someone from Buenos Aires answered my letters and sent me a few pesos. So I flashed her my best smile and nodded several times as I placed the twice-folded bills in my jacket pocket.

"Perfect, ma'am. I think I understand the kind of thing you . . ." I didn't want to look at her as I spoke because I was thinking about Blanes, and I didn't want to see Blanes's humiliating expression in this woman's face as well. "I will spend all afternoon on this and if we could meet . . . tonight? Perfect, right here; by then we'll have the main actor, you can explain the scene to us clearly, and we'll make all the arrangements so that *Dream, A Dream Come True* . . ."

Perhaps it was simply because she was crazy, but it also could have been that she understood, as I understood, that it would be impossible for me to steal her hundred pesos, and that's why she didn't ask for a receipt, she didn't even think of asking for one, and she left after giving me her hand, her skirt making a quarter-turn in the opposite direction with each step, her head held high as she left the half-light of the dining room for the heat of the street, as if she were returning to the temperature of the siesta, which had lasted for so many years and where she had preserved that impure youth that was forever on the verge of rotting away.

I found Blanes in a dark and untidy room, the brick walls poorly concealed behind plants, green reed mats, behind the humid heat of the afternoon. The hundred pesos were still in my jacket pocket and until I found

Blanes, until I got him to help me give that crazy woman what she was asking for in exchange for her money, it was impossible for me to spend a penny. I woke him up and waited patiently for him to wash, shave, return to bed, get up again to drink a glass of milk – which meant he had been drunk the day before – and go back to bed to light a cigarette; because he refused to listen to me before all that, and even then, when I pulled over the ruins of the dressing stool that I was sitting on and leaned over with a serious look on my face, ready to spell out my proposal, he stopped me and said:

"Just look at that roof, will you!"

It was a tiled roof, with two or three greenish-colored beams and wild ginger stalks from who knows where, long and dried out. I looked at it, and he did nothing but laugh and shake his head.

"Well, out with it," he said.

I explained what it was, and Blanes interrupted me constantly, laughing, accusing me of lying, claiming that someone must have sent that woman just to play a joke on me. Then he asked me again what it was about, and I had no choice but to settle things by offering him half of whatever the woman paid me, after expenses, and I told him that the fact was I didn't know what it was or what it was about or what the hell that woman wanted from us. But she'd already given me fifty pesos and that meant we could get to Buenos Aires, or at least I could if he wanted to stay and sleep. He laughed and then got serious; out of the fifty pesos I told him she'd given me as an advance, he wanted twenty right away. So I gave him ten, which I soon regretted, because that night, when he showed up in the hotel dining room, he was already drunk and smiling with his slightly twisted mouth, and, with his head bent over the small bowl of ice, he started by saying:

"You never learn your lesson. The grand patron of Calle Corrientes and every *calle* in the world where there's a flurry of art . . . A man who's been ruined a hundred times because of *Hamlet* is going to selflessly wager on an unknown genius wearing a corset."

But when she arrived, when the woman appeared behind me dressed all in black and wearing a veil, a tiny umbrella hanging off her wrist and a watch on a chain around her neck, and she greeted me and held out her hand to Blanes with that slightly assuaged smile in the artificial light, he stopped harassing me and said:

"Finally, ma'am, the gods led you to Langman, a man who has sacrificed hundreds of thousands to get *Hamlet* just right."

She seemed to be sniggering as she looked briefly at one then briefly at the other; then she grew serious and said that she was in a hurry, that she would explain the whole thing so as to leave no room for the slightest doubt, and she would return only when everything was ready. In the soft, clean light, the woman's face and whatever was shimmering on her body – parts of her dress, the nails on her gloveless hands, the handle of her umbrella, the watch with its chain – seemed to become themselves again, freed from the torture of the bright day; and I immediately felt relatively confident, and all night long I didn't think about her as crazy again; I forgot that there was something about the whole thing that smelled of a scam, and the sense of this being a normal, par-for-the course deal managed to reassure me completely. In any case, I didn't have to deal with anything, for Blanes was now there, behaving himself, drinking constantly, conversing with her as if they'd already met two or three times, offering her a glass of whisky, which she traded for a cup of lime blossom tea. She told him whatever she would have had to tell me, and I didn't protest because Blanes was the lead actor, and the more he managed to understand about the play the better things would turn out. This is what the woman wanted us to stage for her (her voice sounded different when she told Blanes, and even though she didn't look at him, even if she lowered her eyes as she spoke, I felt that she was now telling it more personally, as if she were confessing something intimate about her life, whereas she had told me about it as one tells such a thing in an office, for example, to apply for a passport or some such thing):

"On the stage there are houses and sidewalks, but everything is mixed up, as if it were a town and they'd piled everything up to make it look like it was a big city. I come out, the woman I will be playing comes out of a house and sits down at a green table on the curb. Next to the table is a man sitting on a kitchen stool. That's your character. He's wearing a sweater and a cap. There's a greengrocer across the street with boxes of tomatoes in front of the door. Then an automobile starts to drive across the stage, and the man, you, stands up to cross the street, and I get scared the car will hit you. But you cross in front of it and reach the opposite side of the street at the same moment a woman dressed for an outing comes out holding a glass of beer. You take it from her and drink it down in one gulp and walk back across the street right before another automobile drives by, now in the opposite direction and at full speed; again, you make it across just in time and sit back down on the kitchen stool. In the meantime, I have lain down on the sidewalk, like a child. And you bend over to caress my head."

It was easy to do, but I told her that the difficulty, now that I'd thought about it some more, was with the third person who comes out of the house dressed for an outing with a glass of beer.

"Mug," she said. "It's a ceramic mug with a handle and a top."

Blanes nodded and said:

"Yes, of course, with a picture on it, painted."

She said, yes, and it seemed as if Blanes's words had made her very pleased, happy, that face of happiness that only a woman can have and that makes me want to close my eyes whenever I see it, as if good manners required me to do so. We returned to the subject of the other woman, and Blanes finally held out his hand to her and said that he had everything he needed and we needn't worry about anything. I was obliged to entertain the possibility that the crazy woman's craziness was contagious, because when I asked Blanes what actress he'd found for the role, he said, Rivas, and though I didn't know anybody by that name, I didn't want to say so because Blanes was looking at me angrily. Everything, then, was arranged, arranged between them, and I didn't have to think about the scene at all; I went straight away to find the theater owner, and I rented it for two days for the price of one, after giving him my word that nobody besides the actors would attend.

The following day I found a man who knew about electricity, and for a day's wage of six pesos, he also helped me move around the wings and touch them up with some paint. At night, after working almost fifteen hours, everything was ready, and, sweating and in my shirtsleeves, I sat down to eat sandwiches and drink beer while I listened without paying attention to stories the man was telling me about the town. He paused, then said:

"Today I saw your friend in good company. This afternoon, with that woman who was at the hotel with both of you last night. Everybody knows everything around here. She's not from here; they say she comes in the summers. I don't want to meddle, but I saw them go into a hotel. Yeah, what do you know, you live in a hotel, too. But the hotel they went to this afternoon was different . . . One of those. You know."

When Blanes arrived a while later, I told him that the only thing missing was the famous actress Rivas, and we had to figure out the automobiles, because we'd found only one, which belonged to the man who was helping me. I'd rent it from him for a few pesos, and he'd drive it himself. Then I had an idea: the car was a convertible, so all we had to do was have him drive by first with the top down and then with it up, or the opposite. Blanes didn't say anything because he was quite drunk, and I wasn't able to figure out where he'd gotten the money. Later it occurred to me that he might have had the impudence to obtain it directly from that poor woman. This idea poisoned my thoughts, and I kept eating my sandwiches in silence while he, drunk and humming to himself, walked around the stage, assuming the stances now of a photographer, now of a spy, a boxer, a rugby player, always humming, with his hat pushed back almost onto his neck, looking everywhere, from everywhere, scouring the place for devil knows what. With each passing minute I was growing more and more certain that he'd gotten drunk with money he'd stolen, almost, from that poor sick woman, so I didn't feel like talking to him, and when I finished eating my sandwiches I asked the man to go get me half a dozen more and another bottle of beer.

By then Blanes had grown tired of doing pirouettes; his indecent drunken stupor had made him sentimental, and he came and sat down next to me on a crate, his hands in his trouser pockets and his hat on his lap, his bleary eyes staring, unwavering, toward the stage. Some time passed without a word, and I could see how much he was aging, how his blond hair was faded and sparse. He didn't have many years left to play the leading man or take ladies to hotels or much of anything else.

"I haven't been wasting my time, either," he blurted out.

"Yes, I can imagine," I answered indifferently.

He smiled, looked serious, put on his hat, and stood up. He kept talking to me as he paced back and forth, as he had seen me do so many times as I dictated letters to my secretary in my office full of autographed portraits.

"I asked around about the woman," he said. "Seems like her family or she herself had money and then she had to work as a teacher. But nobody, you understand, nobody says she's crazy. Only that she's always been a bit strange. But not crazy. I don't know why I came here to talk to you, O adoptive father of sad Hamlet, your snout smeared with sandwich cream . . . to tell you this."

"At least," I said calmly, "I don't go prying into other people's lives. Or playing the Don Juan with women who are a bit strange," as I wiped my mouth with my handkerchief and turned to look at him with a bored expression on my face. "And I don't get drunk on money from who knows where."

He was standing there with his hands on his hips, looking back at me, pensive, and kept telling me unpleasant things, but anybody would have realized that he was thinking about the woman and insulting me only half-heartedly, just to be doing something while he was thinking, anything that would prevent me from noticing that he was thinking about that woman. He walked back over to me, bent down, then stood up right away holding the bottle of beer and slowly drank down what was left, his mouth sucking on the bottleneck until it was all gone. He took a few more steps across the stage and sat down again with the bottle between his feet, his hands covering it.

"But I went to talk to her and she told me," he said. "I wanted to know what all this was. I don't know if you understand that it's not just about pocketing some money. I asked her what this was that we were going to perform and that's when I found out she was crazy. Do you want to know? It's all a dream she had, you see? But the craziest part is that she says that the dream doesn't have any meaning to her, that she doesn't know the man who is sitting there wearing a blue sweater, or the woman with the mug, and she's never lived on a street like this ridiculous eyesore you've created. So, why? She says that while she was asleep and having this dream, she was happy, but happy isn't the word, it's something else. So she wants to see it all again. And even though it's crazy, there's something about it that makes sense. Plus, I like that there's no vulgar romance in any of it."

When we left to get some rest, he kept stopping on the street – there was a blue sky and it was very hot – to grab me by my shoulders and my lapels and ask me if I understood, I don't know what, something that he must not have understood very well either, because he never fully explained it.

The woman arrived at the theater at precisely ten o'clock wearing the same black dress as she was wearing the other night, with the watch and chain, which seemed all wrong for that street in that poor neighborhood on the stage and for her to lie down in on the sidewalk while Blanes caressed her head. But it didn't matter: the theater was empty; nobody but Blanes was in the audience, and as usual he was drunk, smoking, wearing a blue sweater and a grey cap folded down over one ear. He'd arrived early and in the company of a young woman, the one who would appear at the door next to the greengrocer and hand him his mug of beer; a young woman who didn't match up, another one, with that character type, the type I imagined, of course, because only the devil knows how she was in reality. She was a sad and skinny young woman, poorly dressed and made up, whom Blanes had, undoubtedly, found in some coffee shop, invited out for an evening stroll, and plied with an absurd story to get her to come. Because she started strutting about like a leading lady, and when I saw her hold out her hand with the mug of beer, I wanted to cry or throw her out of there. The other one, the crazy woman, dressed all in black, stood there looking at the stage for a while as soon as she arrived, her hands pressed together in front of her body, and to me she looked extremely tall, much taller and skinnier than I'd thought until that moment. Then, without saying a word to anybody, still wearing that sickly though now weaker smile, which grated on my nerves, she walked across the stage and disappeared into the wings from which she was supposed to appear. I'd followed her with my eyes, I don't know why, my gaze taking in the exact shape of her long body clothed in black, then pressing against it, clinging to it, my gaze accompanying her body until the edge of the curtain separated them.

Now I was the one in the middle of the stage, and since everything was ready and it was after ten. I lifted my arms to notify the actors with a clap of my hands. But it was at that point, without me fully realizing what was actually going on, that I began to know things and what this was that we were involved in, though I could never say it, the way we know the soul of a person and words are useless to explain it. I decided to call to them with hand signals, and when I saw Blanes and the young woman he'd brought moving into position, I scurried into the wings, where the man was already sitting behind the steering wheel of the old car that started up and shook with a tolerable racket. From there, standing on a crate, trying to hide because I had no part to play in this inanity that was about to begin, I watched her appear at the door of the shack, move her body like a young girl – her hair, thick and almost grey, hanging loose down her back, tied at the shoulder blades with a light-colored ribbon – and take long strides that were, unmistakably, those of a maid who had just finished setting the table and was stepping outside to watch the evening light fade and spend a quiet moment without thinking about anything; I watched her sit down next to Blanes's stool and rest her head on one hand, her elbows leaning on her knees, her fingertips resting on her partially open lips, and her face turned toward a faraway place beyond me, beyond even the wall behind me. I saw how Blanes stood up to cross the street and how he calculated his crossing to precede the automobile with its top up that drove by spewing smoke then promptly disappeared. I saw how Blanes's arm and the arm of the woman who lived in the house across the street met at the mug of beer and how the man drank it down in one gulp and returned the vessel to the hand of the woman, who slowly and quietly slipped back into the doorway. Again I saw the man wearing the blue sweater cross the street an instant before an automobile with its top down drove by quickly and stopped next to me, immediately turning off the engine; and, as the motor's bluish smoke dispersed, I saw the young woman on the sidewalk yawn then lie down on the floorboards, her head resting on her arm and hiding her hair, one leg bent. The man wearing the sweater and the hat then bent down and caressed the young woman's head; he started to caress her, his hand moving up and down, getting tangled in her hair, then he stretched his palm across her forehead, pressed the light-colored ribbon in her hair, and repeated his caresses.

I got down from the crate and let out a sigh, more relaxed now, then tiptoed across the stage. The man with the automobile followed me, smiling shyly, and the skinny young woman whom Blanes had brought emerged from the doorway to join us. She asked me a question, a short question, just one word, and I answered without taking my eyes off Blanes and the woman lying on the sidewalk, Blanes's hand still caressing the woman's forehead and hair, untiringly, without realizing that the scene was over and that this last thing, the caressing of the woman's hair, couldn't go on forever. Blanes was bent over caressing the woman's head, stretching out his arm so his fingers could run along the length of the grey locks from the forehead to the ends that parted over the shoulders and back of the woman lying on the ground. The man with the automobile was still smiling, then coughed and spit to the side. The young woman who had given the beer mug to Blanes started walking toward the woman and the man leaning over her, caressing her. Then I turned and told the owner of the automobile that he could take it out, that way we could leave early, and I came up alongside him, putting my hand in my pocket to give him a few pesos. Something strange was happening on my right, where the others were, and just when I wanted to give that some thought, I bumped into Blanes, who had taken off his hat and was exuding an unpleasant stench of drink, and he punched me in the ribs and shouted:

"Don't you realize she's dead, you swine!"

I stood there alone, doubled over from the blow, and while Blanes paced back and forth across the stage, drunk, in a frenzy, and the young woman with the beer mug and the man with the automobile bent over the dead woman, I understood that this was it, this was what the woman was searching for, what Blanes had been searching for on the stage the night before and still seemed to be searching for, rushing back and forth like a madman: I understood everything as clearly as if it were one of those things one learns forever as a child and words are later useless to explain.

1941

Masquerade

María Esperanza entered the park along the brick path that led to the lake through shadows cast by trees and turned just when it reached the water, colliding with the spotlights, the black backs of the people who were watching boats with streamers and music slip by, and the dancers on the artificial island. She was tired and her high heels, higher than any she had ever worn, made the tendons in her ankles burn like gashing wounds. She stopped; but this wasn't the place, she sensed, without knowing why, why it wasn't, and moreover she was scared of those absorbed, serious or smiling, faces, scared because those faces were so similar to her own under the violent, white, red, and black makeup she had covered hers with, scared that those faces would look and see hers, understand their commonality, and that then they would look at her with hatred for doing what shouldn't be done with a face like that, for she had had one, a few hours earlier, without makeup and clean in front of the mirror: shining, happy, with her uncombed hair dripping wet and shameless.

She walked along the shore of the lake that cut through the shadow and the grove, the dancing music on the island trembling in the air that swirled around her neck. She sat down on a bench and released her heels from her shoes, closed her eyes, puffed out her cheeks as she sighed, happy and drowsy as she resigned herself to what the night contained, distant music and the scent of flowers. But then came the memory of that horrific black thing that had happened a few hours earlier, right after the appearance of her clean face in the mirror, and the malicious face of that memory, of the command to go find men and bring back money, threatened to touch her heart, frighten her limp body on the bench. She rose, walking now toward the part of the park that faced the promenade.

As she approached the lights and began to discern the neon signs of the circus and the colored lights of the kiosks, and the ballet music on the lake died behind her as the marches and the tangos in the cafés drew closer to her cheeks, she stiffened her body, lengthened her stride, slowed her steps, and reenacted the walk she had rehearsed before she went out. Now she also carried the last head, held high, that she had contemplated in the mirror, with eyebrows arched and the promise of a smile.

Now she was in the midst of the noise in the other section of the park, a deafening mixture of music, laughter, calls to waiters, phrases repeated by the waiters at the counters. Just before reaching the intense light and the din, she still had the shadow of a tree she could peer out from to look at the stage and its gathered curtains. A trio of tap-dancers dressed as sailors were pounding the stage.

The small woman moved between two giants. One of the men had a sad, pale face with a nose hanging off it; the other was thin, with a narrow forehead and greasy black hair, and his whole head, his entire narrow body as it swayed, exhibited an incurable, active resentment toward life. She was blond and smiled excitedly, red, smiled with her baby teeth, shaking her hair, unduly marking the beat with her arms, her feet, her hips, she smiled, a white spotlight relentlessly burning her face, its whiteness gnawing away at her nose.

To the right a man in a frock coat was exhibiting a monkey dressed like a bridegroom that crouched on a table, while another monkey, a bigger, sadder monkey with leaden movements squinted as he pressed an accordion between his arms, always playing the same note, the same exhalation that sounded final. The man in the frock coat grimaced while talking in a hoarse voice, and people laughed heartily, always in unison, and María Esperanza – laughing as she leaned against the tree, her hand squeezing a knot in the bark – didn't know if they were laughing at the man, at what the man was saying, or at one of the two monkeys.

To the left, farther away, behind a string of blue and white lights – a blue so sad, so unpleasant, such as she had never seen before, such as she could never have imagined a blue could be – above piano music that seemed to be swirling, always repeating the same thing, a woman dressed as a man wearing a cap and a red scarf around her neck sang in an incomprehensible voice, smoking, looking from side to side as if following the journey of her words through the air and wanting to know how far they might go, how far she could manage to push them and onto the head of which spectator they would fall, under what table, and onto what patch of earth with trampled grass they would land. On the distant stage the woman dressed as a man had no face. María Esperanza stood with her back against the tree, the knot digging into her vertebrae. She couldn't know what the woman was singing about, but a random word from the nocturnal festivities came to offer her a sad happiness like that of a while before, lost in the shadow on the bench. The sky was black and as she looked at it she felt a cold breeze blowing from the beach, a breeze that could extinguish her energy and surrender her once and for all to desolation, she and her body, contemplated by the malicious visage of the memory she shouldn't think about.

She left the tree and began to walk among the tables. As she took her first step nobody looked at her, and as she moved her other leg all the heads turned to look at her, all the smiles, the shining eyes, the sweaty faces turned toward her, but then with the next step she continued alone, unseen by all. She stopped. She stopped hesitantly in front of the table of a fat man with a very dark mustache who was drinking a mug of beer, not looking at her, looking over the froth of his beer at the tap dancers on stage. She was alone as if she had brought the tree with her, as if she were concealing her profile in the slashed bark, and her hand, forgotten, could lean against the knot with polished edges.

A woman displaced a flowery hat as she leaned over laughing, and then the three faces of the tap dancers were looking at her, all the faces had turned toward her, and no matter where she walked, without losing, oh, thank god, that stride so lovingly practiced, she always had to step stupidly into the spot where the light was strongest, where the colored lights converged, the glances of all the people sitting at the tables and strolling by at leisure, alone, in couples, with children, at leisure through the park on the cool summer night. María Esperanza closed her eyes, felt her mouth in a pout, opened her eyes and walked over to the table of the fat man who was drinking his beer and happened to see her and made a friendly face as he slightly adjusted the knot of his tie with his finger, pulled on the bottoms of his vest, and pushed aside his mug of beer. Still looking at her with a friendly expression on his face, so friendly that she whispered *no* and kept walking, her body brushing against a row of reeds with sharp blades that repeated her whisper, dragging it along.

A loud round of applause rang out to the left, while the woman dressed as a man bowed, cap in hand, hair spilling out until it almost touched the white and blue lights, that disgusting blue that was capable of making her, María Esperanza, ill, of breaking her into pieces at that moment, sweating, feeling the makeup on her face softening, and the pain of her heels dig like knives into her ankles.

And right after the applause they turned once again, everybody turned to look at her, and the actor who came on stage after the tap dancers, walking quickly as the orchestra played a *paso doble*, dug a hand into his waist and sang, laughing, looking at her, took two or three steps and sang again for her, looking at her, mocking her, conversing with her alone as a shiver of laughter ran through the heads of the audience at the tables.

At that point she left the wall of reeds and approached a tall, thin man who was standing still and smoking, his straw hat pushed onto the back of his head, and stopped right before she touched him, looking him in the face. The man kept smoking, and his small sad eyes kept staring straight ahead. She turned quickly and continued in a straight line, but now with her own everyday walk, slow, her hands hanging by her sides, to the table of the fat man who was drinking a second mug of beer, which he put down right away when he saw her approach, so he could repeat his friendly smile until she sat down next to him at the small iron table. She saw for an instant that the fat man was looking at her with his friendly face. Then it darkened when he called to the waiter, then, smiling again – that thick syrupy sweetness that seemed to explain that she, María Esperanza, was the daughter of a fat man with a black mustache who was drinking beer in the park on a cool summer night – he took one of her hands from her lap, brought it onto the table covered by his own, and asked her a question, smiled, another question, two questions in all that she didn't manage to understand.

But she understood, happier as much for herself as for the crowd, who can't understand, that she was able to obey the black, hideous memory with its quick command to find men and return with money.

1943

Welcome, Bob

for H.A.T.

There's no question that every day he'll get older, farther away from when he was called Bob, from his blond hair hanging over his temples, from that smile and those sparkling eyes when he'd silently enter the room, murmuring a greeting or slightly moving his hand near his ear, and go to sit down under the lamp near the piano with a book or simply motionless and separate, lost in thought, looking at us for an hour, his face expressionless, his fingers moving every once in a while to handle his cigarette or brush ash off the lapels of his light-colored suits.

Equally as far away — now that he's called Roberto and gets drunk on anything, covering his mouth with his dirty hand when he coughs — from the Bob who drank beer, no more than two glasses even on the longest of nights, a pile of ten-cent coins for the juke box on his table at the tavern in the club. Almost always alone, listening to jazz, his face sleepy, blissful, and pale, barely moving his head to greet me as I walked past, following me with his eyes for as long as I'd stay, for as long as it was possible for me to withstand his blue stare leveled at me indefatigably, effortlessly maintaining his intense disdain and gentler mockery. Or on Saturdays with one or another young man, as furiously young as he, with whom he discussed solos, French horns, and choruses, and the infinite city Bob would build along the river when he became an architect. He'd interrupt himself when he saw me walk by, to briefly greet me, then not take his eyes off my face, balancing muted words and smiles on the corner of his mouth that pointed toward his companion, who always ended up looking at me and doubling the disdain and mockery in silence.

Sometimes I'd feel strong and try to look at him; I'd rest my face on one hand and smoke over my drink, looking at him unblinkingly, maintaining my attention on my own face to keep it cold, a little melancholic. In those days Bob looked a lot like Inés; I could see something of her in his face from across the room in the club, and there might have been a night when I looked at him the way I looked at her. But I almost always preferred to forget Bob's eyes, and I'd sit with my back to him and watch the mouths of the people talking at my table, sometimes keeping quiet and sad so that he would know that I had something in me more than what he'd judged me on, something closer to him; a few drinks would sometimes help, and I would think, *Dear Bob, go tell your little sister*, while I was caressing the hands of the girls sitting at my table or expanding upon a theory about one thing or another, so they would laugh and Bob would hear.

But neither Bob's attitude nor his gaze showed any signs of change all that time, no matter what I did. I recall this only as evidence that he never noticed my antics in the tavern. One night at his house, I was waiting for

Inés next to the piano in the living room when he entered. He had on a raincoat buttoned up to the neck, his hands in his pockets. He nodded at me in greeting, looked around quickly, and walked into the room, as if he had eliminated me with a quick nod; I watched him move about, walking in circles around the table, stepping on the rug with his yellow rubber shoes. He touched a finger to a flower, sat on the edge of the table, and lit a cigarette as he stared at the vase, his serene profile turned toward me as he leaned slightly forward, idle and pensive. Imprudently – I was standing up and leaning against the piano – I played a low note with my left hand and then felt compelled to repeat the sound every three seconds, looking at him.

I felt nothing but hatred and shameful respect for him, and I kept pushing on the key, stabbing it with fierce cowardice in the silence of the house, until suddenly I was on the outside, observing the scene as if from the top of the stairs or from the door, seeing him and feeling him, Bob, silent and lost in thought next to the line of smoke that rose tremulously from his cigarette; feeling myself tall and stiff, a little pathetic, a little ridiculous in the shadows, banging on that low note with my index finger every three seconds precisely. Then I thought that I wasn't playing a note on the piano with some kind of incomprehensible bravado but rather that I was calling to him; that the deep note my finger tenaciously revived on the verge of each previous vibration was the only godforsaken word, finally found, that I could use to ask for tolerance and understanding from his implacable youth. He remained motionless until Inés closed the door to her bedroom before coming down to meet me. Then Bob stood up and walked lazily over to the other side of the piano, leaned his elbow on it, looked at me for a moment, then said with his beautiful smile:

"Is tonight a night of milk or whisky? An impetus toward salvation or a leap into the abyss?"

I couldn't say anything; I couldn't smash his face in with one blow. I stopped playing the note, and I slowly withdrew my hand from the piano. Inés was halfway down the stairs when he said, as he walked away:

"Well, maybe you'll improvise."

The duel lasted for three or four months, and I couldn't stop frequenting the club at night – I remember, incidentally, that there was a tennis championship going on at the time – because when I didn't show up for a while, Bob would greet my return with increased disdain and sarcasm in his eyes, then settle into his chair with a happy grin.

When the time came that I wanted nothing but to marry Inés as soon as possible, Bob and his tactics changed. I don't know how he found out about my need to marry his sister and about how I had embraced that need with all the strength I had left. My love of that need had eliminated the past and every bond with the present. I didn't pay much attention to Bob; but a short time later I would remember how he had changed during that period, and at one point I stood motionless on a street corner, cursing him between clenched teeth, understanding that by then his face had ceased to be mocking and now looked at me gravely and with intense calculations, as one looks at a danger or a complex task, as if trying to assess the obstacle or measure it against one's own strength. But he didn't matter to me anymore, and I even came to think that his set and motionless face was beginning to show some understanding of what was fundamental in me, of an old past that was pure and that my beloved need to marry Inés had drawn out from under the years and the events and had brought me closer to him.

Later I saw that Bob was waiting for night; but I only saw it when he arrived that night and came to sit down at the table where I was sitting alone and signaled to the waiter to go away. I waited a while, staring at him; he looked so much like Inés when he moved his eyebrows, and the tip of his nose, like hers, how it would flatten a little when he talked.

"You are not going to marry Inés," he said at last.

I looked at him, smiled, then looked away.

"No, you are not going to marry her because something like that can be prevented if there is someone who is really resolved to stop it."

I smiled again.

"A few years ago," I told him, "that would have made me want to marry Inés even more. Now it doesn't make any difference at all. But I can listen to you, if you wish to explain . . ."

He lifted his head and remained staring at me in silence; maybe he already had his sentences ready and was waiting for me to complete mine to speak them.

"If you wish to explain to me why you don't want me to marry her," I said slowly, then leaned back against the wall.

Directly I saw that I had never suspected how much or with how deep a resolve he hated me; his face was pale, his smile tight and fixed between his teeth and his lips.

"I'd have to divide it up into chapters," he said, "and the night would never end. But it can be stated in two or three words. You are not going to marry her because you are old and she is young. I don't know if you are thirty or forty, and it doesn't matter. But you are a grown-up man, or rather, a broken-down one, like all men at your age who are not extraordinary," he said, sucking on his extinguished cigarette and looking out to the street then back at me; my head was pressed against the wall, and still I waited. "You probably have your own reasons to believe there's something extraordinary about you, to believe you have rescued something from the shipwreck. But it's not true."

I lit a cigarette, turning my profile toward him; he was a nuisance, but I didn't believe him; he made me feel lukewarm hatred, but I was sure that nothing would make me doubt myself after having recognized my need to marry Inés. No: we were sitting at the same table, and I was as clean and young as he.

"You might be wrong," I told him. "If you would like to name something about me that's broken . . ."

"No, no," he said quickly, "I'm not that childish. I'm not going to play this game. You're selfish; you're a sensualist, in a dirty way. You're attached to miserable things and those things control you. You're not going anywhere, and you don't really want to. That's all, nothing else; you're old and she's young. I shouldn't even be thinking about her in your presence. And you expect to . . ."

Not even then could I smash him in the face, so I decided to be done with him, walked over to the juke box, punched in something, and inserted a coin. I returned to my seat slowly and listened. The music wasn't very loud; someone was singing sweetly between long pauses. Next to me, Bob was saying that not even he, someone like him, had the right to look Inés in the eyes. Poor kid, I thought with admiration. He was going on about how during what he called old age, the most revolting thing, what caused the breakdown, or rather what symbolized the breakdown, was thinking in concepts, including all women in the word *woman*, carelessly pushing them to adapt to the concept created by some pathetic *experience*. But – he also said – the word *experience* was not even exact. There were no experiences anymore, only habits and repetitions, withered names to attach to things and bit by bit create them. That's more or less what he said. And I was gently thinking: what if he dropped dead or found a way to kill me right then and there, what if I described to him the images that he conjured for me when he said that not even he deserved to touch Inés with the tip of his finger, the poor kid, or kiss the edge of her garments, or her footprint, or things like that. After a pause – the music had ended and the lights on the juke box had gone out, increasing the silence – Bob said, "That's all," and walked off with his usual stride, confident, neither fast nor slow.

If that night Inés's face appeared to me in Bob's features, if at some moment the fraternal similarities used the trick of a gesture to give me Inés through Bob, then that was the last time I saw the girl. It's true, I was with her again two nights later for the customary debriefing, and my desperation demanded that we meet one day at noon, futile, knowing beforehand that any recourse to words or presence was futile, that all my monotonous pleas would die in a rather astonishing way, as if they had never even existed, dissolved in the enormous blue of the plaza under the soft green foliage in the middle of the best season of the year.

The small and swift parts of Inés's face that Bob had shown me that night, though directed against me and married to his aggression, shared the girl's enthusiasm and frankness. But how was I to speak to Inés, touch her, convince her through the suddenly indifferent woman of our last two encounters. How to recognize her or even evoke her while looking at that woman with a long stiff body in the armchair at her house and on the bench in the plaza, equally stiff and resolved and held upright on those two different dates and in two different places; that woman whose neck was tense, her eyes staring forward, her mouth dead, her hands planted firmly on her lap. I looked at her and she was *no*, I knew that all the air surrounding her was *no*.

I never found out which anecdote Bob had chosen; in any case, I'm sure he didn't lie, sure that at that time nothing – not even Inés – could make him lie. I never saw either Inés or her stiffened voided form again; I heard she got married and no longer lives in Buenos Aires. At the time, in the midst of my hatred and suffering, I liked to imagine Bob imagining facts about me and choosing just the right one, or the right combination, that was capable of killing me in Inés and killing her for me.

It's been almost a year now since I've been seeing Bob almost every day, in the same café, surrounded by the same people. When he was introduced to me – now he's called Roberto – I understood that the past has no tense and yesterday joins hands with a date from ten years before. There were still some worn-out traces of Inés in his face, and a certain movement of Bob's mouth managed to make me see once again the girl's long body, her calm and poised steps, and make the same unchanged blue eyes look at me again under her loose coiffure, crisscrossed and tied with a red ribbon. Absent and lost forever, she could remain alive and intact, forever unmistakable, identical to her own essence. But it was painstaking to dig into Roberto's face, his words, his gestures, to find Bob and be able to hate him. The afternoon of the first encounter I waited for hours for him to be alone or leave so I could talk to him or beat him up. Still and silent, staring sometimes at his face or conjuring up Inés in the shiny windows of the café, I meticulously composed the insulting sentences and found the patient tone to utter them, and I chose the exact spot on his body to land the first blow. But he left that evening in the company of three friends, and I decided to wait, as I had waited years before, for the propitious night when we would be alone.

The next time I saw him, when we began this second friendship that I hope will never end, I stopped thinking about any kind of assault. It was decided that I would never talk to him about Inés or the past and, in silence, I would hold everything that was alive inside me. That's all I do, almost every afternoon, in the presence of Roberto and the familiar faces in the café. My hatred will be kept warm and new as long as I can continue seeing and listening to Roberto; nobody knows of my revenge, but I live it, with rage and joy, from one day to the next. I talk to him, smile, smoke, drink coffee. The whole time thinking about Bob, his purity, his faith, the audacity of his former dreams. Thinking about the Bob who loved music, the Bob who planned to embellish the lives of mankind by building a city of blinding beauty for five million inhabitants along the banks of the river, the Bob who could never lie, the Bob who proclaimed the struggle of the young against the old; Bob, the owner of the future and the world. Thinking meticulously and calmly about all of that in the presence of the man with tobacco-stained fingers named Roberto, who leads a disgusting life working in some foul-smelling office, is married to a fat woman he calls "the wife"; the man who spends long Sundays sunk in his chair in the café, poring through newspapers and betting on horses by telephone.

Nobody ever loved a woman with the force that I love his debasement, how definitively he has sunk into the filthy life of men. Nobody has been as enthralled by love as I am by his fleeting sorrows, the lackluster projects that a broken and faraway Bob sometimes recites to himself and that serve only to measure the precise extent to which he has been forever besmirched.

I don't know if I ever welcomed Inés with as much joy and love as I welcome Bob into the gloomy and malodorous world of adults on a daily basis. He's still a newcomer, and once in a while he suffers an attack of nostalgia. I have seen him tearful and drunk, throwing insults at himself and promising the imminent return of the days of Bob. I can confirm that at those moments my heart overflows with love and becomes affectionate and sensitive like a mother's. Deep down I know that he will never go anywhere because he has nowhere to go; but I become delicate and patient, and I try to appease him. Like that fistful of native soil, or those photographs of streets and monuments, or the songs immigrants like to carry with them, I set about constructing for him plans, beliefs, and different tomorrows with the light and flavor of the country of youth, from which he arrived some time ago. And he accepts; he always demands that I redouble my promises, but he ends up saying yes, finally he manages the grimace of a smile, believing that some day he will return to that world and the hours of Bob, and he rests in peace in the middle of his thirties, moving without chagrin or missteps among the horrific corpses of former ambitions, the repulsive shapes of dreams that have been ground down under the mindless, constant pressure of so many thousands of unavoidable feet.

1944

A Long Tale

Capurro was in his shirtsleeves leaning on the railing, watching the faded afternoon sun carry the shadow of his head to the edge of the path lined with shrubbery that connected the beach to the hotel. The girl bicycled down the path and disappeared behind the chalet with its Swiss roof, then reappeared a moment later, the rhythm of her pedaling unbroken, her body upright on the mount, her legs wrapped in thick, grey, fluffy socks moving with slow ease, with calm arrogance, her legs with their knees exposed. She stopped the bicycle next to the shadow of Capurro's head and her right foot, disengaged from the machine, stepped for balance on the sparse, now yellow, grass, then she shook her hair off her forehead and looked at the motionless man. She was wearing a dark sweater and a pink skirt. She looked at him calmly and attentively, as if the tanned hand that moved her hair off her brow were enough to conceal her prolonged inspection, as she offered her body against the abating evening landscape, her teeth in tiredness, her hair mussed and that shimmer of sweat and fatigue that the reflection of twilight was gathering up to shield itself and stand out like a phosphorescent mask in the gloom. Then she left the bicycle on the grass and turned again to look at him as her hands touched her waist, her thumbs sinking under the skirt's waistband, and she showed him her profile, her hands clasped behind her, with no breasts, still catching her breath, her eyes on the spot in the afternoon where the sun was going to set. Suddenly, she sat down on the grass, took off her shoes and shook them out, holding her naked feet in her hands one at a time, rubbing them and waving her short toes, letting her reddened feet show over her shoulders, wiggling them in the just barely cool air. She put her shoes back on and stood up and spent a while turning the pedals with quick little kicks until she repeated that hard and hasty movement and turned a defiant expression on the man who was looking at her, her face retreating in the meager light, with defiance in the whole of her disdainful body, making everything that surrounded her – the metallic shine of the bicycle, the shapes and hues of the trees – complicit, as if sequestered by her. She mounted the bicycle and rode off behind the hydrangeas, behind the benches painted blue.

In the room Capurro spent a long time washing, leaving his fingers in the soapy water while he peeked at himself in the mirror, almost in the dark, motionless until he could make out the thin, white, unsmiling face, and he stopped to look indifferently at himself while someone wandered through the garden dragging something and singing *sotto voce*. He dried his hands and pulled his suitcase out from under the bed, shoved it with his foot and rummaged through it without looking, removing a few items of clothes and two small books and finally took out the folded newspaper. In the armchair next to the open blinds he looked at the headline – FUGITIVE BANK CLERK COMMITS SUICIDE – and the black and grey splotches in the photograph of the man staring with a startled face, beginning to laugh under a mustache with downturned ends, and he felt once again as powerfully as on the previous days that he was forever shut away in a private and narrow world, with no friendship or company or possibility of any dialogue other than what that ghost with the listless mustache could offer. Arturo whistled from the garden, climbed over the railing, and leaped into the light of the balcony dressed in his beach robe, shaking his wet head as he crossed the room, seeing as he passed Capurro's moves to hide the folded newspaper between his leg and the chair: "Still that ghost." He closed the shades, turned on the light, and undressed standing next to the bed.

"The belly keeps growing," he said as he pulled the towel back and forth across his shoulders. "I didn't think you were capable of this, of playing at remorse, as if you had killed him. Don't ask me again if in a twenty-dimensional world you're to blame that your brother shot himself."

Now standing on the rug, he pressed gently on his belly.

"I'm leaving tonight, I have to hurry," he continued. "But you never told him to shoot himself, you never told him to steal so he could buy Chilean pesos and change them for liras and the liras for francs and the francs for coronas and the coronas for dollars and the dollars for pounds and the pounds for águilas and the águilas for yellow silk petticoats and tricycles. You didn't tell him to do that, you didn't advise him to steal. So, now what?"

He flexed his legs as he stuffed the balled-up towel under his arm.

"Are you leaving tonight?" Capurro asked.

"Yeah, at nine. I'm already too healthy."

He put on his trousers and began to button them up in front of the mirror.

"What's more," he said, "it doesn't make sense. I once shut myself away with a ghost. But a ghost with a wired mustache?! Ghosts don't come out of nowhere, they come out of the phantasmagorical substance. If you want to call a bank teller with the mustache of a Russian general a phantasma-gorical substance . . ."

Capurro leaned his head against the back of the chair and looked at the bare ceiling.

"I'm to blame in one way, for having spoken to him encouragingly, for having told him things that convinced him that the ten thousand pesos in the till could make him rich."

"You're nuts," Arturo said, and he put on his jacket, whistling, then looked at himself in the mirror from a distance and brushed his hair; then he lit a cigarette and placed his foot on the seat of a chair. "That's all con-voluted nonsense. Well, life is convoluted nonsense. A surplus of subtlety. But I'm going to tell you something that would cure you if you were as subtle as I am. Did he spend the stolen money correctly, did he spend it exactly how you explained?"

"Him?" Capurro stood up, laughing. "What are you talking about. By the time he came to see me, there was nothing to be done. At first he made some good buys, but then he got scared and started doing stupid things. A lovely combination of currency with horse racing and roulette."

"You see? Certificate of lack of responsibility. I'll wait for you down-stairs."

He checked that he had his wallet and left, whistling, and as he walked away, Capurro thought about the man who had walked through the garden a while ago, dragging something, a long hose, perhaps, something heavy and flexible that made noise on the gravel and slid along the grass, slowly, while he was looking at his old face buried in the mirror.

Only after eating his fruit, sitting and facing Arturo in the dining room, did he see the girl next to a window, leaning toward the stormy night air, a pile of hair blown by the wind over her forehead and eyes, with light areas of freckles – now, under the tube of unbearable light in the dining room – on her cheeks and nose, while her watery eyes looked absent-mindedly at the shadow of the sky, her bare arms crossed over her evening dress, yellow, one hand protecting each shoulder.

An old man was sitting next to her and conversing with the woman seated in front of him, her fleshy white back turned toward Capurro, a rose in her hair over her ear; and as she moved, speaking, the small white circle of the flower went in and out of the girl's absentminded profile, and when she laughed, throwing back her head, the skin on her back shimmered, and the girl's face was forsaken in the night.

Capurro longed to remain peacefully by the girl's side and take care of her life while watching her smoke, until the moment came when she lifted her eyes, without uncrossing her arms, moving her head ever so slightly from the sky to the man's face. She looked at him again as she had in the garden, with the same calm and defiant eyes, with the exact same scornful provocation. How could he withstand the girl's gaze and turn his own on that youthful head, fleeing from there to burrow it into the night storm, lending his serious and weary man's face the sweetness and adolescent humility of freckled cheeks and neck, affixing his gaze on the intensity of the sky and spilling it out, laying it over that girl's face observing him motionless and expressionless, becoming lost without wanting to, without knowing, without being able to avoid it, in the blackened landscape of the garden behind the window.

Arturo smiled, smoking his cigarette.

"You've never seen her before?" he asked.

"Once. This afternoon in the garden. Before you came back from your swim."

"Cupid's arrow," Arturo said, shaking his head. "Well, well. And youth, inexperience. Lovely story; but there's someone who can tell it better. Just a second."

The waiter came to the table to clear away the dishes and the fruit bowl. "Coffee?" he asked. He was small, with a dark face, like a monkey.

"Sure," Arturo said, smiling, "whatever you're calling coffee. But the gentleman here would like to know about the bicycle excursions of the young lady at the window."

Capurro unbuttoned his jacket and looked at the girl, but already her head had turned toward the window and the black sleeve of the man wearing eyeglasses who was sitting next to her cut diagonally across her yellow dress, and then the head of the woman with the flower and her beautiful back bent over, hiding the freckled face, leaving only – a trace between her own dark hair and the ear of the man with the eyeglasses – one thick edge of the girl's red hair, heavy and severe along the edges, flaming along the crest where it caught the light.

"Nothing bad," Arturo continued to the waiter. "The gentleman is interested in cycling and would like to know if the young lady . . . Tell me, what happens at night when Mommy and Daddy go to sleep, or do they never surrender?"

The waiter swayed, smiling, the empty fruit bowl held at shoulder height, his slanted eyes darting about.

"Well, nothing," he said. "You know. At midnight the young lady takes off on her bicycle and sometimes goes to the forest, sometimes to the dunes." He managed to look serious, his face showing no malice, and he spoke as if reciting from memory. "What can I say? You know. Just that she comes back with her hair a mess and without makeup; one time I saw her and she gave me two pesos without saying a word to me, she just put them in my hand. Now, the passengers and those English boys from *The Atlantic* who come here to dance say that she always has someone waiting for her, and it's never the same one. But I don't say anything because I haven't seen anything."

Arturo laughed, slapping the waiter's thigh.

"There you have it," he said.

"So, two coffees?" the waiter said, smiled again, then left.

"Well, well," Arturo said. "A more interesting life plan than masturbating with a mustachioed ghost."

As she left the table, the girl looked again at Capurro, now from above, one hand still tangled up in the napkin, fleetingly, as the breeze from the window moved the lock of hair over her forehead like a bronze bell-pull.

On the veranda, holding his suitcase and his coat over his arm, Arturo patted him on the shoulder.

"See you in a week. Happy cycling."

He jumped into the garden and walked toward a group of cars in front of the hotel terrace. As Arturo crossed in front of the lights, Capurro leaned on the railing and smelled the air. He returned to his room and smoked, lying on the bed listening to the music that reached him intermittently from the hotel dining room, where by that time they must have started dancing. He cupped his hand around the warmth of his pipe and slipped into a slow dream, a lubricated, airless world he moved through only with enormous effort, slack-jawed, toward the exit where the indifferent light of day was slumbering, unreachable, while a rhythmic fusillade bellowed in the shadows behind him. He woke up in a sweat and went to sit back down in the armchair, breathing in the air of the storm with the scent of the sea, dense and hot. Almost without moving, he pulled the newspaper out from under him and looked at the headline and the faded photograph. He threw the newspaper on the table, finished smoking his pipe, put on an old suit, his raincoat, turned off the light in his room, and jumped over the railing into the soft earth of the garden and the wind that traced thick s's around his waist. Then he decided to walk across the lawn until he reached the stretch of earth where the girl had been sitting in the afternoon, her feet in her hands and her buttocks flattened against the ground. The forest was to his left, the sand dunes to his right, everything black and the wind hitting him in the face. He heard a noise, then saw the bright smile of the waiter, his monkey face right next to his arm.

"Too bad," the waiter said. "You missed her."

He wanted to punch him but he quickly quieted his hands that were scratching the insides of his raincoat pockets, and he gasped toward the sea, motionless, his eyes downturned, resolved, feeling sorry for himself.

"She must have left ten minutes ago," the waiter continued. Without looking at him, Capurro knew he'd stopped smiling and was twisting his head to the left. "You could wait for her to get back. If she gets a good scare . . ."

Capurro slowly unbuttoned his raincoat without turning, took a banknote out of his trouser pocket, and handed it to the waiter. Once again he saw his smile and imagined the ordinary monkey face around the smile, the little eyes pointing toward the temples, his wayward cynicism. He waited until he no longer heard the other's steps on the way to the hotel, then he lowered his head and planted his feet firmly on the elastic earth and the grass where she had been, wrapped in that memory: the girl's body and its movements on that remote afternoon, protected from himself and his past by an already enduring atmosphere of aimless belief and hope, breathing in the hot air where everything was forgotten.

He walked through the eucalyptus forest, slowly groping the trees under the wind, closing his eyes to protect them from the sting of sand in his face. Everything was dark and he couldn't find the blaze of the girl's bicycle light or the burning ember of a cigarette of some man who was smoking and sitting on the dry leaves, leaning against a tree trunk, his legs gathered in, tired, wet, happy. Now he was at the end of the forest, at the beach, one hundred meters from the sea and in front of the dunes. He felt cuts on his hands and he stopped to lick his fingers, looking at a light that was flickering in the water. He walked toward the sound of the surf, stepping on the packed sand along the shoreline, then turned to the right, toward the dunes, the sea on the left side of his body. There was no light, no movement in the shadows, no voice carried by the wind. He turned from the shore and began to climb up and down the dunes, slipping in the cold sand that spilled into his shoes, pushing aside the bushes with his legs, almost running, happy and furious, excited as if he could never stop, laughing inside the windy night, running up and down the miniature mountains, falling on his knees, his body slackening until he could breathe without pain, his face turned toward the motion of the water. He was alone in everything that was possible to know of the world, and he kept walking, sad and tired as if all despondent thoughts had managed to reach him there in the sand; and slipping, falling on his knees, rising hunched over, he sought halfheartedly the path back to the hotel, thinking about his face, more affectedly sad in the bathroom mirror.

He fell asleep again, half dressed, on the bed as in the sand, his open mouth sensing his entrance into the world of dreams and the storm that was exploding, beaten by thunderclaps, sinking and still parched, into the raging clamor of the rain.

Once again it was a summer morning on the veranda. He finished shaving and stepped out to look at the rain-washed landscape, while he spread the perfumed remnants of talcum powder over his face with both hands.

He saw three children running near the tennis courts and understood that his anguish could blend nonviolently into the morning. A blue Ford groaned as it climbed the hill, appeared on the road behind the chalet with its red roof, and drove past him on its way to the door of the hotel. He saw a policeman get out, an extraordinarily tall man wearing a wide-stripe suit, and a young, blond, hatless man dressed in grey, whom he saw smile with every sentence he spoke, as he held a cigarette between two fingers in front of his mouth. The hotel manager slowly descended the stairs and walked over to them, while the waiter from the night before appeared from behind a column on the staircase, in shirtsleeves, his dark head shining. Everybody spoke with minimal facial expressions, almost without changing the spot where their feet were planted, and the manager pulled a handkerchief out of the inside pocket of his jacket, wiped it across his lips, and put it back in deeply, only to pull it out again a few seconds later with a quick motion, squeeze it, and move it across his mouth. The children had sat down in the shade of the tennis court, leaning against the net. Capurro entered his room to get his pipe and, as he came out once again onto the veranda, as he became aware of his own movements, of the moroseness with which he desired to live and enact each gesture, as if he were trying to caress with his hands the gestures these same hands had made, he felt that he was happy in the morning, that there could be other days awaiting him anywhere. He saw that the waiter was looking down at the ground, and the other four men were lifting their heads toward him.

The young blond man tossed his cigarette far away; then Capurro began to separate his lips until he smiled and greeted the manager with a nod of his head, and then, before the manager could respond, before he could bow his head, while still looking at the veranda and patting his mouth with his handkerchief, Capurro lifted his hand and repeated his greeting. Then he returned to his room to finish getting dressed, placing a white flower in the buttonhole of his chamois jacket. He stopped for a moment in the dining room, watching the guests eat breakfast, and then he decided to have a gin, just one, at the bar, bought cigarettes, then joined the group waiting at the bottom of the staircase. The manager greeted him again, and Capurro noticed that his jaw was trembling, just barely, rapidly. Capurro said a few words and heard that they were talking, the young blond man came up to him and touched his arm; everyone was silent and he and the young blond man looked at each other and smiled. Capurro offered him a cigarette, and he lit it without taking his eyes off the blond man's face; then he took three steps back and looked at him again. He turned his back, walked to the first tree along the road, and leaned one shoulder against it. All of that had some meaning and, without understanding it, Capurro knew that he agreed, and nodded. Then the tall man said:

"Shall we drive to the beach in the Ford?"

Capurro went ahead and sat down in the passenger seat. The tall man and the blond man sat in the back. Capurro could see the manager talking to the waiter, shaking his head from side to side. He had put away his handkerchief, and he kept lifting his hand to his neck. The policeman sat down behind the steering wheel and started the car. Soon they were driving through the peaceful morning; Capurro smelled the cigarette the young man was smoking, he felt the silence, and the other man's quietude, his resolve filling that silence and that quietude. When they reached the beach the car stopped next to a pile of grey stones that separated the road from the sand. They got out, stepped over the stones, and walked toward the sea. Capurro walked next to the young blond man.

"What a day," the young man said.

"If it hadn't rained we would have died of heat," Capurro answered, a few steps later.

They stopped at the shore. All four were silent, their ties blowing in the wind. They all lit cigarettes.

"The weather is unsettled," Capurro said.

"Shall we go?" the young blond man answered.

The man in the striped suit stretched out his arm until he touched the young man on his chest and said in a thick voice:

"Look. From here to the dunes. Almost two blocks."

The other nodded in silence, then shrugged his shoulders as if it didn't matter. He smiled again and looked at Capurro.

"Let's go," Capurro said, and they all returned to the car in silence.

Just as they were about to get in, the tall man stopped him.

"No," he said. "Over there."

Over there was a house and a shed made with damp-stained bricks. The shed had a sheet-metal roof and black letters painted over the door. They waited while the policeman went to the house next door and returned with a key. Capurro turned to look at midday arriving over the beach, the policeman pulled open the padlock, and they all entered the shadows and the cold. The beams were smeared with tar and pieces of sacking hung from the roof. As they walked Capurro felt the shed grow bigger with each step, the long table made out of sawhorses in the middle moving farther away. He looked at the stretched form, wondering *who teaches the dead the demeanor of death*. There was a narrow puddle of water on the ground, and water was dripping from one corner of the table. A barefoot man, his shirt open over his ruddy chest, cleared his throat as he approached and placed a hand on one end of the plank table, allowing his short index finger to be quickly covered, shiny, with the water still dripping. The tall man stretched out his arm and pulled back the tarp, uncovering the face on the planks. Capurro looked at the air, the striped arm of the man that was still stretched out against the light from the door, holding the riveted edge of the tarp. He turned back to look at the hatless blond man, a sad expression on his face.

"Look here," the tall man said.

He could see that the girl's face was twisted back and it seemed that her head, purple, with reddish-purple splotches over a delicate bluish purple, would break off and roll away at any moment, if someone spoke too loudly, if someone struck the ground with his shoe, if time simply passed.

But her head, with the stiffened hair, the flattened nose, the dark mouth, its corners stretched downward, limp, dripping, remained motionless, its volume unchanging in the dismal air that smelled of bilge, his gaze harder and harder with each sweep across her cheeks and forehead and chin, which had still not decided to hang. One after the other they spoke to him, the tall man and the blond man, as if playing a game, taking turns hitting the same question. Then the tall man let go of the tarp, lunged forward, and shook Capurro, grabbing him by his lapels; but he didn't believe in what he was doing – all you had to do was look in his round eyes – and, when Capurro gave him a weary smile, the other hastily, hatefully, showed him his teeth, and opened his hand.

"Okay. Enough already," Capurro said, and everybody grew quiet, while the corner of the table kept dripping. He looked at the young blond man who was waiting, a cigarette between his fingers in front of his chest, turned his face toward the dead girl and stopped to observe the burlap bags hanging from the ceiling. The only thing he had to tell them was a long story, clipped, full of brilliant and mysterious moments that had nothing to do with what interested the men standing there in the shed, looking at his mouth, that also maybe had nothing at all to do with anything concrete that he could imagine. He directed a brief bow of friendship toward each and turned to leave, believing with each step that they would stop him, but he heard the men following him without touching him, without asking him any questions, without hurrying, as if he had just finished telling them the very long story and everybody was walking aimlessly, a little bent over from the fatigue of listening, listening now to the intermittent rustlings that the endless story kept making inside each of their heads.

1944

Ninth of July, Independence Day

Aurora spoke about the history of that fabulous country the night she agreed to go up to Grandi's room late to have tea and walked across the large terrace, expanded by the moon, then scratched at the blinds on the door. He saw her smile, her body hunched over, and enter with quick, silent steps, softly dragging her feet, her hands hidden under her coat and a hood covering her head; filled with mystery, with lawlessness, and with a shifting happiness as she remained behind him to enact the last rite of concealing her face. Then she sat down on the edge of the bed and looked at the base of the cone of light on her shoes, speaking in an unfamiliar tone, her voice held down to an unnecessary whisper, her breathing so rapid it exposed the edges of her teeth in her darkened mouth. And apart from the inevitable, apart from having a young lady in his room at night, Grandi felt no special desire for her, no impulse to draw close to her and touch her, certain, moreover, that the young lady was as empty as he, on that night and the others.

But she was surrounded by and filled with the adventure and feared failure like she feared a wound. Her falseness made her err, garble her movements, forget indispensable sentences that he continued to expect for many minutes after the moment they should have been spoken. Out of the incomprehensible commitment to remain a stranger to him, Aurora extracted odd facial expressions, the smile of a woman, any woman, movements belonging to others that seemed to take place outside her body and that her body revealed to have immediately forgotten. Then she rested, finally, at the night's final moment, with her mouth open and twisted, surprisingly ugly, pulling away from him as her hair rippled through the semidarkness and onto the rug.

Still now he could remember her brushing her hair in front of the wardrobe mirror and inspecting her own face; searching in silence, eager and disappointed, for any trace of a novelty; begging that image of a long-nosed girl with no makeup for a tiny trace, a crease or a glow that had been added and that she could contemplate next day and use as a reliable means of reconstructing the night and meeting the woman who had been with Grandi.

He could also remember her a moment earlier, crouching, bringing her smile close to the slightly bloody light of the stove where the water for tea was whispering, abruptly pulling her face away to inspect him and wink, still smiling; though not with the enchanted smile she had brought to the stove and that isolated her next to the circle of radiance, but rather with one that expressed avowed complicity, which didn't refer to the night and what it might contain, which was beyond sensuality and united them in the understanding of the ineffable in life and the variations of human destiny.

The now motionless gaze, hanging in his sightline just past the zone of air that disrupted the shape of the flowers and attempted to evoke her

– that rounded forehead that blanches in the light, that thick and solid ear, that placated streak of mouth – next to his face on those autumn and winter nights. It evoked the fog of fear in her eyes, the foolish sentence she mumbled when they tussled.

One afternoon she told him she didn't want to see him anymore and asked him to move out. She began to walk past him on the stairway and in the dining room of the boarding house without looking at him, without trying to avoid him, without showing that she was busy constructing something that would help to separate them, as if she herself had suddenly folded like her hands, empty and limp, with nothing to offer. At that time Carlota began to come on some nights to eat with Aurora and the priest, and Grandi amused himself comparing the face of his friend to the other's blond profile, which showed a single solitary eye separated from her straight, angelic nose.

Then there was an excessive forty-eight-hour finale, plunged in remorse and terror and the discovery of sin. Everything at once, shoved inside him forcefully and furiously so that all of it could fit; only once in a lifetime, true, but still unforgettable and agonizing. That same hand that was now holding Grandi's had been clenched around his arm while the taxi advanced in fits and starts, one Ninth of July at eleven in the morning, weaving its way through the crowd waiting for and running after the bus, blasting its unbearably loud horn past the flag-draped houses and the people wearing rosettes on their chests. He could feel Aurora's contained hatred churning in the head she leaned against a corner of the car, and he measured her fear through the spasms of her fingers on his arm, an animal fear in the face of imminent martyrdom, which compelled her to maintain that contact, to connect to another living being, even to Grandi; to spread her consciousness to somebody – anybody – to fracture her solitude with her fingertips pressed against the warmth of an arm so that fear would not overwhelm her.

Grandi came to know the unforgiveable smile and the stiff words of tenderness at the door to the doctor's office; he came to know the boiling coffee gulped down at the bar on the corner, the first telegram published in a five-cent newspaper read again and again, with teeth clenched, without understanding a word. He came to know the slowness of the trembling second hand on the yellowish circle of his wristwatch, the gaze with which he lapped up the faces of people at the counter and through the mirror behind the bar, begging for an expression, any expression, a gesture, any gesture, a defect or a physical peculiarity capable of distracting him and interposing itself between him and the unyielding image of a woman spread-eagle amid urgency, cotton, and blood. Then he was waiting on the street corner, leaning against a tree, distressed when others surrounded him and lost when they left him to go to their cars.

He entered a bakery and phoned Lankin, furiously stabbing his finger into the busy signal he reached. He returned to the corner and started to pace; from the third tree he saw Lankin on the balcony, leaning over, enormous, moving his head to search, his white coat open. At that moment he was certain that the girl had died, and he knew that sin brought punishment; he suddenly felt at peace, lonely and protected from all harm. He slowly climbed the staircase, chatting with the nurse. The waiting room was empty.

When the woman dressed in white left him alone, he opened the door to the room and saw Aurora stretched out on the bed, her legs covered with a coat, and as he approached, hearing the inevitable graze of his shoes on the linoleum, he desperately loved that pale head with its eyes closed and sunken in grimy blueness, and its long nose with dark nostrils. Aurora turned her head and looked at him; she smiled, and he had to lean over, stretch out his arm, and caress the girl's hair. Lankin opened the door and spoke a sentence, laughing. He had never spoken so loudly. Grandi leaned over the cot and looked gratefully at Aurora. Then he conversed with Lankin, who was walking around with a book in his hand, as he heard the voices and the honking in the street, the sounds of the maid in the dining room setting the table for lunch.

Out of all that, afterwards, nothing but Aurora's stare when he would come to pick up Carlota, and they had to wait together. *There shouldn't be a single memory left of her,* he thought, *and we are bound together only by the fact that she can keep her eyes fixed on my face, silent, for a time; and that I can measure in her features, in her movements, and in her way of making sentences out of everything that has been added, everything that was taken away and remains in her, lifeless, with no influence, like the tiny scar she had next to her left eye and that has now descended toward her cheek. And this is enough for her to be a different woman, for her to have never been naked with me, equally far away from my memory and from the girl with the long nose who ate with her back to the fireplace in the boarding house. She would never be able to imagine how that isolated and submerged memory, which continues to live without any sustenance, has become my secret and how important it is in the midst of my confusion when she wants to look at me. More meaningful than anything is the night she bent over next to the stove, and what remains is that day at noon when the taxi drove slowly toward Lankin's house.*

"I'm going out," Lankin said. "I don't want to wait for the two of you."

Twice he paced from one side of the room to the other, walled in by silence. He stopped in front of Grandi and looked at him.

"I'm going out," he repeated, finally.

Grandi nodded and watched him open the door and walk into the hall-way, without hat or coat. *And Hercules on top of it,* Grandi thought; *poor kid. Only I can know how much I dissembled when I talked to him this afternoon and how my gaze took in the worn-out collar of his shirt, the wrinkled tie, the misshapen and opaque shoes that he finally withdrew into the shadow of the table, as if to hide his dirty feet. How might that all be now, with the blood. And the memory of my conversation today, now that he has died, will have to remain in me, will have to be deposited in the same filthy blackness as my nights with Aurora and the abortion at noon. Only I will continue to know with how much protectiveness and scorn I patted his shoulder after talking to him, letting rip the worst of all laughs over his head. And I didn't do it so that he would kill himself; I didn't do it even to convince him that I was right. Only so that he wouldn't continue to look at me and smile with that unsettled expression on his puny adolescent face, with the glimmer of youthful mockery in front of a man he considers definitively over and done with because he is double his age and has kept nothing but his name and one or another corroded feature to testify that he, too, was once an eager and implacable being, in the vanished past, on a cloudy Ninth of July, in a taxi.*

1945

Back to the South

When he sat alone in the corner of the café, Óscar thought once again about Uncle Horacio's pale head lying on the cot, the head that apparently had accepted, once and for all, the expression of vague interest and courtesy he would don like a mask whenever he heard about people and things that had been in or passed through the southern end of Buenos Aires, the foreign zone that started on Avenida Rivadavia ever since Carnival 1938. Uncle Horacio would raise his eyebrows and almost smile as he waited for such conversations to end. Remembering his dead face, it was once again impossible to guess in what way and to what end hatred and scorn had acted upon the images and beings in the southern district of the city, the Barrio Sur, what distortion had been wrought, or – perhaps it was nothing more than this – in what shades of light did hatred and scorn envelop the banished landscapes of the south for Uncle Horacio.

On the first Saturday of Carnival in 1938, Uncle Horacio and Perla went out after dinner to take a walk along Avenida Belgrano; they left their apartment and walked slowly down Tacuarí and Piedras with their arms linked. Óscar knew they had gone to have a beer at a German café and had stayed there talking until after midnight. When they returned, she wandered aimlessly around the house, humming a tune by Albéniz, and shortly thereafter went to bed. Uncle Horacio sat for a while at the table where Óscar was studying. He seemed tired and took off his collar. He played with his watch, sticking a finger in his vest pocket, and stared pensively at the table during the pauses between his absentminded questions. Óscar saw him smiling gently, and he heard him laugh quietly when he got up and stood there for a few moments, legs astride, shaking his head. Then he sighed, asked one last question about books and exams, and went up to his bedroom.

On Sunday they didn't go out; all day long they drifted heavily and in silence through the heat of the house, shabbily dressed, preferring the darker and cooler corners, where they asserted their presence with thick morning newspapers, magazines, and shabby books from ancient times. When Óscar left at nightfall, Uncle Horacio was alone in his study counting out medicine drops. *She wants to leave and he doesn't want to put pressure on her by bringing up his disease,* Óscar thought, *or she wants to leave and he is going to find a way to pressure her by letting her know, without telling her, that he is sick again.*

Monday of Carnival they spent the whole day together and out of the house. Óscar saw them at night, friends once again; Uncle Horacio talked about many things, a bit excited and happy, with sweat on his forehead and little gasps when he smiled. On Tuesday, Óscar returned to Belgrano at dusk; Uncle Horacio was there alone, next to the window, his shirt open, his glasses hanging from his fingers by one temple, and the fifth edition of the newspaper next to his bare feet. They greeted each other, and Óscar saw only sleepiness in his face. Later he couldn't understand – because it represented some other unknown and had nothing to do with Uncle Horacio – finding on the tablecloth in the dining room, next to the glass of milk and the ham sandwich that Perla left him every night, a letter written in very blue ink, open, held in place by the centerpiece, with four very deep folds. The milk, the sandwich, and the letter had been put there by Uncle Horacio, by the man who was sitting next to the window in the other room; he wanted him to know, without questions, that Perla had left with apologies, oblivion, happiness, and the sovereign right to live her own life. They never again spoke of Perla; when Óscar returned at dawn, the letter was no longer on the table, and Uncle Horacio was still looking out the window at the warm Carnival night, his face now sporting the weak expression of benevolent weariness that would distinguish him till the end.

During their time on Belgrano, Horacio's son, Walter, visited them infrequently; but when they moved to a boarding house on Paraná and Avenida Corrientes, he started coming every night, well turned out, perfumed, his stiff and shiny long hair pushed back toward the back of his neck. Óscar heard the tapping of his heels in the hallway and then saw his white face, made of a material that was bloodless and aged, much older than he, as if Walter had lent it out to another man, who used it for years and filled it with squalor and ignoble visions while sporting false and hesitant smiles.

"Hey, how's it going?" the solitary face would say over the lamp between the dark wall and the black suit. He would greet Uncle Horacio and begin to pace back and forth between the balcony and the bed, telling stories about people in the theater and on the radio, about the money he would make that season, about his fabulous winnings at La Plata Racetrack. He constructed the skeleton of his life, and Óscar, with his books, filled it out and covered it with comfortless bruises, abject faces, hatless women in long gowns of dismal colors who chatted endlessly at small square tables and to music, always to the music of bandoneons or trumpets, or populated, in bathrobes, the courtyard of the boarding house during the siesta.

The barrier along Rivadavia was raised thanks to Walter. He didn't have the courage to tell the old man directly; he stood behind Uncle Horacio and spoke to Óscar, who was putting on his tie in front of the mirror.

"I saw Perla at a café along the avenue. She didn't say anything in particular, but she's okay."

Later, on other nights, they heard that Perla had been with a man who played the guitar at a Spanish café, and the dark and greasy face of Perla's lover became, for Óscar, inseparable from the memory of the woman. Uncle Horacio said nothing, he didn't appear to have learned of Perla's nocturnal proximity, just five blocks to the south. Óscar found out that he had heard Walter, because during their evening strolls, when they'd go out for a coffee, he would start to approach Rivadavia along Paraná, where the Plaza del Congreso opened out and toward which he looked night after night with the exact same curiosity; then he'd turn to the left and they would continue their conversation along Rivadavia to the east. Almost every night; past Paraná, Montevideo, Talcahuano, Libertad. Though they never spoke of it, Óscar discovered that Uncle Horacio's city and his world ended in the insurmountable border along Rivadavia; and all the names of streets, shops, and places in the neighborhood to the south were suppressed and soon forgotten. Hence, whenever anybody mentioned any of them in his presence, Uncle Horacio would blink and smile, not understanding, but pretending to, waiting patiently for the story or the characters to cross Rivadavia so that he could place them.

Thus they were throughout 1938, and thus they continued into 1939, until the beginning of the war, both of them gently hitting up against the wall of Rivadavia almost every night, knowing from Walter that the avenue *was full of fat people, and the other day there was a bullfighter.* They also knew that a new café opened almost every week, with songs and music; in each of those Óscar installed the guitar player next to a rejuvenated and loquacious Perla, who drank chamomile tea and clapped her hands to the beat. *It's because of the war in Spain,* Walter said.

But the war in Spain had ended long before, and for many months nocturnal Avenida de Mayo was for Óscar – and, he thought, for Uncle Horacio as well – ten blocks lined with noisy cafés, filled with fat men and women drinking beer on the sidewalks, while during the day bullfighters came and went with rapid footsteps. And the few times Óscar crossed Rivadavia alone at night and saw a recognizable Avenida de Mayo he returned without saying a word to Uncle Horacio and quickly forgot what he had seen. Thus he was sure that within Uncle Horacio the fantastical vision of the lost territory remained frozen, a place where Perla was talking and laughing, and where there was often a Perla in every noisy café, near a bullfighter, near a man with black hair, leaning over a guitar.

The last time Uncle Horacio was sick, the doctor looked at him with weary eyes while giving him the injection. "Who knows how long," he said later. "Maybe he'll live longer than you." Óscar said yes; but Walter didn't want to believe it and mumbled with the cigarette in his mouth – his mouth slightly twisted because of the cigarette, his high profile, exactly as Óscar would see him through café windows: "One day he'll give us a scare."

The scare came one night when the three of them went out for a walk, Uncle Horacio in the middle, on a Saturday at the beginning of summer. Uncle Horacio was walking slowly, talking, enunciating each word, about the association of corn growers in Canada, and Óscar was looking at him out of the corner of his eye, while Walter, his heels tapping, his narrow shoulders pushing forward, agreed, bobbing his head where his small hat left exposed the left side of his shiny hair. He always bobbed his head that way when Uncle Horacio began to repeat, in that familiar, flat tone, what he had read in books or magazines. Óscar thought about Walter, drinking maté in the afternoons at the boarding house, surrounded by the shouts and idleness of the women who shuffled around in their *rouge*-stained robes, repeating in a serious voice the articles his father had transmitted to him about the distribution of goods after the war, the size of diamonds, and the wave of sex crimes in the United States.

Uncle Horacio continued talking about Manitoba and reducing "bushels" to "kilos" on the corner of Talcahuano and Rivadavia and, without pausing, without any warning, without anything that revealed that he understood what he was doing, he kept walking and talking, crossing the invisible barrier on Rivadavia until he reached the opposite sidewalk. He stopped for a moment to catch his breath, then continued walking slowly, covering the short block that led to Avenida de Mayo. Over and behind Uncle Horacio, Óscar exchanged glances with Walter, who flashed him a smile, a sign of joy, as if he had just discovered that his father was no longer ill.

As they walked the two blocks down the avenue, Uncle Horacio said that the only country deserving of total respect among all those involved in the war was China. He mentioned some geographic names, some names of generals and conductors and a prophecy about the future of Asia. In front of the third café with music, Uncle Horacio stopped and looked inside, smiling.

"Okay," he said, "let's have something to drink."

Once again they looked at each other behind his back, and since Walter was now smiling frankly, about to comment on what was happening, Óscar relaxed and initiated their entrance into the small lounge, where a jukebox was playing *Capricho árabe*.

Uncle Horacio ordered three beers, looked around, then began to talk about the industrialization of colonial nations. During a pause, Walter said:

"Not many people here tonight. If we go across the street . . ."

But Uncle Horacio kept talking, his expression good-natured and carefree. When they brought the beer, he remained leaning over for a while, with the glass poised on his lips, not drinking, motionless, his eyes cast down. Óscar looked at Walter, who was checking out the back of the room, arranging the cuffs of his sleeves that showed under his jacket; he couldn't meet his eyes, so he leaned back, observing Uncle Horacio and waiting. He waited until he took a sip, put the glass down on the table, and leaned back in his chair, his mouth open to speak, and began to slide off the chair. Walter jumped up, rushed behind his father, and tried to lift him, taking hold of him under his arms. Standing between the waiter and a man who rushed to the table, Óscar leaned over to loosen the old man's tie. He saw his head move with great effort, then tilt toward one shoulder, then rise. That's when Walter shouted:

"Hurry, run, go get his drops."

Óscar ran out of the café, caught a taxi, and drove to Paraná and Corrientes for the medicine; he didn't want to think about anything except his memory of Uncle Horacio crossing Rivadavia and asking in a patient voice, without pressure, certain that he himself would soon be able to provide the correct answer:

"So, what is the secret of the strength of Canadian farmers?"

Óscar asked the driver to wait and ran up the stairs. There was nobody in the foyer; the good weather had started and it was Saturday, so everyone must have gone out. He entered the room and saw Perla sitting on the bed, one arm extended away from her body, her hand sunk into the bedspread, her breasts protruding farther than when she lived on Belgrano, perhaps fatter overall, and heavily made up. The woman smiled, tilting her head to one side like a little girl; it was the sign she always made to Uncle Horacio, the sign of winning arguments, saying she was sorry, taking him to bed.

"How's it going?" she said, and dropped her head without dropping the smile, until she almost touched her shoulder with her cheek.

Óscar didn't answer and for a moment he forgot about the medicine, the taxi that was waiting, Uncle Horacio slipping off the chair. He removed his hat and leaned on the table, facing her, looking at her. Then he also smiled, because Perla said:

"What's the matter? Surprised to see me, are you? Seems you're not so happy about it," and she began to lift her head. "Did Horacio go out? I wanted to see him . . ."

Óscar put his hat back on, went to get the bottle in the medicine chest, and as he was rummaging through it he spoke:

"He's there, at a café on Rivadavia, he's had an attack."

He heard her get up, walk back and forth and insist several times that it was impossible. She kept repeating: "As soon as now," and Óscar didn't know what she meant. He found the bottle and said:

"I have a taxi waiting to go back to the café. If you want to come, hurry up."

During the first taxi ride they didn't speak; Óscar was leaning forward, watching the street over the driver's arm, the little bottle pressed between his knees. When they reached the café, the phonograph was playing a Pasodoble and the table was empty, and a waiter was standing next to it, chatting with somebody at the next table, as he randomly waved a napkin.

"They took him away," the waiter said. "He was getting worse, and we called from here and they took him. I don't know where. They must have gone to Esmeralda 66. I'll go ask the boss, see if he knows."

The boss didn't know, but they spoke to the guard out front, and he told them that they had taken Uncle Horacio to Esmeralda 66.

"How was he?" Perla asked.

"I don't know," the guard said. "Not good. By the time I arrived he was completely out."

They continued to the public hospital in another taxi, and during this second trip a handkerchief appeared in Perla's hand, and she began to cry, her head bent forward, as if there was somebody nearby whom she could ask for something.

At the public hospital they let them in, led them down a corridor, walked through a labyrinth filled with stretchers, and entered a large room where Walter was pulling perplexedly on his shirt cuffs, and Uncle Horacio was dead, lying on a cot.

During the last ride of the night Perla was curled up in a corner of the seat, her large open hand pressing the handkerchief that covered her face. The car drove slowly down Esmeralda, and when she lowered her hand at a corner, Óscar saw her red eyes and swollen nose; her mouth, painted and shapely, with a bit of down under her nose, was still calm, pressed forward, the expression that helped Óscar identify her when he remembered her, the same as the mouth in the portraits that Uncle Horacio had hidden in his desk drawer.

"They threw me out as if I were . . ." the woman began to complain.

"No; they threw everybody out. There was nothing anybody could do there."

"I wanted to be there."

Óscar preferred to put up with the noise she made when she cried than listen to her talk. Perla leaned back in the seat, not crying now, her hand scrunching the handkerchief in her lap. Óscar remembered Uncle Horacio's head on the gurney and Walter pacing around him, the perfume of his cosmetics, his *compadrito* suit, his white shirt cuffs hiding his wrists, as he repeated — stopping to futilely look for a different phrase — the same words that Perla had uttered: "As soon as now . . ." He sighed, his lips twitching nervously as if shooing away a fly, and continued to drag the refrain around the gurney. "As soon as now." The nurse was standing in a corner, writing, and the doctor was drying his hands on the other side of the room.

"Hey," Perla said, "will you handle the arrangements?"

He looked at her in silence and, against the light that entered and cut across their faces, he saw her trembling with rage.

"Oh," Óscar said a while later. "Walter, that brute, he'll take care of everything."

"Poor Walter," she said. "He's very upset."

Óscar turned to look out the window, thinking: *arrangements*, and *upset* . . . and *Anyway, she's as fat as a cow.*

"You're the same as always," she said bitterly and weakly. "Seems you don't care much at all. Walter, on the other hand . . ."

"Could be," Óscar said. "You're right; Walter does . . ."

He told the car to stop on the corner of Paraná and Corrientes, while she shook her head and the sounds of her crying continued. Óscar waited for a moment, then told her that he was getting off there, but that if she wanted to continue he could give her money for the taxi. She said no and got out, and while Óscar was paying the driver, she waited, leaning against a wall, fatter than before, sunk in the shadows with her light-colored dress;

then they stood looking at each other in silence, and he smelled the perfume that came in waves from Perla's breasts as they rose and fell next to the empty doorway.

Then Óscar went into the café and found a solitary corner, trying to think of the words the woman might have been expecting as she stood motionless in front of him until they parted without speaking, and he could see her back as she walked away toward the avenue, toward the invisible wall of Rivadavia, back to the south.

1946

Esbjerg by the Sea

Good thing the afternoon has grown less cold and sometimes the sun, diluted, lights up the streets and the walls; because at this hour of the day
they must be walking in Puerto Nuevo, near the ship, or passing the time
strolling from one dock to another, from the Coast Guard kiosk to the
sandwich kiosk. Kirsten, stocky, in flat shoes, a hat plastered down over her
yellow hair; and he, Montes, short, bored and nervous, peering at the woman's face, learning the names of ships without meaning to, absentmindedly
following the maneuvers with the ropes.

I imagine him pressing his lower teeth against his mustache as he
weighs his urge to push the woman's peasant body, fattened up by the city
and idleness, and making it fall into that strip of water between the wet
stone and the black iron of the steamers, where there's the clamor of the
boilers and not enough room for someone to stay afloat. I know they are
there because Kirsten came today at noon to pick Montes up at the office,
and I watched them leave and turn toward Retiro, and because she arrived

with her rainy face: a statue's face in winter, the face of someone who fell asleep and failed to close her eyes under the rain. Kirsten is thick, freckly, stiff; maybe she already smells like a storehouse, a fishing net; she might end up with the stationary smell of stables and cream, which I imagine there must be a lot of in her country.

But on other occasions they have to go to the docks at midnight or at dawn, and I think that when the ships' horns allow Montes to hear the noise she makes as she steps on the paving stones, dragging her men's shoes, the poor devil must feel like he's penetrating the night on the arm of misfortune. Here in the newspaper are the lists of the ships' monthly departures, and I swear I can see Montes tolerating immobility from the moment the steamer blasts its horn and starts to move until it is so small that it's no longer worth watching; sometimes turning his eyes – to ask and ask, without ever understanding, without being answered – to the fleshy face of the woman who must be calming down, shrunken for pieces of hours, sad and cold as if it were raining in her dream and she had forgotten to close her eyes, so large, almost beautiful, dyed with the color of the water in the river on days when the mud hasn't been churned up.

I heard the story, without understanding it, the same morning Montes came to tell me that he had tried to steal from me, that he had concealed from me a bunch of bets on Saturday and Sunday, planning to cover them himself, and now he couldn't pay back what he'd lost. I didn't want to know why he'd done it, but he was riled up with the need to tell me, and I had to listen to him as he thought about luck, so good to his friends, but only to them, and above all I had to not get angry, for when all was said and done, if that idiot hadn't tried to steal from me, those three thousand pesos would have had to come out of my pocket. I cursed him until I ran out of words, and I used every possible way of humiliating him that I could think of until it was left without a shadow of a doubt that he was a pathetic man, a bad friend, a bastard, and a thief; and there was also no doubt that he agreed and would have no problem admitting it in front of anybody at all if some day on a whim I ordered him to do so. And also from that Monday on it was established that every time I'd insinuate that he was a bastard, indirectly, mixing the allusion into any conversation whatsoever, no matter what the circumstances, he would have to immediately understand the meaning of my words and let me know, with a quick smile, just barely moving his mustache to one side, that he had understood my meaning and that I was right. We didn't agree to this in so many words, but this is what's been happening ever since. I paid the three thousand pesos without saying a word to him, and for several weeks I kept him ignorant of my decision whether to help him or persecute him; then I called him and said, yes, I accepted his proposal and he could start to work in my office for two hundred pesos a month, which I wouldn't pay him. And in a little more than a year, in less than a year and a half, he would have paid me what he owed me and would be free to go find a rope to hang himself. He doesn't, of course, work for me; I couldn't use Montes to do anything, since it was impossible for him to continue to handle the betting. I have this office for auctions and consignments to make things easier for myself, to meet people here and use the telephones. So he started to work for Serrano, who's my partner for certain things and has a desk next to mine. Serrano pays his salary, actually pays it to me, and he has him all day going from the customs office to the warehouses, from one end of the city to the other. It wouldn't have been good for me if anybody found out that an employee of mine wasn't as safe as a window at the racetrack; so nobody has.

I think he told me the story, or almost all of it, that first day, Monday, when he came to see me, cowering like a dog, his face green, revolting cold sweat shining on his forehead and down the sides of his nose. He must have told me the rest later, the few times we talked.

It started along with winter, with those first dry cold spells that make all of us think, without realizing what we are thinking, that the fresh, clean air is good for business, for outings with friends, for ambitious projects; opulent air, maybe that's it. He, Montes, returned home on one of those evenings and found his wife sitting next to the iron stove staring at the fire blazing inside. I don't see how that matters, but he told it like that and kept repeating it. She was sad and didn't want to say why, and she kept being sad, not wanting to talk, that night and for a whole week. Kirsten is fat, heavy, and she must have very beautiful skin. She was sad and didn't want to tell him what was going on. "It's nothing," she said, as women from every country say. Then she started filling the house with photographs of Denmark, the king, ministers, landscapes full of cows and mountains, or whatever. She kept saying that she was fine, and that idiot, Montes, imagined one thing or another but never found out. Then letters started arriving from Denmark; he didn't understand a word, and she explained that she'd written to some distant relatives and these were their replies, though the news wasn't very good. He said jokingly that she wanted to leave, and Kirsten denied it.

And that night or another soon thereafter, she touched his shoulder just as he was falling asleep and insisted again that she didn't want to leave; he lit a cigarette and agreed with everything she said while she talked, as though reciting words from memory, about Denmark, the flag with the cross and a path over the hill to the church. All of it, and so she could convince him that she was totally happy with America and with him, until Montes fell asleep peacefully.

For a while letters kept coming and going, and suddenly one night she turned off the light when they were in bed and said, "If you let me, I'll tell you something, and you have to listen without saying a word." He said, yes, and remained stretched out and motionless beside her in bed, letting the ash of the cigarette fall into a fold in the sheet, his attention rapt, like a finger on the trigger, waiting for a man to appear in the story she was telling. But she didn't mention any man, and, her voice hoarse and soft, as if she'd just stopped crying, she said that you could leave bicycles in the streets and shop doors open when you went to church or anywhere else because there are no thieves in Denmark; she told him that the trees were much bigger and older than anywhere else in the world, and that they had an aroma, each tree had a totally distinctive aroma, which remained unique even when mixed with the other aromas of the forests; she said that at dawn you woke up when the sea birds started to screech, and you could hear the sounds of the hunters' rifles; and there spring grows hidden under the snow until it leaps out all at once and encroaches upon everything like a flood, and people all talk excitedly about the snowmelt. That's the time, in Denmark, when there's more activity in the fishing villages.

She also kept repeating: "*Esbjerg er nær ved kysten,*" and that was what made the strongest impression on Montes, even though he didn't understand it; he says that this made him want to cry, something in his wife's voice as she was telling him all that, her low voice, that intoning people use without meaning to when they pray. Over and over again. The fact that he didn't understand melted him, filled him with pity for his wife – heavier than him, and stronger – and he wanted to protect her like a lost child. It must have been, I think, because the sentence he couldn't understand was the most remote, the most foreign, and it came from the part of her he didn't know. From that night on he started to feel more and more sorry for her, as if she were sick, sicker and sicker every day, and no chance of recovery.

That's how he came to think that he could do something big, something that would be good for him, that would help him live and that would bring comfort to him for years. It occurred to him to find the money to pay for Kirsten to travel to Denmark. He started asking around before he was really thinking of doing it, and he found out that two thousand pesos would be enough. Afterwards, he didn't realize that he had inside him the need to get hold of those two thousand pesos. It must have been like that, without him knowing what was going on. To get hold of those two thousand pesos and tell her one Saturday night after they'd had dinner at an expensive restaurant, while they were drinking their last glass of wine. Tell her and see in her face, a little flushed from the food and the wine, that she didn't believe him, that she thought he was lying, then after a while, slowly, excitement and joy, then tears and the decision to not accept his offer. "I'll get over it," she would say, and Montes would keep insisting until he'd convinced her, and also convinced her that he didn't want to separate, and he would be here waiting for her however long it took.

Some nights, when he thought about the two thousand pesos in the dark, about how to get hold of them and about that scenario in which they'd be sitting one Saturday night at a reserved booth at Scopelli, and, with a serious expression on his face, a glimmer of joy in his eyes, he'd start to tell her, he'd start by asking her what day she wanted to leave; some nights, when he dreamed about her dream while waiting to fall asleep, Kirsten would speak again about Denmark. In reality it wasn't Denmark, only part of the country, a very small piece of land where she'd been born, learned a language, where she'd danced with a man for the first time and seen somebody she loved die. It was a place she had lost as one loses a thing and can't forget it. She told him other stories, though she almost always repeated the same ones, and Montes believed that he was seeing in their bedroom the paths she walked down, the trees, the people, and the animals.

Very plump, taking over the bed without realizing it, the woman was looking up at the ceiling, talking; and he was always certain that he knew how her nose arched over her mouth, how her eyelids drooped surrounded by fine wrinkles, and how Kirsten's chin just barely trembled as she spoke her sentences in a faltering voice that originated in the depths of her throat, a bit tiresome to listen to.

Then Montes thought about taking out a loan from the bank, from moneylenders, and he even considered the possibility that I would give him the money. One Saturday or Sunday he found himself thinking about Kirsten's trip while he was with Jacinto in my office answering the phones and taking bets for Palermo or La Plata. There are slow days, with barely a thousand pesos worth of bets; but sometimes there's a strong showing and money comes in and it can even top five thousand. He was supposed to call me before each race and tell me the status of the bets; if the odds were high – sometimes you can feel it – I'd try to cover myself by passing on certain bets to Vélez, Martín, or Vasco. Then it occurred to him that he could not tell me, that he could hide three or four of the biggest bets from me, foot the bill on his own, for thousands of tickets, and, if he had the courage, bet his wife's trip against a bullet to the head. He could do it if he dared; Jacinto had no way of finding out how many tickets were in play on each call. Montes told me he'd been thinking about it for almost a month; that sounds reasonable, seems like a guy like him had to have hesitated and gone through a lot before starting to sweat nervously in between calls. But I would wager a lot of money on him lying about this; I would wager he did it at a specific moment, that he made the decision all of a sudden, that he had a burst of confidence and calmly started to steal from me right in front of that idiot, Jacinto, who suspected nothing, who afterwards only said: "I did tell myself that there were too few tickets for an afternoon like that." I'm certain Montes had a hunch and felt that he was going to win and that he hadn't planned it at all.

That's how he stared squirreling away bets that added up to three thousand pesos, and how he started pacing around the office, sweating and despairing, looking at the spreadsheets, looking at Jacinto's gorilla body in a raw silk shirt, looking out the window at the Diagonal, which was starting to fill up with afternoon traffic. So, when he began to realize he was losing and that the dividends kept growing, hundreds of pesos a call, that's when he started sweating that special sweat of cowards – greasy, a little green, cold – that he still had on his face when Monday at noon he finally had enough strength in his legs to return to the office and talk to me.

He had talked to her about it before he tried to steal from me; he told her that something very important and very good was about to happen, that there would be a gift for her that was beyond compare and was something that couldn't be touched. That's why afterwards he felt he had to tell her about his bad luck; and it wasn't in the reserved booth at Scopelli, or drinking an imported Chianti, but rather in the kitchen of their house, sucking on the metal maté straw while her round face, in profile and reddened by the reflection, watched the flames leaping inside the iron stove. I don't know how much they cried; afterwards he made arrangements to pay me back with his labor, and she found a job.

The other part of the story started when she, a short time later, got used to spending hours after work outside the house; she'd come late when they made a date, and sometimes she'd wake up very late at night, get dressed, and go out without a word. He couldn't bring himself to say anything, couldn't bring himself to say a lot and confront it head on, because they're living on her earnings, because he doesn't take home anything from his job with Serrano, except a drink now and then that I sometimes pay for. So he kept his mouth shut and waited his turn to inflict upon her his sullenness, a different sullenness, which was appended to the one that came over them on the afternoon that Montes tried to steal from me, and that I don't think will leave them till the day they die. He didn't trust her, and he was filling himself up with stupid ideas until one day he followed her and saw that she went to the port and dragged her shoes along the stones, alone, and stayed there for a long time, stiff, looking out over the water, near to but always separate from the people who go to see off the passengers. Like in the stories she had told him, there was no man. This time they talked, and she explained it to him; Montes also repeats something else that doesn't matter: he insists, as if I could never believe him, that she explained to him in a perfectly natural voice that she wasn't sad or angry or confused. She said she always went to the docks, at any time of day or night, to watch the ships departing for Europe. He was worried about her and wanted to struggle against this, wanted to convince her that what she was doing was worse than staying at home; but Kirsten kept talking in a perfectly natural voice, and said that it did her good, and she would have to keep going to the docks to watch the ships depart, to make some gesture of farewell or simply watch until her eyes grew tired, as many times as she could.

And he ended up being convinced that his duty was to accompany her, a way to pay off the debt he owed her, as he is paying off the one he owes me; and now, on this Saturday afternoon, like so many other nights and mid-days, when the weather is good, and sometimes when there are rain showers that combine with the one that's always wetting her face, they walk together past Retiro, then along the pier until the ship departs, and they mingle a little with the people with their coats, luggage, flowers, and hand-kerchiefs, and when the ship begins to move, after it blows its horn, they stand still and stiff and watch, they watch until they can't any longer, each with his or her own hidden and distinctive thoughts, but in agreement, without knowing it, in their despair and in the feeling that each is alone, which always turns out to be surprising when we stop to think about it.

1946

The House in the Sand

When Díaz Grey with sheer indifference accepted being left alone, he began to play the game of recognizing himself in the only memory, shifting, by now undated, that he wished to retain. He saw the images from this memory and saw himself as he carried it around and made corrections to it to prevent it from dying, redressing the depletion at every awakening, propping it up with unplanned inventions, as he leaned his head against his office window, as he took off his white coat in the evenings, as he grew bored, smiling throughout long evenings in the hotel bar. His life, he himself, were now nothing more than that memory, the only one worthy of being evoked and corrected, of its meaning being counterfeited, over and over again.

The doctor suspected that with the years he would end up believing that the first memorable part of the story portended everything that happened later with several variations; he would end up acknowledging that the perfume of the woman – it had been wafting toward him throughout the whole trip from the front seat of the car – contained and encapsulated all subsequent events, everything he now remembered denying, everything that would perhaps achieve perfection in his dotage. He would then discover that Red, the shotgun, the violent sun, the legend of the buried ring, the premeditated discrepancies in the crumbling chalet and even the final bonfire, were already in the perfume of unknown brand that on certain nights, even now, he managed to smell on the surface of sugary drinks.

After the trip along the coast, at the beginning of the memory, the car turned off the main road and started to climb, slowly and uncertainly, until Quinteros stopped and turned off the headlights. Díaz Grey did not want to learn about the landscape; he knew the house was surrounded by trees, high above the river, isolated amid the dunes. The woman didn't get out; they walked away. Quinteros handed him the keys and the folded banknotes. The flame of the lighter she brought to her cigarette might have fleetingly touched their profiles.

"Don't leave, and don't get impatient. Along the beach to the right is the town," Quinteros said. "Above all, don't do anything. We'll figure out how to resolve this. Don't try to see me or call me. Understood?"

Díaz Grey climbed to the house, pretending to try to hide his white suit as he zigzagged between the trees. The car drove back to the road and accelerated until the sound of the motor mixed with that of the sea, until he was left listening only to the sea, his eyes closed, tenaciously repeating to himself that he was alive in a month in autumn, remembering the last few weeks spent almost exclusively signing morphine prescriptions in Quinteros's shiny new office, looking slyly at Quinteros's English lover – Dolly or Molly – who put them in her purse and placed ten-peso bills on the corner of the table, never giving them to him directly, never speaking, never even showing that she saw him and was attentively following the quick and obedient movement of Díaz Grey's hand over the prescription pad.

The sunny days that repeated themselves at the beach before Red's arrival turned into one single day in his memory, of normal length but able to contain all the events: an autumn day, almost hot, which could have, in addition, contained his own childhood and the multitude of desires that had never been fulfilled. He did not need to add a single minute to see himself at the left end of the beach chatting with the fishermen as they pulled crabs apart for bait; to see himself walking along the shore toward town, to the store where he bought his food and got just slightly tipsy, returning a monosyllable for every one of the shopkeeper's assertions. On the same almost boiling hot day, he was also swimming in the beach's complete solitude, inventing, among so many other things, a rotten log floating on the waves and a triplet of gulls shrieking over it. He climbed up and slid down the dunes, hunted insects among the stubble of the shrubs, anticipating the spot where the ring would be buried.

And, moreover, while this was taking place, Díaz Grey yawned in the hallway of the chalet, stretched out on a beach chair, a bottle next to him, an old magazine on his lap; rusted, useless, and vertical against the trunk of the vine, the shotgun he found in the shed.

Díaz Grey was with his bottle, his disappointment, his magazine, and the shotgun when Red appeared from the trees and started climbing up to the house, his jacket slung over one shoulder, his large back bent. Díaz Grey waited until Red's shadow touched his own legs; he lifted his head and looked at the unkempt hair, the thin and freckled cheeks; he was filled with a mixture of pity and revulsion, which would remain unchanged in his memory, stronger than any willpower of memory or imagination.

"Dr. Quinteros sent me. I'm Red," he said with a smile; with one arm leaning on his knee, he waited for the astonishing alterations his name would enact on the landscape, on the morning that was beginning to wane, on Díaz Grey and his past. He was much more burly than the doctor, even as he was, hunched over, constructing his premature hump. They barely spoke; Red exposed the edges of his small teeth, like a child's, stuttered, and turned to look toward the river.

Díaz Grey could continue motionless, just as alone as if the other hadn't arrived, as if the other hadn't stretched out his arm and opened his hand to let his jacket fall, as if he hadn't squatted down until he was sitting on the veranda, his legs dangling, his torso bent too far toward the beach. The doctor recalled Red's clinical history, the bombastic description of his pyromania, as written by Quinteros, in which this red-haired semi-moron, known user of matches and petrol cans in the northern provinces, appeared to be attempting to identify with the sun and interject his own immolation into the maternal darkness. Perhaps now, looking at the reflections on the water and the sand, he was evoking, poeticized and imperious, the blazes he had confessed to Quinteros.

"Don't you eat?" Red asked in the afternoon. Then Díaz Grey remembered that the other one was there, bent over, his round head dangling toward the sand, which the swirling winds were beginning to raise. He let him into the house and they ate, he tried to get him drunk in order to find out something that didn't interest him: if he'd come to hide or to keep watch over him. But Red barely talked at all while he ate; he drank every glass he was offered, then went to lie down, barefoot, in a corner of the house.

Then the rainy days began, a stretch of fog that tangled in and hung from the trees, quickly fading, sometimes erasing and at others reviving the colors of the leaves crushed in the sand. *He isn't here*, Díaz Grey thought, looking at Red's huddled and silent body, seeing him walk around barefoot, push through the humidity with his shoulders, shake himself like a wet dog.

With one arm half bent, with a smile that revealed the long wait for an impossible miracle, Red took charge of the shotgun. He began by bending over it at night next to the lamp, to handle it, brooding and awkward, and oil the screws and the springs; in the mornings he would penetrate the fog with the shotgun slung over his shoulder or dangling against his leg.

The doctor looked around for remnants of boxes, paper, rags, gathered a few almost-dry branches, and one night lit a fire in the fireplace. The flames shed light on the hands folded over the open shotgun; Red finally lifted his head and looked at the fire, staring, his face showing only the absentminded expression of one who is helped to dream by the oscillation of the light, the soft surprise of the sparks. Then he stood up to reposition the logs, handling them carelessly; he sat back down on the small kitchen stool that he favored and picked up the shotgun again. Long before the fire burned down, he went outside to inspect the night, where the fog was turning to drizzle and was already sounding on the roof. He returned, shaking off the cold, and the doctor saw him move nonchalantly past the radiance of the embers, which turned his drenched face red, then lie down on his bedding and immediately fall asleep, his face to the wall, hugging the shotgun. Díaz Grey threw a rag over his muddy feet, stroked then patted his head, and let him sleep, transformed into a dog, feeling once again alone for more days and nights until one morning there was intermittent sunshine. Then they went down to the beach – Red saw him go out and followed him, stopping to aim the shotgun at the few birds he was capable of imagining, then trotting until he almost caught up – and they walked along the shore to the town. With a beach bag full of food and bottles they returned under an already sullen sky; the doctor could see Red's wide bare feet pressing into the various spots where the ring would be buried.

It rained all day, and Díaz Grey rose to light the lamp one minute before he heard the sound of the motor on the road. Here begin the moments that feed the rest of the memory and endow it with variable meaning; and, just as the days and the nights before Red's arrival turned into a single day of sunshine, this piece of the memory expanded and was renewed on a rainy afternoon, lived inside the house.

He heard them talking as they climbed to the chalet; he recognized Quinteros's voice, guessed that the woman who stopped to laugh was the same; he looked at Red, motionless and silent, hugging his knees on his stool; he placed the lamp on the table, lit between him and those who were about to enter.

"Hello, hello," Quinteros said. He was smiling, overstating his satisfaction; he touched the woman's shoulder, as if urging her to utter a greeting. "I think you know each other, don't you?"

She held out her hand and in one question mentioned boredom and loneliness. Díaz Grey recognized the perfume, knew her name was Molly.

"Things are almost all arranged," Quinteros said. "You will soon return to your cotton and your iodine, and with squeaky-clean credentials. I had no choice but to send you this beast; I hope he doesn't bother you, and that you can tolerate him. I couldn't arrange anything else; careful with the matches."

Molly went over to the corner where Red was rocking back and forth making the stool creak. She touched his head and leaned over to ask him useless questions, offer her own obvious answers.

Díaz Grey understood, and was touched, that she had been able to discover, with a single glance, perhaps from the smell, that Red had turned into a dog. He leaned over, playing with the wick of the lamp, to hide his face from Quinteros.

"I'm having a great time. The best vacation of my life. And Red doesn't bother me; he doesn't talk, he's in love with the shotgun. I can carry on like this indefinitely. If you'd like something to eat . . ."

"Thanks," Quinteros said. "Just a few more days, everything is being arranged." The woman continued to shrink along with Red's smile, her raincoat sweeping the floor. "But I think I'm going to spoil your holiday. Would it be a problem if Molly stayed here a few days? It's a good idea to take her out of circulation."

"Not for me," Díaz Grey said; he quickly moved the tremor of his hand away from the lamp. "But for her, to live here . . ."

He stepped away from the table, pointing to the walls of the room, moving in and out of the zone of perfume.

"She'll manage," Quinteros said. "That's true, right, you'll manage? Two or three days."

"I have Red here to sing to me."

"She'll explain it to you if she wants," Quinteros said.

He took his leave almost immediately, and the two descended with their arms around each other, slowly, in spite of the rain wetting and flattening the woman's hair.

Now Quinteros disappears until the end of the memory; in the motionless, singular rainy afternoon, she chooses the spot where she will set up her bed and guides Red through the task of emptying out the small room that faces west. When the bedroom is ready, the woman takes off her raincoat, puts on some beach shoes; she adjusts the position of the lamp on the table, imposes a new lifestyle, serves wine in three glasses, deals out the cards, and tries to explain everything using nothing but a smile, as she smoothes down her damp hair. They play one hand after another; the doctor begins to understand Molly's face, her restless blue eyes, whatever hardness there is in her wide jaw, in the ease with which she can liven up her mouth then abruptly render it inexpressive. They eat something and start drinking again; she says goodbye before she goes to bed; Red drags his bed closer to the door of the woman's bedroom and lies down, the shotgun on his chest, one heel grazing the floor so that Díaz Grey knows that he isn't asleep. They play cards again until the moment when she has too much to drink and drops the ones Red has just passed to her, by merely opening her fingers, in a more definitive way than if she had slammed them violently down on the table, thereby establishing that they will not play another round.

Red rises, gathers up the cards, and starts throwing them into the fire. All that's left, the doctor thinks, is to caress Molly or talk to her; to find and say a sentence that is clean but alludes to love. He stretches out his arm and touches her hair, lifts it off her ear, releases it, picks it up again. Red places the shadow of the shotgun on the table, now holding it by the barrel. Díaz Grey lifts her hair and lets it go, each time imagining the soft blow she must feel against her ear.

Red is talking over their heads, shaking the shotgun and its shadow; he repeats the name of Quinteros, finishes then begins the same sentence again, giving it a more confused and transparent meaning, depending on whether Molly looks at him or lowers her eyes. The shotgun slams down on Díaz Grey's wrist and pushes it against the table.

"You can't do that," Red shouts.

Díaz Grey again lifts her hair off her ear with barely outstretched fingers; Molly lifts her hands and brings them together over her yawn. Then Díaz Grey feels the pain in his wrist, and he thinks, now without any recompense, that it might be broken. She places one hand on each of their chests. Red sits back down on his stool next to the dark fireplace, and Díaz Grey strokes the pain that rises up his arm, pushes his painful hand against Molly's mouth, which retreats, resists, and opens. Then comes the moment when the doctor decides to kill Red, and he sinks into the humiliation of concealing the fish-cleaning knife between his shirt and his belly and walks past the other until the cold blade turns warm, until Molly moves forward, from the door, from alternating corners of the room, stretches out her arms and confesses, alluding to a personal and imprecise misfortune.

The doctor, free of the knife, is lying in bed, smoking; he hears the patter of the drizzle on the roof, on the surface of the still afternoon. Red paces back and forth in front of Molly's door, the useless shotgun over his shoulder, four steps, return, four steps.

The sound of the water on the roof and in the foliage grows furious, then expires; now they wander around in expectant silence, scrutinizing the grey landscape from doors and windows, parodying the stance of the statue on the veranda, one arm outstretched, all the senses united on the back of a hand. She and Díaz Grey, at least. Red has a presentiment of misfortune and walks around in circles inside the room; he drags along the floor a groan and the barrel of the gun. The doctor waits for the pace of his steps to increase, become frantic, scare Molly, subside.

When Díaz Grey begins to make trips between the shed and the fireplace, carrying everything that can be burned, the other man keeps pacing and panting, practicing a song, which she doesn't want to hear but that she pretends to accompany with a movement of her head. Leaning against the door frame, she seems both taller and weaker, dressed in her beach pants and her sailor shirt. Red drags his feet and sings; she sways her head with hope and guile, while Díaz Grey lights matches, while the flames rise and resound in the air. Without looking behind him, without trying to find out what's going on, Díaz Grey enters Molly's room. Lying on the bed, he repeats in a whisper the song Red was singing, looks at Molly's fingers on the buckle at her waist, grows quiet as he imagines that matchmaking corresponds to silence. The rain can again be heard, and the clouds pull apart, holding the sad light of the endless afternoon of bad weather. Cheek against cheek at the window they watch Red walk away, cross the beach at a diagonal until he reaches the shore, the strip of sand and water that borders a line of hardened foam.

"Molly," Díaz Grey says. He knows it's imperative to suppress the words so that each can deceive himself or herself, believe in the importance of what they are doing and draw toward them the already reluctant sensation of what is abiding. But Díaz Grey cannot resist calling her by name. "Molly," he repeats, leaning into her last scent. "Molly."

Now Red is standing stiffly next to the cold fireplace, the shotgun resting on the toes of one foot. She is sitting at the table and drinking; Díaz Grey keeps his eye on Red while still seeing Molly's teeth, stained with wine, exposed in a reiterated grimace that never tries to become a smile. She puts down the glass, shudders, speaks English to nobody in particular. Red remains on guard in front of the dead fire when she picks up a pencil and writes down some verses, forces Díaz Grey to look at them and keep them forever, no matter what happens. There is so much despair in the part of the woman's face that Díaz Grey dares to look at that he moves his lips as if he were reading the verses and carefully puts away the piece of paper while she fluctuates between passion and tears.

"I wrote it myself, it's mine," she lies. "It's mine and it's yours. I want to explain to you what it says, I want you to learn it by heart."

Patient and tender, she forces him to repeat, corrects him, encourages him:

> *Here is that sleeping place,*
> *Long resting place,*
> *No stretching place,*
> *That never-get-up-no-more*
> *Place*
> *Is here.*

They go out to look for Red. Arm in arm, they follow the path they saw him take previously, at a different moment of the inclement afternoon; they descend, annoyed; they walk diagonally to the shore and continue along it to town, to the grocery store. Díaz Grey orders a glass of wine and leans on the counter; she disappears inside the shop, shouts and whispers in the corner with the telephone. She wears, upon her return, a new smile, a smile that would strike fear in the doctor if he caught sight of it directed at another man.

They return along the road under the light drizzle that reappears in order to confront them. She stops.

"We didn't find Red," she says without looking at him. She lifts her mouth for Díaz Grey to kiss and leaves a ring in his hand when they pull apart. "We could live on this for months, anywhere. Let's get my things."

As they speed up their steps along the shore, Díaz Grey looks in vain for the sentence and the kind of gaze he'd like to leave for Red. Now there is, near the shoreline, a rotten piece of driftwood rising and falling on the waves; there's a triplet of gulls and their cries swirling in the sky.

She sees the car before Díaz Grey does and starts to run, slipping in the sand. The doctor sees her climb a dune, her arms spread wide, lose her footing, and disappear; he is left alone to face the small desert of the beach, his eyes stinging in the wind. He turns to protect them and ends up sitting down. Then – sometimes late in the afternoon, at other times right in the middle – he digs a hole in the sand, tosses in the ring, and covers it; he does it eight times, in the places Red stepped, in those he himself had marked with a single glance. Eight times, in the rain, he buries the ring, and walks away; he walks to the water, tries to confound his eyes by looking at the dunes, the emaciated trees, the roof of the house, the car on the slope. But he always returns, in a straight line, without hesitating, to the exact spot of the burial; he digs his hands into the sand and touches the ring. Lying down, face up, he rests, gets wet in the rain, and stops worrying; slowly he starts along the path to the house.

Red is stretched out next to the cold fireplace, chewing slowly; he has a glass of wine in his hand. She and Quinteros are whispering rapidly, face to face, until Díaz Grey approaches, until it is impossible for them to deny that they hear his steps.

"Hey," Quinteros says, and smiles at him, stretching out his arm; his hat is still on, awry.

Díaz Grey pulls over a chair and sits near Red; he strokes his head and pats his back, harder and harder, waiting for him to get furious so he can punch him in the jaw. But the other keeps chewing, barely turning to look; then Díaz Grey lets his hand rest on his red hair and looks at her and Quinteros.

"Everything's all arranged," Quinteros says. "The benefit of the doubt, to repeat the words of the judge. If you were worried, I hope that now . . . Though, naturally, you can stay here as long as you want."

He approaches and bends over to give him more folded banknotes. When Molly finishes putting on makeup and buttoning her raincoat up to her neck, Díaz Grey sits up and, under the light, under the woman's face, opens his hand with the ring resting on his palm. Wordlessly – and now it must be accepted that this scene takes place late in the afternoon – she takes his fingers and bends them, one by one, until the ring is hidden.

"For as long as you want," Quinteros says from the door. Díaz Grey and Red hear the sound of the motor driving away, the silence, the whisper of the sea.

Here ends, in memory, the long rainy afternoon that began when Molly arrived at the house in the sand; once again, time can be used to measure.

So, in a dramatic move, as if wishing to prove that he understood everything before Díaz Grey, Red sits up and turns toward the door, toward the rain that has stopped, a face humanized by surprise and anguish. He touches the doctor for the first time, grabs his arm and appears to gain strength from the contact; then he gets up and goes running out of the house.

Díaz Grey opens his hand, brings it up to the light to look at the ring, and blows off the grains of sand that are stuck to it; he places it on the table, slowly drinks a glass of wine, as if it were good, as if he still had things to think about. There's time, he tells himself; he is certain that Red doesn't need any help. When he decides to go out he finds, and examines with indifference the last moment that could be incorporated into the hazy afternoon: a strip of red light stretches high above the river. He lights a cigarette and walks along the side of the house where the shed is; he thinks indolently that he ended up keeping the ring, that he left on the table the piece of paper with the verses, that perhaps deliberate cynicism will be enough to cleanse him of the parody of passion and his ridicule.

When, in his office facing the square in the provincial city, Díaz Grey starts to play the game of knowing himself through this memory, the only one, he is forced to confuse the sensation of his blank past with that of his weak shoulders; that of the head with thin blond hair, bent against the window glass, with the sensation of loneliness suddenly accepted, when it was already insurmountable. He must also assume that his meticulous life, his own body deprived of lust, his bland beliefs, are symbols of the essential vulgarity of the memory he has struggled to keep for so many years.

At the preferred end of his memory, Díaz Grey lets himself collapse onto the wet sand on one side of the house. Red's frenzy as he collects branches, papers, planks, and pieces of furniture, and places them against the wood wall of the chalet makes him laugh out loud, cough, and roll onto the ground; when he breathes in the smell of kerosene, he makes the other man freeze with an imperious whistle, then approaches him, slipping on the dampness and the leaves, takes a box of matches out of his pocket and shakes it next to one ear as he moves forward and slips.

1949

The Album

I saw her from the door of the newspaper office, where I was leaning against the outside wall, under the metal plate with the name of my grandfather, Agustín Malabia, founder. I had come to hand in an article about the harvest or the cleaning of the streets in Santa María, one of those irresistible pieces of nonsense that my father calls "editorials" and that, once printed, become massively dense, barely ventilated by statistics, noticeably weighing down the third page, always in the upper left.

It was a Sunday afternoon, humid and hot, at the beginning of winter. She had arrived from the port or the city carrying a light airplane bag, wrapped in a fur coat that must have been suffocating, taking one step after another along the shimmering walls, under the aqueous and yellow sky, a bit stiff, forlorn, as if she were being carried closer to me by the evening, the river, the waltz wafting over from the plaza, the girls in pairs who made circles around the bare trees.

Now she was walking past El Berna, looking younger, smaller inside her unbuttoned coat, with an odd agility in her feet that was not transmitted to her legs, that did not alter her stiffness, like a statue in a small town.

Vásquez, from sales, came down the hallway and stopped next to me, seeing me watch her, cleaning his nails with a letter opener, equally honored by the two words that made up my grandfather's name. I lit my pipe and waited for the moment to make my move to cross the street diagonally and perhaps brush against the woman, find out for sure her age and then get into the car, the new one my father let me drive, and slam the door. But she stopped on the corner, blocking with her head, with a corner of her wool hat, the faded tankard a mustachioed gringo held up on the pub sign. She stopped with her knees touching, without meaning to, simply because the impulse that had pulled her up the street had just died.

"She must be a little off her head," Vásquez said. "She's been at the hotel, the Plaza, for a week; she came alone, they say with a bunch of trunks. But she spends all morning and afternoon coming and going along the pier with that small bag, at all hours of the day, always when neither dinghies or ferries are coming or going."

"She's ugly, she must be getting on in years," I said, and yawned.

"Depends how you look at it, Jorgito," he said gently. "More than one would try his luck," and he touched my shoulder to say goodbye, then crossed diagonally, almost as I had planned to do, grey and small, with that walk he'd inherited from his friend, Junacadaveres, trying to balance on the slimy asphalt the rotundity of weight he didn't possess. He passed very close to the woman on the corner in front of El Berna, without turning his neck to look at her, and entered the store.

I knew that it wasn't because of me – and perhaps not because of anybody, not even herself – that the woman had settled down on the sidewalk, motionless and ochre in the middle of a Sunday afternoon, passively an-nexed to the heat, humidity, aimless longing. But I didn't move, just kept my eyes on her, until my pipe rattled empty at the exact moment she had to move one foot forward and lower it, then continue moving forward in the direction of the hotel through the desert of the side street that had separated then reunited us, with short, easy steps, steps that meant only to mark the passage of time, liberated through the quivering of the bass drum, the audacity of the clarinet, the beginning of the night, and its weak, reticent smells, the forewarnings of death.

The next day, in the morning, I thought that Vásquez had lied or exag-gerated, or that the woman was no longer in Santa María. I took the early bus to the city to have my tennis racket restrung, I convinced Hans that I would rather die than admit that he'd cut my hair one Monday morning, behind the closed doors of the barber shop, he and I whispering between the gleaming of metal and mirrors in the semidarkness; I bought tobacco for my pipe and walked to the port.

The woman wasn't there and she didn't come, the ferry arrived with few passengers, with bags of flour or corn, with an old jitney with peeling paint.

I walked around smoking then sat down on the dock, my legs dangling over the water. Sometimes, with only the silhouettes, I could see the ac-tivity on the cobblestones at the main door to the red customs building; I didn't know what I should be doing or thinking when the woman and the small bag, and perhaps again her fur coat, her wool hat, surprised me by approaching from behind. The ferry blew its horn and left the dock at one o'clock on the dot. I kept waiting, hungry, disgusted by the pipe. The bags and the jitney had remained on the dock; my father was writing an editorial titled: "Do we need to import wheat? Until recently the soil of Santa María was fertile," or "The valuable contribution of local transportation: The progressive and determined efforts of our community."

Almost leaning against the horizon, tiny, the ferry had stopped moving. I no longer remembered the woman with the bag or felt any love or curiosity for that summons, the allusion that I had seen her place in the air between us, between the corner of El Berna and the corner of *El Liberal*. Desperate and hungry, swallowing the taste of the match in my pipe, I was thinking: *An ill-advised measure, inexplicably approved by the authorities, has just authorized the entry of twenty-seven and a half bushels of wheat to the port of Santa María. The same independent criteria we used previously to commend the work of the new Board should now force us to raise our voices in startling condemnation.*

From La Nueva Italia I called Mother and told her that I would have lunch in town so I could get to school on time. I was certain that the woman had been rejected or dissolved by the imbecility of Santa María, symbolized precisely by my father's articles: *A true affront, we do not hesitate to say, from the Aldermen to the austere and selfless laborers of the surrounding region, who have, generation after generation, fertilized with their sweat the enviable riches we all enjoy.*

After class, Tito insisted on going to El Universal to have a vermouth (he didn't want to go to the Plaza for fear of running into his father) and making me believe a story about his love affair with his second cousin, the schoolteacher; he repeated plausible details, jauntily answered my questions, it was obvious he had been preparing to share his secret for a while. I grew serious, I grew sad, I grew indignant:

"Look," I told him, fiercely trying to meet his eyes, "you've got to marry her. There's no excuse not to; even if your cousin doesn't want to. If what you told me is true, you have to marry her. In spite of everything; even if she does have knees as thick as thighs, even if she does pucker her lips like an old maid."

Tito started smiling and shaking his head, and he was about to tell me that the whole thing was a joke when I stood up and made him blush with fear and doubt.

"I can't and don't want to see you until you've made that commitment. You're paying because you invited me."

I regretted my words for only three steps, crossing the sidewalk in front of the café as I stuffed my notebooks and the English textbook inside the pocket of my raincoat. Chubby, rosy, arrogant, fawning, now perhaps with teary eyes, my friend, an idiot. The weather was still humid, warm at the openings of the street corners, indecisive in the shade of patios, hot along the two-block walk. As I walked down to the port I felt happy despite the strength of my resolve, I started humming the unnamed march that caps the public concerts in the plaza; I presumed the scent of jasmine, I remembered a summer very long ago when the kitchen gardens hurled tons of jasmine at the city, and I discovered, as I came to a standstill, that I already had a past.

I saw her from the landscaped heights of the promenade: her silhouette was growing on the other side of the boardwalk as she advanced toward the haze of the water, revealing and confounding the bag and the winter coat. She went back and forth while I smoked my pipe; sometimes she'd stop on the large stone slabs on the pier, next to the shore, looking at the fog and that distant, unobstructed spot that contained the pink ruins of Latorre's palace; but I was certain that she wasn't waiting for anything, that she was lying. The boats docked then shoved off again down the river;

but she didn't turn her head to find the source of the horn blasts, did not peer into the blurry groups of passengers. She was there, small and hard, looking at the large whitish cloud resting on the waves, inventing surprises, approximations. It was beginning to get dark and cool off when she grew weary and turned around, checking to make sure everything was in order before walking straight across the dock.

I followed her to the hotel, believing that she – without turning, without looking at me – had sensed my presence half a block earlier, and that I was useful to her, that I helped her to walk up the street, to live. She sleepwalked, unaware, as she had the previous afternoon past El Berna and alongside Sunday and the nostalgic music that Fitipaldi conducted in the plaza, assisted only by the switching back and forth of his furious eyes. But now I watched her stop in front of each shop window of the two blocks surrounding the plaza; she looked, her right shoulder pressed against the glass, barely turning her head, spending exactly half a minute on each one, her contours indifferent under the assault of the lights that went on one by one, unconcerned that they were showing her the petticoats, the packets of maté, the fishing rods, the tractor replacement parts.

She finally entered the Plaza Hotel; I continued walking to the club, filled my pipe with tobacco, looked at the fog that a cold wind began to shred, right over the plaza, and returned. She was sitting on a stool at the bar, a small glass in front of her that she looked at without touching, both hands holding her bag on her lap. I sat next to a window, far away from the bar, and started looking through my notebooks. She remained still, withdrawn, hypnotized by the gold rim of the glass. Maybe she saw me in the mirror, maybe she had seen me ever since I arrived at the port with the pipe between my teeth and a recently discovered past. I read in my notebook: "*Why, thou wert better in thy grave than to answer with thy uncovered body this extremity of the skies."* And it was true, she could see me through the mirror, because when I lifted my eyes, she didn't have to turn her head before she took the small glass in her fingers, climbed off the stool, and followed a straight line that she constructed miraculously between the tables, holding the liquid against her chest without spilling it, the bag effortlessly kept away from the invisible play of her knees.

She sat down and placed the glass exactly in the middle of the table, and since the waiter had not yet come, nobody could know if it was hers or mine. I was looking at her with downcast eyes, and I began to get to know her face, to fill with apprehensions as I stashed away my English notebook. In her woolen cap – stripped, old, badly knit – she was ungracefully leaning on one ear, calm and serious, as if meditating before making a final decision, as if it were indispensable for things to begin with a parody of meditation. I knew that the only truly important part of her body – in spite of my hunger, Tito's hunger, all the cowardly voracious hungers of my friends – was her dark, round, young, and faded face, her eyelids curved down toward her cheeks, her large frayed mouth. Then she drank down the contents of her glass in one gulp, looking at me, and she was already smiling at me by the time she placed it back down on the table: a constant angry smile, simultaneously helpless and possessive like a stare, as if she were looking at me also with her teeth, with that thin red line, downy fuzz, and the wrinkles surrounding it.

"May I speak freely with you?" she said. "We made this afternoon's date a long time ago, didn't we? It doesn't matter when, because as you see we weren't able to forget it, and here we are, right on time."

Her face and, moreover, her voice. When the waiter came she asked for another drink, and I didn't want anything; I started to work on my pipe, blushing, letting myself go, confident that she was not making fun of me, that explanations were not necessary. Her face, always, and that voice that behaved like her feet, free and unheeded, persuasive, without ever resorting to pauses.

But all of this is prologue, because the real story began one week later. Also as prologue is my visit to Díaz Grey, the doctor, to get him to introduce me to a traveling salesman for a drug company who had set up shop, with half a dozen briefcases full of samples, on the first floor of the hotel, along the same hallway as the woman's room; and my interview with the traveling salesman, and how, that afternoon in his disorderly room, his settled cynicism, his silk shirt with rolled-up sleeves, his small damp mouth all so painlessly humiliated the memorized sentences that I tried to repeat nonchalantly. Before he said yes, he was laughing at me, almost noiselessly, lying on the bed in his stocking feet, puffing on his cigarette, telling me dirty memories. We went downstairs together and explained to the manager that I would be coming to his room every afternoon to help him type up his reports. "Give him a key." He shook my hand with the strong, serious grip of a man of his age, with a strange pride in his small, happy eyes.

I didn't fancy inventing another lie to tell my parents; I repeated the story about the reports that the traveling salesman had hired me to type, not mentioning the money I would have to collect and record them. Every afternoon, as soon as school was out – and sometimes before, when I managed to escape – I entered the hotel, smiled at whoever was on duty at the reception desk, and rode the elevator or took the stairs. The traveling salesman – Ernesto Maynard, according to the labels on the samples – was making a tour of all the pharmacies along the coast; the first few days I spent a lot of time examining the tubes and flasks, reading the promises and instructions in the prospectuses printed on tissue paper, enchanted by their impersonal, sometimes obscure style of measured optimism. Pressed against the door, I then listened to the silence in the hallway, the noise from the bar and the city. It happened.

The woman always pretended to be asleep and wake up slightly startled, uttering various men's names, dazzled by the remnants of a dream that neither my presence nor any reality could compensate for. I was hungry and my hunger was always being renewed, and it was impossible for me to imagine myself without her. Nevertheless, the satisfaction of this hunger, with all its considered and inevitable complications, soon became, for the woman and for me, a price we needed to pay.

The real story began one very cold night when we were listening to the rain, and both of us were motionless and curled up, each forgotten by the other. There was a narrow strip of yellow light under the bathroom door, and I reconstructed the solitude of the street lamps in the plaza and along the promenade, the perpendicular threads of rain without wind. The story began when she suddenly said, without moving, when her voice rose and hovered in the semidarkness, half a meter above us:

"What does it matter if it's raining, even if it rains like this for a hundred years, this isn't rain. It's falling water, but not rain."

There had been, also prior to this, the woman's great invisible smile, and it's true that she didn't speak until the smile was fully formed and had taken over her face.

"Nothing but falling water, and people have to give it a name. So, in this god-forsaken town, or city, they call falling water rain; but it's a lie."

I had no reason to suspect, not even when the word *Scotland* arrived, what she was initiating: her voice fell softly and unceasingly over my face. She explained to me that only what falls without purpose or meaning is rain.

"The castle was in Aberdeen and it was so old that the wind whistled through the hallways, the rooms, the stairwells. There was more wind there than in the night outside. And the rain that had been piling up for two days against the fireplace as tall as a man finally drew us to the broken windows. So we didn't speak, we spent morning till night shut away in the drawing room, our noses pressed up against the pane of one window, as still as stone figures in a church. Until the third day, I think, when MacGregor announced that it wasn't raining anymore, that it would start to snow, that the roads would remain closed, and that it was up to each of us to think that this was better or worse than the rain."

This was the first story; she repeated it several times, almost always because I asked for it when I was sick of the heat in India or the camp-sites of Amatlán. Maybe there's nobody else in the world who knows how to lie like that, I thought. Or maybe nobody hunted foxes until she burst out laughing, shaking her head, struggling lethargically with a memory of faded shame, only to immediately tie her horse to a tree and hide behind a *lord* or a *sir* or a *lord's lackey* in a crumbling pavilion, take a tumble on the inescapable mattress of leaves, while she orbited around them – right there, next to me, with no effort, with divine and impersonal pleasure – in the hackneyed landscape of splendid cold that she had just created, the first fox hunt that ever shook the land, the recollected frenzy that she conducted with ambitious and withered words: pomp, leash, riding coast, glade, tracker, useless violence, a small drab death.

And at the center of each lie was the woman, every story was she herself, next to me, undeniable. I was no longer interested in reading or dreaming, I was certain that when I took the trips I was planning with Tito, the landscapes, the cities, the distances, the world, everything would reveal to me meaningless faces, portraits of absent faces, irrevocably shorn of any true reality.

There was, always, the hunger; but listening to her was the vice that was most mine, most intense, most delicious. Because nothing could compare to the dazzling power that she had lent me, the gift of dithering for several hours between Venice and Cairo before our meeting, hermetic, astutely vulgar, among the twelve poor boys who watched perplexing words take shape on the blackboard and in Mr. Pool's mouth; nothing could take the place of the desired returns, and all I had to do was request in a whisper to have them, never the same, altered, approaching perfection.

We had gone from New York to San Francisco – for the first time, and what she described disillusioned me because of its similarity to an advertisement for soda pop in one of the foreign magazines that arrive daily: a meeting in a hotel room, the enormous curtainless windows opening onto the marble city under the sun, and the anecdote was almost a plagiarism of the one about the Hotel Bolívar in Lima – and we had just *wept from the cold on the East Coast, and before the day was out, incredibly, we were swimming at the beach*, when the man showed up.

He was short and wide, and I wanted to know only the few particulars that to this day suffice for me to assemble him and hold him: thick eyebrows, the collar of the shiny striped shirt, a pearl, the fashionable cut of his lapels. Perhaps also, though unnecessary, his small, stubborn half-moon smile, his hairy hands on the table like things he had brought to exhibit and apply pressure and that he wouldn't forget when he left. They were sitting near the dining room at seven in the evening. She was leaning over the glasses and the ashtray, a wand of smoke slicing her face; under the man's black eyebrows was placid embarrassment, hesitation at interrupting an impassioned eulogy.

I rode the elevator and shut myself up in Maynard's room; lying on the bed, smoking my pipe, I listened to the sounds in the hallway, read a story of dramatic and partial victories over Parkinson's Disease, and found out that pernicious anemia is a disease common to blue-eyed blonds. Until suddenly, it occurred to me that she could come up with the man, her quick steps, unaware of the ground or their destination, escorted by grave, slow, masculine heels. I went downstairs. They were at the table and were still thinking about the same things, her face leaning toward his black eyebrows, his toward the hands placed on the tablecloth.

I crossed the plaza without jealousy, sad and irritated, conjuring up omens of ill fortune. I turned down Urquiza and went to the hardware store. Sitting on a ladder, covered to his ankles in iron-grey, dust-grey coveralls, the clerk had a wood box on his lap and was examining nuts to see if the thread went to the left or the right. After checking them, he sorted them. The old woman was behind the counter, a black shawl around her shoulders, solemn, miserly, much more nearsighted than the week before.

"Tito is upstairs studying."

She didn't answer my greeting, she didn't invite me upstairs, she was looking at me as if she suspected that it was my fault her grey hair disgusted me. So I had to waste my smile, a glint, a special form of candor with two tiny points of insolence in my eyes. After a bit of a struggle:

"Why don't you go on up?"

"I will, for just a minute, thanks. I want to get some notes from him."

I crossed the courtyard, saw Tito's sister behind a door, ironing; the cold stood still, a black cat silently avoided my kick and my spit. Tito hid the magazine he was reading under the pillow and made secret and affectionate signs before rummaging through the closet and holding up a bottle of rum.

"But I've got only one glass."

He was content, chubby, confused. Majestic, a bit melancholic, I nodded, shared his spittle, placed my elbow on the torn oilcloth, slowly lit my pipe.

"I read the poem again," he said, and he lifted his filthy glass, decorated with flowers, bought as a toothbrush holder or for herbal infusions. "And whatever you say, it isn't bad. It's smoky in here. Can you open a window?"

In Santa María, when night falls, the river disappears, it retreats without waves into the shadows like a rolled-up rug; gradually, the countryside invades from the right – at that moment, we are all facing north – occupying us and occupying the riverbed. Nocturnal solitude, in the water or along the banks of the river, can, I suppose, offer memory, or nothingness, or a willed future; night on the prairie that spreads, punctual and indomitable, only allows us to encounter ourselves, lucid and in the present tense.

"That's not a poem," I said gently. "You make your father believe that you're studying, and you shut yourself up in your room and read a dirty magazine I lent you. It's not a poem, it's the explanation that I had a reason to write a poem and I couldn't."

"I'm telling you it's good," he said, barely bringing his fist down on the table, rebellious, thrilling.

When night falls we are left without a river, and the sirens that resound at the port turn into the bellowing of lost cows, and the eddies in the water sound like a dry wind in the wheat fields, over bowed mountains. May each man be alone and look until he rots, without memories or tomorrows, at his own face without secrets for all of eternity.

"And your sister is going to marry the clerk at the hardware store, not this year, obviously, but when your old man has no choice but to give his authorization. And you, one day you'll be standing behind the counter, not to fight against the clerk for your sister, as would be right and poetic, as I would do, but to prevent the two of them from robbing you blind."

He offered me the glass with a tolerant, good-naturedly cynical smile. I drank it down while trying to remember what I had come to do in the attic with him, my friend. I brought a match up to the squeaking of the pipe. I had come there to think, in Tito's incomprehensible refuge, that I was not jealous of the man with the eyebrows and the pearl; that she had not looked at me nor could she look at me with that burning need for humiliation that I had glimpsed when I walked through the bar; I truly feared only the loss of adventures and geographies, the loss of dissolute diners in Naples, where she made love to the strumming of mandolins; the office in San Pablo where in some way or other she helped a thick-lipped and contrite man correct the architecture of temperate and hot regions. Not fear of solitude; fear of the loss of a solitude that I had inhabited with a feeling of power, with a kind of good fortune that the days could never again give me or compensate for.

The following afternoon came without a trace of the man, neither she nor I mentioning the mishap of the day before. (Also part of my happiness was avoiding reasonable questions: finding out why she was in Santa María, why she wandered around the pier with her bag.) Maybe she was more protective that afternoon, more demanding, more meticulous. The only thing certain is that she wasn't there, was not named, did not embrace a single man during her prolonged story on the Rhine, on a boat that sailed in bad weather from Mainz to Cologne. And the other certainties are questionable: the intention of her smile in the dark, the alarming intensity of the cold, the fearful love with which she prolonged the details of the journey, her desire to suppress the essential, to mix up meanings. In any case, she gave me only things I knew by heart: a raft on a river, blond and undaunted people, the always misplaced hope for a definitive catastrophe.

And, also, in any case, as I got dressed, placed my beret on my head, and tried to quickly reassemble my confidence in the world's imbecility, I forgave her the failure, I continued to work on the style of forgiveness that would reflect my tumultuous experience, my weary maturity.

I remember her with tousled hair, satisfied, letting me go, helping me leave, bidding farewell to my skinny body, my ineptness, my ears.

And just as, by saying goodbye to the woman on the evening of the tempestuous journey down the Rhine, I was separating from my mother, I ran into my father the following day, at six in the evening. He was sitting at the bar, watching the front door with his flushed and enthusiastic profile, confident that he, a little drunk, would catch me as I walked past, by calling himself Ernesto Maynard. He had only to move his thumb to summon me.

"How's it going?" I said in my deepest voice; I sat down next to him, arranged my books and my notebook on my lap, accepted the drink he wanted.

We drank in silence, slowly. Then he placed a hand on my shoulder, lightly, without dominance, without pity. I will continue to remember him lovingly for years, sitting next to me, chewing on his cigar, pulling it away so he could look with small and satisfied eyes at the length and color of the ash, coarse and certain, looking with his coarse, simple head for the formula that would not hurt too much but that would still contain the particular acrimony that strengthens and instructs.

"Well, she left. I know the whole story. Me, sitting in a hotel room or traveling along the coast, coaxing doctors, dentists, pharmacists, and quacks. I can sell anything, I always knew I could, ever since I was much younger than you, it's a gift. Working hard. But I never missed out on an item of gossip, I foretell them before they begin to take shape; all the cuckoldry, all the abortions, all the swindles. She left this morning, or rather, she didn't return last night. She left a letter asking them to keep her trunk, saying she'd come get it and pay what she owes, about three hundred pesos. Just the trunk; and it must be full of rocks, or old clothes, or bills from other hotels. I also knew that you were going to arrive at the hotel at six fifteen. I waited so I could tell it to you straight, that she won't return and that it doesn't matter that she won't return. And it's not possible for you to live like all those pathetic men who buy their shirts, or their wives buy them for them, at La Moderna, and pick their suits out of the Gath & Chaves catalogue. Waiting for women and deals to fall from the sky, or no longer waiting for anything. You've got to take off. One day, I guarantee it, you're going to thank me."

I thanked him and left, really knowing for the first time that I had nobody to be with. That night I tried to remake the world, every place she had given me, every fable. I no longer remembered her face by the time light came through the window.

And it wouldn't do any good to borrow money. In the morning I went to the bank and left only five pesos in my savings account; I went to Salem's shop and pawned the watch I'd inherited from my brother (silent and melodramatic, my sister-in-law had removed it from my dead brother's wrist). Before noon I was standing in front of the reception desk at the hotel, full of money, power, a dark need for insult and attrition. I explained that the woman had sent me the three hundred pesos for the trunk; they gave me a receipt, they made me sign another one: "for Carmen Méndez." I arranged with Tito for us to carry the trunk to the hardware store garage while his parents were sleeping. All day I was thinking about Dr. Díaz Grey, imagining that I was doing all this for him, for the vague prestige of chivalry that he represented in town: small, well-dressed, banished, tenderly exaggerating the limp he assisted with his cane.

So, exhausted and proud, twenty-four hours after the woman left Santa

María, I shut myself away in the garage with Tito, and we opened a bottle while we talked about wedding nights and the repercussions of deaths, sitting on the trunk, gently kicking it with our heels. When the bottle was half gone and he asked that we not talk about his sister's body, I broke the padlock and we started removing unusable and dirty clothes, not perfumed, with the scent of long use and sweat and confinement, old magazines, two books in English, and a leather-bound album with the initials C. M.

Crouching down, older, trying to hold my pipe with evident pride, I saw the photographs where the woman – less young and more credulous the more I leafed angrily through the pages – rode horseback in Egypt, smiled at golfers in a Scottish meadow, embraced movie actresses in a California cabaret, sensed death in the windstorm in Rouen, making real, defaming, each and every one of the stories that she had told me, every afternoon I was loving her and listened to her.

1953

The Tale of the Rosenkavalier
and the Pregnant Virgin from Lilliput

From the very first moment, the three of us believed we'd always known the man and would forevermore. We were drinking warm beer at a table in front of El Universal just as an end-of-summer night was setting in; the air around the banana trees became alert and the blusterous thunderclaps showed signs of approaching over the river.

"Over there," Guiñazú whispered, leaning back in his wrought-iron chair. "Look, but not too much. At least don't stare and, in any case, have the prudence to remain skeptical. If we look nonchalantly, it might last, they might not vanish, at some moment they might manage to sit down, order something from the waiter, drink, truly exist."

We were sweaty and dazzled, our eyes turned toward the table in front of the door to the café. The girl was tiny and perfect; she was wearing a tight dress that was open at the neckline, over her stomach, and up her thigh. She looked very young and determined to be happy, incapable of closing her smile. I wagered she had a good heart, and I predicted episodes of sadness. With a cigarette in her wide and avid mouth, with one hand on her hair, she stopped next to the table and looked around.

"Let's assume everything is in order," Old Man Lanza said. "Too close to perfect to be a midget, too confident and demagogic to be a child dressed as a woman. She even looked over at us, maybe she's blinded by the light. But her intentions are what matter."

"You can keep looking," Guiñazú said, "but don't talk yet. Maybe they are precisely as we see them. Maybe it's true that they're in Santa María."

The man had many mannerisms and all of them, restive and variable, worked together toward the goal of keeping him sharp, solid, unmistakable. He was young, thin, very tall; he was shy and insolent, dramatic and cheerful.

Indecision on the woman's part; then she moved one hand to dismiss the tables on the sidewalk and their occupants, the commotion of the storm, the planet onto which she had just stepped lacking delicacy and surprises. He took one step forward to offer her a chair and help her sit down. He smiled at her, caressed her hair, then her hands, then lowered himself slowly until he touched his own chair with his grey trousers, very tight around the calves and ankles. With the same smile he used for the girl and had taught her to mimic, he turned to call to the waiter.

"A drop just fell," Guiñazú said. "It's been threatening to rain since dawn and now it decides to start. It's going to erase this, dissolve what we were seeing and what we almost started to accept. Nobody will want to believe us."

For a while, the man's head was turned toward us, maybe looking at us.

With the dark and glossy lock that shrunk his forehead, with the anomalous grey flannel suit on which the tailor had pinned a small hard rose, with his alert and hopeful indolence, with his alliance to life, which was older than he.

"But it just might be," Guiñazú said, "that all the other inhabitants of Santa María will see them and be suspicious, or at least afraid and resentful, before the rain finally erases them. It just might be that somebody will walk by and feel them as strange, too beautiful and happy, and sound the alarm."

When the waiter arrived, it took them some time to make up their minds; the man caressed the girl's arms, patiently made suggestions, a master of time and sharing his mastery with her. He leaned over the table to kiss her on the eyelids.

"Now we are going to stop looking at them," Guiñazú recommended.

I was listening to Old Man Lanza's breathing, the cough provoked by every drag off his cigarette.

"The sensible thing is to forget about them, not be able to give anybody an explanation."

The downpour started, and we remembered no longer hearing the thunderclaps over the river. The man took off his jacket and placed it around the girl's shoulders, almost without needing to move, without ceasing to worship her and tell her with his smile that living is the only happiness possible. She tugged on the lapels and amused herself by looking at the quick dark stains that spread over the yellow silk shirt that the man had exposed to the rain shower.

The light of the U of "Universal" glowed in the dampness of the inscrutable and miserly rose stretching the jacket's buttonhole. Without taking her eyes off her husband – I had just discovered the rings on their hands clasped on the table – she turned her head to brush her nose against the rose.

In the doorway where we had taken refuge, Old Man Lanza stopped coughing and told a joke about the knight of the rose, the Rosenkavalier. We broke out laughing, separated from the couple by the racket of the rain, believing that this term defined the young man and that we were starting to make his acquaintance.

II

Everything we were learning about them was of no interest to me until a month later, when the couple moved into Las Casuarinas.

We heard that they attended the dance at Club Progreso but not who'd invited them. One of us spent the whole night watching the girl dance, tiny and dressed in white, never forgetting, when she walked up to the long dark counter of the bar, where her husband was, talking to the oldest and most important customers, never forgetting to smile at him with such a tender, spontaneous, and steady glint in her eyes that it was impossible not to forgive her.

As for him, listless and tall, listless and delighted, once again listless and with the privilege of ubiquity, he danced only with the women who could tell him – even if they didn't – about their husbands' lack of understanding and their children's selfishness, about other dance parties with waltzes, one-steps, and the final *pericón*, with lemonade and watered-down *clericot*.

He danced only with them and agreed to bend his tall body clothed in dark garments, his lovely head, his smile with no past or precautions, his confidence in eternal good fortune over daughters and single women for only a few seconds. And even this with merely polite and fleeting amusement. According to the observer, the virgins and young wives of Santa María, who in keeping with the abbreviated feminine lexicon had not yet begun to live and those who had stopped doing so prematurely and brooded, perplexed, over grudges and deceits, seemed to be there for no reason other than to unfailingly offer him a bridge between women and older men, between the dance floor and the uncomfortable bar stools in the shadows, where people sipped slowly and talked about wool and wheat. According to the observer.

They danced the last number together and lied stubbornly and in unison to bow out of dinner invitations. He kept bending, patient and restrained, over the aged hands he pressed but dared not kiss. He was young, lean, strong; he was everything it occurred to him to be, and he did not make mistakes.

During dinner, nobody asked who they were and who had invited them. One woman waited for silence to recall the coursage the girl wore on the left side of her white dress. The woman spoke parsimoniously, without giving her opinion, naming only the bird-of-paradise coursage fastened to the dress with a gold pin. Picked perhaps from a bush along some deserted street or from the garden of a boarding house, from the room or the hole where they were living right after they left the Victoria, and that none of us managed to discover.

III

Almost every night, Lanza, Guiñazú, and I talked about them at El Berna or El Universal, when Lanza had finished correcting the newspaper galleys and he came up to our table limping, slow, kindhearted, dying, and on top of the patches of sunlight that had fallen without wind from the tipu trees.

It was a humid summer, and I was on the verge of salvation, nearly accepting that old age had begun; but not yet. I would get together with Guiñazú, and we would talk about the city and the changes it had undergone, about heirs and illnesses, about droughts, betrayals, about the horrific speed with which strangers multiplied. I was waiting for old age, and maybe Guiñazú was waiting for wealth. But we never discussed the couple before the variable hour when Lanza would leave *El Liberal*. He would arrive, limping and ever thinner, stop coughing and cursing the editor and the entire race of Malabias, order a coffee as an aperitif, and clean his eyeglasses with his filthy handkerchief. In those days I looked at and listened to Lanza more than Guiñazú, trying to learn how to grow old. But it didn't do any good; that and two other things can never be learned from others.

One of us, any one of us, would mention the couple, and the rest would contribute what we could, unconcerned whether it was a little or a lot, like true friends.

"They dance, they're dancers, that can be ascertained, and it's impossible to say anything else if we've sworn to tell only truths in order to discover or formulate the truth. But we haven't sworn anything. So the lies that each of us might approach, as long as they are firsthand and align with the truth that the three of us suspect, will be useful and welcome. The Plaza Hotel is no longer modern and luxurious enough for them. I'm talking about foreigners in general, and I'm pleased that's the case. As for them, they came on the ferry and went straight to the Victoria, two rooms with a bathroom and no board. We can imagine them in each others' arms on the ferry (looking with interest and dislike, bracing themselves against the dangers of scorn and optimism) as soon as the boat began to keel over in the current in the middle of the river and turn toward Santa María. They calculated every meter of every building with more than one storey, they calculated the size of their field of operations, foresaw weak points and ambushes, assessed the intensity of one of our summer days at noon. They: he with his left arm almost entirely sheltering the body of that perfect midget, and she looking toward us like a pensive child, chewing on the petals of the rose that he had gotten off to buy for her at the dock in Salto. They, afterwards, riding toward the Victoria in the latest model taxi they could find in the noisy lineup at the landing, followed an hour later by the wagon loaded with their suitcases and a trunk. They carried a letter for Latorre's fat, effete great-grandson; and they had to have known since the afternoon of the first day that we didn't know him, that we weren't interested, that we were trying to forget about him and segregate him out of the myth of Latorre, constructed with impatience, candor, and malice by three generations of nostalgic and aimless men. They learned, in any case, that the great-grandson was in Europe.

"It doesn't matter," he said, with his quick precise smile. "It's pleasant here, we can stay for a while."

So they stayed, but not at the Victoria. They moved out of their two rooms with a bathroom, they hid successfully, and we were able to see them only at their one meal at night at the Plaza, at El Berna, or at one of the restaurants along the coast, so much cheaper and more picturesque. So it went, for a week or ten days, until the dance at the Club Progreso. And, then, right away, a pause during which we thought they were gone forever, when we described with some wit their arrival at another coastal city, confident and a bit vain, a bit complacent because of the monotonous regularity of their triumphs, where they would keep performing *Life Will Always Be Beautiful*, or *The Sham of Perfect Love*. But we never agreed on the name of the impresario, and I was determined to oppose all vulgar theories with a theological interpretation no more absurd than the end of this story.

The pause ended when we found out that they were living, or at least sleeping, in one of the small red-roofed houses on the beach, one of the dozen that Specht had purchased – at the price he wanted, but with cash – from Old Man Petrus, when the shipyard closed down, and we, the downhearted, began to say that no train would ever ride on the rails that had been laid over half the distance, one quarter then another quarter, between El Rosario and the shipyard at Puerto Astillero. They slept in the small house in Villa Petrus, from twelve midnight till nine in the morning. Specht's chauffeur – at that time Specht was president of Club Progreso – took them and picked them up. We never found out where they ate breakfast; but they took their other three meals at Specht's house, facing the old, circular plaza, or Brausen Plaza, or Founder's Plaza.

We also learned that they never signed a lease for the house on the beach. Specht wasn't interested in talking about his guests or in avoiding the subject. At the club he confirmed:

"Yes, they visit us daily. They entertain her. Since we don't have children."

We thought that Mrs. Specht, if she cared to, could give us the key to the couple, recommend definitions and adjectives. The ones we'd invented didn't wholly convince us. They, she and he, were too young, fearsome, and happy for their fee and the future to consist of the compensation meted out to servants: room, board, and whatever pocket money that Mrs. Specht insisted they take without them asking for it.

This period might have lasted about twenty days. It was when summer was being overtaken by autumn, making room for a few vitreous skies at twilight, stiff and silent mid-days, flat and colorful leaves on the streets.

For those twenty days, the young man and the small woman came to the city every morning at nine o'clock in Specht's car from the coolness of the beach to the lagging summer in the old plaza. We were able to see them — for me it was easy — smiling at the chauffeur, at the scent of leather in the car, at the streets and the waning morning bustle, at the trees in the plaza and the ones that peeked out over garden walls, at the iron and marble entryway of the house, at the maid and Mrs. Specht. Smiling afterwards, all day, the same smile of solidarity with the world, though hers less pure and convincing, with sheens and aspects that were just a bit misguided. And, in spite of everything, making themselves useful from morning till their return, inventing chores for themselves, repairing furniture, cleaning the piano keys, preparing in the kitchen one of the recipes he knew by heart or improvised. And they were useful, principally, in altering Mrs. Specht's clothing and appearance, then celebrating those alterations with discreet and plausible admiration. They were useful in prolonging their evenings till Specht's first yawn, agreeing with his immortal and disillusioned clichés, or simply listening eagerly to his autobiographical exploits. (She, not fully, of course; she, whispering with Mrs. Specht in a duet of background melodies — fashion, preserves, and misfortunes — that well suited the epic themes of masculine conversation.)

"Not the Rosenkavalier," Lanza finally suggested, "but rather the *chevalier servant*. Said without scorn, probably. That remains to be seen."

It was known that Specht threw them out nonviolently the morning after a party he gave at his house. As usual, the chauffeur arrived at the beach chalet that Sunday morning at nine; but instead of picking them up he handed them a letter, four or five decisive and polite lines written in the neat and unhurried penmanship of daybreak. He threw them out because they had gotten drunk; because he found the young man embracing Mrs. Specht; because they stole a set of silver spoons engraved with the coats of arms of Swiss cantons; because the tiny woman's dress was indecent over her chest and one knee; because at the end of the party they danced together like sailors, like comics, like negroes, like prostitutes.

The last version could become true for Lanza. Very early one morning, after the newspaper and then El Berna, he saw them at one of the cafés on Caseros Street. A hot and humid night was beginning to end, and the door to the place was open, no plush curtain, no promises or tricks. He had stopped to light a cigarette, and saw them, alone on the dance floor, surrounded by the hybrid fascination of the few people still sitting at the tables, dancing any old dance, a rumble, a giddy romp, a mating ritual.

"Because that would, I'm certain, have a name that is merely a euphemism. Nor did it go beyond a tribal dance, a betrothal rite, the bride's twists and turns to surround and trap the groom, the offer deferred to aggravate the demand. But this time, it was she who let herself go, a bit clumsy, her movements restricted, brushing her feet along the ground and not lifting them, swinging her ample and tiny body, pursuing the man with her patient and dazzling smile and the palms of her hands, which she had raised to protect herself and to plead. And he was the one dancing in a circle, swinging his hips as he came and went, pledging and withdrawing with his face and his feet. They danced like that because the others were there, but they danced only for themselves, in secret, protected from any intrusion. The young man's shirt was open to his belly button; and all of us could see how happy he was to be sweating, a little drunk and in a trance, how happy he was to be watched and awaited.

IV

Then, for the first time and as predicted, they came to us. One day, mid morning, the man arrived at Guiñazú's office, recently bathed and smelling of cologne, his fingers wrapped around a fifty-peso banknote folded the long way.

"I can't afford any more, at least not in cash. Tell me if it's enough to cover the price of a consultation.

"I told him to take a seat while I thought about the two of you, not certain it was he. I leaned back in my armchair and without answering I offered him a cup of coffee, requesting his permission to finish signing some papers. But when I sensed that my baseless antipathy could not be sustained and that curiosity as well as an almost impersonal form of envy were starting to replace it, when I admitted that what anybody would have called insolence or effrontery could be something else, extraordinary and almost magical because so rare, I understood without any doubt that my visitor was the man with the yellow shirt and the rose in his button-hole whom we had seen that rainy night on the sidewalk in front of El Universal. What I mean, even if I persist in my animosity: a man congeni-tally convinced that the only thing that matters is to be alive and, therefore, is convinced that anything that allows him to live is important and good and worthy of being felt. I said, yes, for fifty pesos, the rate I charge my friends, I could tell him how long a sentence, give or take a few months, he could expect from the statutes, the tax authorities, and the courts. And, that one could attempt to have the sentence suspended. I wanted to listen to him and, above all, I wanted to take away from him the green banknote that he twisted distractedly between his fingers as if he were certain that all he had to do was show it to me.

"Finally, he unfolded the banknote and placed it on the desk; I put it in my wallet, and we talked for a few minutes about Santa María, landscapes and climate. He told me a story about the letter he had brought for Latorre and asked me if it was possible for him to stay at the beach chalet – he and she, of course, so young and expecting a child – in spite of his estrangement from Specht, in spite of there being nothing but what he called a verbal rental agreement.

"I thought it over and decided to tell him that it was; I slowly explained to him his rights, citing numbers and dates of laws, cases that established precedence. I recommended that he offer to deposit with the courts a reasonable sum in lieu of rent, and subpoena Specht for the execution of the existing contract, oral and de facto.

"I could see he was pleased with my words; he nodded with a pleasant half smile, as if he were listening to his favorite music, remote and well executed. He asked that I repeat one or two sentences, apologizing for not having understood. But that was all, unfortunately he showed no real enthusiasm or relief. Because when I called an end to the pause and told him in a sleepy voice that everything I said was strictly according to the law as it applied to this case, but that, in the dirty Santa María tradition, it would be enough for Specht to talk on the phone with the police chief so that he and his young wife, who was expecting their child, could be removed from the chalet to any spot two leagues beyond the boundaries of the city, he started to laugh and looked at me as if I were his friend and had just told him a memorable joke. He was so keen that I pulled out my wallet to give him back the fifty pesos. But he didn't take the bait. He removed from the front pocket of his trousers a small gold watch that had at one point been called a chatelaine and lamented having other commitments and being uncertain if this transaction could one day turn into the dialogue of a real friendship.

I shook his hand vigorously, suspecting I was indebted to him for things of greater importance than the fifty pesos I had just cheated him out of."

V

Then they disappeared, were spotted in the company of tourists on Saturdays at the Club Comercial, once again nothing was known about them, and suddenly they were living at Las Casuarinas.

This time, very close to us and to scandal. Because Guiñazú was the lawyer of Doña Mina Fraga, owner of Las Casuarinas; I would go there on house calls when Dr. Ramírez was away from Santa María; and the previous winter Lanza had finished polishing an obituary titled, "Doña Herminia Fraga," of precisely seven column centimeters, carping but ambiguous, that mainly alluded to the colonizing virtues of Doña Mina's deceased father.

Close to scandal because Doña Mina, between puberty and her twentieth birthday, had escaped three times. She left with a ranch hand and Old Man Fraga brought her back with the help of the lash, according to the legend, which also throws in the death of her seducer, his secret burial, and a financial arrangement with the commissioner in 1911. She left, not with but in the wake of a circus magician, who was appropriately happy with his job and his wife. The police brought her back, at the insistence of the magician. She left, at the time of the almost revolution of 1916, with a veterinary medicine salesman, a mustachioed, foppish, and determined man, who had done some good business deals with Old Man Fraga. This was her longest absence, and she returned without being summoned or brought back.

At that time, Fraga was building Las Casuarinas, a mansion in the city, as a dowry for his daughter and because he was sick of living on the ranch.

One heard chatter about the young woman's religious crisis, her entering a convent, and an improbable priest who refused to approve the plan because he didn't believe in Doña Mina's sincerity. What's certain is that Fraga, who claimed without boasting that he had never stepped foot in a church, had a chapel built at Las Casuarinas before the house was completed. And when Fraga died, the young woman rented out the ranch and all the land she'd inherited at the highest possible price, moved into Las Casuarinas, and turned the chapel into quarters for guests and gardeners. For forty years she went from one name to another, from Herminia to Doña Herminita and Doña Mina. She ended up old, alone, and with arteriosclerosis, neither defeated nor wistful.

There they were, then, the lovers who'd fallen upon us from the heavens one stormy afternoon. Settled, as if forever, into the chapel of Las Casuarinas, now performing day and night under the ideal conditions of décor, audience, and ticket sales, the play whose dress rehearsal they had held at Specht's house.

Las Casuarinas is fairly far from the city, to the north, along the road that leads to the coast. They were seen there by Ferragut, the notary who worked with Guiñazú, one Sunday morning. The three of them and the dog.

"It had been raining at daybreak; a few hours of water and wind. By nine the air was clean and the earth was slightly damp, dark, and fragrant. I left the car at the top of the hill and saw them almost immediately, like in a small painting, the kind with wide gilded frames, motionless and surprising as I walked down toward them. He, in the background, wearing his blue gardener's overalls, I would swear, custom tailored; on his knees in front of a rose bush, looking at it without touching it, offering a smile of proven efficacy against the ants and the aphids; surrounded, for the benefit of the creator of this painting, with the attributes of his circumstances: the shovel, the rake, the pruners, the lawnmower. The young woman was sitting on a mat, with a straw hat that almost touched her shoulders, her huge belly about to burst, her crossed legs covered by a large and colorful skirt, reading a magazine. And next to her, on a wicker chair with a sun shade, Doña Mina smiled at the glory of God's morning, the disgusting and flatulent dog on her lap. Everybody was serene and gracious, each of them innocently playing their role in the recently created paradise of Las Casuarinas. I stopped, intimidated, at the wooden gate, knowing that I was unworthy and intrusive; but the old woman called to me and was already waving her hand and squinting to make me out. She was disguised in a sleeveless dress, open at the neckline. She introduced me to the young woman ("my own darling"), and when the man finished threatening the ants and walked over jauntily and armed with a smile, Doña Mina started to laugh affectedly, as if he had paid her a lewd compliment. Ricardo was the man's name. He'd been scratching in the soil until he'd dirtied his fingernails, and now he was looking at them with concern but without losing confidence: 'We are going to be able to save almost all of them, Doña Mina. As I told you, they planted them too close together. But it doesn't matter.' It didn't matter, everything was easy; to bring withered rose bushes back to life or turn water into wine."

"Excuse me," Guiñazú said. "Did he know that you were the notary, that the old woman had called you, that there is such a thing as a will?"

"He knew, I'm sure he did. But that didn't matter, either."

"He did, he must be sure."

"When the old woman handed the dying and crusty-eyed dog to the young woman, who kept pressing her buttocks into her heels, and groped blindly for the cane to stand up and accompany me to the house, the man jumped to her side, and bent over her to offer her his arm. They walked ahead of me, very slowly; he was explaining to her, as he thought it up, the idiosyncrasies of the unknown person who had planted the roses; she stopped to laugh, to pinch him, to dab her eyes with her handkerchief. In the office, the man handed her over to me already seated and requested my permission to continue his conversation with the ants."

"Okay," Guiñazú said, playing with his glass. "Maybe Santa María is right to denounce what is going on at Las Casuarinas. But if the money, instead of going to a country relative, falls to the amateur gardener and his female companion and the child who is not yet born . . . How long can the old woman live?" he asked me.

"Impossible to say. Two hours or five years, in my opinion. Since she took in guests, she no longer keeps to her diet. For better or for worse."

"Yes," Guiñazú continued, "they can help her." He turned to Ferragut: "Does she have a lot of money? How much?"

"She has a lot of money," Ferragut said.

"Thank you. Did she change her will that Sunday?"

"She confessed to me, because the whole time she was talking to me in a confessional tone, that it was the first time in her life that she really felt loved. That the pregnant midget was better to her than any real daughter imaginable, that the man was the best, most refined and understanding of men, and that if death came for her now, she, Doña Mina, would have the happiness of knowing that her disgusting, incontinent dog would be left in good hands."

Lanza started laughing convulsively, choking, choking on gloomy sounds. He looked at our faces and lit a cigarette.

"We have little nourishment," he said. "And everything is hereby deemed worthwhile. But this is an old story. It's just that rarely, as far as I know, has it played out so perfectly. In the previous will, you say, she left her fortune to priests or relatives."

"Relatives."

"And this morning she changed her will."

"And this morning she changed her will," Ferragut replied.

VI

They lived at Las Casuarinas, exiled from Santa María and the world. But on certain days, once or twice a week, they drove to the city in the old woman's wobbly Chevrolet to do the shopping.

Old-time residents could evoke the remote and brief existence of the brothel, the women's Monday outings. In spite of the years, in spite of changes in fashion and demography, the city inhabitants continued to be the same. Timid and spoiled, forced to pass judgment in order to prop each other up, always judging out of envy or fear. (The most important thing to say about these people is that they lack spontaneity and joy; this can produce only lukewarm friendships, unfriendly drunkards, women who chase after security and are as identical and interchangeable as twins, swindled and lonely men. I'm talking about the people of Santa María; perhaps travelers have learned that human solidarity, under wretched circumstances, is a disappointing and astonishing truth.)

But the hesitant scorn with which the inhabitants viewed the couple who visited the cleanly swept and progressive city once or twice a week was of a different essence than the scorn they had shown years before in order to measure the steps, the stops, and the itineraries of the two or three women from the house on the coast, who played at going shopping on Monday afternoons for a few months. Because we all knew a few things about the listless and smiling young man and the miniature woman, who had learned to balance her growing belly on high heels, who strolled through the streets of the town center, not too slowly, leaning back, her neck resting on her husband's open hand. We knew they were living off Doña Mina's money; and it had been settled that, in this case, their sin was dirtier and unforgiveable. Perhaps because they were a couple and not only a man, and because the man was much too young, or because we found them both simpatico and they appeared not to know.

But we also knew that Doña Mina's will had been changed; hence, when we saw them walk by, we added to our scorn a timid and calculated offer of friendship, of understanding and tolerance. Soon we would see how, whenever it became necessary.

What was seen sooner was Doña Mina's birthday party. Guiñazú saw it for us.

They said – and rich old ladies, who were invited and sent their regrets, were saying it – that it was impossible for Doña Mina to have a birthday in March. They even offered to pull out moldy photographs, images saved from Doña Mina's respectable childhood, where she had to be front and center, the only girl wearing a hat, in the unfinished garden of Las Casuarinas, at her own birthday party, surrounded by girls wearing furry caps and coats with lapels, collars, and fur braiding.

But they didn't take out the pictures or attend. In spite of the young man promising or, at least, doing everything possible. He ordered invitations on cream-colored paper with black embossed lettering (Lanza corrected the proofs). For three or four days they crisscrossed the city streets and the neighborhood roads in a Tilbury gig, mysteriously unearthed and now with new rubber tires, newly painted in dark green and faded black, and a gigantic statuesque horse – fat, asthmatic, a mill and plow animal, enraged, drooling, and on the verge of keeling over – now pulling the couple. And they went around in their invitation-distributor uniforms, sitting stiffly behind the beast's round rear end, with their twin absentminded smiles and their idle whip.

"But they achieved nothing, or very little," Guiñazú told us. "It occurs to me that maybe if he'd made himself seen and heard by each of the old ladies when he went to their houses to beg. . . The truth is, that Saturday they didn't manage to attract anybody, neither man nor woman, who had the indisputable right to be mentioned on the society page of *El Liberal*. I arrived closer to nine than eight, and already there were people with bottles settled into the darkness of the garden. I climbed the staircase without really wanting to, or wanting to be finished with it quickly, inhaling the tenderness of burnt firewood at some nearby site, listening to music wafting outside, noble, thinned out, and proud music, which had not been made or played for me or any of the inhabitants of the house or garden.

"In the dimly lit foyer a dark-skinned woman wearing an apron and a cap towered over a pile of hats and women's coats. I thought that they had dressed her up and placed her there for the purpose of announcing the names of the guests.

"First, by chance, because he was near the velvet and naphthalene curtain, I saw the man, the young man, the man with the rose in his buttonhole. Then I made my way through the dregs of society in their Sunday best and went to say hello to Doña Mina. She fit poorly in the recently reupholstered, spiral-legged armchair; she didn't stop petting the snout of the foul-smelling hound. She wore lace on her hands and around her neckline. I uttered two pleasantries and took one step back; then I quickly saw the eyes, hers and those of the perfect midget, sitting on the rug, her head leaning on the armchair.

"The pregnant woman's eyes had an expression of stupid sweetness, of unshakeable physical happiness.

"The old woman's eyes looked at me, telling me something, confident that I was capable of discovering what it was, mocking my lack of comprehension and also anticipating what I might understand in error. Her eyes, establishing a moment of contemptuous complicity with me. As if I were a child; as if she were stripping in front of a blind man. Her still shining eyes, not resigned, trapped by time, sparking momentarily with her impersonal revenge amid the wrinkles and the sagging lids.

"The young man with the rose played records for another half hour. When he'd had enough or felt confident, he went to his pregnant midget, swept her off her feet, and they started to dance in the center of the room, encircled by the spontaneous retreat of the others, determined to live, to endure with joy, to dispense with concrete hopes. He, swaying indolently, his feet intertwining on the flattened, wine-stained rug; she, even slower, miraculously unaltered by her enormous belly that grew with each turn of the dance she knew by heart and could perform without a false step, deaf and blind."

And that was all till the end, till the exasperated construction of the vegetal monument that lends interest to this story and deprives it of meaning. Nothing very important till the multicolored, luscious, and overwhelming pyre of unknown intent, burned in three days through the frost of May.

Lanza and Guiñazú had seen much more, had been, on two or three occasions, closer than I to the deceptive heart of the affair. But the futile revenge of going to Las Casuarinas at three in the morning fell to me; the young man coming to get me with his gigantic wheezy horse in the middle of the cold and blue night; he, helping me put on my coat with absent-minded good manners wholly devoid of insult; he, anticipating along the way – as he affectionately swore at the horse and paid excessive attention to the reins – the end we had foreseen and even wished for, out of the simple necessity for things to happen.

The nostrils of the snorting horse moved rhythmically under the moon, the hollow sound of its trot, ready to carry me anywhere. The young man was keeping his eyes on the deserted road, hoping to spot dangers and obstacles, his hands protected by thick old gloves, held unnecessarily far away from his body.

"Death," he said. I looked at his rabid teeth; his overly well-wrought nose; his expression appropriate for an autumn night, for the cold we rode through, for me, for what he assumed he'd find at the house. "Agreed. But not fear, or respect or mystery. Disgust, indignation at the final injustice that simultaneously renders all previous injustices unimportant and unforgiveable. We were sleeping and were awoken by the bell; I had placed a bell next to her bed. She tried to smile and everything seemed fine, according to her wishes and with her permission, as always. But I'm sure she didn't see us, her whole face waiting for a sound, a voice. Propped up on her pillows, hoping to hear something that we ourselves couldn't tell her. And since the voice didn't come, she started to move her head, to invent an unknown language in order to speak with some other, so rapidly that it was impossible to respond to her as she jumped ahead of the answers, defended herself against interruption. Personally, I think she was arguing with a childhood friend. And after about ten minutes of giddy mumblings it became clear that her friend, almost a child, was being defeated and that she, Doña Mina, was going to be left forever with the afternoon laden with jasmine and wisteria, with the man with slow curly eyelashes, a jacaranda walking stick under his arm. At least that's what I understood, and I still believe it. We surrounded her with hot water bottles, we made her take some pills, I saddled the horse, and I came to get you. But it was death. You can only sign the certificate and request an autopsy tomorrow. Because all of Santa María is doomed to think that I poisoned her, or that we, my wife, the fetus, and I poisoned her for the inheritance. But, fortunately, as you will confirm when you cut her open, life is much more complicated."

The tiny woman, dressed in black, as if she had carried those splendid black garments in her suitcases in anticipation of that very night, had lit candles next to Doña Mina's bewildered head, had spread a few precocious and pale violets around the foot of the bed and waited for us on her knees with her back turned, with her face in her hands on top of the cheap white bedspread, brought perhaps from the maid's room.

They kept living in the house and, as Lanza would tell us at El Berna as he glanced over at Guiñazú's face – more refined at that stage, craftier and more professional – nobody could throw them out until they read the will and it was shown that there was somebody with the right to throw them out, or that it was their right to leave after the place had been sold. Guiñazú agreed and smiled:

"There's no rush. As executor of the will, I can wait three months before I file it with the court. Unless some relative with a reasonable claim appears. In the meantime, they're still living in the house; and they're that rare kind of people who fit in well anywhere, who improve or give meaning to places. We all agree. I've watched them come to shop every week, as usual, and I could even discover how they've managed things to be able to keep buying. But I didn't talk to them. There's no reason to rush things. Most likely they've taken the large drawing room at Las Casuarinas for themselves, and they're turning it into a museum to honor Doña Mina. I believe they have enough dresses, hats, parasols, and bootees to illustrate that heroic life from the Paraguayan War to our present day. And maybe they've discovered bundles of letters, daguerreotypes and corsages, pills to enhance the bust, a carved marble fountain pen, and vials of aphrodisiacs. With those items, if they know how to use them, they will make it possible for any visitor to the museum to easily reconstruct Doña Mina's personality, a source of pride to all of us, constrained as we are by history to the poverty of a single hero, Brausen the Founder. There's nothing rushing us."

(But I suspected that he was being rushed by the impure hope that the young man of the rose would pay another visit to his office to ask for the the will to be opened. That he was waiting for this so he could get even for the confusing enchantment wrought upon him by the young man on that morning he paid him a visit and fifty pesos for nothing.)

"There's nothing rushing us," Guiñazú continued, "and for the moment, to all appearances, there's nothing rushing them, either. Because, for the people of Santa María, the tacit curse that had exiled Doña Mina's personal filth from our collective filth half a century ago was left without cause or effect after the night of the wake. Since then, after the period of mourning had passed, the most discreet among us, the farmers and small businessmen, and even the families descended from the first wave of immigrants, began to love the couple freely, with all their desire to love. They began to offer them their houses and unlimited credit. Speculating on the will, of course, making prudent and bold investments in prestige and merchandise, betting on the couple. But, moreover, I insist, doing all of this with love. And they, the dancer, the Rosenkavalier and the pregnant virgin from Lilliput, show that they have risen to the heights of the new circumstances, the exact height of this high tide of affection, forbearance, and adulation that the city raises to draw them in. They buy only the bare min-imum to eat and be happy, they buy white wool for the child and special biscuits for the dog. They are grateful for invitations and can't accept them because they are in mourning. I imagine them alone in the large draw-ing room, with nobody to dance for, near the fire or surrounded by the first disorderly items of the museum. In exchange for listening to them, I would gladly return the fifty pesos in fees and would add to that another banknote. In exchange for listening to them, for knowing who they are and how we seem to them."

Guiñazú didn't say a word about the will, about the changes the old woman dictated to Ferragut, until the exact moment he felt like doing so. Perhaps he grew weary of waiting for a visit from the young man, for the tacit confession that would authorize him to pass judgment on him.

He felt the urge to do it one hot autumn noon. He ate lunch with us, placed on the window sill in El Berna the brown briefcase he'd bought be-fore he graduated and that will always look brand new, as if it were made out of the hide of a young and still living animal, with no traces of litiga-tions, courthouse corridors, accumulated dirt. He covered it with his hat and told us that he was filing the will with the court.

"May man's justice be done," he laughed. "I spent a lot of time, I amused myself imagining the clauses that divine justice could have dictated. Trying to guess what the will would have been if God had written it instead of Doña Mina. But when we think about God we think about ourselves. And the God that I can think of (I repeat, I dedicated a lot of time to the prob-lem) would not have done things any better, as will soon be seen."

We watched him walk toward the plaza and cross it hurriedly, upright and without slumping his shoulders, with the briefcase hanging from two fingers, confident of what he was doing under the strong yellow sun, confident that what he was taking to court, for us, for the whole city, was the best, what we had managed to deserve.

We started to find out the following day, quite early. We heard that Guiñazú drank coffee and cognac with the judge, for a while they spoke little and kept looking at each other, serious and sighing, as if Doña Mina had just died and as if her death mattered to them. The judge, Canabal, was a burly man, with cold bulging eyes, his voice nasal, and whom I, going a bit overboard, had forbidden from drinking alcohol since the end of the year. He shook his heavy head over the will, becoming more and more distraught as he turned each page with a single expert finger. Then he stood up, huffing, and walked with Guiñazú to the door.

"If we lose the harvest, as well, we're going to have fun," said one of the two.

"Now that they're practically giving the wheat away to Brazil," said the other.

But before the door had closed, Canabal started to laugh, a laugh without prologue composed entirely of mature guffaws.

"The dog!" he shouted. "That sentence, so cynical and harsh, about love and the dog. How I long to see their faces! And I think I'm going to see them in this very office. They thought they'd bagged her and now . . . the dog and five hundred pesos!"

Guiñazú returned to the room and smiled silently. Canabal wiped his face with a grief-stricken handkerchief.

"Forgive me," he grunted, "but never in my life, not even as an ambulance chaser, have I ever seen anything so comical. The dog and five hundred pesos."

"I was thinking the same thing," Guiñazú said, tolerantly. "Ferragut is also impatient to see their faces, and it's true, the whole thing seemed comical to me," he continued, smiling, until he reached the window that opened onto the straight, narrow street, embellished by the humidity and the yellow light, above the infantile and dissolute music that crept up from the radio and record store. "But if we keep in mind that the deceased left behind a fortune..."

"Precisely," Canabal said, and started laughing again.

"A fortune and some cousins and nieces who have maybe never seen her and almost certainly hated her, and several dozens of thousands of people nobody knows and who will have to be pursued with banns all over the country... If we take into account, Judge, that the couple was taking care of her and made her happy for months, and that she was certain (as we ourselves are, without any proof other than vilifying experience) that the couple were confident they would be the heirs. If we admit that the old woman thought about that when she called Ferragut to determine that the young man, the midget, and the fetus would receive in payment the subsequently revealed five hundred pesos, so they could be set for life against any economic difficulty..."

"But, Guiñazú..." said the judge, smelling the dry and sad perfume of his handkerchief. "That's exactly why I was laughing. Therein lies the charm: in the coming together of all the things you have just listed."

His eyes are colorless, Guiñazú thought. *They merely shine and are convex; he could spend hours looking without blinking, with a rose leaf stuck to his cornea.*

"But I don't find it amusing anymore," Guiñazú continued. "The story is too comical, too monstrously comical. So, I ended up taking it seriously, distrusting what appeared to be obvious. For example, and in parting, think about the dog; tell me tomorrow why she left it to him and not to the millionaire cousins."

He closed the door dramatically and heard almost immediately Canabal's burst of laughter, the slobbery questions he asked himself out loud to keep himself laughing.

We also learned that Guiñazú – who had stopped joining us at the café and at El Berna – visited Las Casuarinas the following day. We heard he drank tea in the garden with the couple, that he inspected the burlap and tin defenses against frost and ants set up around the rose bushes.

We learned, when Guiñazú wanted to talk about it, when winter arrived and Las Casuarinas was left abandoned and the inhabitants of Santa María forgot about the cold and the hail in order to talk about the confusing and immortal story of the will, we learned that on that humid autumn afternoon Guiñazú arranged for the official transfer of the dying and diarrhetic dog and the five one-hundred-peso bills.

Though the fact was that a long time ago we'd had no choice but to suspect that Guiñazú had transferred the dog and the money. We had to imagine him doing it on that same syrupy Sunday morning when someone came to tell us that the midget had settled in to wait among piles of suitcases and round hat boxes, her legs outstretched to make room for the eleven-month fetus and the matted, mucous-eyed dog on the staircase at the docks, in front of the ferry berth.

The dual transfer had to have been known about at the very moment that someone else came to tell us that the young man, since daybreak of that same day, whipping the horse for the sake of it, had been driving in the wobbly seat of Las Casuarinas's gig through every neighborhood buying flowers. He had no preferences, paid out of pocket without asking questions, placed the bunches under the hood, said yes to a glass of *vineta*, then climbed back onto the coachman's seat. He drove up and down dirt roads, stopped to open and close gates, forced the animal to gallop under the imperfect circle of the moon, around skinny dogs, flecked and invisible, faced headlights and suspicions, began to feel weak and penniless, hungry and sleepy, deprived of his initial faith and the memory of any purpose.

It was morning when the horse stopped, its head drooping, next to the cemetery wall. The young man took his hands off his knees to protect himself from the disgusting perfume of kilos of flowers that weighed down the cart, and started thinking about dames, death, dawns, all while he waited for the ringing of the bells that would open the gates of the cemetery.

Perhaps he bribed the caretaker with smiles and promises, with the exhaustion and blind desperation of his body and face, older now and with a longer nose. Or perhaps the caretaker had felt what we – Lanza, Guiñazú, and I – thought we knew: that those who love the gods too much die young. He must have smelled it, hesitantly, thrown off for a moment by the scent of the flowers. He must have touched it for a moment with his cane until he recognized it and treated it like a friend, like a guest.

Because they let him bring in the carriage, guide it by pulling on the steaming jawbone of the horse until it reached the columned vault with a black angel with broken wings and metal dates and exclamation marks.

Because they saw him on his feet and on his knees in the coachman's seat, and then standing up on the swelling, black, and always damp earth, on the impetuous and irregular grass, constantly moving his arms, panting through a determined and exhausted grimace that exposed his teeth, as he haphazardly carried the recently cut flowers from the carriage to the grave, one bundle after another, without sparing a single petal or leaf, until he had returned the five hundred pesos, until he had raised an insolent and irregular mountain that expressed, for him and for the dead woman, what we could never know for certain.

1956

Most Dreaded Hell

The first letter, the first photograph, was delivered to him at the newspaper between midnight and closing. He was banging on the typewriter, a little hungry, a little sick from coffee and tobacco, dedicated with familiar pleasure to the march of the sentence and the compliant appearance of words. He was writing, "It is worth noting that the commissioners noticed nothing suspicious or even out of the ordinary in Play Boy's crowning triumph, when he took full advantage of the wintry track and shot ahead like an arrow at the decisive moment," when he saw the red hand stained with ink from *Politics* between his face and the typewriter, holding out the envelope.

"This is for you. They always mix up the mail. Not a single damn notice from the clubs, and then they come crying before the elections and complain about there never being enough space for them. It's already midnight, and I've got nothing to fill the column with?"

The envelope had his name, "Horse Racing," and *El Liberal* written on it. The only odd thing was a couple of green stamps and the Bahia post-mark. He finished the article just when they came up from typesetting to ask for it. He felt weak and satisfied, almost alone in the unduly large news-room, mulling over the last sentence: "We once again assert, with the same objectivity that informs all our assertions, that our duty is to the fans." Someone in the back was looking through envelopes in the files, and the older woman from *Society* was slowly taking off her gloves in her glass-walled cubicle, when Risso casually opened the envelope.

It contained a photograph, postcard size, poorly lit, where hatred and squalor gathered around the dark edges forming thick, wavering swaths, like embossing, like bands of sweat around an anguished face. He saw it with surprise, he didn't fully understand, he knew that he would give any-thing to forget what he had seen.

He stuffed the picture into his pocket and had started putting on his overcoat when *Society* came out of her glass lair smoking and with a fan of papers in her hand.

"Hi," she said. "Here I am, at this time of night, the soiree just now over."

Risso looked at her from above. Her fair, dyed hair, the wrinkles on her neck, the double chin that hung, round and sharp like a small belly, the tiny and undue gaieties that decorated her garments. *She, too, is a woman. I am now looking at the red scarf around her neck, her periwinkle nails on her old, tobacco-stained fingers, her rings and bracelets, her dress given to her on credit by a dressmaker not a lover, her endless and possibly crooked high heels, the sad curve of her mouth, the almost frenetic eagerness she instills in her smiles. All of it will be easier if I convince myself that she, too, is a woman.*

"Seems like you do it for the fun of it, deliberately. When I come, you leave, as if you were always taking shots at me. The temperature's glacial out there. They give me material, as promised, but not a single name, not a single quote. Take a guess, get it wrong, publish some nonsensical fantasy. I have no names other than the betrothed, thank god for that. Affluence and poor taste, that's all there was. They feted their friends with a spectacular reception at the home of the bride's parents. Nobody who's anybody gets married on Saturday anymore. Button up, a glacial wind is blowing up from the promenade."

When Risso married Gracia César, we all joined together in silence and kept our pessimistic prophecies under wraps. In those days she was staring at the inhabitants of Santa María from the billboards of El Sótano Theatre Cooperative, from the walls made more dilapidated by the end of autumn. Sometimes intact, sometimes with a pencil mustache or lacerated by spiteful fingernails, other times by first rains, her head was turned slightly to look at the street, alert, a little defiant, a little deluded with the hope of convincing and being understood. Betrayed by the sparkle over her tear ducts added on to Orloff Studio's blowup, her face also contained the farce of lifelong love, cloaking the determined and exclusive search for joy.

All of which was fine, he must have thought, it was desirable and necessary, it coincided with the results of multiplying the number of months of Risso's widowerhood by the total number of countless identical Saturdays at dawn, which he had repeated with aptly polite demonstrations of patience and familiarity in the brothel on the coast. A sparkle, the one in the eyes on the poster, was linked to the frustrated skill he employed to retie the knot of the always smart and sad mourning tie in front of the portable oval mirror in the bedroom at the brothel.

They got married, and Risso thought that it was enough to keep living as he always had, but devoting to her, without thinking about it, almost without thinking about her, the passion of his body, the deranged need for absolutes that possessed him on those long, drawn-out nights.

She imagined in Risso a bridge, an exit, a beginning. She had emerged from two courtships — one director, one actor — a virgin, perhaps because for her the theater was a calling as well as a game, and she thought that love should be born and remain apart, not contaminated by what one does to earn money and oblivion. With one then the other she was condemned to feel, during their trysts in the plazas, along the promenade or in the café, the fatigue of rehearsals, the effort of being adequate, maintaining vigilance over her voice and her hands. She always anticipated her own face one second before it took on an expression, as if she could look at it or touch it. She acted excited and incredulous, irrevocably measured her farce and that of the other, the sweat and dust of the theater that covered them, inseparable, signs of age.

When the second photograph arrived, from Asunción and with a visibly different man, Risso feared above all that he would be incapable of tolerating an unknown feeling that was neither hatred nor pain, that would die with him unnamed, that was linked to injustice and doom, to the first fear of the first man on earth, to nihilism and the beginning of faith.

The second photograph was given to him by *Police/Crime* one Wednesday night. Thursdays were days he could spend with his daughter from ten in the morning till ten at night. He decided to tear up the envelope without opening it, so he put it away and only on Thursday morning, while his daughter was waiting for him in the living room of his boarding house, did he allow himself to take a quick look at the envelope before ripping it apart over the toilet: here, too, the man was shown from the back.

But he had looked at the photo from Brazil many times. He kept it for an entire day and at dawn he was imagining a joke, a mistake, a fleeting absurdity. It had already happened to him, he had woken many times from a nightmare, smiling obsequiously and gratefully at the flowers on the walls of his bedroom.

He was lying on the bed when he pulled the envelope out of his jacket and the photo out of the envelope.

"Alright," he said out loud, "it's fine, it's true, and that's the way it is. It doesn't matter at all, even if I didn't see it I'd know what was going on."

(When she took the photograph with a self-timer, under the red and encouraging light of the lamp, she probably foresaw Risso's reaction, this challenge, this refusal to set himself free through rage. She had also foreseen, or simply desired, with little and mostly unfamiliar hope, that he would dig out of the obvious insult, the stunning indignity, a message of love.)

Once again he protected himself before looking: *I am alone and freezing to death in a boarding house on Calle Piedras in Santa María, at the dawn of any day whatsoever, alone and regretting my solitude as if I'd sought it out, proud as if I'd deserved it.*

In the photograph, the headless woman conspicuously digging her heels into the edge of the divan, awaiting the impatience of the dark man, enlarged by the inevitable foreground, would have been certain that showing her face was not necessary for her to be recognized. On the back, her calm handwriting said: "Mementos from Bahia."

On the night that corresponded to the second photograph, he thought that he could understand the totality of ignominy and even accept it. But he knew that the deliberation, persistence, and organized frenzy required to carry out revenge was beyond his reach. He measured the disparity, he felt unworthy of so much hatred, so much love, so much willingness to cause suffering.

When Gracia met Risso, she was able to assume many current and future things. She guessed his solitude from his stubble and a button on his vest; she guessed that he was bitter but not defeated, and that he needed to settle a score and didn't want to admit it. Many Sundays she watched him in the plaza, before the show, making careful calculations, his ardent and dour face, his greasy hat forgotten on his head, his large indolent body that had begun to get fat. She thought about love the first time they were alone together, or about desire, or about the desire to soothe the sadness of the man's cheekbone and cheek with her hand. She also thought about the city, about how the only wisdom possible was to become resigned in time. She was twenty and Risso was forty. She started to believe in him, she discovered intensities of curiosity, she told herself that you are only truly alive when every day brings a surprise.

For the first few weeks she locked herself up to laugh by herself, she forced herself into fetishistic worship, she learned to determine moods based on smells. She was guiding herself in the discovery of what lay behind the voice, the silences, the preferences, and the attitudes of the man's body. She loved Risso's daughter and reconfigured the girl's face, extolling the resemblance to her father. She didn't leave the theater because the Municipality had just started giving it a subsidy, and she began to receive a steady salary at El Sótano, a world apart from her house, her bedroom, her frenzied and indestructible man. She didn't want to extricate herself from debauchery; she wanted to rest and forget it, allow debauchery to rest and forget. She made plans and carried them out, she was confident in the infinitude of the universe of love, confident that every night they would be offered a different and recently invented wonder.

"Everything," Risso insisted, "absolutely everything can happen to us, and we are going to always be happy and in love. Everything; whether God invents it or we do."

The truth is he'd never held onto a woman before, and he believed he was fabricating what was now being imposed upon him. But it wasn't she who was imposing it on him, Gracia César, Risso's handiwork, separated from him in order to render him whole, like air for the lungs, like winter for wheat.

The third photo arrived three weeks later. It also came from Paraguay and didn't arrive at the newspaper but rather the boarding house, and the housemaid brought it to him late one afternoon when he was waking up from a dream in which he'd been advised to defend himself against terror and dementia by keeping all future photographs in his wallet and rendering them anecdotal, inoffensive, through hundreds of daily distracted glances.

The maid knocked on the door, and he saw her place the envelope on the slats of the blinds, began to perceive how its damaging nature, its quivering threat, filtered through the darkness, the dirty air. He stared at it from bed as at an insect, as at a poisonous creature that is crushed at a moment of carelessness, of propitious error.

In the third photograph, she was alone – pushing against the shadows of a poorly lit room with her whiteness, her head thrown painfully back, toward the camera, her loose black hair partially covering her shoulders, robust and quadrupedal. As unmistakable now as if she'd had her picture taken in a studio and had posed with her most tender, meaningful, and oblique smile.

He, Risso, now had only irremediable pity for her, for himself, for all lovers in the world who had ever loved, for truth and the error of his beliefs, for the simple absurdity of love, and for the complex absurdity of the love that is created by men.

But he also tore up that picture, and he knew that it would be impossible for him to look at another one and go on living. But on the magical level where they had begun to understand each other and engage in a dialogue, Gracia had an obligation to know that he was going to tear up the pictures as soon as they arrived, each time with less curiosity, less remorse.

On the magical level, all vulgar or timid men with a sense of urgency were nothing but obstacles, indispensable postponements of the ritual act of choosing, in the street, in a restaurant, or in a café, the most credulous and inexperienced man, the man who could lend himself, without arousing suspicion and with comic pride, to be exposed in front of the camera or timed shutter, the least unpleasant among those who believed the memorized pitch of the traveling salesman.

"It's just that I've never had a man like you, so unique, so different. And I never know, involved as I am in the life of the theater, where I will be tomorrow or if I will ever see you again. At least I want to look at you in a photograph when we will be far apart and I'll miss you."

And after the almost always easy persuasion, thinking about Risso or putting off those thoughts till tomorrow, fulfilling the duty she had imposed on herself, she set up the lights, the camera, and aroused the man. If she thought about Risso, she evoked an ancient event, again reproached him for not having struck her, for having pushed her away forever with a lackluster insult, an intelligent smile, a comment that confounded her with all other women. And without understanding; proving despite the nights and the sentences spoken that he had never understood.

Without a surplus of hope, she bustled and sweated in the always hot and seedy hotel room, measuring lights and distances, correcting the position of the man's stiff body. Forcing – through any means, decoy, dissolute lie – the man of the hour to turn his cynical and mistrustful face toward her. She tried to smile and goad, mimicking the affectionate clucks made to newborns, counting the seconds, at the same time calculating the intensity with which the picture would allude to her love with Risso.

But since she could never know this, since she didn't even know if the photographs found their way to Risso, she began to intensify the evidence in the pictures, converting them into documents that had very little to do with them, with Risso and Gracia.

She ended up allowing and demanding that the faces, thinned by desire, stupified by the ancient masculine dream of possession, would face the hole in the camera with a tough smile, with shameful impudence. She considered it necessary to slide backwards and insert herself in the photograph, make her head, her short nose, her large undaunted eyes descend from the nothingness beyond the borders of the photo in order to include the filth of the world, the awkward, erroneous photographic vision, the satires of love that she had sworn to send regularly to Santa María. But her real mistake was to change the addresses on the envelopes.

The first separation, six months after the wedding, was welcome and excessively anguished. El Sótano – now Teatro Municipal de Santa María – traveled to Rosario. There, she repeated the same old hallucinatory game of being an actress among actors, of believing in what was happening on stage. The audience grew excited, applauded, or resisted the pull. Programs and reviews were printed promptly; and people accepted the game and prolonged it till the end of the night, talking about what they had seen and heard, and had paid to see and hear, conversing with a kind of desperation, a kind of goaded enthusiasm about performances, stage decorations, speeches, and plotlines.

Hence the game, the cure, alternatively melancholic and intoxicating, which she began as she slowly approached the window overlooking the fjord; shuddering and whispering for the entire theater to hear: "Perhaps . . . but I also carry within me a life of memories that remains unknown to others," was also accepted in Rosario. Playing cards were always dropped in response to the one she discarded, the game became formalized, and it was no longer possible to drift off and look at it from the outside.

The first separation lasted exactly fifty-two days, and Risso tried to copy in each of them the life he had led with Gracia César for their six months of married life. To go at the same time to the same café, the same restaurant, see the same friends, repeat silences and solitudes along the promenade, walk back to the boarding house stubbornly suffering the anticipation of the encounter, stirring up in front of him or in his mouth exaggerated images that were born out of perfected memories or unattainable ambitions.

It was ten or twelve blocks, now alone and more slowly, through nights disrupted by warm and freezing winds along the unsettled line that separated spring from winter. He used them to measure his need and his distress, to learn that the madness they shared had, at least, the grandiosity to lack a future, to not be a means to anything.

As for her, she had thought that Risso was giving their shared love a motto when he whispered, lying down, with fresh astonishment, overwhelmed:

"Everything can happen and we are always going to be happy and in love."

Already the sentence was not a judgment, not an opinion, did not express a wish. It was dictated to them or imposed, it was a confirmation, an old truth. Nothing they might do or think could weaken the madness, the love with no exit or modification. All human possibilities could be used and everything was condemned to serve as nourishment.

She believed that beyond them, outside the room, there stretched a wall devoid of meaning, inhabited by beings who didn't matter at all, teeming with worthless facts.

So she thought only of Risso, of them, when the man began to wait for her at the door of the theater, when he invited her and guided her, when she herself began to undress.

It was the last week in Rosario, and she thought it was useless to mention it in her letters to Risso; because the incident was not separate from them and at the same time had nothing to do with them; because she had behaved like a strange and lucid animal, with some pity for the man, with some scorn for the shabbiness of what she was adding to her love for Risso. And when she returned to Santa María, she preferred to wait for a Wednesday evening – because Risso didn't go to the newspaper on Thursdays – for a night without time, for a dawn identical to the twenty-five they had already lived.

She began to tell it before undressing, with the pride and tenderness of having invented, as simple as that, a new caress. Leaning on the table, in his shirtsleeves, he closed his eyes and smiled. Then he undressed her and asked her to repeat the story, now from standing, moving barefoot on the rug and almost without changing position, facing him and in profile, turning her back, her body swaying as she shifted her weight from one leg to the other. At moments she saw Risso's long, sweaty face, his heavy body leaning on the table, protecting the glass of wine with his shoulders, and sometimes she only imagined them, distracted by her thirst for fidelity in the story, by the joy of reliving that peculiar intensity of love that she had felt for Risso in Rosario, next to a man with a forgotten face, next to nobody, next to Risso.

"Good. Now you get dressed," he said, in the same hoarse and astonished voice that had repeated that everything was possible, that everything would be for them.

She scrutinized his smile and put on her clothes. For a while the two of them looked at the patterns on the tablecloth, the stains, the ashtray with the bird with a broken beak. Then he got fully dressed and left, spent his Thursday, his day off, talking with Guiñazú, convincing him of the urgency of a divorce, mocking in advance any attempts at reconciliation.

There was then a long and unwholesome period in which Risso wanted her back and simultaneously hated the pity and disgust of any imaginable encounter. Then he decided that he needed Gracia, and now a little more than before. That a reconciliation was necessary and that he was willing to pay any price as long as his volition played no part, as long as it would be possible to have her at night again without saying *yes*, not even with his silence.

Once again he started spending his Thursdays with his daughter and listening to the list of the predictions that had come to pass, which the grandmother ticked off after meals. He received cautious and vague news from Gracia, and he began to imagine her as an unknown woman whose gestures and reactions had to be guessed or deduced; as a preserved and lonely woman among people and places, who was preordained for him and whom he would have to love, perhaps at first sight.

Almost one month after the beginning of the separation, Gracia passed out contradictory addresses and left Santa María.

"Don't worry," Guiñazú said. "I know women well, and I was expecting something like this. This confirms desertion and simplifies the case, which cannot be adversely affected by the obvious delay tactics exhibited by the defendant's unreasonableness.

That was at the humid beginning of spring, and many nights Risso returned on foot from the newspaper, the café, giving names to the rain, stoking his suffering as though blowing on an ember, pushing it away from himself in order to see it as better and unbelievable, imagining acts of love never lived, only to then remember them with desperate lust.

Risso had destroyed the last three messages without looking at them. Now, and forever, he felt, whether at the newspaper or the boarding house, like vermin in its lair, like a beast listening to the echoes of the hunters' gunshots at the entrance to its cave. He could save himself from death and the idea of death only by pushing himself into quietude and ignorance. Curled up, he rubbed his whiskers and his snout, his paws; he could do nothing but wait for the other's rage to be spent. Without allowing himself either words or thoughts, he found himself forced to begin to understand; to confound the Gracia who sought and chose men and positions for the photos with the girl who had arranged, many months earlier, dresses, conversations, makeup, caresses for his daughter in order to win over a widower devoted to grief, that man who earned a meager salary and who could offer women only an astonished, loyal lack of comprehension.

He had started to believe that the girl who had written him long and hyperbolic letters during the brief summer separations of their courtship was the same one who pursued his despair and annihilation by sending him the photographs. And he came to think that any lover who has managed to inhale in the comfortless tenacity of a bed the dismal scent of death is condemned to pursue – for him and for her – destruction, the final peace of nothingness.

He thought about the girl who walked arm in arm with two girlfriends in the afternoon along the promenade dressed in the full-skirted appliqué dresses of starched fabric that memory invented and imposed, and who walked through the overture to *The Barber of Seville* that topped the bill of the Sunday band concert to look at him for a second. He thought about that bolt of lightning when she turned her enraged expression full of offer and challenge, when she showed him directly the almost masculine beauty of her capable and thoughtful face, in which she chose him, besotted by widowhood. And, little by little, he came to admit that this was the same naked woman, a little bit heavier, with a certain air of composure and having settled down, who sent him photographs from Lima, Santiago, Buenos Aires.

Why not, he came to think, why not accept that the photographs, their laborious preparation, their prompt dispatch, originated in the same love, in the same capacity for nostalgia, in the same congenital loyalty.

The next photograph came to him from Montevideo; not to the newspaper and not to his boarding house. And he never saw it. He was leaving *El Liberal* one night when he heard Old Man Lanza's limp pursuing him down the stairs, the tremulous cough behind him, the innocent and duplicitous introductory sentence. They went to eat at the Baviera, and afterwards Risso could have sworn that he was aware that the unkempt, bearded sick man who sat at the table, moving a damp cigarette in and out of his sunken mouth, who avoided looking him in the eyes, who made trite comments about the latest wires from UP that had arrived at the newspaper, was impregnated with Gracia, or with the frenzied absurd aroma that love exudes.

"From one man to another," Lanza said with resignation. "Or from one old man who has no joy left in life other than the disputable one of being alive. From one old man to you; and I don't know, because one never knows, who you are. I know a few facts and I've heard people talk. But I no longer have any interest in wasting my time believing or doubting. It doesn't make any difference. Every morning I verify that I'm alive, without bitterness and without gratitude. I drag a lame leg and arteriosclerosis through Santa María and the newsroom; I remember Spain, I correct galleys, I write, and sometimes I talk too much. Like tonight. I received a dirty photograph and there's no doubt who sent it. There's also no way to guess why they chose me. On the back it says: "To be donated to the Risso Collection," or something of the sort. It arrived on Saturday, and I spent two days thinking about whether or not to give it to you. I reached the conclusion that I should tell you because sending it to me is abject madness, and maybe it would be good for you to know that she's mad. Now you know; I only ask your permission to tear it up without showing it to you."

Risso said *yes*, and that night, looking at the light of the streetlamp on the ceiling of his room till morning, he understood that the second misfortune, revenge, was in essence less serious than the first, betrayal, but also much harder to bear. He felt his long body exposed like a nerve to the pain of the air, unprotected, unable to conjure up any relief.

The fourth photograph not sent to him was thrown on the table by his daughter's grandmother the following Thursday. The girl had gone to bed, and again the picture was inside the envelope. It fell between the soda bottle and the candy bowl, exposed, pierced and tinted by the reflection of the bottle, sporting eager letters of blue ink.

"You understand that after this . . ." the grandmother stuttered. She stirred her coffee and looked Risso in the face, peering at his profile in search of the secret of universal corruption, the cause of her daughter's death, the explanation for so many things that she had suspected without the courage to believe them. "You understand," she repeated with rage, in her aged and comical voice.

But she didn't know what needed to be understood, and Risso didn't understand, either, even though he made an effort, looking at the envelope that had been placed in front of him, one corner resting on the edge of the plate.

Outside, the night was heavy, and the city's open windows mingled the milky mystery of the sky with the mysteries of the lives of men, their efforts and their habits. Flipped over on his bed, Risso believed he was starting to understand that, like an illness, like well-being, understanding was taking place inside him, freed from will or intellect. It was taking place, simply, from the contact between his feet and his shoes to the tears that ran onto his cheeks and his collar. Understanding was taking place inside him, and he wasn't interested in knowing what it was that he understood, as he remembered or was seeing his tears and his calm, the extended passivity of his body on the bed, the camber of clouds through the window, ancient and future scenarios. He saw death and friendship with death, the hubris of disdain for the rules that all men had agreed to obey, the authentic awe of freedom. He tore up the photograph over his chest, without moving his eyes from the whiteness of the window, slowly and skillfully, afraid of making noise or being interrupted. He then felt the movement of a new breeze, perhaps one he'd breathed as a child, which began to fill the room and spread with inexpert idleness through the streets and the unwary buildings, to await him and offer him protection tomorrow and in the days that followed.

Until dawn he was getting to know, like cities that had once seemed out of reach, indifference, unfounded joy, acceptance of solitude. And when he awoke at noon, when he loosened his tie and his belt and his wristwatch as he made his way to the putrid scent of storm at the window, he was over-taken for the first time by paternal affection for men and for what men had done and built. He had decided to find out where Gracia lived, call her or go live with her.

That night at the newspaper he was a slow and happy man, behaving with the awkwardness of a newborn, and he fulfilled his quota with the distractions and mistakes that are commonly forgiven in a stranger. The big news was that Ribereña wouldn't be running in San Isidro, because we are now able to report that the offspring of El Gorrión, the famous stud, woke up today showing signs of pain in one of his front legs, indicating inflammation of the tendon, which speaks clearly to the magnitude of the pain he is suffering.

"Recalling that he covered the races," Lanza said, "one tries to explain the bewilderment of comparing him to the man who bet his wages on a tip he was given and that was then confirmed by the caretaker, the jockey, the owner, and the horse itself. For although he had, as we will find out, the best reasons to suffer and swallow all the bottles of sleeping pills from all the pharmacies in Santa María, what he showed me half an hour before doing that was nothing more than the reasoning and the attitude of a man who'd been cheated. A man who'd been safe and sound, and was no longer, and can't explain how that could be, what error in calculation produced his collapse. For at no moment did he call the filly who was passing out filthy pictures around the city a bitch, and he didn't even agree to walk across the bridge I held out to him, insinuating, without believing it, the possi-bility that the filly (naked and raised in the way she liked to expose herself, imitating on stage the ovarian problems of other fillies made famous in universal dramas), the possibility that she was stark raving mad. Nothing.

He had made a mistake, not by marrying her but at a different moment he didn't want to name. It was his fault, and our conversation was incredible and horrific. Because he'd already told me that he was going to kill himself, and he'd already convinced me that it was useless and also grotesque and again useless to argue to try to save him. And he spoke to me coldly, not accepting my pleas for him to get drunk. He'd made a mistake, he insisted; he and not that miserable wretch who sent the photograph to the little one, to her Catholic school. Maybe thinking that the Mother Superior would open the envelope, maybe hoping that the envelope would come into Risso's daughter's hands intact, certain then to have hit on what Risso had that was truly vulnerable."

1957

The Face of Disgrace

for Dorotea Muhr, neglected dog of bliss

I

In the evening I was in my shirtsleeves, in spite of the annoying wind, leaning on the hotel railing, alone. The light carried the shadow of my head through the bushes to the edge of the sandy path that connects the road and the beach to the hamlet.

The girl appeared bicycling down the path then quickly disappeared behind the chalet with its Swiss roof, empty, and its sign with black lettering on top of the letter box. It was impossible for me to not look at the sign at least once a day; in spite of its rain-punished surface, afternoon naps, and the wind from the sea, its luster endured and made one believe its words: "My Refuge."

A moment later the girl reappeared over the sandy strip surrounded by weeds. Her body was vertical in the seat, she moved her legs with slow ease, calm arrogance, her legs swaddled in grey socks, thick and fluffy, spiked with pine needles. Her knees were astonishingly round, fully formed, in comparison to the youth betrayed by her body.

She stopped the bicycle next to the shadow of my head, and her right foot, disengaged from the bicycle, stepped for balance on the short dead grass, already brown, now in the shadow of my body. She then moved her hair off her forehead and looked at me. She was wearing a dark sweater and a pink skirt. She looked at me calmly and attentively, as if the tanned hand that removed her hair from her brow would be enough to conceal her inspection.

I figured there were twenty meters and fewer than thirty years between us. Resting on my forearms, I held her gaze in mine, changed the position of my pipe between my teeth, continued to look at her and her heavy bicycle, the colors of her thin body against the landscape of trees and sheep, which was abating in the afternoon.

Suddenly sad and impassioned, I looked at the smile the girl offered up to fatigue, her stiff and mussed hair, her thin upturned nose that moved with her breath, the childish angle at which her eyes had been inserted into her face – and that no longer had anything to do with age, that had settled there once and for all and unto death – and the excessive space this left for the sclera. I looked at that glow of sweat and fatigue as the first or the last light of dusk caught her, covering and silhouetting her like a phosphorescent mask in the looming darkness.

The girl gently rested the bike against some shrubs and turned to look at me again as her hands touched her waist, her thumbs sinking under the waistband of her skirt. I don't know if she was wearing a belt; that summer all the girls wore wide belts. Then she looked around. Now I saw her in profile with her hands clasped behind her, still with no breasts, still oddly catching her breath, her face turned toward the spot in the afternoon where the sun was going to set.

Abruptly, she sat down on the grass, took off her sandals, and shook them out; she held her naked feet one hand at a time, rubbing her short toes and wiggling them in the air. Over her narrow shoulders I saw her wave her dirty and reddened feet. I saw her stretch her legs, take a comb and a mirror out of the large monogrammed purse hanging over the front of her skirt. She brushed her hair carelessly, almost without looking at me.

She put her sandals back on and stood up, then spent a while giving the pedal quick little kicks. She repeated her hard and hasty motion, then turned toward me, still standing alone at the railing, still motionless, looking at her. The scent of the honeysuckle began to rise and the light from the hotel bar spread pale blotches over the grass, over the sandy areas, and over the circular driveway that surrounded the terrace.

It was as if we had seen each other before, as if we knew each other, as if we did not have pleasant memories. She looked at me defiantly as her face sank into the meager light; she looked at me with defiance in her entire scornful body, in the nickel-plated shine of her bicycle, in the landscape with a chalet with a Swiss roof and privets and young eucalyptus trees with milky trunks. It was like that for a second: everything surrounding her was sequestered by her and her absurd stance. She mounted the bicycle and rode off behind the hydrangeas, behind the empty benches painted blue, then more quickly past the line of cars in front of the hotel.

I emptied my pipe and watched the sun die between the trees. Already I knew, and perhaps too much, what she was. But I didn't want to name her. I thought about what was awaiting me in my hotel room until dinner. I tried to measure my past and my guilt with the yardstick I had just discovered: the thin girl in profile against the horizon, her tender and impossible age, her blushing feet that one hand had banged and squeezed.

Next to the bedroom door I found an envelope with the hotel bill for the fortnight. As I bent over to pick it up, I surprised myself, smelling the perfume of the honeysuckle that by then was groping its way into the room, with feelings of sadness and expectation, without any new reason I could put my finger on. I lit a match to reread the *Avis aux passagers* framed on the door, and relit my pipe. I spent several minutes washing my hands, playing with the soap, and I looked at myself in the bathroom mirror, almost in the dark, until I could make out the thin, white, poorly shaved face, maybe the only white one among the hotel guests. It was my face, and the changes of the last few months really didn't make any difference. Someone walked through the garden, singing sotto voce. My habit of playing with the soap, I realized, began with Julián's death, perhaps the very night of the funeral.

I returned to the bedroom and opened the suitcase after taking it out from under the bed. It was an idiotic ritual, it was a ritual; but maybe it would have been better for everyone if I'd faithfully abided by this form of madness until I had worn it out or been worn out myself. I searched without looking, removing clothes and two small books, finally locating the folded newspaper. I knew the article by heart; it was the fairest, the most inaccurate and respectful of all those that had been published.

I brought the armchair closer to the lamp and was looking at it without reading the black full-page-width headline, which was beginning to fade: FUGITIVE BANK CLERK COMMITS SUICIDE. Underneath, the picture, the grey splotches that constituted the face of a man looking at the world with an expression of astonishment, his mouth almost beginning to smile under the downturned mustache. I remembered the sterility of having thought of the girl, minutes before, as the possible beginning of a sentence that would echo in a different sphere. This, my world, was a specific, narrow, and irreplaceable world. There was no room in it for a friendship, company, or dialogue other than what could be established with that ghost with the listless mustache. Sometimes I was allowed, by him, to choose between Julián and the Fugitive Bank Clerk.

Everyone accepts that they can influence, or have influenced, a younger brother. But Julián was – until a month and a few days ago – a bit more than five years older than I. However, I have to write *however*. I could have been born, and continue living, in order to sabotage his condition as an only child; I could have forced him, through my fantasies, my indifference, and my meager responsibility, to turn into the man he became: first into the poor devil so proud of his promotion, then into a thief. Also, of course, into the other, the relatively young deceased man that we all looked at but only I recognized as a brother.

What do I still have of his? A shelf of detective novels, a stray childhood memory, clothes I can't wear because they're too tight and too short. And the picture in the newspaper under the big headline. I disparaged his acceptance of life; I knew that he was single because of lack of momentum; many times I went by, almost drifted by, the barber shop where he went for a daily shave. His humility irritated me, and I had difficulty believing in it. I knew he received visits from a woman, punctually, every Friday. He was very affable, incapable of being a nuisance, and from the time he turned thirty, his jacket exuded the smell of old age. A smell impossible to define, provenance unknown. When he had doubts, his mouth twisted into the same grimace as our mother's. If I were free of him, he never would have become my friend, I never would have chosen him or accepted him for that. Words are beautiful or strive to be so when they try to explain something. All these words are, from birth, deformed and useless. He was my brother.

Arturo whistled in the garden, climbed over the railing, and was immediately inside the room, dressed in his beach robe, shaking sand off his head as he made his way to the bathroom. I watched him rinse off in the shower, and I hid the newspaper between my leg and the back of the chair. But I heard him shout:

"Still that ghost."

I didn't answer and relit my pipe. Arturo came in from the bath whistling and closed the door that opened onto the night. Throwing himself down on one of the beds, he put on his underwear then continued getting dressed.

"The belly keeps growing," he said. "I barely ate lunch, I swam out to the breakwater. And the result: the belly keeps growing. I would have bet anything, that of all the men I know, this couldn't have happened to you. But it's happening, and in a serious way. It's been about a month, hasn't it?"

"Yes. Twenty-eight days."

"You've even counted them," Arturo continued. "You know me pretty well. I say this without any disrespect. Twenty-eight days ago that poor slob shot himself, and here you are, even you, playing at remorse. Like a hysterical old maid. Because there are different kinds. Hard to believe."

He sat down on the edge of the bed to dry off his feet and put on his socks.

"Yeah," I said. "Since he shot himself, I guess he wasn't too happy. Not as happy, at least, as you are at this moment."

"No choice but to joke about it," Arturo said. "As if you were the one who killed him. And don't ask me again . . ." he stopped to look at himself in the mirror, "don't ask me again if in some world with seventeen dimensions it's your fault that your brother shot himself."

He lit a cigarette and stretched out on the bed. I stood up, placed a cushion over the newspaper that had so quickly aged, and started pacing in the heat of the room.

"Like I said, I'm leaving tonight," Arturo said. "What are your plans?"

"I don't know," I answered quietly, indifferently. "For now, I'm staying. Summer's still got a ways to go."

I heard Arturo sigh and I listened to how his sigh turned into a whistle of impatience. He got up, tossing the cigarette into the bathtub.

"As it turns out, I have the moral obligation to give you a couple of kicks and take you with me. You know it's different there. When you'll be nice and drunk, in the wee hours of the morning, well distracted, everything will be over."

I shrugged my shoulder, only the left one, and recognized a gesture that Julián and I had both inherited without any choice in the matter.

"I'm telling you again," Arturo said, stuffing a handkerchief in his breast pocket. "I'm telling you, I'm repeating, with a little bit of anger and the respect I mentioned earlier. Did you tell your poor brother to shoot himself to get out of the trap he was in? Did you tell him to buy Chilean pesos and change them for liras and the liras for francs and the francs for Baltic coronas and the coronas for dollars and the dollars for pounds and the pounds for yellow silk petticoats? No, don't shake your head. Cain in the depths of the cave. I want a *yes* or a *no*. Actually, I don't need an answer. Did you advise him — and here's the only thing that matters — to steal? Not ever. You aren't capable of that. I told you again and again. And you'll never find out if that's praise or criticism. You didn't tell him to steal. So, now what?"

I sat back down in the armchair.

"We already talked about this, many times. Are you leaving tonight?"

"Yeah, on the bus at nine something. I've got five more days of vacation and I don't intend to keep saving up more health just to squander it in the office."

Arturo chose a tie and started putting it on.

"It just doesn't make sense," he said again in front of the mirror. "I have to admit, I once shut myself away with a ghost. The experiment always ends badly. But with your brother, like you're doing now . . . A ghost with a wired mustache? Never. The ghost doesn't come out of nowhere, obviously. This time he came out of misfortune. He was your brother, we know. But right now he's the ghost of a bank teller with the mustache of a Russian general . . ."

"One last time, I promise?" I asked in a whisper; I wasn't asking for anything: I just wanted to do my duty and to this day I don't know by whom or by what.

"One last time," Arturo said.

"I see the logic. I didn't tell him to, I didn't remotely insinuate that he should use the money from the bank to do currency trading. But when I explained to him one night, just to boost his spirits, or so his life would be less boring, to show him that there were things that could be done in the world to make money and to spend it, other than collecting his salary at the end of every month . . ."

"I know, I know," Arturo said, sitting back down on the bed and yawning. "I swam too much, I'm too old for heroics. But it was the last day. I know the whole story. Explain it to me once and for all, but I'm warning you, the summer's over, it won't do you any good to stay shut away here. Explain why it's your fault that he did such a stupid thing."

"I'm to blame in one way," I mumbled, my eyes down, my head leaning back in the chair; I pronounced the words slowly, disjointedly. "I'm to blame for my encouragement, maybe my lie. I'm to blame for having talked to Julián, the first time, about something we can't define and that's called the world. I'm to blame for having made him feel (I don't say believe) that if he accepted the risks, that thing I called the world would be his."

"So what?" Arturo said, taking a step back to look at his hair in the mirror. "My friend. That's all convoluted nonsense. Well, life is also convoluted nonsense. One of these days you'll get over this stage; then come visit me. For now, get dressed and let's go have some drinks before we eat. I've got to leave early. But, before I forget, I'll leave you with one final argument. Maybe it'll help."

He touched my shoulder and looked me in the eyes.

"Listen," he said. "In the middle of all that happy convoluted nonsense, did Julián, your brother, use the money he stole properly, did he faithfully do the stupid things you were telling him to do?"

"Him?" I stood up, astonished. "Come on. By the time he came to see me, there was nothing to be done. At first, I'm pretty sure, he made some good buys. But then he got scared and did some unbelievable things. I don't know many details. It was something like a combination of securities and foreign currencies, of red and black and horseracing."

"You see?" Arturo said, nodding his head. "Certificate of lack of responsibility. I'm giving you five minutes to get dressed and think it over. I'll wait for you at the bar."

III

We had a few drinks while Arturo insisted on looking through his wallet for the picture of a woman.

"It's not here," he said finally. "Lost. The picture, not the woman. I wanted to show it to you because there's something unmistakable about her that few notice. And before you went crazy, you understood such things."

And there were, I was thinking, childhood memories that would emerge and become clearer in the coming days, weeks, or months. There was also the deceptive, perhaps deliberate, distortion of memories. There would be, in the best-case scenario, the choice I never made. It would show us, fleetingly or in a nightmare, dressed in ridiculous suits, playing in the wet garden or beating each other up in the bedroom. He was older, but weak. He was tolerant and kind, he took the blame for me, he lied gently about the marks on his face my blows had left, about a broken cup, a late arrival. It was strange that none of that had begun during that month-long fall holiday at the beach; perhaps, without meaning to, I was holding back the torrent with newspaper articles and evocations of the last two nights. In one, Julián was alive, in the next, dead. The second night didn't matter and all interpretations of it had grown confused.

It was his wake, his jaw was starting to hang, the bandage around his head had aged and turned yellow long before dawn. I was very busy serving drinks and comparing the similarities of the lamentations. Five years older than I, Julián had left his fortieth year behind a while ago. He'd never asked for anything important from life; maybe, yes, for them to leave him alone. He went around, as he had since childhood, asking permission. This sojourn on earth, not astonishing but definitely long, prolonged by me, hadn't worked well for him, not even to make a name for himself. All those hushed and listless imbibers of coffee or whisky concurred in their judgment and pity of suicide as a mistake. Because with a good lawyer, after a couple of years in prison . . . And moreover to everybody, the end, which they began to get a whiff of, seemed totally out of proportion and grotesque in relation to the crime. I thanked them and shook my head; then I moved back and forth between the hall and the kitchen, carrying drinks or empty glasses. I tried to imagine, without any information whatsoever, the opinion of the cheap whore who visited Julián every Friday and every Monday, days on which she had fewer clients. I wondered about the invisible, never revealed, truth of their relationship. I wondered what her judgment would be, attributing to her an impossible intelligence. What might she think, she who every day endured the burden of being a prostitute, about Julián, who accepted being a thief for a few weeks but, unlike her, couldn't tolerate that the imbeciles who occupy and make up the world would know about his failure. But she didn't come all night or at least I didn't recognize a face, an impudence, a perfume, a humility that could be attributed to her.

Without moving from the stool at the bar, Arturo had purchased the bus ticket and seat assignment. Nine forty-five.

"There's more than enough time. I can't find the picture. It's useless to keep talking to you today. Another round, waiter."

As I said, the night of the wake didn't matter. The previous one was much shorter and more difficult. Julián could have waited for me in the hallway of my apartment building. But he was already thinking about the cops and chose to pace back and forth in the rain until he saw a light in my window. He was soaked – he was a man born to use an umbrella and had forgotten his – and sneezed several times, apologizing, mockingly, before sitting down near the electric heater, before using my house. All of Montevideo knew the story about the bank and at least half the newspaper readers hoped, idly, not to hear anything more about the clerk.

But Julián had not endured an hour and a half in the rain to see me, say goodbye with words, and inform me of his suicide. We had a few drinks. He accepted the alcohol without fuss, without resistance:

"Anyway, by now. . ." he mumbled, almost laughing, shrugging one shoulder.

He had, however, come to say goodbye in his own way. Memories were inevitable, thoughts of our parents, our childhood vacation home, now razed. He wiped his long mustache and said, worried:

"It's strange. I always thought that you knew and I didn't. Ever since I was a kid. And I don't think it's a matter of character or intelligence. It's something else. There are people who instinctively find their place in the world. You did and I didn't. I always lacked the necessary faith," he said, rubbing his unshaven jaw. "And it's not a question of having to make up for some kind of vice or deformity. There was no handicap; at least none I ever knew about."

He paused and emptied his glass. As he lifted his head, the one I have looked at every day for the past month on the front page of the newspaper, he exposed his healthy and tobacco-stained teeth.

"But," he continued as he stood up, "your combination was very good. You should have given it to somebody else. Failure is not your thing."

"Sometimes they work and sometimes they don't," I said. "You're not going out in this rain. You can stay here forever, for all the time you want."

He leaned back in his chair and mocked me without looking at me.

"In this rain. Forever. All the time," he said as he walked up to me and touched my arm. "Forgive me. There will be hassles. There're always hassles."

He'd already left. He was saying goodbye with his always cowering presence, with his well-groomed well-meaning mustache, with his allusion to all the death and dissolution that blood, however, was and is capable of reconstituting in minutes.

Arturo was talking about the cheating at the racetrack. He looked at his watch and asked the bartender for one last drink.

"But with more gin, please," he said.

Then, without listening, I surprised myself by connecting my dead brother to the girl on the bicycle. I didn't want to remember him in childhood or his passive goodness, but rather his impoverished smile, his body's humble posture during our last meeting – if that's what I can call what I allowed to happen between us when he came into my apartment, drenched, to say goodbye in accordance with his own sense of etiquette.

I didn't know anything about the girl on the bicycle. But then, suddenly, while Arturo was talking about the jockey Ever Perdomo or the poorly managed tourism sector, I felt a wave of that old, unfair, almost always misplaced pity rising in my throat. Without a doubt I wanted her and wished to protect her. I couldn't imagine from what or against what. I sought, frantically, to guard her against herself and any danger. She had seemed to me insecure yet defiant, I had watched her lift her proud face of disgrace. This can last but always gets paid off prematurely, disproportionately. My brother had paid for his excess of simplicity. In the case of the girl – whom

I might never see again – there were different debts. But both, along such different paths, coincided in a desired nearness to death, to the definitive experience. Julián, by not being; she, the girl on the bicycle, by trying to be everything and in a rush.

"But," Arturo said, "even if you have proof that all the races are fixed, you'll still bet. See, now that I'm leaving, it looks like it's going to rain."

"Of course," I answered, and we moved into the dining room. I saw her immediately.

She was sitting next to a window, breathing in the stormy night air, a pile of sturdy dark hair blown in the breeze over her forehead and eyes; areas of light freckles – now, under the unbearable tube of light in the dining room – on her cheeks and nose, while her childish and watery eyes looked absent-mindedly at the shadow of the sky or the mouths of her fellow diners; with her thin, strong, bare arms in front of what could be called a yellow evening gown, one hand protecting each shoulder.

An old man was sitting next to her and conversing with the young woman in front of him, her fleshy white back turned toward us, a wild rose in her hair, over her ear. As she moved, the flower's small white circle went in and out of the girl's absentminded profile. When the woman laughed, throwing back her head, the skin on her back shimmering, the girl's face was forsaken to the night.

Talking with Arturo, I looked down at the table, trying to guess the source of her secret, the sensation she created of being something extraordinary. I longed to remain peacefully by the girl's side and take care of her life. I watched her smoke with her coffee, her eyes now glued onto the slow mouth of the old man. Suddenly she looked at me as she had from the path, with the same calm and defiant eyes, accustomed to contemplating or surmising scorn. With inexplicable desperation I withstood the girl's gaze, turning my own toward that youthful head, long and noble; fleeing from the incomprehensible secret in order to burrow into the night storm, to conquer the intensity of the sky and spill it out, lay it over that girl's face, which was observing me, still and expressionless. The face that let flow, unintentionally, the sweetness and adolescent humility of the violet and freckled cheeks.

Arturo smiled, smoking his cigarette.

"And you, Brutus?" he asked.

"And me what?"

"The girl on the bicycle, the girl at the window. If I didn't have to leave right now . . ."

"I don't understand."

"That one, in the yellow dress. You've never seen her before?"

"Once. This afternoon, from the veranda. Before you came back from the beach."

"Love at first sight," Arturo said, nodding. "Youth intact, and experience covered with scars. A lovely story. But, I must confess, there's someone who can tell it better. Just a sec."

The waiter came to the table to clear away the dishes and the fruit bowl.

"Coffee?" he asked. He was small, with the dark face of a monkey.

"Sure," Arturo said, smiling, "whatever you're calling coffee. Like they call the girl in yellow next to the window a young lady. My friend here is very curious; he would like to know something about her nighttime excursions."

I unbuttoned my jacket and sought the girl's eyes. But her head had already turned to one side and the black sleeve of the old man cut diagonally across the yellow dress. At that moment the flower-studded hair of the woman leaned over, covering the freckled face. The only thing remaining of the girl was some of her very dark hair, metallic along the crown that received the light. I remembered the magic of her lips and her gaze; *magic* is a word I cannot explain but that I write now irrevocably, with no possible substitute.

"Nothing bad," Arturo continued to the waiter. "The gentleman, my friend, is interested in cycling. Tell me. What happens at night when mommy and daddy, if that's what they are, go to sleep?"

The waiter swayed, smiling, the empty fruit bowl held at shoulder height.

"Nothing special," he said finally. "Everyone knows. At midnight the young lady goes out for a bicycle ride; sometimes to the forest, sometimes to the dunes," he said, managing to sound serious and then continued without malice: "What can I say. I don't know anything else, no matter what they say. Just that she comes back with her hair in a mess and without makeup. One night I was on duty and I saw her and she put ten pesos in my hand. The English boys at the Atlantic talk a lot. But I don't say anything because I haven't seen anything."

Arturo smiled, slapping one of the waiter's legs.

"There you have it," he said, as if he had just scored a victory.

"Excuse me," I asked the waiter, "how old might she be?"

"The young lady?"

"Sometimes, like this afternoon, she looked like a child; now she looks like a grown up."

"I know this for sure, sir," the waiter said, "because of the register. She's fifteen, her birthday was a few days ago. So, two coffees?" he leaned over before leaving.

I tried to smile under Arturo's gleeful gaze; my hand holding the pipe was shaking on the corner of the tablecloth.

"Anyway," Arturo said, "whether it works out or not, it's a more interesting life plan than living behind closed doors with a mustachioed ghost."

As she was leaving the table, the girl looked at me again fleetingly, now from above, one hand still tangled up in the napkin, as the breeze from the window ruffled the stiff hairs on her forehead, and I stopped believing what I had told the waiter and that Arturo had accepted.

On the veranda, holding his suitcase and with his coat over his arm, Arturo patted me on the shoulder.

"One week and we'll see each other. I'll drop in at Jauja and I'll find you at a table savoring the flowers of wisdom. Happy, long cycling."

He jumped into the garden and walked toward a group of cars parked in front of the terrace. As Arturo crossed in front of the lights, I lit my pipe, leaned on the railing, and smelled the air. The storm seemed far away. I returned to the bedroom and stretched out on the bed, listening to the music that reached me intermittently from the hotel dining room, where they might have started to dance. I cupped my hand around the warmth of the pipe and slipped into a slow dream, into a lubricated, airless world that I was condemned to move through with enormous effort and no desires, slack-jawed, toward the exit where the indifferent light of the morning was slumbering, unreachable.

I woke up in a sweat and went to sit back down in the armchair. Neither Julián nor my childhood memories had appeared in the nightmare. I left the dream forgotten in bed, breathed in the stormy air that entered through the window, scented with woman, oafish and hot. Almost without moving, I pulled the paper out from under me and looked at the headline, at Julián's faded photo. I let the newspaper fall, put on my raincoat, turned off the light, and jumped over the railing onto the soft earth of the garden.

The wind formed thick *s*'s and encircled my waist. I decided to walk across the lawn until I reached the stretch of sand where the girl had been sitting that afternoon. Her grey socks, spiked with pine needles, then her bare feet in her hands, her slim buttocks flattened against the ground. The forest was to my left, the sand dunes to my right, everything black and the wind hitting me in the face. I heard footsteps and soon saw the bright smile of the waiter, his monkey face right next to my shoulder.

"Bad luck," the waiter said, "you missed her."

I wanted to punch him but I quickly quieted my hands that were scratching the insides of my raincoat pockets, and I gasped toward the sound of the sea, motionless, my eyes downturned, resolved, and feeling sorry for myself.

"She must have left ten minutes ago," the waiter continued. Without looking at him, I knew he'd stopped smiling and was twisting his head to the left. "What you can do is wait for her to get back. If she gets a good scare . . ."

I slowly unbuttoned my raincoat without turning, took a banknote out of my trouser pocket and handed it to the monkey. I waited until I no longer heard the waiter's steps on the way to the hotel. Then I lowered my head, my feet planted firmly on the elastic earth and the grass where she had been, wrapped up in that memory, the girl's body and her movements on that remote afternoon, protected from myself and my past by an already enduring atmosphere of aimless belief and hope, breathing in the hot air where everything was forgotten.

I saw her suddenly, under the excessive autumn moon. She was walking alone along the shore, avoiding the rocks and the shining and expanding pools of water, pushing her bicycle, now without that comical yellow dress, wearing tight trousers and a pea coat. I had never seen her in those clothes and there had not been time for her body and her gait to become familiar to me. But I immediately recognized her and crossed the beach almost in a straight line toward her.

"Evening," I said.

A while later she turned to look at me; she stopped and flipped the bicycle around to face the water. She looked at me carefully for a moment, and there was already something solitary and helpless about her when I repeated my greeting. Now she answered. On the deserted beach her voice squealed like a bird's. It was a bleak and distant voice, so removed from her, from her lovely face, so sad and thin; it was as if she had just learned a language, a subject of conversation in a foreign tongue. I reached out my arm to hold the bicycle. Now I was looking at the moon and at her, protected by the shadows.

"Where were you going?" I said, then added: "Little girl."

"Nowhere," her strange voice sounded laborious. "I always like to walk along the beach at night."

I thought about the waiter, about the English boys at the Atlantic; I thought about everything I had lost forever, through no fault of my own, without being consulted.

"They say . . ." I said. The weather had changed: it was neither cold nor windy. Helping the girl hold the bicycle on the sand at the edge of the roar of the sea, I had a sensation of loneliness that nobody had ever before allowed me to have; solitude, peace, and trust. "If you have nothing else to do, they say that nearby there's a boat that's been converted into a bar and restaurant."

The harsh voice repeated with inexplicable joy:

"They say that nearby there's a ship that's been converted into a bar and restaurant."

I heard her breathe wearily; after a rest, she added:

"No, I have nothing to do. Are you inviting me? In these clothes?"

"I am. In those clothes."

When she averted her eyes I saw her smile; she wasn't mocking me, she seemed happy and not used to happiness.

"You were at the next table with your friend. Your friend left tonight. But I got a flat tire right after I left the hotel."

It irritated me that she would think of Arturo; I took the handlebars from her and we started walking along the shore toward the ship.

Two or three times I uttered a dead sentence, but she didn't respond. The heat and the storminess in the air increased. I felt the girl was growing sadder by my side; I peeked at her resilient footsteps, the resolute verticality of her body, her boyish buttocks squeezed into the ordinary pants.

The ship was there, beached and dark.

"There's no boat, there's no party," I said. "I'm sorry for having made you walk all the way here for nothing."

She had stopped to look at the freighter perched under the moon. She stood for a while, her hands behind her back, as if she were alone, as if she had forgotten about me and her bicycle. The moon was descending toward the horizon of the water or rising from there. Abruptly the girl turned and came toward me; I didn't let go of the bicycle. She took my face in her rough hands and moved it until it was in the light.

"What?" she wheezed. "You spoke. Again."

I almost couldn't see her but I remembered her. I remembered many other things that she, effortlessly, symbolized. I had started to love her and the sadness began to pour out of her and spill all over me.

"Nothing," I said. "There's no ship, no party."

"No party," she repeated, enunciating each syllable. I glimpsed her smile in the shadows, white and brief like the foam of the small waves that came within a few meters of the shore. Suddenly she kissed me, she knew how to kiss, and I felt her hot face, wet with tears. But I didn't let go of the bicycle.

"No party," she said again, now with bent head, smelling my chest. Her voice was more confused, almost guttural. "I had to see your face," and again she lifted it up to the moon. "I had to know that I wasn't wrong. Understood?"

"Yes," I said, lying; and then she took the bicycle from me, mounted it, and rode in a large circle around me in the damp sand.

When she was beside me, she leaned with one hand against my neck and we started back to the hotel. We walked away from the rocks and took a detour toward the forest. I didn't do it nor did she. She stopped next to the first pine trees and dropped her bicycle.

"Your face. Again. I don't want you to get angry," she begged.

I meekly looked at the moon, at the first clouds appearing in the sky.

"Something," she said in a strange voice. "I want you to say something. Anything."

She placed a hand on my chest and stood on tiptoes to bring her childish eyes to my mouth.

"I love you. And it's no good. And it's another form of disgrace," I said after a while, speaking almost as slowly as she.

Then the girl whispered, "Poor thing," as if she were my mother, in her strange voice, now tender and vindictive, and we began to burn and kiss. We helped each other strip her of the essentials and suddenly I had two things that I had never deserved: her face enthralled by tears and happiness under the moon, the disconcerting certainty that nobody had ever entered her before.

We sat near the hotel on the dampness of the rocks. The moon was covered. She started throwing pebbles; sometimes they landed in the water with a loud noise; at others, they barely reached beyond her feet. She didn't seem to notice.

My story was serious and definitive. I told it to her in a serious masculine voice, furiously resolved to speak the truth, not caring if she believed it or not.

All the facts ended up losing their meaning and could only have, from then on, the meaning she wished to give them. I spoke, of course, about my dead brother; but now, starting that night, the girl had become – retreating in order to be stuck like a long needle into bygone days – the main subject of my story. Every once in a while I heard her move and say *yes* in her strange, poorly formed voice. It was also obligatory to mention the years that separated us, lament too much, feign a desolate belief in the power of the word *impossible*, show tactful discouragement in the face of the inevitable struggles. I didn't want to ask questions, and her affirmations, not always placed precisely in my pauses, did not seek to make confessions either. There was no question, the girl had freed me from Julián and a lot of other wreckage and dregs that Julián's death represented and had brought to the surface; there was no question that, as of a half hour ago, I needed her and would continue to need her.

I accompanied her almost to the hotel door and we separated without telling each other our names. As she walked away, I thought I saw that the two bicycle tires were full of air. Perhaps she had lied to me about that, but nothing mattered now. I didn't even see her enter the hotel, and I slipped straight into the shadows in front of the veranda that led into my room; I continued laboriously to the dunes, finally hoping to not think about anything, and await the storm.

I continued walking and then, already far away, returned through the eucalyptus grove. I walked slowly between the trees, between the twisting wind and its lament, under the thunder that threatened to rise above the invisible horizon, closing my eyes to protect them against the sand pecking at my face. Everything was dark and – as I had to tell it several times afterwards – I did not see a bicycle light, supposing that someone would use one on the beach, not even the tip of a burning ember of a cigarette of someone walking or sitting, resting on the sand, on the dry leaves, leaning against a tree trunk, their legs gathered in, tired, wet, happy. That had been me; and though I didn't know how to pray, I was expressing my gratitude, refusing to accept, incredulous.

Now I was at the end of the trees, one hundred meters from the sea and in front of the dunes. I felt cuts on my hands and I stopped to suck on them. I walked toward the sound of the sea until I reached the wet sand on the shore. I did not see, I repeat, any light, any movement in the shadows; I heard no voice that sundered or distorted the wind.

I left the shore and began to climb up and down the dunes, slipping in the cold sand that spilled crackling into my shoes, pushing aside the bushes with my legs, almost running, furious and with a joy that had been pursuing me for years and had now caught up with me, excited as if I would never be able to stop, laughing inside the windy night, running up and down the miniature mountains, falling on my knees, my body slackening until

I could breathe without pain, my face turned toward the storm that was approaching from the water. Then, it was as if all the discouragements and resignations were also chasing me; for hours I looked unenthusiastically for the path back to the hotel. Finally, I came across the waiter and I repeated the act of not talking to him, of placing ten pesos in his hand. The man smiled and I was too tired to believe that he had understood, that everybody understood and would forever.

I fell asleep again half dressed on the bed as in the sand, listening to the storm that had finally settled in, beaten by thunderclaps, sinking parched into the wrathful clamor of the rain.

V

I'd finished shaving when I heard the strum of fingers on the glass door that gave onto the veranda. It was very early; I knew that the fingernails were long and painted with zeal. Without putting down the towel, I opened the door; it was terrible, there she was.

Her hair was dyed blond and perhaps at twenty she had been blond; she was wearing a tailored tweed suit that time and ironings had pressed against her body, and a green umbrella with an ivory handle that may never have been opened. Of the three things, I had guessed two – or assumed correctly – throughout my life and at my brother's wake.

"Betty," she said as she turned to me, with the best smile she could muster.

I pretended I'd never seen her, didn't know who she was. It was, just barely, a kind of compliment, a twisted form of the delicacy that no longer interested me.

This was, I thought, and would never be again, the woman I glimpsed faintly through the dirty windows of a café in the slums, touching Julián's finger during those long prologues to the Fridays or Mondays.

"Forgive me," she said, "for coming from so far away to bother you and at this time of day. Especially at these moments when you, as the best of Julián's brothers . . . I swear, I still can't accept that he's dead."

The morning light aged her, and she must have looked different in Julián's apartment, even in the café. I had been, until the very end, Julián's only brother; neither better nor worse. She was old, and it seemed easy to placate her. Not even I, in spite of everything I had seen and sensed, in spite of the memory of the previous night at the beach, fully accepted Julián's death. Only when I lowered my head and invited her with one arm to enter my room did I discover that she was wearing a hat and had decorated it with fresh violets surrounded by ivy leaves.

"Call me Betty," she said, and she chose the armchair where the newspaper, the picture, the headline, the decisively dissolute account were hidden. "But it is a matter of life and death."

There were no traces of the storm and the night might have never transpired. I looked at the sun through the window, the yellow splotch that was beginning to seek the rug. There was no doubt, however, that I felt different, that I was greedily breathing the air, that I had the urge to walk and to smile, that indifference – as well as cruelty – appeared to me as possible forms of virtue. But all of this was muddled, and I came to understand it only later.

I approached the armchair and offered my excuses to the woman, to that unwonted expression of filth and misfortune. I extracted the newspaper, lit several matches, and made it dance in flames over the railing.

"Poor Julián," she said behind me.

I returned to the middle of the room, lit my pipe, and sat down on the bed. I suddenly discovered that I was happy, and I tried to calculate the number of years that separated me from my last sensation of happiness. The smoke from the pipe irritated my eyes. I lowered it to my lap and looked with delight at that trash in the chair, that badly treated piece of dirt leaning back, unconscious, into the newborn morning.

"Poor Julián," I repeated, "I said that many times at the wake and afterwards. I'm sick of it, it's time. I waited for you at the wake and you didn't come. But, understand me, thanks to the task of waiting for you I knew what you were like, I could have picked you out on the street."

She examined me suspiciously and smiled again.

"Yes, I think I understand," she said.

She was not that old, still much younger than me or Julián. But our lives had been very different, and what she offered me from the chair was nothing but fatness, the wrinkled face of drink, suffering and veiled spite, the goop of life stuck forever to her cheeks, to the corners of her mouth, to the bags under her eyes surrounded by furrows. I felt like slapping her and throwing her out. But I remained calm, took another puff, and spoke to her in a gentle voice:

"Betty. You gave me permission to call you Betty. You said it was a matter of life or death. Julián is dead, problem solved. What else, then, who else?"

She again leaned back in the faded cretonne armchair, on top of the upholstery of large wild flowers, and looked at me as if I were a possible client: with inevitable hatred and strict calculations.

"Who's going to die now?" I insisted. "You or I?"

Her body relaxed, and she was preparing an expression of stirring emotions. I looked at her, admitted that she could be convincing; and not only to Julián. Behind her stretched the autumn morning, cloudless, a small glory offered to men. The woman, Betty, turned her head and a bitter smile began to appear on her face.

"Who?" she said facing the wardrobe. "You and I. You better believe it, this is just the beginning. There are IOUs with his signature, without collateral, that are now showing up in the courts. And there's the mortgage on my house, the only one I have. Julián assured me that it was just an offer; but the house, my home, has been mortgaged. And it has to be paid now. If we want to save something from this shipwreck. Or if we want to save ourselves."

Based on the violets in her hat and the sweat on her face, I sensed that it was inevitable I would hear, sooner or later on that sunny morning, a sentence of that sort.

"Yes," I said, "seems you're right, we have to join together and do something."

It had been many years since I'd derived so much pleasure from lies, farces, and evil. But I had turned young, and I didn't have to explain anything, not even to myself.

"I don't know," I said incautiously, "how much you know about my guilt, about my involvement in Julián's death. In any case, I can assure you that I never advised him to mortgage your house, your home. But I'm going to tell you everything. I saw Julián about three months ago. A brother having a meal in a restaurant with his older brother. And we were the kind of brothers who saw each other no more than once a year. I think it was somebody's birthday; his, our dead mother's. I don't remember and it doesn't matter. The date, whatever it was, seemed to depress him. I told him about the exchange market, currency trading; but I never told him to steal money from the bank."

She let some moments pass, succoring herself with a sigh and stretching her high heels toward the square of sun on the carpet. She waited for me to look at her, then smiled at me again; now it seemed like any birthday whatsoever, Julián's or my mother's. It was tenderness and patience; she wanted to guide me without tripping up.

"Dear boy," she whispered, her head resting on one shoulder, her smile reaching the limits of tolerance. "Three months ago?" she sighed as she shrugged her shoulders. "Julián had been stealing from the bank for five years. Or four. Don't remember. You spoke to him, you child, about some deal with dollars, right? I don't know whose birthday it was that night. And I don't mean to show disrespect. But Julián told me all about it, and I couldn't get him to stop laughing. He never even considered the dollars deal, whether it was good or bad. He stole and bet on the horse races. He won and he lost. He'd been doing it for five years, since before I met him."

"Five years," I repeated, chewing on my pipe. I stood up and walked over to the window. There were still traces of water on the grass and in the sand. The cool air had nothing to do with us, with anybody.

In one or another hotel room, above me, the girl would be sleeping peacefully, stretched out, starting to move between the stubborn despair of dreams and the hot sheets. I imagined her and still loved her, I loved her breathing, her smells, the supposed allusions to the nocturnal memory, to me, whatever might fit into her morning daze. I returned with a heavy heart from the window and looked without disgust or pity at what fate had placed in the chair of my hotel room. She straightened out the lapels of her tailored suit, which, after all, maybe wasn't tweed; she smiled into the air, awaited my return, my voice. I felt old and without much strength left. Perhaps the neglected dog of bliss was licking my knees, my hands; maybe it was just that other thing, that I was old and tired. But, in any case, I saw that I had to let time pass, relight my pipe, play with the match flame, with its splutter.

"For me," I said, "everything is just fine. Surely Julián did not put a gun to your head and force you to sign the mortgage. And I never signed an IOU. If he forged my signature and was able to live like that for five years (I think you said five), he had enough, you both had enough. I look at you, I think about you, and I don't give a damn if they take away your house or throw you in prison. I never signed any IOU for Julián. Unfortunately for you, Betty, and that name seems inadequate, I'm sorry to say it no longer suits you, there's no danger or threat that will work. We can't be partners in anything, and that's always sad. I think it's sadder for women. I'm going out onto the veranda to smoke and look at how the morning is developing. I'd be very grateful, Betty, if you left right away, if you don't make much of a fuss."

I went outside and swore at myself under my breath, looking for defects in the prodigious autumn morning. I heard, from far away, the lackadaisical curse that rang out behind me. I heard, almost immediately, a door slam. A blue Ford appeared near the hamlet.

I was little, and it all seemed undeserved, orchestrated by the poor, uncertain imagination of a child. Always, since adolescence, I had shown my defects, I was always right, I was eager to converse and argue, without reservations or silences. Julián, on the other hand – I began to like him and feel a wholly other kind of pity for him – had deceived all of us for many years. This Julián whom I'd only gotten to know dead had been laughing at me, slightly, ever since he started to confess the truth, to lift his mustache and his smile in his coffin. Perhaps he was still laughing at all of us a month after his death. But it didn't do me any good to invent resentment or disenchantment.

The memory of our last meeting, above all, irritated me, the gratuitousness of his lies, the fact that I couldn't understand why he had come to see me, with all the risks that entailed, to lie one last time. Because Betty's only use to me was for pity or scorn; but I was buying her story, I felt confident in the constant filth of life.

A blue-painted Ford groaned as it climbed the hill, appeared on the road behind the chalet with a red roof, and drove past the veranda, continuing to the door of the hotel. I saw a policeman wearing a faded summer uniform get out, an extraordinarily tall and skinny man wearing a wide-stripe suit, and a young, blond, hatless man dressed in grey, whom I saw smile with every sentence he spoke, as he held a cigarette between his long, slender fingers.

The hotel manager came slowly down the stairs and walked over to them while the waiter of the night before appeared from behind a column on the staircase, in shirtsleeves, his black head shining. Everybody spoke with minimal facial expressions, almost without changing the spot where their feet were planted, and the manager pulled a handkerchief out of the inside pocket of his jacket, wiped it across his lips, and stuffed it back in only to again pull it out a few seconds later with a quick motion and squeeze it and move it across his mouth. I went back inside to make sure that the woman had left; when I returned to the veranda, when I became aware of my own movements, of the moroseness with which I longed to live and enact each gesture, as if I were trying to caress with my hands the gestures these had made, I felt that I was happy in the morning, that there could be other days awaiting me anywhere.

I saw that the waiter was looking down at the ground, and the other four men lifted their heads and turned their faces of distracted observation toward me. The young blond man tossed his cigarette far away; then I began to separate my lips until I smiled and greeted, with a nod of my head, the manager, and then, before he could respond, before his head lowered, still looking at the veranda, patting his mouth with his handkerchief, I lifted my hand and repeated my greeting. I returned to my room to finish getting dressed.

I stopped for a moment in the dining room, watching the guests eat breakfast, and then I decided to have a gin, just one, at the bar, I bought cigarettes, then joined the group waiting at the bottom of the staircase. The manager greeted me again, and I noticed that his jaw was trembling, just barely, rapidly. I said a few words and I heard that they were talking; the young blond man came up to me and touched my arm. Everyone was now silent, and the blond man and I looked at each other and smiled. I offered him a cigarette and he lit it without taking his eyes off my face; then he took three steps back and looked at me again. Perhaps he had never seen the face of a happy man; the same thing was happening to me. He turned his back, walked over to the first tree in the garden, and leaned one shoulder against it. All of that had some meaning and, without understanding it, I knew that I agreed, and nodded. Then the very tall man said:

"Shall we take the car to the beach?"

I went ahead and settled into the passenger seat next to the driver. The tall man and the blond man sat in the back. The policeman sat down unhurriedly behind the steering wheel and started the car. Soon we were driving quickly through the peaceful morning; I smelled the cigarette the young man was smoking, I felt the silence, and the other man's quietude, his resolve filling that silence and that quietude. When we reached the beach the car stopped next to a pile of grey rocks that separated the road from the sand. We got out, stepped over the rocks, and walked toward the sea. I walked next to the young blond man.

We stopped at the shore. The four of us were silent, our ties blowing in the wind. We all lit cigarettes.

"The weather is unsettled," I said.

"Shall we go?" the young blond man said.

The tall man in the striped suit stretched out his arm until he touched the young man on the chest and said in a thick voice:

"Look. From here to the dunes. Two blocks. Not much more or less."

The other nodded in silence, shrugging his shoulders as if it didn't matter. He smiled again and looked at me.

"Let's go," I said, and I started back to the car. Just as I was about to get in, the tall man stopped me.

"No," he said. "It's over there, on the other side."

In front of us there was a shed built with damp-stained bricks. It had a sheet-metal roof and dark letters painted over the door. We waited for the policeman to return with the key. I turned to look at noon arriving over the beach; the policeman pulled open the padlock, and we all entered the shadows and the unexpected cold. The beams were shiny black, lightly smeared with tar, and pieces of sacking hung from the roof. As we walked through the grey semidarkness I felt the shed grow bigger with each step, the long table made out of sawhorses in the middle moving farther away. I looked at the stiff form, thinking, *who teaches the dead the demeanor of death.* There was a narrow puddle of water on the ground and water was dripping from one corner of the table. A barefoot man, his shirt open over his reddened chest, cleared his throat as he approached and placed one hand on one end of the plank table, allowing his short index finger to be quickly covered, shiny, with the water that continued to drip. The tall man stretched out his arm and pulled back the tarp, uncovering the face on the planks. I looked at the air, the striped arm of the man that was still stretched out against the light from the door holding the riveted edge of the tarp. I turned again to look at the hatless blond man, a sad expression on my face.

"Look here," the tall man said.

I could see that the girl's face was twisted back, and it looked like her head, purple, with reddish-purple splotches over a delicate bluish purple, would break off and roll away at any moment, if someone spoke too loudly, if someone struck the ground with his shoe, if time simply passed.

From the back, invisible to me, somebody began to recite in an ordinary, hoarse voice, as if speaking to me. Who else?

"On the hands and feet, the skin is slightly bleached and wrinkled at the tips of the fingers and toes, and under the nails there is a small amount of sand and silt. There are no abrasions, no chafing on the hands. On the arms, and particularly on the front, above the wrists, there are several overlapping ruptured blood vessels, transversal, the result of violent pressure applied on the upper limbs."

I didn't know who was talking, I didn't want to ask. All I had, I repeated to myself, my only defense, was silence. Silence for us. I approached the table, feeling the obdurate bone of the skull. Maybe those five men were expecting something else; and I was ready for anything. The monster, still from the back of the shed, kept reciting in his vulgar voice:

"The face is stained with a bluish and bloody liquid, originating from the mouth and nose. After a thorough washing, we saw extensive chafing with broken blood vessels around the mouth, and fingernail marks dug into the flesh. There are two analogous marks under the right eye, where the lower lid is heavily bruised. In addition to the signs of violence carried out while the victim was alive, you will notice numerous scratches, puncture marks on the face that are not red, no broken blood vessels, only the drying of the epidermis caused by the body scraping against the sand. Notice that coagulated blood has infiltrated both sides of the larynx. The integuments have already undergone putrefaction, and we can see vestiges of bruising and broken vessels. Inside the trachea and the bronchial tubes there is a small quantity of a muddy, dark liquid, not foamy, mixed with sand."

It was a good dirge, everything was lost. I leaned over to kiss her forehead and then, out of mercy and love, the reddish liquid that formed bubbles between her lips.

But her head with the stiffened hair, the flattened nose, the dark mouth, its corners stretched downward in the shape of a sickle, limp, dripping, remained motionless, its volume unchanging in the dismal air that smelled of bilge, my gaze harder and harder with each sweep across her cheeks and forehead and chin, which had still not decided to hang. One after the other they spoke to me, the tall man and the blond man, as if playing a game, lobbing the same question back and forth between them. Then the tall man let go of the tarp, lunged forward, and shook me by the lapels. But he didn't believe in what he was doing; all I had to do was look into his round eyes, and when I smiled wearily, he hastily, with hatred, showed me his teeth, and opened his hand.

"I understand, I imagine, you have a daughter. Don't worry: I'll sign whatever you want, without reading it. The funny thing is, you're wrong. But it doesn't matter. Nothing, not even this, really matters at all."

Facing the violent light of the sun, I stopped and asked the tall man in a suitable voice:

"I'm curious, and please forgive me: do you believe in God?"

"I'll answer you, of course," the giant said, "but first, and only if you wish, for it's not relevant to the case, but, as with you, I'm just curious . . . Did you know that the girl was deaf?"

We had stopped right in between the vigorous heat of summer and the cool shade of the shed.

"Deaf?" I asked. "No, I was only with her last night. She never seemed deaf. But that's not the point anymore. I asked you a question; you promised to answer it."

The lips were too thin to call the face the giant made a smile. He looked at me again with scorn, with sad astonishment, and he crossed himself.

1960

Jacob and the Other

Half the city must have been at the Cine Apolo last night, watching the event and even participating in the tumultuous finale. I was at the poker table in the Club, bored, and I got involved only when the doorman came to tell me of an urgent call from the hospital. The Club has only one telephone line, but by the time I left the booth, everybody knew the news much better than I. I returned to the table to turn in my chips and pay my losses.

Burmestein hadn't moved; he slobbered a little more on his cigar and in a thick and level voice said:

"Excuse me, but if I were you, I'd stay to take advantage of your streak. Anyway, you can sign the death certificate here."

"Not yet, it seems," I said, trying to laugh. I looked at my hands as they handled the chips and the banknotes; they were steady, a bit tired. I'd slept only a few hours the night before, but this had almost become a habit by then; I'd had two cognacs that evening and mineral water with dinner.

The people at the hospital knew my car and all its diseases by heart, so the ambulance was waiting for me at the door to the Club. I sat next to the Spaniard and heard only his greeting; he waited quietly, out of respect or excitement, for me to begin the conversation. I lit a cigarette and didn't talk until we rounded the Tabárez curve, and the ambulance entered the spring night along the cement roadway, white and windy, cold and warm, with disorderly clouds that grazed the windmill and the tall trees.

"Herminio," I said, "what's the diagnosis?"

I saw the joy the Spaniard was trying to conceal, imagined the sigh with which he feted the return to normal, to the old sacred rituals. He started to speak in his humblest and most astute tone of voice; I understood that the case was serious or lost.

"I barely saw him, Doctor. I picked him up in the ambulance from the theater, took him to the hospital at ninety or a hundred because that kid Fernández was rushing me, and also because it was my duty. I helped unload him, and then they instructed me to go get you at the Club."

"Okay, Fernández. But who's on duty?"

"Doctor Rius, Doctor."

"Why doesn't Rius operate?" I asked out loud.

"Well," Herminio said, waiting until he'd dodged a pothole full of shimmering water, "he probably started right away, but with you by his side . . ."

"You loaded and unloaded. That's all you need. What's the diagnosis?"

"Oh, Doctor . . ." the Spaniard smiled affectionately. We caught the first glimpses of the hospital lights, the whiteness of the walls under the moon. "He didn't move or moan, he started swelling up like a balloon, ribs in the lungs, a tibia sticking out, concussion almost for sure. But he fell on his back over two chairs, so if you'll excuse me, the problem must be in the spine. Whether or not there's a fracture."

"Will he die or won't he? You've never been wrong, Herminio."

He'd been wrong many times, but always with excuses.

"I won't say this time," he said, shaking his head as he came to a stop.

I'd changed clothes and was starting to wash my hands when Rius came in.

"If you want to get to work," he said, "he'll be ready for you in two minutes. I did almost nothing because there's nothing to do. Morphine, in any case, so that he and all of us can stay calm. We might as well toss a coin to decide where to start."

"It's that bad?"

"Multiple injuries, coma, pallor, thready pulse, rapid breathing, and cyanosis. Right hemothorax, crepitation and angulation of the sixth rib on the right. Dullness at the base of the right lung with hyper-resonance at the apex of the lung. Coma is deepening and the acute anemia is getting worse. Possible rupture of intercostal arteries. Enough? I'd leave him be."

I took refuge in my threadbare sentence of mediocre heroism, in the legend that surrounds me like the one on a coin or a medal, circumscribing an effigy and that might remain attached to my name for a few years after my death. But that night I was no longer twenty-five or even thirty years old; I was old and tired, and, face-to-face with Rius, the oft-repeated sentence was nothing but a familiar joke. I said it with the nostalgia of lost faith, as I put on my gloves. I repeated it, listening to myself, like a child who carries out the absurd and magical ritual that allows him to enter or remain in a game.

"My patients die on the operating table."

Rius laughed, as usual; he squeezed my arm and left. But almost immediately, as I was trying to figure out which broken pipe was dripping in the lavatories, he reappeared and said:

"Hey, man, I forgot one thing. I didn't tell you about the woman. I don't know who she is, the one who was kicking or trying to kick the soon-to-be corpse in the theater, and approached the ambulance to spit on him while the Spaniard and Fernández were loading him in. She was hanging around here and I had her thrown out; but she swore that she'd be back tomorrow and that she has the right to see the deceased, maybe so she can spit on him at her leisure."

I worked alongside Rius till five in the morning then asked for a liter of coffee to help us through the wait. At seven Fernández appeared in the office with that suspicious look God gives him to confront major events. His narrow, childlike face makes his eyes squint, he leans forward a little, his mouth on guard, as if to say: *Somebody's cheating me, life is nothing but a vast conspiracy to deceive me.*

He walked up to the table and stood there, white and twisted, not saying a word.

Rius stopped droning on about grafts, avoided looking at him, and snatched the last sandwich off the plate; then he wiped his mouth with a piece of paper and turned to the iron inkwell, with its eagles and two dry reservoirs, and asked:

"Ready?"

Fernández inhaled audibly and placed one hand on the table; we shook our heads and looked at him, upset and suspicious, thin and weary. Dazed by hunger and lack of sleep, the young man stood up straight out of loyalty to his fanatical desire to alter the order of things, the world in which we understand each other.

"The woman's in the hallway, sitting on a bench, with a thermos and her maté. They forgot and let her in. She says she doesn't mind waiting, that she has to see him. Him."

"Yes, my friend," Rius said slowly; I recognized in his voice the usual malignancy of exhausting nights, the excitement so expertly calibrated. "Did she at least bring flowers? Winter is over and every ditch in Santa María must be full of wildflowers. I'd like to punch her in the face and in a moment I'm going to ask the chief if I can take a turn through the hallways. But in the meantime that filly might visit the deceased and toss him a flower and then spit on him, and then another flower."

I was the chief, so I asked:

"What happened?"

Fernández swiftly rubbed his thin face, effortlessly verified the existence of all the bones Testut's anatomy textbook had promised him, and turned to look at me as if I were responsible for all the cheating and deception that leaped out at him with mysterious regularity. Without hatred, without violence, he ignored Rius, kept his suspicious eyes on my face and said:

"Improvement in pulse, respiration, and cyanosis. Exhibiting periods of lucidity."

This was much better than I expected to hear at seven in the morning. But it was not a firm basis for confidence, so I nodded in gratitude and took my turn looking at the bronze eagle on the inkwell.

"Dimas arrived a while ago," Fernández said. "I passed everything on to him. May I go?"

"Yes, of course," Rius said, leaning against the back of the chair, and he began to smile, looking at me; maybe he'd never seen me so old, perhaps he'd never loved me so much as that spring morning, maybe he was verifying who I was and why he loved me.

"No, my friend," he said once we were alone. "I'll go along with any farce, but not the farce of modesty, indifference, that crap that gets soberly translated as, 'I just did my job.' You did it, Chief. If that animal hasn't croaked yet, he's not going to. At the Club they suggested you just sign a death certificate (that's what I would've done, with a lot of morphine, of course, if for some reason you weren't in Santa María), and now I suggest you give the guy a certificate of immortality. With an easy conscience and the official endorsement of Doctor Rius. Do it, Chief. Then go straight to the lab and mix up a cocktail of sedatives and sleep for twenty-four hours. I'll deal with the magistrate and the police, and I promise to organize the spittle of the woman who is pumping herself up on maté in the hallway."

He stood up and patted me on the back, just once, but the weight and warmth of his hand lingered.

"Okay," I said. "You'll decide if I need to be sent for."

As I took off my coat, with a slowness and dignity that did not come exclusively from tiredness, I admitted that the success of the operation, of the operations, mattered to me as much as fulfilling an unachievable dream: to fix the engine of my old car, once and for all, with my own hands. But I couldn't say this to Rius because he would understand it effortlessly and enthusiastically; I couldn't tell Fernández because, fortunately, he wouldn't believe me.

So I kept my mouth shut, and on the way back in the ambulance I listened with equanimity to the admiring profanities of Herminio, the

Spaniard, and in response to his story, I agreed in silence that the resurrection that had just occurred in the hospital of Santa María could not have been brought about even by the doctors in the Capital.

I decided that once again my car could wake up in front of the Club, and I had the ambulance take me to my house. The morning, ravenously white, smelled like honeysuckle, and you could begin to smell the river.

"They threw stones and they said they were going to set fire to the theater," the Spaniard said when we reached the plaza. "But the police showed up and there were only the stones I already told you about."

Before taking the pills, I understood that I could never know the truth about that story, but with a dose of good luck and patience I might learn the half that belonged to us, the city's inhabitants. I had no choice but to resign myself, accept as unattainable the knowledge of the part the two strangers brought with them and would take away with them, each in his own mysterious way, forever.

At the very same moment, with the glass of water in my hand, I remembered that all of it had begun to reveal itself almost a week earlier, on one cloudy and hot Sunday, as I watched the comings and goings in the plaza from the window of the hotel bar.

The restless and agreeable man and the moribund giant walked diagonally across the plaza and the first yellowish sunlight of spring. The smaller man was carrying a wreath of flowers, a small wreath suitable for the modest funeral of a distant relative. They kept walking, indifferent to the curiosity aroused by the slow-moving, two-meter-tall monster; with determination but no hurry, the restless man marched on with sovereign dignity, lifting a diplomatic smile, as if he were flanked by soldiers in ceremonial dress, as if someone, a stage bedecked with banners and serious men and old women, were waiting for him somewhere. It was said that as the children joked and one or another threw a pebble, they left the wreath at the foot of the monument to Brausen.

From here the trail gets a bit more confused. The little one, the ambassador, went to El Berna to rent a room, have an aperitif, and discuss prices dispassionately, passing out bows, curtseys, and casual invitations. He was between forty and forty-five, had a wide chest, and was of average height; he had been born to persuade, to create the damp, warm atmosphere where friendship flourishes and hope is accepted. He had also been born to be happy, or at least to stubbornly believe in happiness, against all odds, against life and its blunders. He had been born, above all and most importantly, to impart quotas of well-being to as many people as possible. With invincible and natural wit, without ever setting aside his personal goals, without worrying too much about the uncontrollable futures of others.

At noon he was at the offices of *El Liberal*, and he returned in the afternoon to be interviewed by *Sports* and obtain free advertising. He unwrapped the album with photographs and yellowed newspaper cuttings with large headlines in foreign languages; he showed off diplomas and documents reinforced at the folds with gummed paper. Over and above the aging of memories, over and above the years, the melancholy and failure, floated his smile, his untiring and noncommittal love.

"He's in his prime. Maybe a kilo or two extra, but that's precisely why we're doing this South American tour. Next year, at the Palais de Glace, he'll win back his title. Nobody can beat him, no European or American. And how could we pass up Santa María on this tour, which is the prologue to the world championship? Santa María. With such a coastline, such a beach, such air, such culture."

His tone of voice was Italian, but not exactly; in his vowels and his *s*'s there was always a sound that could not be located, a friendly connection to the complicated breadth of the world. He walked through the newspaper offices, played with the linotype machines, embraced the typesetters, improvised some astonishment at the foot of the printing press. He obtained, the following day, the first cold but free headline: "Former World Wrestling Champion in Santa María." He paid a visit to the offices every weeknight, and the space devoted to Jacob van Oppen grew daily, in the lead-up to the Saturday of the challenge and the match.

At noon on the same Sunday I saw them parade through the plaza with the cheap wreath; the moribund giant spent half an hour on his knees in the church, praying in front of the new altar of the Blessed Virgin; they say he confessed, they swear they saw him pound his chest, they presume that he then hesitantly placed his enormous and childish face, soaked with tears, under the golden light of the atrium.

II. AS TOLD BY THE NARRATOR

The cards said "Comendador Orsini," and the talkative and fidgety man generously handed them out all over the city. Copies can still be found, some of them with autographs and added adjectives.

On the first – and last – Sunday, Orsini rented the auditorium at the Apollo for the training sessions, charging a one peso entrance fee on Monday and Tuesday and half of Wednesday, and two pesos on Thursday and Friday, once the challenge had officially been announced and the curiosity and patriotism of the people of Santa María began to fill the theater. That same Sunday the poster for the challenge was nailed up in the new plaza, with the corresponding permission from the municipality. In an old photo, the former world heavyweight wrestling champion showed off his biceps and his gold belt; loud red lettering detailed the terms of the challenge: five hundred pesos for anyone who enters the ring with Jacob van Oppen and remains standing for three minutes.

One line below, the challenge was forgotten and a demonstration of Greco-Roman wrestling was promised between the champion – that's what he would be once again within a year – and the best athletes of Santa María.

Orsini and the giant arrived on the continent in Colombia and made their way from there through Peru, Ecuador, and Bolivia. The challenge was accepted in only a few towns and always van Oppen had been able to win in seconds, after the first clinch.

The posters conjured up nights of heat and shouting, in theaters and tents, audiences full of Indians and drunken spectators, admiration and laughter. The referee lifted his arm, van Oppen returned to his sadness, thinking eagerly of his bottle of fierce alcohol waiting for him in his hotel room, and Orsini smiled as he stepped out under the white lights of the ring, dabbing the sweat off his brow with a handkerchief, which was even whiter.

"Ladies and gentlemen . . ." It was the moment to express gratitude, to speak of enduring reminiscences, to cheer the country and the city. For months those communal memories had been shaping America for them; at some point, one night, once they were far away, and before the year was out, they would be able to talk about America and recognize it effortlessly, with the help of only three or four moments that were repeated and devout.

On Tuesday or Wednesday, Orsini drove the champion in a car to El Berna after the nearly empty training session. The tour had already become routine, and there was scarcely a difference between the estimate of pesos to be earned and pesos already earned. But Orsini considered it in-dispensable for their mutual well-being to maintain his vigilance over the giant. Van Oppen sat down on the bed and drank from the bottle; Orsini gently took it away from him and brought from the bathroom the plastic cup that he used in the morning to rinse his dentures. He repeated the old sentence in a friendly voice:

"There's no morale without discipline," he spoke French as he did Spanish, his accent never definitively Italian. "You still have your bottle, and nobody will take it away from you. But if you drink from a cup, it's different. There's discipline, there's gallantry."

The giant turned to look at him; his blue eyes were murky, and he seemed to be using his half-open mouth to see. *Again, shortness of breath, anxiety*, Orsini thought. *Better that he get drunk and sleep till morning.* He filled the glass with caña, took a sip, and stretched his hand out to van Oppen. But the monster leaned over to take off his shoes, then, panting, second symptom, stood up and looked around the room. With his hands on his hips, he looked first at the beds, the useless rug, the table and the ceiling; then he took a few steps and tested the resilience of the doors with his shoulder, the one to the hallway and the one to the bathroom, the resil-ience of the window that didn't lead anywhere.

Now it's starting, Orsini continued thinking, *the last time was in Guayaquil. It must be cyclical, but I don't understand the cycle. One random night he'll strangle me, and not out of hatred, just because he has me within reach. He knows I'm his only friend.*

The giant turned slowly, barefoot, in the middle of the room, his smile full of mockery and scorn, his shoulders slightly hunched forward. Orsini sat down next to the flimsy table and stuck his tongue into the glass of caña.

"*Gott*," van Oppen said and began to sway gently, as if he were listening to halting and distant music; he was wearing a black sweater, too tight, and blue jeans Orsini had bought him in Quito. "No. Where am I? What am I doing here?" and with his enormous feet planted firmly on the ground, he moved his body, looking at the wall above Orsini's head. "I'm waiting. I'm always somewhere that is a hotel room in a country full of smelly darkies, and I'm always waiting. Give me the cup. I'm not scared; that's what's wrong, nobody is ever going to come."

Orsini filled the cup and stood up to hand it to him. He scrutinized his face, the hysteria in his voice, he touched his moving back. *Not yet*, he thought, *but soon.*

The giant drank down the caña and started coughing without dropping his head.

"Nobody," he said. "The jogging, the stretching, the shots, Lewis. For Lewis. At least he lived and was a man. Exercise isn't a man, wrestling isn't a man, all of this isn't a man. A hotel room, the gym, dirty Injuns. Out of this world, Orsini."

Orsini made another calculation and stood up with the bottle of caña. He filled the cup van Oppen was holding against his belly and caressed the giant's shoulder and cheek.

"Nobody," van Oppen said. "Nobody," he shouted. His eyes looked desperate, then enraged. He smiled, humorous and wise, and emptied the cup.

Now, Orsini thought. He placed the bottle in one hand and began to push his hip against the giant's thigh, guiding him to the bed.

"A few months, a few weeks," Orsini said. "That's it. Then they'll all come, we'll be with all of them. We'll go there."

Sprawled out on the bed, the giant drank from the bottle and snorted, shaking his head. Orsini turned on the bedside light and turned off the one overhead. Sitting back down at the table, he cleared his voice and sang quietly:

Vor der Kaserne
Vor dem großen Tor
Stand eine Laterne.
Und steht sie noch davor
So wolle'n wir uns wiegder seh'n
Bei der Laterne wollen wir steh'n
Wie einst, Lili Marleen
Wie einst, Lili Marleen.

He sang the song one and a half times, until van Oppen put the bottle down on the ground and started to cry. Then Orsini rose with a sigh and an affectionate taunt and tiptoed to the door and out into the hallway. Just like on nights of glory, he descended the stairs of El Berna, wiping his brow with his spotless handkerchief.

III

He descended the stairs without meeting anybody to whom he could pass out smiles and tips of the hat, but with a friendly expression, primed. The woman, who had been waiting for hours, determined and patient, sunk into the leather armchair in the lobby, ignoring the magazines on the small table, smoking one cigarette after another, stood up and faced him. Prince Orsini had no escape, nor did he look for one. He heard the name, doffed his hat, and bowed rapidly to kiss the woman's hand. He wondered what favor he could do for her, and he was willing to do whatever she asked. She was small, intrepid, and young, with very dark hair and skin and a small hooked nose, her eyes very light and cold. *Jewish, or some such thing,* Orsini thought. *She's pretty.* Straightaway the prince heard language so concise as to be almost incomprehensible, almost preposterous.

"That poster in the plaza, those ads in the paper. Five hundred pesos. My fiancé is going to fight the champion. But today or tomorrow, tomorrow is Wednesday, you have to deposit the money in the bank or with *El Liberal.*"

"Signorina," the prince smiled and dangled an expression of despair. "Fight the champion? You'll end up without a fiancé. And I would be so sorry if such a lovely young lady . . ."

But she, small and now more resolute, effortlessly dismissed Orsini's middle-aged chivalry.

"Tonight I'm going to *El Liberal* to accept the challenge. I saw the champion at Mass. He's old. We need those five hundred pesos to get married. My fiancé is twenty and I'm twenty-two. He's the owner of the Porfilio's grocery store. Go and check him out."

"But, young lady," the prince said, his smile expanding, "your fiancé, that most fortunate of men, if you allow me to say so, is twenty years old. What has he done till now? Buying and selling?"

"He also did farm work."

"Oh, farm work," the prince whispered, overjoyed. "But the champion has devoted his entire life to this, to wrestling. Is he a few years older than your fiancé? Indeed he is, young lady."

"Thirty, at least," she said, with no need to smile, confident in the coldness of her eyes. "I saw him."

"But those were years dedicated to learning how to effortlessly break ribs, arms, or how to gently pull out a clavicle, dislocate a leg. And if you have a healthy fiancé, twenty years old . . ."

"You called a challenge. Five hundred pesos for three minutes. Tonight I'm going to *El Liberal*, Mr. . . ."

"Prince Orsini," the prince said.

She nodded, not wasting any time on the joke; she was small, beautiful, and compact, and had hardened into steel.

"I'm happy for Santa María," the prince smiled, bowing again. "It will be a great sporting event. But you, young lady, will you be going to the newspaper on your fiancé's behalf?"

"Yes, he gave me a piece of paper. Go check him out. Porfilio Grocery Store. They call him the Turk. But he's Syrian. He has the document."

The prince understood that it was inappropriate to kiss her hand again.

"Very well," he joked, "single and widowed. As of Saturday. A very sad destiny, young lady."

She held out her hand then walked to the door of the hotel. She was as hard as a lance, no more graceful than necessary to make sure that the prince kept watching her from behind. The woman stopped abruptly and retraced her steps.

"Single, no, because we'll get married with those five hundred pesos. Not a widow, either, because the champion is old. He's bigger than Mario, but he won't beat him. I saw him."

"I see. You saw him leave Mass. But I can assure you that when things get serious, he's a monster. And I swear to you, he knows what he's doing. World Champion, Super Heavyweight, young lady."

"Fine," she said, suddenly weary. "As I told you, the grocery store of Porfilio Hermanos. Tonight I'm going to *El Liberal*, but tomorrow you can find me, as always, at the store."

"Young lady..." he kissed her hand again.

Clearly the woman wanted to close the deal. So Orsini went to the restaurant and ordered a stew with meat and pasta; then, crunching some numbers and sucking on his gold-ringed maté straw, he watched over the movements and grumblings of Jacob van Oppen while he slept.

Just as he was about to fall asleep above the silence of the plaza, he allocated himself a twenty-four-hour vacation. It would be inadvisable to rush his visit to the Turk. Moreover, he thought, as he turned off the light and analyzed the giant's snores: *He's suffered enough, Lord knows, we've both suffered; and I see no reason to rush.*

The next day Orsini was present when the champion awoke; he brought him aspirin and hot water, heard with satisfaction to van Oppen swearing under the shower, and listened with delight as the coarse sounds transformed into an underwater version of "The Good Comrade." Like all men, he had decided to lie, to lie to himself, and to have faith. He organized van Oppen's morning, the slow walk through the city, his enormous torso covered in a wool sweater with the big blue letter on his chest, the *C* that meant, in every conceivable language and alphabet: World Super Heavyweight Champion. He accompanied him at a good pace to the street that descended to the promenade. There, for the few curious onlookers at eight in the morning, he repeated one of the scenes from the old farce. He stopped to take off his hat and wipe his forehead, smiled with the admiring smile of a good loser, and slapped Jacob van Oppen on the back.

"What a man this is," he muttered for nobody in particular; then, his head twisted around, his arms hanging in defeat, his mouth gasping for air, he repeated for all of Santa María to hear: "What a man this is."

Van Oppen continued at the same prudent pace, his shoulders pushing into the future, his jaw hanging, to the promenade; then he turned toward the canning factory, skirting the astonishment of fishermen, bums, and ferry employees; he was too big for anybody to dare taunt him.

It's possible that all day the taunts, never spoken aloud, surrounded Prince Orsini, his clothes, his manners, his inadequate good breeding. But he had wagered on being happy and was able to hear only pleasant and good things. At *El Liberal*, in El Berna, and in the plaza, he held what in his memory he would call "press conferences"; he drank and chatted with the curious and the idle, told stories and terrible lies, showed again and again the newspaper clippings, yellowed and brittle. There had been a time, and this was indisputable, when things had been thus: World Champion van Oppen, young, with an invincible swivel, taking trips that weren't flights into exile, overwhelmed with offers that could be turned down. Though old-fashioned, faded, the photographs and the printed words were right there, tenacious in their nearness to the flames, irrefutable. Never drunk, even after the fourth or fifth shot, Orsini believed that past evidence guaranteed the future. No personal changes were necessary in order to comfortably inhabit an impossible paradise. He had been born at age fifty, cynical, kind, a friend for life, a proponent of things happening. The miracle required only the transformation of van Oppen, his return to the years before the war, to his flat belly, his glowing skin, bright whites of eyes in the morning.

Yes, the future Mrs. Turk – a little lady, with all due respect, pleasant and hardheaded – had been to *El Liberal* to formalize the challenge. The head of *Sports* already had pictures of Mario working out; but the pictures cost them a speech about freedom of the press, democracy, and the free exchange of information. Also about patriotism, according to *Sports*: "The Turk would have broken our heads, mine and the photographer's, in spite of everything, if the fiancée hadn't intervened and calmed him down with a few words. They were whispering in the back room and then the Turk came out, not as big, I think, as van Oppen, but much rougher, more dangerous. Well, you understand those things better than I do."

"I understand," the prince smiled. "Poor kid. He won't be the first," he said, spreading his sadness over El Berna's chips and olives.

"The man was furious, but he controlled himself, and he put on his fishing shorts and went out to exercise in the sun; all the exercises Humberto, the photographer, wanted or invented, out of revenge and to get even for the fright he'd had. And the whole time she was sitting on a barrel, as if she were his mother or his master, smoking, not saying a word, just watching him. And when you think, she isn't even a meter and a half tall, doesn't weigh even forty kilos . . ."

"I know the young lady," Orsini said, nostalgically. "And I've seen so many examples . . . Ah, personality is such a mysterious thing; it doesn't show in the muscles."

"It wasn't for publication, obviously," said *Sports*, "but are you going to make the deposit?"

"The deposit?" the prince said piously, opening his hands. "This afternoon, tomorrow morning. Depends on the bank. Sound okay, tomorrow morning at *El Liberal*? It will be good advertising, and free. To stand up to Jacob van Oppen for three minutes . . . As I always say," he flashed his gold molars and called over the waiter, "sports on one side, business on the other. What can one do, what can *we* do, if at the end of this training tour, someone suicidal shows up? And, what's more, if he has help."

IV

Life had always been difficult and beautiful, irreplaceable, and Prince Orsini didn't have the five hundred pesos. He'd met the woman, sensed an
adjective to define her precisely and carry her into the past; now he started
to think about the man whom the woman represented and concealed,
about the Turk who'd accepted the challenge. So he took a vacation from
apathy and joy, and at nightfall, after lying to the champion, checking his
mood and his pulse, he began to walk toward the grocery store of Porfilio
Hermanos, the yellow album under his arm.

First, the rotting ombú tree, then the streetlamp hanging from the tree
and its daunted circle of light. Then the barking dogs and the corresponding shouts: *get out, shush, shoo.* Orsini crossed the first light, was able to
see the round, watery moon. He reached the sign for the store and entered
respectfully. A man wearing baggy *bombacha* pants and espadrilles was finishing up his gin at the counter and saying goodbye. They were left alone:
he, Prince Orsini, the Turk, and the woman.

"Good evening, young lady," Orsini said, smiling and taking a bow.
The woman was sitting in a wicker armchair, knitting; she looked up at
him from the needles, nodded, and she might have smiled. *A baby blanket,*
Orsini thought, incensed. *She's pregnant, knitting the layette, that's why she
wants to get married, that's why she wants to steal five hundred pesos.*

He made a beeline to the man, who had paused from filling paper bags
with tea and was waiting for him, stupidly, behind the counter.

"This is the man I told you about," the woman said, "the impresario."

"Impresario and friend," Orsini said, correcting her. "After so many
years . . ."

He shook the man's open and rigid hand and reached his left arm forward to pat him on the back.

"At your service," the storekeeper said, and lifted his thick black mustache to show him his teeth.

"My pleasure, my pleasure," but he had already breathed in the faint and acrid smell of defeat, had already calculated the Turk's unworn youth, the perfection with which his hundred kilos were distributed around his body. *There's not a gram of excess fat, or a gram of intelligence or sensitivity; there's no hope. Three minutes; poor Jacob van Oppen.*

"I came about those five hundred pesos," Orsini began, getting a feel for the density of the air, the shabbiness of the light, the couple's hostility. *They're not against me; they're against life.* "I came to reassure you; tomorrow, as soon as I receive the wire from the Capital, the money will be deposited at *El Liberal.* But I also wanted to talk about a few other things."

"Didn't we already talk about everything?" the woman asked. She was too small for the rickety wicker chair; the shiny knitting needles were too long. She could be good or evil; now she had chosen to be implacable, overcome some long and dark deferral, exact her revenge. Under the light of the lamp, the outline of her nose was perfect and her light eyes sparkled like glass.

"Everything, true, young lady. I don't intend to say anything that hasn't already been said. But I consider it my duty to tell it to you straight. To tell Mr. Mario the truth," he smiled, repeating his greeting with a nod; his truculence was just barely vibrating, deep and muted. "May I ask, sir, that you serve a round for the three of us. It's on me, of course; whatever you'd like."

"He doesn't drink," the woman said, taking her time, not taking her eyes off her knitting, nestled in her atmosphere of ice and irony.

The hairy monster behind the counter finished closing a package of tea and turned slowly to look at the woman. *The chest of a gorilla, two centime-ters of forehead, no expression in the eyes,* Orsini noted. *Never really thought, never could have really suffered, couldn't even imagine that tomorrow might be a surprise or not come at all.*

"Adriana," the Turk muttered. "Adriana, me, vermouth. I do drink."

She gave a quick smile and shrugged her shoulders. The Turk formed his mouth into a circle to take small sips of the vermouth. Leaning on the counter, with his warm green hat pushed back onto his neck, brushing the album cover, looking for inspiration and kindness, the prince mentioned the harvest, rains and droughts, farming methods and transportation routes, the aged beauty of Europe and the youthfulness of America. He was improvising, doling out auguries and hopes, while the Turk nodded in silence.

"The Apollo was full this afternoon," the prince said, suddenly on the attack; "since they heard that you'd accepted the challenge, everyone wants to watch the champion train. I raised the price of the tickets so they wouldn't bother him too much; but people are still paying. Now," as he started to pull aside the paper wrapped around the album, "I'd like you to take a look at this," he said, caressing the leather cover then lifting it. "Almost everything is in other languages, but the pictures help. Take a look, you'll understand. World champion, gold belt."

"Was, he was world champion," the woman clarified from the creaking of the wicker chair.

"Yes, young lady," Orsini said without looking at her, exclusively for the Turk, as he turned the pages of torn newspaper clippings. "And he will be again within six months. An incorrect ruling, the World Wrestling Federation has already intervened . . . Look at the headlines, eight columns, front page, look at the pictures. This is a champion, look. Nobody in the entire world can beat him. Nobody can stay standing for three minutes without being thrown on their backs. In fact, one single minute would be a miracle. The European champion couldn't, the United States champion couldn't. I'm speaking seriously, man to man; I've come to see you because as soon as I talked to the young lady I understood the problem, the situation."

"Adriana," the Turk corrected him.

"Yes," the prince said, "I understood everything. But everything has a solution. If you get into that ring at the Apollo . . . Jacob van Oppen is my friend, and our friendship has only one limitation; our friendship vanishes when the bell rings and he starts fighting. Then he isn't my friend, he isn't a man; he's the world champion, he has to win and he knows how to do it."

Dozens of traveling salesmen had stopped their Fords in front of Porfilio Hermanos to smile at the now dead owners or at Mario, have a drink, show their samples, catalogues, and lists, sell sugar, rice, wine, and corn. But Prince Orsini was making an effort, with smiles, friendly pats, and sympathetic looks, to sell the Turk a strange and difficult item: fear. Alerted by the woman's presence, cautioned by memories and instinct, he limited himself to selling prudence, trying to strike a deal.

The Turk still had half a glass of vermouth; he raised it to moisten his small pink mouth, without drinking.

"It's five hundred pesos," Adriana said from the armchair. "And it's closing time."

"You said . . ." the Turk started to say; his voice and thoughts were trying to understand, approach some equanimity, extricate themselves from three generations of stupidity and greed. "Adriana, first I have to take the bags downstairs. You were saying, if I get on the stage at the Apollo on Saturday."

"I was saying. If you get on that stage, the champion will break some of your ribs, a bone or two; he'll throw you on your back in half a minute. Then there won't be any five hundred pesos, though you might have to spend much more on doctors' bills. And who will take care of the shop while you're in the hospital? All of that, without even mentioning the loss of face, the ridicule." Orsini considered this to be the right moment for a pause and meditation; he asked for another shot of gin, glanced at the Turk's impassive face, his nervous movements; he heard a giggle from the woman, who had dropped her knitting onto her lap.

Orsini drank down his gin and slowly started to wrap up his tattered album. The Turk smelled of vermouth and was trying to think.

"I don't mean to say," the prince mumbled offhandedly and under his breath, making it sound like a mutually agreed-upon epilogue, "I don't mean to say that you aren't stronger than Jacob van Oppen. I understand a lot about these things, I've devoted my life and my money to finding strong men. Moreover, as Miss Adriana has so intelligently said, you are much younger than the champion. More energy, more youth; I'm ready to write it down, sign you up. If the champion (just for example) bought this business, six months later he'd be begging on the streets. You, on the other hand, will be rich within two years. Because you, my friend Mario, you understand business and the champion doesn't." The album had been wrapped up; he placed it on the counter and leaned on it to continue with the gin and the conversation. "By the same token, the champion knows how to break bones, how to bend knees and waists to throw you on your back on the mat. That's what they call it, or called it. On the mat. To each his own vocation."

The woman had stood up and turned off the light in the corner; now she was standing there, her knitting between her belly and the counter, small and hard, without looking at either of the men.

The Turk looked at her face, then grunted:

"You said that if I don't get on that stage at the Apollo . . ."

"I said?" Orsini asked in surprise. "I think I was giving you folks some advice. In any case, if you withdraw your challenge, we can come to an agreement, agree to some compensation. We can discuss."

"How much?" the Turk asked.

The woman raised her hand and dug her fingernails into the monster's hairy arm; when the man turned his head to look at her, she said:

"There'll be no more and no less than five hundred pesos, understood? We aren't going to lose them. If you don't go on Saturday, all of Santa María will know that you chickened out. I'm going to tell them so, house by house, person by person."

She didn't speak passionately; her nails kept digging into his arm, but she talked to the Turk patiently and teasingly, like a mother talks to her child, chiding and threatening.

"Just a moment," Orsini said; he raised his hand and with the other brought the glass of gin to his lips and drank it down. "I thought about that, too. About what people will say, in the city, among themselves, if you don't show up at the Apollo on Saturday. But it can all be worked out," he smiled at the hostile faces of the woman and the man, and his voice grew more wary. "For example . . . let's say, instead, that you do go, you do get into the ring. You try not to enrage the champion, because that would be fatal to our plans. You get into the ring, figure out with the first clinch that the champion knows what he's doing, and let yourself get thrown, clean, without a scratch."

The woman again dug her nails into the gigantic hairy arm; with a yelp, the Turk pushed her aside.

"I understand," he said. "I go and I lose. How much?"

Suddenly, Orsini accepted what he had been suspecting since the beginning of the interview: that whatever agreement he might reach with the Turk, the skinny and hell-bent woman would spend the rest of the night undoing it. He understood, without any doubt, that Jacob van Oppen was condemned to fight the Turk on Saturday.

"How much . . ." he mumbled as he fit the album under his arm. "We can talk about a hundred, a hundred and fifty pesos. You get in the ring . . ."

The woman took one step away from the counter and stabbed her needles into the ball of yarn. She looked down at the dirt and cement floor and her voice sounded calm and sleepy:

"We need five hundred pesos, and he's going to win them on Saturday without any tricks or deals. Nobody's stronger, nobody can beat him. Least of all that worn-out old man, even if he was a champion. Time to close?"

"I have to take the bags downstairs," the Turk said again.

"Okay, so be it," Orsini said. "Charge me and give me a final shot," and he placed a ten-peso note on the counter and lit a cigarette. "Let's have a toast; please join me."

But the woman turned the light in the corner back on and sat down in the wicker armchair to keep knitting and smoking a cigarette; and the Turk poured only one glass of gin. Yawning, he started to carry the bags of tea that were piled up against the wall toward the trapdoor of the basement.

Without knowing why, Orsini tossed one of his cards onto the counter. He spent ten more minutes in the store, smoking and drinking down the gin's yeasty flavor, and watched with astonished terror, his eyes blurry, sweating, the Turk's methodical labor of transporting the bags, watched how easily he moved, with the same visible effort as he, Prince Orsini, would use to move a pack of cigarettes or a bottle.

Poor Jacob van Oppen, Orsini reflected. *Getting old is a good calling for*

me. But he was born to always be twenty years old; and now, instead, it's this
gigantic son of a bitch twisted around the finger of this pregnant fetus who's
twenty. This beast is twenty, and nobody can take that away from him and give
it back to somebody else, and he will still be that age on Saturday night at the
Apollo.

V

From the offices of *El Liberal*, standing shoulder-to-shoulder with *Sports*,
the prince called the Capital, requesting they urgently wire one thousand
pesos. He used the direct line to avoid the operator's curiosity; he shouted
lies in front of the staff, composed now of skinny and mustachioed young
men, one or another young lady smoking through a cigarette holder. It was
seven in the evening; he became almost crass when it seemed obvious that
the man listening to him on that remote telephone was hesitating, a man
in a room that could not be imagined, sniffling through his bewilderment
in some cubicle in the big city, one evening in October.

He hung up with a tolerant, annoyed smile.

"Finally," he said, blowing into his linen handkerchief. "Tomorrow
morning we'll have the money. Minor hiccups. Tomorrow at noon I'll deposit it with management. With management, seems more serious, doesn't
it . . . ? Here's the porter. If anybody wants some refreshments . . ."

They thanked him, the noise of one of the typewriters stopped; but nobody took him up on the invitation. *Sports* leaned his thick eyeglasses over
the table as he marked up some photographs.

Leaning on a table, smoking a cigarette, Orsini looked at the men bent
over their typewriters and their tasks. He knew that for them he no longer

existed, was no longer in the office. *And tomorrow, too,* he thought with faint sadness, smiling and resigned. Because everything had been postponed till Friday night, and Friday night began to grow, at the tail end of a reddening and tender twilight, beyond the windows of *El Liberal*, along the river, above the first shadows that surrounded the deep sirens of the ferries.

He pushed through the indifference and the distrust, forcing *Sports* to shake his hand.

"I hope tomorrow will be a great night for Santa María; and may the best man win."

That sentence would not be quoted in the newspaper, would not back up his smiling and friendly face. From the lobby of the Apollo – Jacob van Oppen, World Champion, training here from 6 to 8 p.m., three pesos – he heard the buzz of the audience and the stomping of the champion in the improvised ring.

Van Oppen couldn't fight, break bones, or risk his own being broken. But he could jump rope, endlessly, never tiring.

Sitting in the narrow office, Orsini checked the box office receipts and crunched some numbers. Without counting the triumphal night of Saturday at five pesos a ticket, their stay in Santa María was showing a profit. Orsini took a sip of coffee and signed his name at the bottom of the forms after counting the money.

He was alone in the dark, foul-smelling office. The rhythmic sound of van Oppen's footsteps on the wood floor was approaching.

"A hundred and ten animals with their mouths hanging open because the champion is jumping rope; any girl in a schoolyard does it better."

He remembered van Oppen when he was young, or at least not yet old; he thought about Europe and the States, about the real lost world; he tried to convince himself that van Oppen was as responsible for the passage of time, for decay and disgusting old age, as if it were a vice he had acquired and accepted. He tried to hate van Oppen in order to protect himself.

I should have talked to him before, during one of those strolls along the promenade when he walks at the pace of a fat lady; yesterday or this morning; spoken to him in the open air, near the river, the trees, the sky, all those things the Germans call nature. But Friday arrived: Friday night.

He gently patted the banknotes in his pocket and stood up. Outside, punctual and warm, Friday night was waiting for him. One hundred and ten idiots inside the movie theater; the champion must have finished the final number, the exercise session when all his muscles expanded and overflowed.

Orsini walked slowly toward the hotel, his hands clasped behind him, looking for details of the city he could remember and say goodbye to, so he could blend them into those of other faraway cities, so he could join all of them together and continue to live.

The counter of the hotel bar reached all the way around until it butted up against the concierge's desk. While he had a drink with a lot of soda, the prince planned out the battle. Taking a hill can be more important than losing an ammunitions dump. He placed some banknotes on the counter and asked for the bill for the days they'd spent in the hotel.

"Forgive me, it's for tomorrow, so I won't have to rush. Tomorrow, as soon as the match is over, we have to leave by car, in the middle of the night or at dawn. Today I made a phone call from *El Liberal* and found out we have new bookings. Everybody wants to see the champion, you see, before the tournament in Antwerp."

He left an extravagant tip and went up to his room with a bottle of gin under his arm to pack the suitcases. There was an old black one, Jacob's, that couldn't be touched; there was also the collection of impressive objects – robes, sweaters, braces, ropes, fur-lined shoes – on the stage at the Apollo. But he would find some excuse to collect all of that afterwards. He finished packing his suitcases and the ones that Jacob had not declared sacred; he was in the shower, snorting with relief, paunchy and determined, when he heard the bang of the door to the room. Above the sound of the water he heard footsteps and silence. *It's Friday night, and I don't even know if it's better to get drunk before or after I talk to him. Or before and after.*

Jacob was sitting on his bed, his legs crossed, looking with childish joy at the logo on the sole of his shoes, the word *Champion*; somebody, perhaps Orsini himself, had once said jokingly that those shoes were made exclusively for van Oppen, to remember him and pay tribute to him on the feet of thousands.

Wrapped in his bathrobe, dripping wet, Orsini entered the room, cheerful and chatty. The champion had grabbed the gin bottle and after taking a sip he continued to look at his shoe, not listening to Orsini.

"Why did you pack? The match is tomorrow."

"To save time," Orsini said. "That's why I started. But then . . ."

"It's at nine? But it always starts late. And after the three minutes are over I have to juggle and lift weights. And also celebrate."

"Well," Orsini said, looking at the bottle leaning against the champion's mouth, counting the sips, calculating. "Of course we're going to celebrate."

The champion put down the bottle and started to rub the white sole of his shoe. He was smiling, mysterious and skeptical, as if he were listening to some faraway music he hadn't heard since childhood. Suddenly he grew serious, took his foot with the logo that alluded to him in both hands, and slowly lowered it until he had placed the sole on the narrow rug next to the bed. Orsini saw the quick, curt smirk that had taken the place of the vanished smile; hesitantly, he approached the champion's bed and picked up the bottle. By pretending to take a sip, he could ascertain, based on the sound and the weight, that there was still two-thirds of a liter of gin left.

Motionless, collapsed, his elbows resting on his legs, the champion prayed: "*Verdammt, verdammt, verdammt.*"

Without making a sound, Orsini dragged his feet along the floor; behind the champion's back, accompanied by a yawn, he pulled the gun out of the jacket hanging on the back of a chair and placed it in his bathrobe pocket. Then he sat down on his bed and waited. He'd never had any need for a gun with Jacob, not even to show it. But the years had taught him to anticipate the champion's actions and reactions, to respect his violence, the degree of his madness, and also the precise point on the compass that marks the beginning of madness.

"*Verdammt,*" Jacob said, still praying. He filled his lungs with air and stood up. He clasped his hands behind his neck and his chest swayed, to left and to right, bending at his waist. "*Verdammt,*" he shouted, as if he were looking at somebody who was challenging him; then he reassembled his suspicious smile and began to undress. Orsini lit a cigarette and put his hand into his bathrobe pocket, his knuckles resting against the crispness of the gun. The champion took off his sweater, his T-shirt, his pants, the shoes with his logo; everything hit the corner between the wardrobe and the wall and formed a pile on the floor.

Leaning against the bed and the pillows, Orsini searched for other rages, other prologues, wishing to compare them to what he was seeing. *Nobody told him we were leaving. Who could have told him we were leaving tonight?*

Jacob was wearing only his fighting jersey. He lifted the bottle and drank half of what was left. Then, keeping hold of his smile, full of mystery, of allusions and memory, he started doing exercises, stretching and flexing his arms as he bent at the knees to do squats.

All this flesh, Orsini thought with his finger on the trigger; *the same muscles, or more, that he had in his twenties; a little bit of fat on the belly, on his back, around the waist. White, fearful enemy of the sun, gringos, and women. But those arms and those legs are as strong as ever, maybe stronger. Time hasn't passed as far as they're concerned; but it always passes, it always seeks and finds a spot where it can enter and stay put. We were all promised old age and death, either all at once or stutteringly. This poor devil didn't believe in promises, that's why the results are so unfair.*

Lit by the last light of Friday through the window and by the light that Orsini had left on in the bathroom, the giant was shimmering with sweat. He finished his exercises by throwing himself on his back and pushing himself up with his hands. Then he nodded briefly and slowly at the pile of clothes next to the wardrobe. Panting, he took another sip from the bottle, lifted it into the ashen air, and without taking his eyes off it he approached Orsini on the bed. He remained standing, enormous and sweaty, breathing noisily and with difficulty, his gaping mouth expressing the beginning to the end of his rage. He kept looking at the bottle, looking for explanations on the label, in its round and secretive shape.

"Champion," Orsini said, retreating until he touched the wall, lifting one leg in order to more comfortably grip the gun. "Champ. We have to order another bottle. We have to celebrate starting now."

"Celebrate? I always win."

"Yes, the champion always wins. And he's going to win in Europe, too."

Orsini sat up on the bed and used his legs to help him into an upright seated position, his hand still deep in his bathrobe pocket.

In front of him were Jacob's enormous thighs, his muscles taut. *There never were better legs than these,* Orsini thought with fear and sadness. *All he has to do is bring the bottle down to crush me; you need much less than a minute to break open a head with the bottom of a bottle.* He got up slowly and hobbled away, flashing a happy and paternal smile until he reached the other corner of the room. He leaned on the corner of the small table and stood there with his eyes down, muttering a Catholic and magical formula.

Jacob hadn't moved; he stood next to the bed, his back to Orsini, the bottle still in the air. The room was almost dark, the light from the bathroom weak and yellow.

Using only his left hand, Orsini lit a cigarette. *I've never tried this.*

"We can celebrate right now, Champ. We'll celebrate till dawn and at four we'll get on the bus. Goodbye, Santa María. And thank you very much, we didn't do badly here at all."

White, enlarged by the shadows, Jacob slowly lowered his arm that was holding the bottle and made the glass sound against his knee.

"We're leaving, Champ," Orsini added. *Now he's thinking. Within three minutes, maybe he'll understand.*

Jacob turned, as if his body were in a pool of salt water, and bent his knees to sit down on the bed. His thin but still not grey hair showed the tilt of his head in the night.

"We have bookings, real bookings," Orsini continued, "in the south. But we have to leave right away, we have to take the four o'clock bus. This afternoon I spoke on the phone at the newspaper with an impresario in the Capital."

"Today. Now it's Friday," Jacob said slowly, no hint of inebriation in his voice. "The fight is tomorrow night. We can't leave at four."

"There won't be a fight, Champ. It's not a problem. We're leaving at four, but first we celebrate. I'll order another bottle right now."

"No," Jacob said.

Orsini became motionless again leaning against the table. From pity for the champion, so exacerbated and painful over the last few months, he began to feel sorry for Prince Orsini, condemned, like a nanny, to take care of, lie to, and be bored with his charge, though fortunately his charge earned him a living. Then his pity became depersonalized, almost universal. *Here, in a town in South America that has a name only because somebody wanted to comply with the custom of baptizing a bunch of houses. He, even more lost and weary than I, older and happier and more intelligent, guarding him with a gun, which I'm not sure even works, ready to pull it out should it become necessary, but certain that I will never pull the trigger. Pity for the lives of men, pity for whoever arranges things in this awkward and absurd way. Pity for those I've had to cheat, just so I could continue to live. Pity for the Turk from the grocery store and his fiancée, for all those who don't really have the privilege of choosing.*

From far away, in bursts, came the piano of the Conservatory; despite the hour, the heat was increasing in the room and along the tree-lined streets.

"I don't understand," Jacob said. "Today is Friday. If that crazy man no longer wants the challenge, I still have to do the show, at five pesos a head."

"That crazy man . . ." Orsini began; from pity he moved to rage and hatred. "No; it's us. We aren't interested in the challenge. We're leaving at four."

"The man wants to fight? He didn't cancel?"

"The man wants to fight, and he doesn't have permission to cancel. But we're going to leave."

"Without fighting, before tomorrow?"

"Champ," Orsini said. Jacob's head shook, hanging and shaking in denial.

"I'm staying. Tomorrow at nine o'clock I'll be waiting for him in the ring. Will I be alone?"

"Champ," Orsini repeated as he approached the bed; he affectionately brushed against Jacob's shoulder and picked up the bottle to take a small sip. "We're leaving."

"I'm not," the giant said, and he began to rise, to grow. "I'm going to be in the ring. Leave me half the money and go. Tell me why you want to run away, why you want me to run away, too."

Having forgotten about the gun, no longer gripping it, the prince spoke to the arc of the champion's ribs.

"Because we have bookings waiting for us. Because that thing tomorrow isn't a match, it's a stupid challenge."

Without hurrying, Orsini moved toward the window, toward Jacob van Oppen's bed. He didn't dare turn on the light, he was in no mood to win with smiles and grimaces.

He preferred the shadows and persuasion through tones of voice. *Maybe it's better to put an end to this here and now. I've always been lucky, something new always showed up and often better than what I'd just lost. Never look back, leave him alone, like an elephant without a master.*

"But we called the challenge," Jacob's voice said, surprised, almost laughing. "We always call it. Three minutes. In the newspapers, in the plazas. Money to whoever lasts three minutes. And I've always won, Jacob van Oppen always wins."

"Always," Orsini said; suddenly he felt weak and jaded; he placed the gun on the bed and pressed his hands together between his bare knees. "The champion always wins. But also, each time, I saw beforehand the man who accepted the challenge. Three minutes on his feet," he recited. "Nobody ever lasted half a minute, and I knew they wouldn't long before the bell rang. (*I can't tell him that once I was successful in my threats and also that I paid so that it wouldn't last more than thirty seconds; but I might have no choice but to tell him.*) And this time, I also did my duty. I went to see the man who accepted the challenge, I weighed and measured him. With my eyes. That's why I packed the suitcases, that's why I suggest we get on the four o'clock bus."

Van Oppen had stretched out on the floor, his head resting against the wall, between the bedside table and the light from the bathroom.

"I don't understand. This guy, this shopkeeper from some town in the middle of nowhere, who's never seen a match, this guy is going to beat Jacob van Oppen?"

"Nobody can beat the champion in a match," Orsini said patiently. "But this isn't a match."

"It's a challenge," Jacob exclaimed.

"That's right. A challenge. Five hundred pesos for staying on his feet for three minutes. I saw the man." Orsini paused and lit another cigarette; he was calm and dispassionate; it was as if he were telling a story to a child to help him fall asleep, as if he were singing "Lili Marleen."

"He'll stand up to me for three minutes?" van Oppen said mockingly.

"Well. He's a monster. Twenty years old, 110 kilos; all I did was make my assessment, but I'm never wrong."

Jacob bent down until he was sitting on the floor. Orsini heard him breathing.

"Twenty years old," the champion said. "I was twenty once, and I wasn't as strong as I am now, and I knew less."

"Twenty years old," the prince repeated, turning a yawn into a sigh.

"That's all? That's it? How many twenty-year-old men have I thrown on their backs in less than twenty seconds? So what makes you think this idiot can last three minutes?"

That's how it is, Orsini thought with a cigarette in his mouth. *As simple and terrible as suddenly discovering that we don't like a woman and we're impotent and we understand that nothing can be fixed or eased with explanations; as simple and terrible as telling a sick person the truth. Everything is simple when it happens to others, when we remain separate, and we can understand and feel pity, repeat comforting words.*

The piano of the Conservatory had disappeared in the heat of the dark night; crickets could be heard and a jazz record, much farther away, was playing.

"He's going to last three minutes?" Jacob insisted. "I saw him, too. I saw the pictures in the newspaper. A good body to move barrels around."

"No," Orsini replied, sincere and impartial. "Nobody can stand up to the world champion for three minutes."

"I don't understand," Jacob said. "I don't understand. Is there something you're not telling me?"

"The man won't last three minutes. But I'm sure he'll last more than one. And these days, a temporary situation but still indisputable, the world champion doesn't have the breath to fight for more than a minute."

"Me?" Jacob said, now on his knees, leaning on his fists. "Me?"

"Yes," Orsini said; he spoke quietly and nonchalantly, as if it didn't matter very much. "Once we finish this training tour, everything will change. We'll also have to quit the booze. But today, tomorrow, Saturday night in

Santa María or whatever this hole in the wall is called, Jacob van Oppen can't clinch or resist a clinch for more than a minute. Van Oppen's chest can't do it; his lungs can't do it. And that monster won't be thrown in a minute. That's why we have to take the bus at four in the morning. The bags are packed, I paid the hotel bill. Everything's settled."

Orsini heard the grunt and the cough on his left, measured the spread of silence through the room. He picked up the gun and warmed it between his knees.

After all is said and done, he thought, *it's odd that I beat around the bush, took so many precautions. He knows it better than I do and has for longer. But maybe that's precisely why I went round and round and took so many precautions. And here I am, at my age, as pitiful and ridiculous as if I'd told a woman that I no longer love her and was waiting, apprehensive and curious, for her reaction, her tears, her threats.*

Jacob's body had folded, but the strip of light from the bathroom revealed the shimmer of his tears on his head pitched back. Orsini held on to the gun and walked over to the telephone to order another bottle. As he passed he brushed against the champion's shaved head, then returned to the bed. Lifting his legs, he could feel against his thighs the round weight of his belly. From the kneeling man there came the sound of gasping, as if van Oppen had reached the end of a day of training or a particularly long and difficult match.

It's not his heart, Orsini remembered. *It's not his lungs. It's everything. One point ninety-five meters of a man who had started to grow old.*

"No, no," he said out loud. "It's just a pause along the way. Within a few months everything will get back to how it was before. The quality; that's what's important, that's what you'll never lose. Even if you want, even if you try to lose it. Because every man has suicidal periods in his life. But this can be overcome, this can be forgotten." The dance music had gotten louder as the night wore on. Orsini's voice vibrated, satisfied, lingering in the throat and on the palate.

There was a knock on the door and the prince went silently to get the tray with the bottle, the glasses, and the ice. He put it down on the small table and chose to sit on a chair to continue the evening and the lesson in optimism.

The champion sat in the shadows, on the floor, leaning against the wall; his breathing was no longer audible; he existed for Orsini only through his enormous, undeniable, crouching presence.

"Quality, that's the thing," the prince added. "Who has it? We are born with quality or we die without quality. There's a good reason everybody makes up funny and idiotic nicknames, a few little words to put on the posters. The Buffalo of Arkansas, The Crusher of Liege, Mihura de Granada. But Jacob van Oppen is only ever called World Champion."

Orsini's speech perished in the silence and fatigue.

The prince filled a glass, stuck in his tongue, and stood up to bring it to the champion.

"Orsini," Jacob said. "My friend, Prince Orsini."

Van Oppen pressed on his knees with his large hands; like the jaws of a trap, his knees held his bent head fast. Orsini left the glass on the floor after passing it over the giant's neck and back.

"A drink, Champ," he whispered, sweet and paternal. "It always does you good."

He was straightening up with a grin, touching the tiredness in his waist, when he felt the fingers encircling his ankle and pinning him to the ground. He heard Jacob's slow, happy, relaxed, and sluggish voice:

"Now the prince is going to finish off the whole glass in one gulp."

Orsini leaned back to keep his balance. *That's all I needed, for this monster to believe that I want to put him to sleep or poison him.* He bent down slowly, picked up the glass, and drank it down quickly, feeling Jacob's fingers relax around his ankle.

"Okay, Champ?" he asked. Now he could see the other's eyes, part of a lifted smile.

"Okay, Prince. A full glass for me."

Keeping his legs apart, trying not to fall over, Orsini went to the small table and refilled the glass. He leaned on the table to light a cigarette and was able to see, in the small flame of the lighter, that his hands were shaking with hatred. He returned with the glass, the cigarette in his mouth, a finger on the trigger of the gun hidden in the pocket of his bathrobe. He crossed the strip of yellow light and saw Jacob standing up, white and enormous, swaying gently.

"Cheers, Champion," Orsini said, offering him the drink with his left hand.

"Cheers," repeated van Oppen's voice from above, with a weak trace of excitement. "I knew they were going to come. I was in the church praying for them to come."

"Yes," Orsini said.

There was a pause, the champion sighed, the night brought them the shouts and applauses from the faraway dancehall, a tugboat called out three times from the river.

"Now," Jacob said with difficulty, "the prince will finish his drink in one gulp. We are both drunk. But I don't drink tonight because it's Friday. The prince has a gun."

For a second, holding the glass in the air and looking at van Oppen's belly button, Orsini imagined a biography of perpetual humiliation, tasted the flavor of disgust, knew that the giant wasn't even challenging him, that he was simply offering him a target for the gun he was gripping in his pocket.

"Yes," he said a second later; he spit out the cigarette and again drank down the gin. His stomach rose into his chest as he threw the empty glass toward the bed, as he retreated with difficulty and placed the gun on the table.

Van Oppen hadn't changed places; he continued to sway in the darkness with mocking slowness, as if aping classic exercises for the waist muscles.

"We're crazy," Orsini said. He had no use for memories, or for the weak scorching of the summer night that was touching the window, or for plans for the future.

"'Lili Marleen,' please," Jacob said.

Leaning on the table, Orsini put down the cigarette he was planning to light. He sang in a muted voice, with one last hope, as if his only calling had ever been crooning idiotic lyrics, easy-listening music, as if he had never done anything else to earn a living. He felt older than ever, diminished and paunchy, alienated from himself.

There was silence and then the champion said, "Thank you." Sleepy and weak, picking up the cigarette he had left on the table next to the gun, Orsini watched the large stark-white body, released from age by darkness.

"Thank you," van Oppen repeated, almost touching him. "Again."

Astonished, indifferent, Orsini thought, *It is no longer a lullaby, it no longer makes him get drunk, cry, sleep.* He cleared his throat again and began: "*Vor der Kaserne, vor dem großen Tor . . .*"

Without moving his body, the champion lifted his arm from his hip and hit Orsini's jaw with his open hand. An old habit prevented him from using his fist except in desperate situations. With the other arm, he held the prince's body and stretched him out on the bed.

The heat of the night and the party had swung the windows open. The jazz music from the dance seemed to be rising now from the hotel, out of the middle of the darkened room.

It was a city risen out of the river, September, five centimeters, more or less, south of Ecuador. I woke up, without pain, in the morning in the hotel room full of light and heat. Jacob was massaging my stomach and laughing to facilitate the release of insults that ended up as a single one, repeated until I could no longer pretend to be asleep and I sat up:

"Old swine," in pure German, almost Prussian.

The sun was already licking the leg of the little table, and I thought sadly that nothing would be salvaged from the wreck. At least – I started to remember – that was what was best to think, and my face and my words had to adjust themselves to that sadness. Something warned van Oppen because he made me drink a glass of orange juice and placed a lit cigarette in my mouth.

"Old swine," he said, as I filled my lungs with smoke.

It was Saturday morning, we were still in Santa María. I moved my head and looked at him, took a quick measure of his smile, his happiness, and our friendship. He was wearing his expensive grey suit, his buckskin shoes, his Stetson was resting on the back of his head. All of a sudden I thought that he was right, that life is always definitely right, that the victories and the defeats don't matter.

"Yes," I said, removing his hand, "I'm an old swine. Years pass and things get worse. Is there a match today?"

"There is," he nodded enthusiastically. "I told you they were going to come back and they did."

I sucked on the cigarette and stretched out on the bed. All I had to do was look at his smile to understand that, even if they broke his spine on that warm Saturday night as anybody could predict, Jacob had won. He had to win in three minutes; but I was charging more. I sat up in bed and rubbed my jaw.

"There's a match," I said, "the champion decides. But, regrettably, the manager has nothing more to say. No bottle and no blow is capable of suppressing everything."

Van Oppen started laughing and his hat fell onto the bed. His laughter had been neglected over the years, it was the same.

"No blow and no bottle," I confirmed. "We agreed that the champion doesn't have enough breath, for now, to withstand a match, a real effort, that lasts more than a minute. That's settled. The champion won't be able to break the Turk. The champion will die a mysterious death when he gets to the fifty-ninth second. We'll see it in the autopsy. I believe, at least, that that's what we agreed."

"That's what we agreed. No more than one minute," van Oppen nodded, once again happy, young, impatient. Morning now filled the entire room, and I felt ashamed of my sleepiness, my misgivings, my bathrobe weighed down by the unloaded gun.

"And then," I said slowly, as if wanting to take revenge, "there's us not having five hundred pesos. Agreed, we all know, the Turk can't win. But it's already Saturday, and we have to deposit the five hundred pesos. All we have is enough for our tickets and a week in the Capital. And then it's up to God."

Jacob picked up his hat and laughed again. He shook his head like a father sitting on a park bench next to his wary little boy.

"Money?" he said without asking. "Money for the deposit? Five hundred pesos?"

He gave me another lit cigarette and placed his left foot, the more sensitive one, on top of the small table. He undid the laces of his grey shoe, took it off, and came over to show me a roll of green banknotes. It was real money. He peeled off five ten-dollar bills and had to keep showing off.

"More?"

"That's fine," I said. "More than enough."

A lot of money went back into the shoe; between three and five hundred dollars.

So I changed the money at noon; and since the champion had disappeared – no monogrammed sweaters or little jogs along the promenade that morning – I went to the restaurant in the Plaza and ate like a gentleman, like I hadn't eaten in a long time. I had a coffee made at my table and some appropriate liqueurs and a cigar that was very dry but easy to smoke.

I ended my lunch with a tip befitting a drunkard, or a thief, and called the hotel; the champion wasn't there; what remained of the afternoon was cool and cheerful, Santa María was going to have its big night. I left the newspaper's number with the receptionist so Jacob could coordinate the trip to the Apollo with me, and a few minutes later I sat down at the table with *Sports* and two other faces. I showed them the money:

"Just so there aren't any doubts. But I prefer to hand it over directly in the ring. In case van Oppen dies of a heart attack, or I have to contribute to the Turk's funeral expenses."

We played poker, I lost and won, until I was informed that van Oppen was in the theater. It was still a long half hour till nine o'clock; but we put on our jackets and took old taxicabs to ride the few blocks through town, to highlight the carnivalesque, the ridiculous.

I entered through the back door and went to the room lined with posters and photographs, fiercely pervaded by the smell of rancid urine and slop. There was Jacob, in his sky blue shorts, in honor of Santa María, and his World Champion belt, he was doing pushups. All I had to do was take one look at him – his childlike eyes, clean and clear; the brief curve of his smile – to understand that he didn't want to talk to me, didn't want any prologues, nothing that separated him from what he was determined to be and remember.

I sat on a bench, not hearing whether or not he answered my greeting, and lit a cigarette. Now, at this moment, within a few minutes, the end of the story would be coming. Of this story, the story about the World Wrestling Champion. But there would be others, there would also be an explanation for *El Liberal*, Santa María, and the neighboring towns.

"Temporary physical indisposition," I liked better than "Overtraining resulted in the Champion's defeat." But tomorrow they wouldn't use the capital "C" and perhaps not even the dubious title. Van Oppen continued to do pushups, and I fought off the smell of ammonia by lighting a cigarette with the one before, not forgetting that the cleanliness of the air is the most important condition for exercising.

Jacob raised and lowered his body as if he were alone, moving his arms horizontally, it seemed, thinner and heavier. Through the stench, into which his sweat was being blended, I tried to hear him breathe. The noise from the hall also penetrated the fetid room. Perhaps the champion had enough wind to last a minute and a half, but never two or three. The Turk would remain standing until the bell rang, with his furious black mustache, his modest knee-length shorts that I had pictured him in – and I wasn't wrong about – his small and hard fiancée howling in triumph and rage next to the planks of the stage in the Apollo Theater, next to the threadbare rug that I will keep calling a mat. There was no longer any hope, we would never recover the five hundred pesos. The noise of the rabble in the full and impatient hall was growing.

"Time to go," I told the dead man, who was doing calisthenics.

It was exactly nine o'clock according to my watch; I left the stench and walked down the dark hall to the ticket booth. By nine-fifteen I'd finished checking and signing the box office forms. I went back to the filthy room – the shouting announced that van Oppen was already in the ring – and took off my jacket after stuffing the money in my pants' pocket, and walked the other way down the hall until I entered the auditorium and strode onto the stage. They applauded me and hurled insults, I thanked them with nods and smiles, certain that there were more than seventy people in the Apollo who had not paid. Anyway, I'd never get the fifty percent I was due.

I took off Jacob's bathrobe, walked across the ring to greet the Turk, and had a little more time for a bit more buffoonery.

The bell rang, and it became impossible to not breathe and understand the smell of the throng that filled the Apollo. The bell rang, and I left Jacob alone, much more and forever alone than I had left him at dawn on so many days, on street corners and in bars, when I would start to get tired and bored. The worst part was that on that night, as I walked away from him to take a seat in the VIP box, I wasn't tired or bored. The first bell was to empty the ring. The second was to begin the match. Greased, almost young, not showing the extra kilos, Jacob started to turn around, bent over, until he was in the middle of the ring and there he waited with a smile on his face.

He spread his arms and waited for the Turk, who seemed to have gotten wider. He waited for him, smiling, until he was close, took one step back then suddenly lunged forward for the clinch. In defiance of all the rules, Jacob held up his arms for ten seconds. Then he planted his legs and turned; he placed one hand on the challenger's back and the other, as well as the forearm, against his thigh. I didn't understand that, and I continued not to understand for the exact half minute that the match lasted. Then I saw the Turk fly out of the ring, struggling to break through the howls of the people of Santa María, and disappear in the dark depths of the audience.

He had flown, with his big mustache, with the absurd flailing of his legs that searched in the dirty air for support and stability. I saw him pass just under the ceiling, between the lights, gesticulating. We hadn't reached fifty seconds and the champion had either won or not, depending on how you looked at it. I climbed into the ring to help him put on his robe. Jacob was smiling like a child, he didn't hear the shouts and the insults of the spectators, the growing clamor. He was sweating, but not very much; and as soon as I heard his breathing I knew that his fatigue was due to his nerves, not exhaustion.

Then pieces of wood and empty bottles began to fall into the ring; I was ready with my speech, my exaggerated smile for the strangers. But the projectiles kept falling, and the shouts would have drowned out my words.

Then the soldiers started to move in enthusiastically, as if they had never done anything else since their first day on the job, under orders or not; they knew how to spread out and organize themselves and start to break heads with their shiny new sticks until the only ones left in the Apollo were the champion, the judge, and I in the ring, the soldiers in the hall, and the poor dead kid, twenty years old, draped over two chairs. It was then, and nobody knew from where, and I know less than anybody, that the small woman, the fiancée, appeared next to the Turk and started to kick and spit at the man who had lost, the other, as I congratulated Jacob discreetly, and the nurses and doctors appeared at the door carrying the stretcher.

1961

As Sad as She

for M.C.

Dear Assad:

I understand that, in spite of our numerous and unspeakable bonds, the time has come to thank each other for the closeness of the last few months and say goodbye. It will be all to your advantage. I think we never really understood each other; I accept the blame, the responsibility, and the failure. I try to forgive myself – only between us, of course – by citing the difficulty of remaining on the fence for x number of pages. I also accept, as merited, the moments of joy. In any case, forgive me. I never looked you straight in your face, never showed you mine.

J. C. O.

Years before, which could be many or meld into yesterday during scarce moments of happiness, she had been in the man's room. An imaginable bedroom, a dirty and dilapidated bathroom, a shaky elevator; that's all she remembered about the house. It was before the wedding, a few months before.

She wanted to go there, she longed for something to happen – the cruelest, the most anemic and disappointing thing – something of use to her loneliness and ignorance. She didn't think about the future and she felt capable of denying it. But a fear that had nothing to do with her old sorrow forced her to say no, to defend herself with her hands and a stiffening of her thighs. She acquired, accepted, only the flavor of the man stained by sun and beach.

At dawn, already separate and far away, she dreamed that she was walking alone through a night that could have been a different night, almost naked in her short nightdress, carrying an empty suitcase. She was condemned to despair and dragged her bare feet along deserted and tree-lined streets, slowly, her body unbowed, nearly defiant.

Heartbreak, sadness, saying yes to death could be tolerated only because, at a whim, the taste of the man would rise into her throat at every street corner where she asked for it and commanded it to come. The painful steps became slower until they were stilled. Then, partially naked, surrounded by shadows, the pretense of silence, a distant pair of lights, she would stop and noisily take in the air. Weighed down with the weightless suitcase, she savored the memory and continued on her return walk.

Suddenly she saw the enormous moon rising over the grey, black, dirty village; with each step it became more silvery and the bloody edges containing it were rapidly dissolving. With each step she understood that she and her suitcase were not moving any closer to a goal, a bed, a room. The moon by now was a monstrosity. Almost naked, standing erect, her small breasts piercing the night, she continued walking until she was able to plunge into the extravagant moon that continued to grow.

The man became skinnier every day and the color in his grey eyes was fading, diluting, a long way away now from curiosity and entreaty. It had never occurred to him to cry, and the years, thirty-two, had at least taught him the futility of all renunciation, of all hope for understanding.

He watched her every morning without candor or lies across the cluttered, lopsided breakfast table they had set up in the kitchen for the delights of summer. Maybe it wasn't all his fault, maybe it would be useless to try to figure out whose fault it was, whose it still is.

Secretly, she looked at his eyes. If you can call wariness, a cold bolt of lightning, her calculations, "a look." The man's eyes, without giving themselves away, became larger and lighter each time, every morning. But he wasn't trying to conceal them; he simply wanted to deflect, without being rude, what his eyes were condemned to ask and say.

He was at that time thirty-two years old and from nine to five each day he kept expanding into offices of a large place of business. He loved money, as long as there was plenty of it, the way other men feel attracted to tall and fat women and put up with their age without caring. He also believed in the happiness of tiring weekends, in the good health that fell on everyone from the sky, the great outdoors.

He was there or here, he expected mastery over all sorts of good luck, of temptations. He had loved the small woman who gave him food, who had given birth to a baby boy who cried incessantly on the second floor. Now he looked at her in astonishment: she was, fleetingly, something worse, lower, deader than a stranger whose name has never reached us.

At their irregular breakfast hour the sun shone in through the high windows; at the table the scents from the garden grew more complex, though still faint, like the simplistic beginning of a suspicion. Neither of them could deny the sun, the springtime; at the very least, the demise of winter.

A few days after the move, when nobody had thought yet about transforming the wild and overgrown garden into a sepulchral row of fish tanks, the man rose at dawn and waited for the sun to rise. At first light he hammered a can into the araucaria tree and took a few steps back, the small gun with its mother-of-pearl handle in one hand. He raised his arm and heard only the frustrated clicks of the firing pin. He returned to the house with an overblown feeling of ridicule and ill humor; carelessly, without respecting the woman's sleep, he tossed the gun into a corner of the closet.

"What happened?" she mumbled as the man undressed to get into the bath.

"Nothing. Either the bullets are rusty, I bought them less than a month ago, they've cheated me, or the gun has had it. It was my mother's or my grandmother's, the trigger is loose. I don't want you to be alone here at night without something to defend yourself. But I'll deal with it today."

"It doesn't matter," the woman said as she walked on bare feet to pick up the baby. "I have good lungs and the neighbors will hear me."

"I'm aware of that," the man said, and laughed.

They looked at each other with affection and humor. The woman waited for the sound of the car, then went back to sleep with her baby hanging on a nipple.

The maid came in and out and it was not always possible to know why. The woman was used to it, she no longer believed in the entreaty in the man's eyes, glimpsed so many times, as if his glance, his expression, his humid silence didn't matter more than the color of his iris, the inherited slant of his eyelids. He, for his part, was now incapable of accepting the world; not the business deals, not the nonexistent daughter, often forgotten, often alive, tenacious, toughened, distinct in spite of his premeditated drinking bouts, his inescapable business deals, his companies, and solitude. It's also likely that by now neither she nor he believed fully in the reality of the nights, in their brief and predictable moments of happiness.

They expected nothing from the time they spent together, but they didn't accept this impoverishment, either. He kept playing with his cigarette and the ashtray; she spread butter and jam on toast. On those mornings, he didn't try to actually look at her; he merely showed her his eyes, like a beggar – almost apathetically and without faith – who exhibits a scar, a stump.

She talked about what was left of the garden, about the suppliers, about the pink baby boy in the room upstairs. When the man grew tired of waiting for the impossible sentence or word, he bent over to kiss her forehead and left orders for the workers who were building the fish tanks.

Every month the man confirmed that he was wealthier, that his bank accounts were growing without effort or intentionality. He was unable to invent a true, coveted goal for the new money.

Until five or six in the afternoon he sold parts for automobiles, tractors, all kinds of engines. But from four o'clock on he used the telephone, patiently and without hard feelings, to assuage his anxiety, to make certain of a woman in a bed or at a table in a restaurant. He made do with little, with what was strictly necessary: a smile, a caress on his cheek that could be taken for tenderness or understanding. Later, of course, the acts of love, scrupulously paid for with clothes, perfumes, useless objects. Also paid for – the vice, the control, the entire night – by resigning himself to fickle and asinine conversations.

Upon his return at dawn she would inhale the ordinary, undeniable scents and keep her eye on the bony face that so mistakenly sought serenity. The man had nothing to tell her. He'd look at the row of bottles in the cabinet and randomly choose one. Sunk in his armchair, listless, with one finger between the pages of a book, he drank facing her silence, facing her pretense of sleep, facing her eyes, fixed and staring at the ceiling. She wouldn't scream; for a while she tried to understand without disdain, wanting to bring to bear on him some of the pity she felt for herself, for life and its end.

In the middle of September the woman began, at first imperceptibly, to find solace, to believe that existence, like a mountain or a stone, is simply there, that we do not make it ourselves, that neither one of them was making it.

Nobody, nobody can know how or why this story began. What we are trying to recount here began on a quiet autumn afternoon, when the man cast a shadow over the still sunlit twilight of the garden and stopped to look around, to sniff the grass, the last flowers on the wild and stunted bushes. For a while he didn't move, his head leaning to one side, his arms hanging down and seemingly dead. Then he advanced until he reached the hedge of the Jerusalem thorn bush and from there began to measure the garden in regular, reticent paces, each about one meter long. He walked from south to north, then from east to west. She watched him from behind the curtains on the upper floor; anything outside the routine could be the birth of a hope, the confirmation of misery. The baby had been squealing since the late afternoon, and nobody could ascertain if he was already dressed in pink, if they had dressed him like that from birth or before.

That night, Sunday, the saddest day of the week, the man in the kitchen, stirring his cup of coffee, said:

"So much land and it's all useless."

She eyed his ascetic face, his diluted, unfathomed torment. She saw a new malignant lassitude, the birth of resolve.

"I always thought . . . ," the woman said, understanding as she spoke that she was in fact lying, that she had not had either the time or the desire to think about it, realizing that the word *always* had lost all meaning. "I always thought about fruit trees, about planting beds built according to a design, about a real garden."

But she had been born there, in the old house far away from the water of the beach, which Old Man Petrus, using some excuse, had baptized. She had been born and raised there. And when the world came looking for her, she didn't fully understand it, protected and tricked by the capricious and stunted bushes, by the mystery – in light and shadow – of the gnarled and intact old trees, of the innocent, tall, vulgar grass. She had a mother who bought a machine to cut the grass, a father who was good at making promises, after every evening meal, that he would start work tomorrow. He never did. Sometimes he oiled the machine for hours or lent it to a neighbor for months.

But the garden, that deformed parody of a jungle, was never touched. Thus the little girl learned that no word is comparable to *tomorrow*: never, nothing, permanence, and peace.

As a young girl she discovered the affectionate banter of the bushes, the grass, any of the anonymous and gnarled trees; she laughed when she discovered that they threatened to invade the house, only to retreat a few months later, shrunken, sated.

The man drank his coffee and then started moving his head, slow and resolute. He paused or he let the pause come and settle in.

"Next to the windows we can leave a corner for lounging and enjoying cold drinks in summer. But the rest, everything, has to be paved over with concrete. I want to build fish tanks. Rare species, difficult to grow. There are people who make a lot of money doing that."

The woman knew the man was lying. She didn't believe he was interested in money, she didn't believe anybody could chop down the sick and useless old trees, kill the neglected grass, the flowers with unknown names — pale, fleeting, downcast.

But the men, the workers, three of them, gathered to talk one Sunday morning. She watched them from the upstairs window; two were standing, surrounding the almost horizontal chaise lounge where the instructions, the questions about cost and time were coming from; the third, squatting, with a beret, huge and calm, was chewing on a stem.

She remembered him till the end. The oldest one, the boss, slouching, with thick, white hair, his hands hanging down, stopped for a moment with his back to the wrought-iron gate. She contemplated without surprise the dispossessed trees, the large area of jumbled weeds. The other two kept walking, uselessly loaded down with scythes and shovels, pickaxes, and the bewilderment that fettered their legs. The youngest and biggest, the laziest one, kept chewing on his stem, at the end of which was a small, rose-colored flower. It was a Sunday morning and spring was shaking the garden leaves; she watched them trying to make mistakes, the baby's mouth latched onto her breast.

She was familiar with resentment, with the man's desire to hurt her. But everything had been talked about so many times, understood to the point of believing that one was understood and understood the other, that she didn't believe that revenge, the destruction of the garden and her own life, was possible. Sometimes, when they both gave into the dream of having forgotten, the man would find her knitting somewhere in the garden and would start up again without any preamble: "Everything's fine, everything's as over as if it had never happened." The gaunt and obsessive face refused to look at her. "But why did it have to be a boy? Buying pink yarn for so many months and this was the result, a boy. I'm not crazy. I know, deep down, it doesn't make any difference. But a girl could end up being yours, exclusively yours. That poor thing, on the other hand . . ."

She sat still for a bit, her hands settling, and finally looked at him. Skinnier, his light eyes even bigger, he stood next to her with his legs astride, shattered and sarcastic. He was lying, they both knew the man was lying, but they understood the lie in different ways.

"We've already talked about it so much," the woman said, bored. "I've had to listen to you so many times . . ."

"Possibly. Fewer of course than my urges to bring the subject up. It's a boy, he has my name, I pay for his upkeep and will have to educate him. Can we take a step back, look at it from the outside? Because if we do, I'm either a gentleman or a dupe. And you, you're a clever little slut."

"Shit," she said quietly, without hatred, without it being knowable whom she was speaking to.

The man looked back at the dimming sky, the certain spring. He turned and started walking toward the house.

Perhaps the whole story was born out of this, so simple and terrible: the choice depends on whether one wants to think about it or gets distracted: the man believed only in disgrace and good fortune, in good luck or bad, in all the sadness and joy that can befall us, whether or not we deserve it. She believed she knew something more; she thought about fate, about mistakes and mysteries, she acknowledged her guilt and in the end came to admit that living brings enough guilt for us to accept the price, whether reward or punishment. The same thing, when all is said and done.

Sometimes the man would wake her up to talk about Mendle. He'd light his pipe or a cigarette and wait till he was certain that she was resigned and listening. Maybe he was waiting for a miracle in his soul or in that of the naked woman, anything that could be exorcised and would give them peace or an equivalent deception.

"Why Mendle? You could have picked from many better, so many who would have embarrassed me less."

He wanted to hear again the story of the woman's trysts with Mendle; but in the end he always recoiled, afraid to know everything once and for all; resolved deep down to save himself, to disregard the whys. His madness was humble and could be respected.

"Mendle or anybody else. Same thing. It had nothing to do with love."

One night the man tried to laugh:

"But that's how it turned out. Because things have gotten so complicated, or harmonious, that today I could send Mendle to jail. Mendle himself, nobody else, only Mendle. A falsified document, his signature. And I'm not motivated by jealousy. He has a wife and three kids who are his and his alone. A house or two. He still seems happy. It's about envy, not jealousy. It's difficult to understand. Because for me, personally, it doesn't do me any good to destroy all of that, to sink Mendle or not. I've wanted to do it since long before I found out, since before I knew it was possible. I imagine, you know, the possibility of pure envy, without any concrete motive, without resentment. Sometimes, very rarely, I find it possible."

She didn't answer. Curled up against dawn's first chill, she was thinking about the baby, waiting for his first cry of hunger. He, on the other hand, was waiting for the miracle, the resurrection of the pregnant girl he'd known, his very own, the girl of the love they believed in, or built, for months, with determination, without deliberate deception, forsaken so close to bliss.

The men started to work one Monday, unhurriedly sawing down trees, which they hauled away at the end of the day in a beat-up truck, roaring with age, also gnarled. Days later they began to scythe the flowering weeds, the grass that had grown tall and succulent. They didn't keep to a regular schedule; perhaps they'd been hired for the whole job, directly, so they didn't have to worry about daily wages, no-shows, or slacking off. They did not, however, show any signs of being in a hurry.

The man never talked to her about what was happening in the garden. He was still gaunt and quiet, still smoked and drank. The concrete now spread over the land and its memories – white, soon grey.

Then, at the end of one breakfast, the man, resentful and unwary, stubbed out his cigarette in a cup and, almost smiling, as if he truly understood the fate of his words, said slowly, without looking at her:

"It would be a good idea for you to keep an eye on the well diggers. Between nursings. I don't see them making much progress with the cement."

From that moment on the three workers became well diggers. They soon brought large sheets of glass to construct the tanks – enormous, placed with deliberate symmetry, out of proportion to any kind of fauna that would be raised there.

"Yes," she said. "I can talk to the old man, go to where the garden used to be and watch them work."

"The old man," the man said mockingly. "Does he even know how to talk? I think he manages them by moving his hands and his eyebrows."

She began to go down to the concrete on a daily basis, in the morning and in the afternoon, taking advantage of the wayward schedule they kept. It might be said that she too was resentful and unwary.

She walked slowly, taller now above the hard flat ground, bewildered, moving diagonally, reclaiming her old detours, her lost shortcuts once determined by trees and planting beds. She looked at the men, watched the enormous fish tanks rise. She sniffed the air, awaited the solitude of five in the afternoon, the daily ritual, absurdity conquered, very nearly turned into habit.

At first it was the incomprehensible excitement of the well itself, the black hole sunk into the earth. It would have been enough for her. But soon she discovered, at the bottom of it, the two men working, their torsos bare. One of them, the one with the chewed stem, moved his enormous biceps incautiously; the other, tall and thin, slower, younger, evoked pity, a longing to help him and hand him a rag to wipe his sweaty brow.

She didn't know how to move away and lie to herself alone.

The old man was smoking, sitting awkwardly on a log. He looked at her impassively.

"They're working?" she asked with indifference.

"Yes, ma'am, they're working. Exactly what they should do every day, every shift. That's what I'm here for. For that, and for other things I figure out. But I'm not God. I just barely see ahead and help out whenever I can."

The well diggers greeted her with a nod of their polite and taciturn heads. Only rarely could they invent a subject of conversation, excuses that could be batted back and forth for a few minutes. She and the pair of well diggers: the calm giant, always wearing his beret and chewing on a weed that he no longer could have picked from the walled garden; the other, very young and thin, dim-witted from hunger, sickly. Because the old man didn't talk and could remain motionless for the entire day, standing or sitting on the ground, rolling cigarettes, one after the other.

They dug, measured, and sweated as if some part of this could matter to her, as if she were alive and capable of participating. As if she had once owned the vanished trees and dead grass. She would talk about anything, be overly polite, respectful, a form of sadness that helps to bring people together. She would talk about anything and always leave her sentences unfinished, waiting for five in the afternoon, waiting for the men to leave.

The house was surrounded by a hedge of Jerusalem thorn bushes. They had grown to be like trees, almost three meters high, though their trunks maintained their adolescent slenderness. They had been planted very close together, but they knew how to grow without getting in each other's way, using each other for support, their thorns intermingling.

At five in the afternoon the well diggers imagined they heard a bell, and the old man raised his arm. They put away, or rather tossed the tools into the cool shade of the shed, waved, and left. The old man out in front, then the beast with the beret, and the hunched skinny man behind, so that the clouds and what remained of the sun would learn of their respect for hierarchies. All three walked slowly, smoked calmly, half-heartedly.

Upstairs, her back to the din in the cradle, the woman kept her eye on them just to be certain. She stood there without moving for ten or fifteen minutes. Then she went downstairs toward what had once been her garden, avoiding obstacles that no longer existed, treading on the concrete till she reached the hedge. Obviously she didn't always go to the same spot. She could leave through the large iron gate used by the well diggers, the imaginary guests; she could escape through the garage door, always open when the car wasn't there.

But she would choose, without conviction, without a longing for truth, the bloody and useless game with, against, the Jerusalem thorns, be they bushes or trees. She'd seek, for nothing, with no goal, to find a path between the trunks and the thorns. She'd pant for a while, opening her hands. She'd always end in failure, accepting it, saying yes to it with a grimace, a smile.

Then she'd move through the twilight, licking her hands, looking at the sky of this newborn spring and the tense, promissory sky of future springs that her son might enjoy. She cooked, she took care of the baby, and always with a poorly chosen book she'd begin to wait for the man in one of the flowery armchairs or lying in bed. She'd hide the clocks and wait.

But every night the man's returns were identical, easily confounded. Near October she happened to read: "Imagine the growing sorrow, the urge to flee, the impotent disgust, the submission, the hatred." The man hid the car in the garage, walked across the concrete, and climbed the stairs. He was the same as always, the sentence she had just read was not enough to transform him. He would pace around the bedroom, rattling his keys, telling simple or complicated stories about his day at work, lying to her, sometimes cocking his gaunt face, his eyes growing during the pauses. As sad as she, maybe.

That night the woman yielded, insisted, as she had not done for many months. Everything that would make them happy or help them forget was welcomed, sacred. Under the small, half-hidden light, the man finally fell asleep, almost smiling, quieted. Sleepless again, she discovered without astonishment, without sadness, that since childhood she'd known no true solid happiness other than the garden greenery, now snatched from her. That was all there was, those things that changed, those colors. And it occurred to her, before the baby's first cry, that he intuited this, that he wanted to deprive her of the only thing that actually mattered to her. Destroy the garden; keep staring at her meekly with those light, haggard eyes; play at smiling, ambiguous, indirect.

At the first sounds of the morning, the woman would bare her teeth to the ceiling, thinking again and again of the first part of the Hail Mary. Only the first, because she could not accept the word death. She admitted to never having been tricked, she accepted that she'd been right about her confusions, her fears, her childhood doubts: life was a mixture of inaccuracies, cowardices, blurry lies, not necessarily always intentional.

But she would remember, even now and more intensely, the sensation of being defrauded when childhood ended, then its attenuation in adolescence by desires and hopes. She had never asked to be born, had never wanted the union – perhaps momentary, fleeting, routine – of a couple in a bed (mother, father, afterwards and forevermore) to bring her into the world. And, above all, she had not been consulted about the life she was forced to know and accept. A single a priori question and she would have rejected, with equivalent horror, bowels, and death, the need for words to communicate or to strive for another's comprehension.

"No," the man said when she brought breakfast from the kitchen. "I don't plan to do anything against Mendle. Not even help."

He was dressed with strange care, as if he were on his way to a party rather than the office. Seeing the new suit, the white shirt, the brand-new tie, she spent minutes remembering and believing in her memory. That's how it had been for her during their courtship. She was speechless and incredulous as she moved around, relieved of anguish and years.

The man dipped a piece of bread in the sauce and pushed the plate away. The woman saw the new look shining in his eyes, timid and tempting, that reached her from the table or that she had to invent.

"I'm going to burn Mendle's check. Or I can give it to you. In any case, it's only a matter of days. Poor man."

She had to wait a bit. Then she managed to pull herself away from the fireplace and went to sit, not suffering and patient, in front of the thin man, waiting for him to leave.

When she heard the sound of the car die on the road, she went up to the bedroom; she soon found the small, useless gun with the mother-of-pearl handle and looked at it without touching it. Outside of her, summer had also not yet arrived, though spring was advancing with a fury, and the days, the little things, could not and would not have wanted to stop.

In the afternoon, after the ritual with the thorns and the idle streaks of blood on her hands, the woman learned to whistle with the birds and knew that Mendle had disappeared along with the thin man. It's possible neither had ever existed. The baby remained on the upper floor and did nothing to attenuate her solitude. She'd never been with Mendle, she'd never met him or seen his squat, muscular body; she never knew his tenacious masculine will, his easy smile, his nonchalant rapport with joy. The cut on her forehead now bled slowly, dripping all the way down her nose.

The baby cried and she had to go upstairs. The old man was smoking, sitting on a stone, so still, so nothing, that he seemed to be part of his seat. The other two were invisible at the bottom of the well. Upstairs, she soothed the baby and saw the man's wrinkled suit on the floor. She started rummaging around, looked at incomprehensible pieces of paper covered with numbers, coins, a document. Finally, the letter.

The handwriting was feminine, quite lovely and legible, impersonal. It didn't quite cover both sides of the page, and the signature teased an incomprehensible message: *Másam*. But the message of the letter, the accumulation of nonsense, oaths, phrases that simultaneously feigned ingenuity and talent, was very clear. *She must be very young*, the woman thought, without pity or envy; *that's how I used to write to him*. She found no photographs.

Under *Másam*, the man had written in red ink: *She will be sixteen and will come naked from over and under the earth to be with me for as long as this song and this hope shall last.*

She never became jealous of the man, nor could she hate him, though maybe life, a little, her own lack of understanding, the nebulous dirty trick the world had played on her. For weeks they continued to live as always. But it wasn't long before he felt the change, before he perceived that the rejections and the apologies were turning into meek distance without hostility.

They spoke to each other but didn't really converse. She impassively avoided the flashes of entreaty that sometimes leapt from the man's eyes. *It would be the same if he'd died months ago, if we'd never met, if he weren't sitting next to me.* Neither of them had anything to hope for. The words didn't come, they averted their eyes. The man fiddled with his cigarette and the ashtray; the women spread butter and jam on her bread.

When he'd return at midnight, the woman would stop reading, pretend to sleep, or talk about the work in the garden, about the poorly washed shirts, about the baby and the price of food. He'd listen to her without asking questions, indifferent, without anything reliable of his own to tell. Then he'd take a bottle out of the cabinet and drink till dawn, alone or with a book.

She, in the summer night air, would keep her eye on his sharp profile, on the back of his head, where grey hairs, unexpected days before, were appearing, where the hair had begun to thin. She'd stopped feeling pity for herself and hung it on him. Now, when he came home, he'd refuse to eat. He'd head straight for the cabinet and drink through the night, through daybreak. Lying in bed, he'd sometimes speak in someone else's voice, addressing neither her nor the ceiling; he'd tell of happy and incredible things, invent people and events, simple or dubious circumstances.

The decision was made one night when the man arrived very early, didn't want to read or get undressed, and smiled at her before speaking. *He wants me to help pass the time. He will tell me a lie for precisely as long as it is convenient for him. Something absurdly embedded in our lives, in the dull story we are living.* The man held a glass just barely half full and offered her a full one. He knew, had known for years, that she wouldn't touch it. She hadn't had time to get into bed, he'd surprised her in the large armchair as she looked at the book again and again, at the words she knew by heart: "Imagine the growing sorrow, the urge to flee, the impotent disgust, the subjugation, the hatred."

The man sat down in front of her, listened to the news of the day, nodded in silence. When the end of the pause was approaching, he said, in different words:

"The old man. The one you pay, who smokes, watches nonchalantly as the laborers work. He studied at a seminary for a year, architecture for a few months. There's talk about a trip to Rome. How could he afford it, the poor devil? I don't know how long afterwards, several years in any case, he decided to show up around here, in the city. He was dressed as a priest. He lied, not by boasting, just by confusing and misleading. Nobody knows how, he managed to live two days and two nights in the seminary. He tried to find support to build a chapel. He displayed, unfurled, blue-tinted plans, with a tenacity akin to fury. Finally, they threw him out, despite him offering to take on the cost, to personally raise the necessary money.

"Maybe it was then, not before, that he put on the cassock and went from door to door asking for help. Not for him but for the chapel. It seems he was persuasive, what with his passion and the vague story of his failure. He was clever enough to deposit the money he collected with the courts. So that when the real priests intervened they'd have no choice but to settle for a fine, which he didn't pay, and a few days in jail. Afterwards nobody could stop him from spending his time building houses. He put roofs on so many of the horrors that surround us here, in Villa Petrus, that people call him 'the builder.' Maybe some call him 'Mr. Architect.' I don't know if this story is true or false. Who would waste their time finding out."

"What if it were true?" she mumbled over the glass.

"In any case, it's not our story."

She turned over in bed. She thought about anybody who was alive or had carried out the incomprehensible ritual of living, about anybody who was living or had been centuries before, posing questions that received only that proverbial silence. Man or woman, it didn't matter. She thought about the giant well digger, about anybody, about compassion.

"As long as he does his job . . . ," he began to say; then the telephone rang, and the man got up, thin and agile, his long strides slowing. He spoke in the dark hallway and returned to the bedroom with an annoyed, almost irate, look on his face.

"It's Montero, from the office. He stayed to do the accounting and now . . . Now he tells me there's something wrong, he needs to see me right away. If it's okay with you . . ."

She had no need to examine his face in order to understand, to remember that she had known the reason for the incongruous story about the old man from the beginning; that he had talked and she had listened only so that they could wait together for the phone call, the confirmation of the tryst.

"Más Am," the woman pronounced, barely smiling, feeling pity grow without it turning on her. She drank down her drink in one gulp and stood up to get the bottle and place it on the small table next to her.

The man didn't understand, he remained neither understanding nor answering.

"But if you'd rather I stay...," he insisted.

The woman smiled again, looking straight at the curtain swaying lazily over the window.

"No," she answered. She filled the glass again and leaned over to drink it down without spilling it, without using her hands.

The man stood there for a while, silent and still. Then he returned to the hallway to get his hat and coat. She waited calmly for the sound of the car; then, almost happy in the exact center of loneliness and silence, she shook her befuddled head and once again poured cognac into the glass. She had made a decision, certain by now that it was inevitable, suspecting that she'd wanted to from the moment she saw the well and, inside it, the thorax of the man who was digging, his huge white arms effortlessly maintaining the pace of his labors. But she could not relinquish distrust: she could not manage to convince herself that she was the one choosing, thought that some other person, persons, or thing had decided for her.

It was easy, and she'd known it would be for a long time. She waited in the garden, in its ruins, knitting disinterestedly as always, until the beast came out of his cave, picked up a water jug and went looking for a faucet. She waved to him and summoned him to her. Next to the garage, she hazarded some stupid questions. They didn't look at each other. She asked if flowers and plants, bushes and weeds, any form of vegetation and greenery, could grow there again.

The man knelt down, scratching with his dirty and broken fingernails the piece of sandy earth available to him.

"Possible," he said as he stood up. "It's a matter of wanting to, a little patience and care."

Quickly and whispering and willful, without having heard him, with her hands clasped behind her back, looking at the cloudy sky and its threat, the woman instructed:

"After you all leave. And nobody can know. Promise?"

Unperturbed, detached, clueless, the man touched his temple and agreed with a heavy voice.

"Return at six and enter through the gate."

The giant walked away without saying goodbye, slowly, swaying. The old man was listening to the angels who announced that it was five o'clock and instructed them to leave. That afternoon, she left the Jerusalem thorn bushes alone; slowly, sleepwalking, contrite, and incredulous, she climbed the stairs and tended to the child. Then, from the window, she began to watch the road, to see the increasing indigo of the sky. *I'm crazy, or I was and I still am, and I like it,* she repeated to herself with a happy invisible smile. She wasn't thinking about revenge, about retribution; barely, glancingly, about her remote and incomprehensible childhood, about a world of lies and disobedience.

The man arrived at the gate at six, the chewed stem adorning his ear. She let him walk very slowly for a while along the concrete covering the murdered garden. When the giant stopped, she ran downstairs – the rapid and rhythmic drumbeat of the treads under her heels – and was smaller as she approached him until she almost touched his enormous body. She smelled his sweat, contemplated the stupid and suspicious look in his blinking eyes. Stretching up, with a burst of frenzy, she stuck out her tongue to kiss him. The man gasped and turned his head to the left.

"The shed," he suggested.

She laughed quietly, tersely; she was looking calmly at the Jerusalem thorn bushes, as if bidding them farewell. She had grabbed hold of one of the man's wrists.

"Not in the shed," she said, finally and sweetly. "Too dirty, too uncomfortable. Either upstairs or not at all." She guided him like a blind man to the door, helped him climb the stairs. The baby was sleeping. Mysteriously, the bedroom remained identical, undefeated. The large reddish bed, the sparse furniture, the drinks cabinet, the restless curtains, the same trifles, vases, paintings, candlesticks: they all persisted.

Deaf, distant, she let him talk about the weather, gardens and harvests. When the well digger was finishing his second glass she brought him over to the bed and gave other instructions. She had never imagined that a naked man, real and hers, could be so admirable and fearsome. She acknowledged desire, curiosity, an old feeling of health that had been slumbering for years. As she watched him approach, she began to become aware of her hatred for his physical superiority, for the masculine, for the one who gives orders, for someone who has no need to ask useless questions.

She summoned and held the well digger, stinking and compliant. But it was impossible, over and over again, because they'd been created definitively, insurmountably, haphazardly different. The man pulled away, grumbling, his throat stuck and hateful:

"It's always like this. It always happens to me," he said sadly and wistfully, without a trace of pride.

They heard the baby's cry. Without words, without violence, she had the man get dressed, told him lies as she caressed his bearded cheek.

"Another time," she whispered as goodbye and comfort.

The man went back into the night, probably chewing on a stem, tamping down anger, the old unjust failure.

(As for the narrator, he is only authorized to attempt calculations in time. He can repeat, at dawn, in vain, the forbidden name of a woman. He can beg for explanations, he is allowed to fail and upon waking wipe away his tears, his snot, and his curses.)

It might have happened the following day. The old man, with his thin, expressionless face, which was older than he, might have waited a little longer. Half a week, let's say. Until he saw her sauntering through what had been a garden, between the house and the shed, hanging diapers on the line.

He lit the dangling cigarette and mumbled grumpily to his workers before moving: "I want to find out if they'll pay us two weeks in advance."

Very slowly, almost groaning, he managed to stand up and hobbled over to the woman. He found her without hope, more childish than ever, almost as liberated from the world and its promises as he was. The seminarian architect looked at her with pity, fraternally.

"Listen, ma'am," he said. "I don't need an answer. With you, not even words."

Laboriously, he pulled out of his pant pocket a fistful of recently opened roses, prodigiously small, common, with broken stems. She took them without hesitating, wrapped them in a damp rag and continued to wait. She wasn't mistrustful; and the only thing the tired eyes of the old man did was open the way to an ancient desire to cry, a desire no longer connected to her current life, to herself. She didn't say thank you.

"Listen, my dear," the old man asked of her again. "Those, the roses, are for you to forget or forgive. It's the same thing. It doesn't matter, we don't want to know what we're talking about. When the flowers die and you have to throw them out, consider that we are, whether we like it or not, siblings in Christ. They have surely told you many things about me, even though you live in isolation. But I'm not crazy. I see and I endure."

He lowered his head to say goodbye and left. Tired out by the monologue, he started to hear in the still and stormy afternoon air the prelude
to the five peals of the bell.

"Let's go," he said to the well diggers. "There's no advance, it seems."

After several nights wavering between waiting and a directionless hope,
one night facing the boredom of the book and indomitable sleep, she heard
the sound of the car in the garage, the muted whistle carefully rising with
the stairs. Ignorant, definitely innocent of so many things, the man was
whistling "The Man I Love."

She watched him move around, the expression on her face greeted him,
she accepted the glass he handed her.

"Did you go to the doctor?" the woman asked. "You promised you
would. Or did you swear it?"

His bony profile smiled without turning, happy to give her something.

"Yes, I went. There's nothing. A naked skeletal man standing in front
of a mild-mannered fat man. The customary X-rays and tests. A fat man in
a lab coat, perhaps not overly clean, who had no faith in his little hammer,
in his stethoscope, in the instructions he wrote down. No, there's nothing
going on that they can understand, or cure."

She accepted, for the first time, another overflowing glass. She moved
her fingers and took a cigarette. She was laughing and stiffened her body
to stifle a cough. The man looked at her, astonished, almost happy. He took
a step to sit down on the bed; but she slowly moved away from the sheets,
from the paternal caress. She still had half a cigarette and kept smoking,
cautious.

Her back was turned to him when she asked: "Why did you marry me?"

The man looked at her thin contours, the tangled hair on the back of her neck; then he walked away, toward the armchair and the table. Another glass, another cigarette, quick and confident. The woman's question had aged, grown wrinkled, spread in disarray like ivy clinging by its nails to a wall. But he had to stall for time; because the woman, though they never knew it, though nobody ever knew it, was more intelligent and more wretched than the skinny man, her husband.

"You didn't have any money, so that wasn't it," the man tried to joke. "The money came later, through no fault of my own. Your mother, your brothers."

"I already thought about that. Nobody could have guessed. And anyway, you don't care about money. Which is even worse, I sometimes think. So, again: why did you marry me?"

The man smoked for a while in silence, nodding, stretching his pale lips over the glass.

"Everything?" he asked finally; he was filled with cowardice and pity.

"Everything, of course." The woman sat up in bed to watch his hard, determined head shrink.

"I didn't do it because you were pregnant with Mendle's baby, either. There was no compassion, no desire to help somebody else. So it was very simple. I loved you, I was in love. It was love."

"And it's gone," she said from bed, almost shouting. But also, inevitably, asking.

"After so much guile and dissembling and betrayal. It's gone. I couldn't say if it needed weeks or months or preferred to fade away slowly, one hour then another hour. It's so difficult to explain. Assuming I know, understand. Here, in the resort that Petrus invented, you were the girl. With or without a fetus inside you. The girl, the almost woman, who can be contemplated sadly, with the dreadful sensation that it is no longer possible. The hair goes, the teeth rot. And, above all, to find out that curiosity was being aroused in you when I was beginning to lose mine. It's possible that my marriage to you was my last real curiosity."

She kept waiting, in vain. Finally she got up, put on a robe, and stood facing the man sitting at the table.

"Everything?" she asked. "Are you sure? I'm asking you, please. And if necessary, I'll get on my knees . . . For this little bit of the past that we are helping each other trample, without a commitment, freely, for this little bit of the past that we crouch down over to find relief, shoulder to shoulder, for reasons of space . . ."

The man, his cigarette hanging out of his thinned mouth, turned toward her and the vertebrae cracked in his neck. Without pity or surprise, listless out of habit, she was looking at the face of a corpse.

"Everything?" the man said scornfully. "More of everything?" he was talking to the glass he held up, to lost moments, to what he believed himself to be. "Everything? Maybe you didn't understand. I was talking, I think, about the girl."

"About me."

"About the girl," he insisted.

The voice, the confusion, the careful slowness of his movements. He was drunk and approaching vulgarity. She smiled, invisible and happy.

"That's what I said," the man continued slowly, watchful. "What every normal man looks for, invents, finds, or is made to believe he's found. Not a woman who understands, protects, pampers, helps, makes right, corrects, improves, supports, advises, directs, manages. None of that, thank you."

"I?"

"Yes, now; and all the bloody rest," he said and leaned on the table to get up to go to the bathroom.

She took off her robe, the orphan-girl slip, and waited for him. She waited for him until she saw him emerge clean and naked from the bathroom, until he gave her a vague caress and, lying next to her in bed, began to breathe like a child, peacefully, without memory or sin, submerged in the unmistakable silence where a woman stifles her cries, her tamed exasperation, her atavistic sense of injustice.

The second well digger, thin and languid, who appeared to not understand life or ask it for meaning, solutions, turned out to be easier, more hers. Perhaps because of the man's way of being, perhaps because she had him many times.

After five she'd wound herself on the Jerusalem thorn bushes, her eyes closed. She'd slowly lick her hands and wrists. Gangly, hesitant, not understanding, the second well digger would arrive at six and let himself be led to the shed that smelled of confinement and sheep.

Naked, he'd become childlike and fearful, pleading. The woman employed all her memories, her sudden inspirations. She usually spit on him and slapped him, she was able to find, inside the metal walls and the ceiling, an old riding crop, not oiled, forgotten.

She enjoyed whistling for him to come, like to a dog, snapping her fingers. One week, two weeks or three.

Nevertheless, each blow, each humiliation, each payment, and each joy carried her into the fullness and sweat of summer, into a culmination that can only be followed by a descent.

She was happy with the young man and sometimes they cried together, not knowing each other's reasons. But, slowly and fatefully the woman had to return from desperate sex to the need for love. It was better, she believed, to be alone and sad. She didn't see the well diggers again; she went down at dusk, after six, and cautiously approached the hedge.

"Blood," the man said, waking her up when he returned at dawn. "Blood on your hands and your face."

"It's nothing," she answered, waiting for sleep to return. "I still like to play with the trees."

One night the man returned and woke her up; he poured himself a drink as he loosened his tie. Sitting on the bed, the woman heard him laugh and contrasted it to the clear, fresh, irrepressible sound she used to hear from him years before.

"Mendle," he finally said. "Your marvelous, irresistible friend Mendle. And, therefore, my bosom buddy. He was arrested yesterday. Not because of my papers, my documents, but because it had to end like this."

She asked for a shot without soda and drank it down in one gulp.

"Mendle," she said in astonishment, incapable of understanding, of figuring it out.

"And as for me," the man mumbled in a truthful tone, "all day I didn't know if it would be better for him if I turned the dirty papers over to the judge or burned them."

Then, in the middle of summer, the afternoon arrived, the one foreseen long ago, when she still had her wild garden and the well diggers had not yet come to destroy it.

She walked through the garden flattened by the concrete and, smiling, threw herself with old and familiar skill against the Jerusalem thorn bushes and the pain.

She glanced off them in softness and docility, as if the plants had suddenly turned into rubber canes. The thorns no longer had the strength to wound, and they barely leaked milk, a slow and viscous liquid, white, sluggish. She tried other trunks and they were all the same – malleable, inoffensive, oozing.

At first she despaired and then she ended up accepting; that was her custom. It was already after five in the afternoon and the workers had left. On her way she pulled on some flowers and leaves and then stopped to pray, standing under the immortal araucaria tree. Someone was screaming, hungry or frightened, upstairs. With a crushed flower in her hand, she began to climb the stairs.

She nursed the baby until she felt him fall asleep. The she crossed herself and shuffled into the bedroom. She rummaged around in the closet and found, almost immediately, among the shirts and underpants, the useless, impotent Smith and Wesson. It was all a game, a ritual, a preamble.

But she recited again, as she looked at the bluish polish of the weapon, the first two verses of Hail Mary; she slipped until she fell on the bed, reconstructed the first time and had to surrender, crying, see again the moon from that night, yielding like a child. The cold barrel of the dead gun went past her teeth and rested against her palate.

Back in the baby's room she stole the hot water bottle. In the bedroom, she wrapped the Smith and Wesson in it, waiting patiently for the barrel to reach body temperature for her eager mouth.

She acknowledged, without shame, the farce she was enacting. Then she heard, unhurriedly, fearlessly, the three failed strikes of the firing pin. She heard, for a split second, the fourth shot of the bullet that smashed through her head. Without understanding, she spent some time in that first night and its moon, she believed that once again she had in her throat the spilled taste of the man, so like fresh grass, happiness, and summer. She advanced persistently into every corner of the destroyed dream and brain, into every moment of fatigue as she climbed the endless hill, half naked, bent under her suitcase. The moon kept growing. Pushing her small breasts, radiant and hard as zinc, through the night, she kept walking until she sank into the boundless moon that had waited for her, confidently, for years, not many.

1963

On the Thirty-First

At the very moment the entire city became aware that midnight had finally arrived, I was alone and almost in the dark, looking at the river and the light of the streetlamp from the coolness of the window while I smoked and once again endeavored to find a memory that would thrill me, a reason to feel sorry for myself and blame the world, contemplate with some kind of exhilarating hatred the lights of the city that were advancing to my left.

I had completed earlier than expected the drawing of the two children in their pajamas who were astonished anew each morning to see the pile of Christmas gifts – horses, dolls, cars, and scooters – spilling over the shoes placed carefully on the hearth to receive them. According to the agreement, I had copied the drawing from an advertisement published in *Companion*. The most difficult part was to capture the fawning expressions on the faces of the parents peeping out from behind a curtain and to stop myself from scrawling feathery letters across the drawing in crimson with a sable-hair brush: "Long Liv Hapines!"

Instead, I spent the forty minutes that separated me from the New Year, from my birthday, and from my promised return to Frieda, painting a new sign for the bathroom in green lettering. The old one was faded and splashed with soap and toothpaste. Moreover, it was written in horrible cursive handwriting, the kind used on those little plaques idiots hang on their walls: SMALL HOUSE BIG HEART, WELCOME, YOUNG SHIP OLD CAPTAIN.

I bought a present for Frieda and it was waiting for her, wrapped in blue paper, next to her glass, the bottle of caña, the small plate of shiny fruit, some turrón and nuts at the place at the table where she usually sat. I also bought her a cigar and a pack of razor blades so she could cut her hair. Although we'd only been living together for a short time, such gifts were customary for the anniversaries we observed and invented. She expressed her gratitude with astonishingly obscene insults that were sometimes convincing and promised revenge, and she always ended up accepting my good intentions, my regard, and my careless understanding. Her gifts, on the other hand, were jobs, ways of earning money, gimmicks to make me forget that I was living off her.

On Saturday nights, when lots of people were around, as she started to get drunk, Frieda would go sit on the toilet and, for a few minutes or quarters of an hour, as long as nobody went to look for her, she'd sit nearly motionless, her knickers around her knees, cutting her bangs with a razor blade, staring greedily with the alert eyes of a bird at the little sign tacked up between the medicine cabinet and the sink, the one I was replacing to surprise her, with those verses of Baudelaire's that say: "Thank you, dear God, for not making me a woman, or black or Jewish or a dog or short of stature." Nobody who used the toilet could leave without having prayed those words.

But on that New Year's Eve we had wanted – or we had wrapped ourselves in lies until we were committed – to be alone and attempt to feel happy. She had sworn she'd drop everything – her dance students, her clients at the dress shop, unexpected propositions – to be alone with me before midnight. I didn't have much to drop to do likewise; on New Year's Eve, someone, some female member of that sinister tribe, would spend her time till dawn in contemplation of the oscillations of the old year's head.

It wasn't happiness but it was the least possible amount of effort. Frieda would arrive, though she didn't, before the New Year. We would eat something and we would spend our time, expertly putting things off so as not to ruin them, getting drunk; I would ask questions with feigned interest to encourage her to repeat the monologue about her childhood and her adolescence in Santa María, the story of her expulsion, the whimsical, variable evocations of that lost paradise.

Perhaps, at the end of the night, we would make love in the large bed, on the rug in the main room, or on the balcony. I wouldn't care if we did or not; but I'd never met a woman so skilled at continuing to surprise, so willing to confess. Whenever she felt like sleeping with me and her drunkenness forced her to converse, it was like possessing a dozen women and finding out about them all. She might, moreover, agree to celebrate the New Year stretched out on her back on the floor or the mattress.

I was at the window, smoking and drinking booze with lots of water, when the honking and gunshots began. It was impossible for me to think about myself, so I thought about María Eugenia and Seoane, my son; I forced myself to suffer and blame myself, I remembered anecdotes that didn't manage to mean anything.

Everything had been or was like that, just like that, although perhaps otherwise, and every person imaginable could offer a different version.

And undoubtedly not only could I not be pitied but I wasn't even credible. Others existed, and I watched them live, and the love I gave them was nothing more than the manifestation of my love for life.

In Montevideo they'd already forgotten about midnight. The lights toward Ramírez Beach began to grow sparse and the couples dancing at the Parque Hotel would already be traipsing to and from the sand by the time the New Year really began. Some Candombe drums again rang out, deep, lonely, unvanquished, from the area around the barracks, and blurred the words.

But I recognized Frieda's voice – insecure, yielding, running out of steam. She shouted *Himmel* and I walked through the apartment silently and in the dark took a few steps down the brick staircase, which led into the garden and the gate.

The only light out there came, diluted, from El Proa. But I could see her, all decked out, between two dry flowerbeds, athletic, swaying with strength, while that miscarried fetus of tubercular parents, dark-skinned and wearing a skirt, her head miraculously enlarged by a day of work in a cheap beauty salon, said to her: "'Cause how I see it, bitch, you thought you were gonna play me, 'cause if you're with me you ain't with nobody else." She slapped her and Frieda let her; then she started hitting her with her purse, methodically and without stopping.

I sat on a step and lit a cigarette. *Frieda can crush her with one hand*, I thought. *Frieda can send her flying into the river with a single kick.*

But Frieda had chosen to begin her year in this way: with her hands on her ass, expanding the width of her shoulders in her tailored suit, letting herself get beaten up, and enjoying it, answering the blows of the purse with her hoarse *Himmel*, which sounded like it was asking for more.

When that piece of shit got tired of hitting her, the two of them cried and walked out of the garden and into the street. I saw them stop, out of breath, then start up again, their arms around each other. Then I went upstairs to turn on all the lights and prepare a proper New Year's homecoming for Frieda.

I held her under the lavishness of the standing lamp, or she was there alone, in the armchair, her blond hair covering her forehead, her mouth twisted with sin and bitterness, her right eyebrow raised as usual and now curving over a black eye. With her lips split and bleeding, blood she didn't want to stanch, she obliged me to begin the New Year with a conversation about Santa María. Her family had thrown her out, and they sent her money on a monthly basis because, since the age of fourteen, she had spent her time getting drunk and creating scandals and making love with all the sexes envisaged by divine wisdom.

I say this in tribute to her, who acted more Catholic every Sunday, and who every Saturday, every Saturday at dawn, filled my apartment – which she paid for – with women who were increasingly older, more astonishing and wretched. She talked about her provincial childhood and her family of *junkers*, totally to blame for the fact that now, in Montevideo, she had no choice but to get drunk and reiterate scandal and dissolute love. She spoke until daybreak of that first of January, about missed opportunities and others' guilt, already drunk before she arrived, caressing her half-closed eye, enjoying the pain of her split and swollen lips.

"I thought . . . ," she said, smiling, "you're not going to believe me . . . I thought I saw Seoane on the corner."

"At this time of night? Anyway, he would have come up to see me."

"Maybe he didn't come to see you."

"Yes, my dear," I said.

"Not to visit you. Maybe to spy on the house, to see if you were coming or going."

"Could be," I said, because I don't like to talk about Seoane with Frieda or maybe with anybody.

She talked, like all women do, about an ideal Frieda; she was amazed by the incessant triumph of injustice and incomprehension; she looked for, offered up, guilty parties without hating them.

She didn't say anything about that inexplicable monstrosity who'd been hitting her in the face with her purse. I was already used to her need for increasingly cheap and filthy lovers. Since time lacks importance, since simultaneity is a detail that depends on the whims of memory, it was easy for me to recall nights when the apartment where Frieda allowed me to live was inhabited by numerous women she'd brought from the street, from the bars in the port, from Victoria Plaza. Some were beautiful and well dressed, wearing only a little bit of jewelry, anklets, dark suits complemented by pearls.

But lately there had been an abundance of insolent and filthy mestiza women, with burning cigarettes hanging from their foul mouths. Frequently their acrimonious dialogues prevented me from sleeping, and I'd jump out of bed and run through the apartment chewing on a cigarette as if it were an olive branch, making my way with difficulty past women crouching, sitting on the table, spread-eagle on the divan, kneeling in the kitchen, changing their clothes in the bathroom, lying in the sun or the moonlight on the balcony's red tiles.

"Herrera paid," Frieda said. "He did the right thing, so he could start the year off right, and maybe it'll bring him good luck."

The banknotes had fallen off my chest and onto the table. I picked them up without taking off the rubber band around them; they were hundred-peso bills.

"He paid all of it?" I asked.

Frieda started laughing then sucked on her split lip.

"Give me a drink and a smoke. That poor tramp. But it's so lovely to keep surrendering, to let them do whatever they want, and they don't have a clue who you are. To surrender until it suddenly occurs to somebody that it's over and then you stop tolerating it and getting pleasure from surrendering, and then you do the most outrageous thing in the world with all your desire and happiness. Out of revenge; and not out of pride or a desire to get even, but because pleasure suddenly consists of hitting and not letting yourself be hit. Right?"

"I understand," I said. I listened to her while I made the roll of banknotes dance on my hand.

"Are you going to help me? When the time comes, I mean, if it comes."

"Of course," I said, putting the money in my pants pocket; I filled a glass with caña and gave it to her, placed a cigarette in her mouth, and lit it with a match. "Whenever you want. Did he pay or didn't he? I mean, did he pay everything once and for all?"

Frieda got up bursting with laughter and fell on her side, spraying the floor with spit.

"I think that dirty . . ." and she pressed on her ribs then made a childish face as she listened to what remained of the night. "That filthy bitch kneed me in the stomach. It's nothing. Yes, he paid everything. I told him it was the last payment. I don't know if that's true, I don't know if within a week, when he's playing with his kids and their Christmas presents, I'll show up and ask him for more money. And I don't care about Herrera's money. You see, you already took it. I care about messing him up, that's my relationship with him and it's got to stay that way."

"Frieda," I said in a very loud voice. She wriggled in the armchair and finally lifted her head. She was drunk, smiling like a little girl, and tears began to fall from her eyes. I put the money on the table, taking care it didn't roll off. "That's no good. You have to put an end to things with Herrera."

She shrugged her shoulders and kept looking at me as if she loved me, with such a sad and astonished smile, as she lazily stuck out her tongue to lick her tears.

"As you wish," she said. "Give me another drink, let's go celebrate the New Year."

1964

The Kidnapped Bride

There was nothing happening in Santa María; it was autumn, with just a touch of the bright sweetness of a moribund, punctual, slowly extinguishing sun. There was nothing happening for a whole range of people of Santa María, who looked up at the sky and down at the earth before consenting to the suitable futility of work.

Without consonants, there was nothing happening that autumn I spent in Santa María until the fifteenth of March when everything started, without violence, as soft as the Kleenex that women carry discreetly in their purses, as soft as paper, tissue paper, silky, slipping between their thighs.

There was nothing going on in Santa María that autumn until the arrival of the appointed hour – whether accursed or fatal or definitive and ineluctable – the happy hour when the lie arrived and yellow seeped in around the edges of the Venetian lace.

They told me, Moncha, that this story had already been written and also, less importantly, lived, by a different Moncha in the south, which the Yankees had liberated and destroyed, in some fluctuating place in Brazil, in a shire in an England with the Old Vic.

I told you, Moncha, that it doesn't matter because this is, barely, a letter of love or affection or respect or loyalty. You always knew, I think, that I was fond of you and that the words that come before or after are weaker because they are born out of pity. You preferred compassion. I'm telling you this, Moncha, in spite of everything. Many will be called upon to read this, but only you, now, have been chosen to hear.

You are now immortal, and for all those years that you may or may not remember, you managed to avoid wrinkles, whimsical varicose drawings on swollen legs, the deplorable ineptitude of your small head, old age.

Just a few hours ago, Moncha, I was drinking coffee and anisette, surrounded by witches who stopped talking in order to stare at you, to visit the washroom, or to sniffle behind hankies. But I know more and I know better, and I swear to you that God approved of your hoax and also knew how to reward it.

They tell me, moreover, that if I persist in doing this, I should begin at the end then return to the perplexing progress you made on all fours when you were a year old, skip over the fright of your first menstruation, then alight again with mystery and deception upon the end, go back to when you were twenty and took that trip, then immediately to your first, sinister, inconsolable abortion.

But you and I, Moncha, have coincided so often in our ignorance of the scandal that I prefer to tell it to you from the beginning that matters and end with the wave, the farewell. You will thank me, you will laugh at my memory, you will not shake your head when you hear what I probably shouldn't tell you. As if you were already trained to know that words are more powerful than events.

No, not ever, not for you. Deep down you never understood any words that didn't mutely announce money, security, something that would allow you to settle those large hips and that skinny torso into a wide, accommodating armchair that belonged to someone recently widowed.

This is not a love letter or a eulogy; it is a letter of having been fond of you and understood you from the immemorial beginning to the repeated kiss on your yellow feet, oddly dirty and odorless.

Moncha, once again, I remember and I know that regiments saw you naked and made use of you. That you opened yourself up without any violence but your own, that you kissed in bed, that they did almost the same to you.

Now the ladies are arriving to see your new and definitive nakedness; to cleanse you with rotten sponges and concentrated puritanical tenacity. Your feet are still frail and dirty.

Compared to your mouth, soft and kind now for the first time, nothing I can tell you from memory matters. Compared to the odor pervading you and surrounding you, nothing matters. Least of all myself, of course, among everybody, I, who begin to smell the first, timid, almost pleasant signs of your putrefaction. Because I was always too old for you, and you never inspired in me any possible desire other than, one far-off day, to write you a sort-of love letter, a brief letter, scarcely even a letter, a lineup of words that would tell you everything. A short letter, I repeat, that I could not foresee when I would see you, grotesque and sorrowful, walking down the streets of Santa María, or when I would find you, grotesque and sorrowful and impassive, in the obstinate resolve of your costume among the ubiquitous and never-revealed taunts, and I would contribute wordlessly to the creation and imposition of the respect that had been owed to you for centuries, for being a woman and for demurely and ineluctably carrying your person between your legs.

And it's a lie, but I saw you parade past the church when Santa María rid itself of its first, timid, almost innocent brothel; young, energetic, and awkward, tripping over yourself, an expression on your face of abstinence and defiance behind the placard boldly and bashfully blazing with tall and narrow black lettering: WE WANT CHASTE FIANCÉS AND HEALTHY HUSBANDS.

The letter, Moncha, unforeseeable, but that I now pretend to have foreseen from the beginning. The letter conceived on an island that is not called Santa María, that has a name pronounced with a guttural *f*, even though it might be called *Bisinidem*, without any possible *f*; a solitude for us; a persistent fixation for the obsessed and the bewitched.

With cunning, means, humility, love of truth, the desire to be clear and to establish order, I abandon the I and pretend to lose myself in the we. Everybody did the same.

Because the indolence of the umbrella of a pseudonym, of signing without a signature, is easy: J.C.O. I've done it many times.

It's easy to play when writing; according to what Old Man Lanza said, or what some reckless person told us he said about her: a defiant look in the eyes, a sensual and scornful mouth, the strength of her jaw.

It was already done once.

But the Basque girl, Moncha Insurralde or Insaurralde, returned to Santa María. She returned, as everybody returned, returns, after a certain period of time, everybody who had their goodbye-forever party and now wanders, stagnates, attempts to survive by leaning against anything small and solid, a square meter of land far away, in Europe, in a place called Paris, far away from the dream, the great dream. We could say they return, turn back. But the fact remains that we have them back with us in Santa María, and we listen to their explanations for their unforgettable failure, for the unfair why-not. They protest under their breaths with rage until they begin to wail like newborns. In any case they protest, explain, complain, spurn. But we grow bored; we know they will cheerfully disguise their failures and their embellished memories, falsified out of necessity, without any conscious intention. We know they came back to stay and continue to live, once again.

So the key, for a patriotic and friendly narrator, is, has to be, somebody else's incomprehensible lack of comprehension, bad luck, somebody else's, also, and equally incomprehensible. But they do return and cry, squirm, settle in, and stay.

That's why, in the very different Santa María of today, with its raised roadways, we have what any big city can and does have without the need for tedious expropriations at sad but rock-bottom prices. We acknowledge the appropriate ratio: ten to a hundred, a hundred to a thousand, a thousand to a million. But in Santa María there is and always will be, accompanied by new faces and elbows that replace the last ones to have vanished, our Picasso, our Béla Bartók, our Picabia, our Lloyd Wright, our Ernest Hemingway – a bearded and abstemious heavyweight, a hale and hearty hunter of flies who are paralyzed by the cold.

Many more failures, caricatures that start us thinking, awkward and obstinate replicas. We say yes, we accept, and we must, it seems, try to keep on living.

Everyone, however, came back, even if not everyone went away. Díaz Grey came without ever having left us. Insurralde, the Basque girl, was here but then she fell from the sky and still we don't know; that's why we're telling.

It's still a mystery that Moncha Insurralde came back from Europe and didn't speak to any of us, the notables. She locked herself up in her house, refused to receive anybody, and we forgot about her for three months. Then, without us seeking word of her, it arrived at the Club and at the Plaza Bar. It was inevitable, Moncha, that there would be divisions among us. Some of us didn't believe it and we asked for another round of drinks, a deck of cards, a chessboard, in order to change the subject. Others believed we were impartial, and we allowed the already dead winter evenings to drag themselves past the hotel windows while we played poker, while we waited with motionless faces for the expected and undeniable confirmation. Others knew it to be true, and we drifted between the impossible lust of understanding and a sealed secret.

The first bits of news made us uncomfortable, but they brought hope, took flight after being born in another world, so different, so alien. That scandal would not reach the city, would not graze its temples, the peace of Santa María's households, especially the nocturnal postprandial peace, those perfect hours of digestion and hypnotism in the face of a world so inept as to be absurd, of the crass and joyfully shared idiocy that flickered and stuttered out of television sets.

The idly high walls surrounding the house of Insaurralde, the dead Basque man, protected us from the cries and the vision. Crime, sin, the truth, and weak madness could not touch us, did not drag themselves among us, leaving behind as insult or lucidity a thin quivering line of silver drool.

Moncha locked herself up in the house, shut away behind four brick walls of extraordinary height. Moncha – also protected by a housekeeper, a cook, an idle chauffeur, a gardener, servants of both sexes – was a distant lie, easy to forget and disbelieve, a remote and white legend.

We knew, it was known, that she slept like the dead in the mansion, that on dangerous moonlit nights she wandered around the garden, the orchard, the neglected lawn, dressed in her wedding gown. She moved slowly back and forth, upright and solemn, from one wall to the other, from nightfall till the moon dissolved into the dawn.

And we, all of us in Santa María, were safe, ignorance and oblivion permitting, protected by the high-walled quadrilateral, serene and ironic, able to disbelieve the faraway, absent whiteness, the ambulatory white ray under the always greater whiteness of the round or horned moon.

The woman descending from the four-in-hand carriage, from the scent of citron, from the Russian leather. The woman advancing implacably and calmly through the garden we deem enormous, where we let exotic plants grow, not detouring around rhododendrons and rubber trees, not brushing up against the straight trees with orchids, not fracturing their nonexistent perfume, always and weightlessly hanging on the arm of her godfather. Until he whispered without lips, tongue, or teeth the insincere, ritual, and ancient words to give her, without violence, with just a touch of unavoidable and elegant manly resentment, to the groom in the abandoned garden, white with moon and gown.

And then, slowly, on each clear night, the ceremony of the hand, now childlike, held out with its slight and reawakened tremor, awaiting the ring. In this other deserted and freezing park, she, on her knees facing his ghost, listening to those obligatory Latin words that slid down from the heavens. To love and to obey, for better or for worse, in sickness and in health, until death do us part.

All of this so beautiful and unreal, each inexorable white night repeated tirelessly and without hope. Shut away behind the insolent height of four walls, separated from our peace, our routine.

At that time in Santa María there were many newer and better doctors, but almost immediately after her return from Europe, and before she shut herself away behind those walls, Moncha Insaurralde, the Basque girl, called Dr. Díaz Grey, made an appointment, climbed the two flights of stairs one afternoon, and smiled stupidly, short of breath, her hand pressed to her chest and lifting her left breast so that it would rest where she thought she had her heart, too close to her shoulder.

She said she was going to die; she said she was going to get married. She seemed, or was, so different. The inevitable Díaz Grey tried to remember her from a few years before, when she escaped from Santa María, from the phalanstery, when she thought that Europe promised at least a change of skin.

"Nothing, I don't have any symptoms," the girl said. "I don't know why I came to see you. If I were sick I would have gone to a real doctor. I'm sorry. But one day you'll realize that you are more than that. My father was your friend. Maybe that's why I came."

Skinny and heavy, she rose, swaying without coquetry, propelling her unbalanced body with weary resolve.

Still a beautiful filly, a purebred mare with painful splints, the doctor thought. *If I could wash your face and examine it, that's all, your invisible face under the violet, the red, the yellow, the thin black lines that elongate your eyes without any certain or comprehensible intent.*

If I could see you once again challenging Santa María's idiocy, without defenses or protection or masks, with your hair loosely tied back in a ponytail, with just the right masculine ingredient that makes a woman, without fuss, into a person. That incomprehensible fourth or fifth sex that we call a girl.

Another madwoman, another sweet and tragic madwoman, another Julita Malabia so soon among us, right here with us, and we can do nothing but suffer her and love her.

She approached his desk as Díaz Grey unbuttoned his coat and lit a cigarette; she opened her purse upside down and spilled everything out, and a tube – a feminine fetish – rolled slowly away. The doctor didn't look: he saw only her, wanted only to see her face.

She took out the banknotes, counted them in disgust, and put them down next to the doctor's elbow.

Madwoman, incurable, no questions possible.

"I'm paying," said Moncha. "I'm paying for you to prescribe something for me, to cure me, to repeat after me: 'I'm going to get married, I'm going to die.'"

Not touching the money, not refusing it, Díaz Grey stood up, pulled off his very white, very starched coat, and looked at the tense profile, the vulgar makeup, its astonishing combination of colors now changing against the light from the window.

"You are going to get married," he repeated obediently.

"And I am going to die."

"That is not a diagnosis."

She smiled briefly, reclaiming her adolescence, as she put everything back into her purse. Pieces of paper, cards, jewelry, perfume, toilet paper, a golden powder compact, candies, pills, a half-eaten biscuit, perhaps a crumpled envelope musty with time.

"But it's not enough, doctor. You have to come with me. My car's down-stairs. It's not far away; I'm living, for a few days or forever, who knows who wins, at the hotel."

Díaz Grey went and saw, as a father. While looking at the secret, he absentmindedly caressed Moncha's restless nape; he grazed her elbows, his gestures brushed against a breast.

He, Díaz Grey, saw one tenth of what a woman would have seen or been able to explain. Silks, laces, picots, sinuous foam across the bed.

"Do you understand now?" the woman said without asking. "It's for my wedding gown. Marcos Bergner and Father Bergner," she laughed as she looked at the whiteness rippling across the dark mattress. "The whole family. Father Bergner is going to marry me to Marcos. We still haven't decided on a date."

Díaz Grey lit a cigarette as he took a step back. The priest had died in his sleep two years earlier; Marcos had died six months before, after food and alcohol, on top of a woman. But, he thought, none of that mattered. The truth was what could still be heard, seen, perhaps touched. The truth was that Moncha Insaurralde had returned from Europe to marry Marcos Bergner in the cathedral with the blessings of Bergner, the priest.

He agreed and said, as he stroked her back:

"Yes. It's true. I was sure of it."

Moncha got on her knees to kiss the lace, soft and meticulous.

"I couldn't be happy there. We arranged everything by mail."

It was impossible for the entire city to participate in the conspiracy of lies and silence. But Moncha was surrounded, even before the gown, by lead, by cork, by a silence that prevented them from understanding or even hearing the distortions of her truth, the one we'd created for her, the one we'd kneaded along with her. Father Bergner was in Rome, always returning on colorful postcards with the Vatican in the background, always shuffling from one chamber to another, always bidding farewell to cardinals, archbishops, silk robes, an infinite theory of ephebi dressed as altar boys, flagons, swift swirls of incense smoke.

Marcos Bergner was always returning on his yacht from mythical coasts, always tied to the mainmast through unavoidable and always weathered storms, every day or night playing at the helm, maybe a little drunk, his unforgettable face accompanying his return, with the salt and the iodine that lengthened his beard and turned it red, like the happy tip of an English brand of cigarette.

This: not knowing the dates of safe returns, the indubitable and unverifiable value of the word or the promise of an Insaurralde, a Basque word or the word of a Basque man that was dropped and carried weight without needing to be spoken once and for all forever after. One thought, just barely, perhaps never, thought out fully; the ambition of a promise inserted into the world, hanging there indestructible, always defiant, stronger and more decisive if concealed by bad weather, rain, wind, hail, moss, the furious sun, and time alone.

So we, all of us, without premonitions or regrets, helped her sink during that first brief stage, during the prologue written for the sake of the ignorant. We said to her, yes, we accepted that it was urgent and necessary, and it's possible that we even touched her on the shoulder so that she would board the train; it's possible that we waited, that we hoped not to see her again.

And that's how Moncha, Moncha Insaurralde or Insurralde, encouraged by our good will, our well-earned hypocrisy, went to the Capital – in the language of the scribes at *El Liberal* newspaper – so that Madame Caron would turn her silks, laces, and picots into a wedding gown worthy of her, of Santa María, of the deceased Marcos Bergner – dead but on his yacht – of the deceased Father Bergner – dead but endlessly bidding farewell from the Vatican, from Rome, from the crumbling church of the town we were able to dream up.

Once again, though, she went to the Capital and returned to us with a wedding gown that the disappointed reporters on the social page would be able to describe in their hermetic, nostalgic style: "The day of her wedding, held in the Basílica del Santísimo Sacramento, she wore a crepe gown with *strass* embroidery around a high waist. A *strass* headdress shaped like a snood adorned her head and held the tulle veil; she carried a bouquet of *phalaenopsis* and the wedding was held in the Basílica de Nuestra Señora de Socorro, the bride wearing a princess gown of embroidered organza. On top of her bouffant hairdo was a crown with small flowers atop the bun, from which hung a tulle veil, and in her hand she carried a rosary. At San Nicolás de Bari, in the meantime, the bride wore an A-line gown with an overskirt whose hem was edged with satin camellias, a motif that was repeated in the headdress that held the tulle veil; and again in the main church of Santa María she showed up in an original A-line gown, a long tulle veil attached to her hair with mother-of-pearl flowers stretching down both sides of her sleeves and fastened at her wrists, and in her hand she carried a bouquet of tulips and citron blossoms."

She left, bounced, rebounded, like a fully inflated soccer ball, not yet flattened and dead. She left and came back to us, to Santa María.

And then we all believed; we confronted the improbable guilt. She, Moncha, was crazy. But we had all contributed out of love, kindness, good intentions, languid mockery, the respectable desire to feel comfortable and sheltered, the desire that nobody – not even crazy, dead, alive, healthy, admirably dressed Moncha – would make us lose a moment of sleep or everyday pleasure.

We accepted her, in the end, and we had her. May God – Brausen – forgive us.

She didn't tell us about the ceilings of hotels, about country outings, monuments, ruins, museums, historical names that referred to battles, artists, or plunders. She gave to us when wind or light or a whim forced her to. She gave, had been giving to us, without questions, without beginnings or ends:

"I arrived in Venice at dawn. I barely slept all night, my head leaning against the window, watching as the lights of cities and towns that I was seeing for the first and last time passed by, and when I closed my eyes I smelled the strong scent of the wood, the leather of the uncomfortable seats, and I heard voices that now and then whispered sentences I couldn't understand. When I got off the train and left the station that had its lights still on it was about five thirty in the morning. I walked half asleep through the empty streets to San Marcos, which was totally deserted except for the pigeons and some beggars leaning against the columns. From far away it was so exactly like the postcards I'd seen, the colors were so perfect, the complicated silhouettes of the domed roofs against the rising sun, it was all as unreal as the fact that I was there, that I was the only person there at that moment. I walked slowly, as if sleepwalking, and I sensed that I was sobbing – it was as if that solitude, seeing that it was as perfect as I had expected, became part of me forever, though it was the closest thing to a waking dream one can have. And afterwards – it happened before, one night in Barcelona – there was the boy dressed as a torero with tight red pants who danced inside the circle formed by the tables. I remember when we went upstairs and sat at a table looking over the dance floor, when almost everybody had left, and the two boys danced very close together, both the same height, both dark-skinned, and the owner who offered me a partner, and how afraid I was, not knowing if he was offering me a man or a woman. And a street, I don't know where, the old houses painted in faded garish colors, the clothes hanging across the narrow street, the ragged children, their bare feet slipping over wet paving stones between stands that sold fish and octopus in strange shapes and colors."

After the undeniable months-long nightmare that was called, that we notables called in order to forget it, Corpse Collector, the male or female apprentice at Barthé's pharmacy grew broad and strong, and only the sudden whiteness of a smile recalled his shyness of years past.

"Barthé was playing with fire," said the most idiotic among us on some unspecified date as he was dealing out cards at the table in the club.

We. We knew it was so, that Barthé, the pharmacist, had been playing with fire, or with that robust animal who had at one time been a child, that he had played and ended up getting burned.

Parenthetically, however, it might be fitting to point out that the pharmacy apprentice's face, his smile, never had the brilliant radiance of cynicism. Without meaning to, he displayed, exhibited, goodness and the simple acceptance of being situated, or adapting to life, to the world that was limitless for him, to Santa María.

One of us, while dealing or being dealt cards during a poker game, spoke of the absent sorcerer, the solitary sorcerer's apprentice. We didn't respond because talking is prohibited while playing poker.

"I'll see you."

"Call. And fold."

"See you and raise you ten."

The police reports mentioned nothing, and the gossip column of *El Liberal* never found out. But all of us, sitting together around the card or drink table, knew that the Basque girl, Insaurralde, so different now, was shutting herself away at night in the pharmacy with Barthé – whose pharmacist degree was framed and exhibited, unmistakable and high on the wall behind the counter – and the apprentice, male and female, who now smiled distractedly at everybody and was, based on facts of unknown origin, the owner of the pharmacy. The three of them were inside, and all that was left for our aging curiosity, for guessing games and slander, was the blue button over the small lighted plate: EMERGENCY SERVICES.

We shuffled cards and chips, we muttered names of games and challenges, we thought voicelessly; all three; two, and one watches; two, and the one who calls, watches, I fold, I don't call, but I'm always watching. Or again: all three and the drugs, liquids or powders hidden in the pharmacy of the confused, shifting, interchangeable proprietor.

Everything was possible, even the physically impossible, for us, for four old men sitting around the cards, legitimate cheating, a variety of drinks.

As the head waiter, Francisco, would say, each of the four of us had learned, perhaps even before we'd learned to play, to sit for hours without moving a single muscle in our faces, to maintain a dead, unchanging glimmer in our eyes, to repeat weary, monotonous, bored words with indifference.

But by squashing any expression that might transmit joy, disappointment, calculated risk, large or small cunning, it became necessary, inevitable, that we show other things in our faces, the things we were determined to hide, accustomed to hiding on a daily basis, for years, every day, from the end of our dreams, every day of the week, until the beginning of our dreams.

Because it wasn't long before we found out and laughed discreetly, shaking our heads with feigned pity, with a simulacrum of comprehension, that Moncha was shut away inside the pharmacy with Barthé and his apprentice; she, always wearing her wedding gown; the boy, always exposing his naked torso without remembering; the pharmacist, always with his gout, his slippers, and the eternal, indefinable sullenness of a spinster.

The three of them poring over tarot cards and other witchcraft, pretending to believe in returns, strokes of good luck, death evaded, betrayals both predictable and expected.

Just for a moment; Barthé's fat whiteness, his eager and scowling mouth; the growing muscles of the boy who no longer needed to raise his voice to give orders; the improbable wedding gown that Moncha dragged around past counters and shelves, past those enormous caramel-colored flasks with white labels, all or almost all of them illegible.

But the strange tarot cards were always on the table and it was irresistible to return to them, be amazed, afraid, or hesitant.

And one must point out, for the benefit or discomfort of future, and likely, exegetes of the life and passion of Santa María, that those two men had ceased to belong to the novel, to the indisputable truth.

Barthé, fat and asthmatic, in hysterical retreat with grotesque and tolerated outbursts, was no longer an alderman, was nothing other than his pharmacy diploma soiled by age and dead flies hanging on the wall behind the counter, nothing other than the sporadic leader of one of ten Trotskyist organizations, each one made up of three or four dangerous revolutionaries who, with menstrual regularity, wrote and signed manifestos, declarations on and protests against diverse and exotic issues.

The boy wasn't or hadn't ever been anything more than a shy, aggrieved cynic who one winter evening approached Barthé while he lay in bed terrorized by fear, the flu, his bad conscience, the great beyond, a thirty-eight- degree fever, and said clearly and cautiously: "Two things, sir, if you'll forgive me. Make me your partner and I'll bring the notary. Or I'll leave; I'll shut the pharmacy. And the business will be finished."

They signed the contract, and the only thing Barthé still had that allowed him to believe in survival was the sadness that things hadn't turned out differently, that the partnership he had planned so long before as a belated wedding gift had been imposed through extortion and not the harmonious maturity of love.

Hence Moncha, of the three of them, in spite of her partial madness and death that can be considered a mere detail, a characteristically personal way of being, was the only one who had remained – Brausen would know for how long – alive and functional.

Like an insect? Could be. Also admissible, for being equally original, is the metaphor of the siren mercilessly removed from the water, patiently enduring the lurching and land-sickness in the den of the pharmacy. To repeat: like an insect in the sticky half-light, ensnared in the strange cards that distilled the yesterday and the today, that exhibited the inexorable future in confusion, without much commitment. The insect with its carapace of old-fashioned whiteness flying in tired circles around the sad light that fell on the table and the four hands, moving away only to crash into the carafes and window panes, slowly and awkwardly dragging its long, mute, train, so disparaged, which one long-ago day Madame Caron herself had designed and made.

And every night, after the pharmacy closed and the purple light on the wall outside that announced night service was switched on, the long white insect traced out its habitual large circles and small horizons, only to return to stillness, rubbing together or only touching its antennae over the tarot's whispered promises, over the babbling of those cards with hieratic and threatening faces, which repeated good fortunes attained after grueling labyrinths, which mentioned dates both inevitable and vague.

And, though of minor importance, it gave the half-naked boy fraternal feelings he didn't fully understand; and it gave Barthé an unsolvable problem to chew on toothlessly for what remained of his old age, sunk into the armchair that he now inhabited, twiddling his thumbs over his never diminished belly:

"If she was here and this house was like her own. If she hung around and looked around and poked around. If we both always loved her, why didn't she steal poison, which anyway wouldn't have been stealing, and finish herself off more quickly and with less suffering?"

And then it started happening to us, and it continued happening to us until the end and even a bit beyond.

Because, we insisted, just as Moncha had once returned from the phalanstery, had passed through Santa María and left us to go to Europe, she now arrived from Europe and disembarked in the Capital and returned to live with us in this Santa María that, as some have said, isn't what it used to be.

We couldn't protect you, Moncha, not in the large grey and green spaces of the avenues; we couldn't winnow out so many thousands of bodies; we couldn't reduce the height of the incongruous new buildings to make you feel more comfortable, more united with us or more alone among us. We could do very little against scandal, irony, indifference, only what was absolutely indispensable.

In a city that was erecting a wall of concrete or glass every day, that was so much greater than and so alien to us, the old men, we insisted on denying time, on pretending, on believing in the static existence of the Santa María that we saw, that we strolled through; and Moncha was enough for us.

There was something else, which didn't matter. Just as easily, with the same effort and the same pretense that we used to forget the new undeniable city, we tried to forget Moncha over our glasses and playing cards at the Plaza Bar, at our favorite restaurant, in the Club's brand-new building.

It's possible someone imposed respect, silence, with some poorly chosen sentence or other. We accepted it, we forgot Moncha, and once again we talked about the harvest, the price of wheat, the still river and its ships – and what came in and out of the holds of the ships – the fluctuations of the currency, the health of the governor's wife, the lady, Our Lady.

But nothing was working or had ever worked, neither childish tricks nor descents into exorcism. Here we were with Moncha's curse, the seventy-five-thousand-dollar illness of our lady, first installment.

So we had to wake up and believe, tell ourselves, yes, we'd been seeing it for months, and Moncha was in Santa María, and she was the way she was.

We'd seen her, found out that she rode around in taxis or in that dilapidated 1951 Opel, that she paid weary courtesy calls, remembering – perhaps with orchestrated ill-will – the dates of bygone and irredeemable anniversaries. Births, weddings, and deaths. Possibly – they exaggerate – on the exact day it became advisable and acceptable to forget a sin, an elopement, a swindle, a soiled form of farewell, cowardice.

We didn't know if she knew it all by heart, and we never found a notebook, a simple almanac with optimistic lithographs that could explain it.

Santa María has a river; it has ships. If it has a river, it has mist. The ships use horns, sirens. They blast warnings, they are there to the misfortune of the fresh-water swimmer and gazer. With your hat, your robe, your bathing suit, your picnic basket, your wife and children, you, in a quickly forgotten moment of imagination or weakness, can, could, would be able to think of the hoarse and tender cry of a baby whale calling to its mother, of the hoarse and frightened call of a mother whale. It's alright; this is what happens, more or less, in Santa María when the mist extinguishes the river.

If we could swear that the ghost lived among us and persisted for three months, the truth is that Moncha Insaurralde left her house nearly every day by taxi or in the Opel, always dressed and with that aroma and appearance of eternity – as it turned out – in the wedding gown that Madame Caron had sewn in the Capital, fashioning the silk and lace that Moncha had brought from Europe for her marriage to one of the Marcos Bergners, whom she had invented from afar, and blessed by a Father Bergner who was unchangeable, grey, and made of stone. She was the only one who had yet to die.

All things are as they are and not otherwise; even if it were possible to deal out four times thirteen after it had already been dealt out and was irretrievable.

Various surprises, categorical assertions made by old people who refuse to let go, inevitable confusions prevent us from establishing the precise day, the night of the first great alarm. Moncha arrived at the Plaza Hotel in her sputtering car, told the chauffeur to leave, and walked as if in a dream toward the table set for two that she had reserved. The bridal gown, dragging along the ground, was met with stares, and she spent hours, more than one hour, almost calm as she faced the emptiness – plates, forks, knives – she held in front of her. Vaguely pleased and affable, she queried the void and held a morsel, a cup, in the air while she listened. Everybody perceived the pedigree, the undeniably pampered upbringing. Everyone saw, in their own way, the yellowed bridal gown, the lace, torn and hanging loose in places. Fear and indifference protected her. The better ones, if there were any, merged the gown with a memory of good fortune, also worn out by time and failure.

Neither too soon nor too late, the *maître* personally – Moncha's name is Insaurralde – brought the folded check on a small plate and left it precisely in the middle between her and the other absent one, invisible, separated from us, from Santa María, by an incomprehensible distance of nautical miles, by the appetite of fish. He inquired; he was hardly even there; he bowed his fat, impassive, smiling head. He seemed to bless and consecrate; it seemed like a habit. The summer-autumn tuxedo could also be understood as a credible surplice.

The secret and solitary pilgrimages to the restaurant where she ate with Marcos had to be organized. A difficult and complex task because it wasn't an issue of mere physical displacement. It required the previous and lasting creation of a state of mind, sometimes felt, lost forever, a spirit suitable for awaiting an encounter and knowing that it would last, with pleasure, irrefutably, till the end of the night, till the exact hour when it can be confirmed that everything in Santa María is closed. And there's more: the state of mind had to be maintained and last past the hour of closing, remain in nocturnal solitude and engender the sweetness of dreams. Because it must be understood that all the rest, all that we of Santa María insisted on calling reality, was for Moncha simply a physiological feat carried out in good health. To call the *maître* of the Plaza, reserve a table that was "not too near and not too far away," announce Marcos's return and the corresponding celebration, provocatively discuss the choices on the menu, demand Marcos's favorite wine, wine that no longer existed, that no longer came to us, wine that used to be sold in tall thin bottles with confusing labels.

Old and unsmiling Francisco, the *maître*, kept up the telephone game with composure, did not abandon his long-held convictions, confirmed that the impossible wine should be served, of course, *chambré*, not too far from and not too close to the ideal, unattainable temperature.

The date is documented and appears to be irrevocable. Nevertheless, somebody, anybody, can swear that they saw, forty years after this story was written, Moncha Insaurralde at the corner of the Plaza Hotel. The details of this vision, the progress of Santa María's public works that *El Liberal* would extol, don't matter. The only thing that matters is for everybody to contribute to her sighting and manage to agree. Much smaller, with her wedding gown now dyed black for mourning, wearing a hat, a *canotier* with opaque ribbons, exceedingly small even for the fashion of forty years later, almost leaning on a thin ebony cane, on the compulsory silver handle, alone and resolved at the start of an autumn night – the air so gentle, the wailing of the tugboats so discreet – and waiting with playful and patient eyes for the departure of the occupants of precisely that table, the one situated not too near and not too far away from the entrance door and the door to the kitchen. And always, in that infinite amount of time that will exist when forty years have passed, the true and promised moment arrived, the moment when the table was empty and she could make her way forward, coquettishly pretending to use the cane, greeting Francisco and Francisco's grown-up grandson, make her way to Marcos's impatience, and apologize not very emphatically for being late. God was in heaven and ruled over the earth; Marcos, already drunk, undying, forgave her as he joked and cursed, holding out to her over the tablecloth a bouquet of the first violets of that forty-year-old autumn.

As had been agreed, we, the old folks, went our separate ways. Words were not needed for there to be respect and understanding. Some forgot for as long as they needed to, and they could have continued to construct their oblivion for years and dozens of years. They forgot, they didn't know that Moncha Insaurralde in her wedding gown was wandering through the streets of Santa María, entering shops, visiting the mansions of the wealthy and the farms that try to reach all the way to the shore, waiting for Marcos to return in order to gather up the prescribed white flowers, fresh and hard.

Some thought of Insaurralde, the Basque man, also dead, of remaining loyal to his memory, of the same bewildered woman who dragged along the unavoidable filth adhering to the train of her gown. And they chose to also take care of the ghost, pretend they believed in it, use the wealth, the prestige, what was left of the ashes, still unburied, of tender adolescent brutality.

There was very little for these as for the others; in any case, they saw and found out much less. They simply saw.

If there are lilies and jasmines, if there is wax and candles, if there is a light over a table and blank sheets of paper on the table, if there are verges of foam along the river, if there are dentures for young girls, if there is the whiteness of dawn growing above the whiteness of the milk that pours hot and white into a cold bucket, if there are women's aged hands, hands that never worked, if there is a short hem of a slip showing for the first date with a boy, if there is miraculously well-made absinthe, if there are shirts hanging out to dry in the sun, if there are soap bubbles and shaving cream or toothpaste, if there are the falsely innocent whites of children's eyes, if there is, today, intact, newly fallen snow, if the emperor of Siam keeps a herd of elephants for the viceroy or governor, if there are cotton burrs brushing against the chests of black men who sweat and scythe, if there is a woman in distress and suffering who is capable of denial and emergence, capable of not counting coins or the immediate future so she can give something useless as a gift.

This, so long, and the impossibility of telling the story of the inadmissible wedding gown – disintegrating, twisted, and old – in a single three-line sentence. But so it was: a gown, a negligee, a nightshirt, and a shroud. For everybody, for those who would have preferred to prudently take refuge in ignorance, for those who had chosen to become a dislodged garde du corps, to acknowledge her existence and proclaim that we would safeguard, to whatever extent possible, the wedding gown that was aging by the day, that was irremediably turning into a rag, protect the gown and the unknown, the unpredictable, that it carried inside.

The sterile, silent, contrary, never bellicose positions of us, the old men who met at the Plaza or in the new Club building, didn't last long. Less than three months, as has already been said.

Because suddenly, so gently that it then became sudden, when we found out or when we were beginning to forget, all the imaginable dying whitenesses – yellower by the day and with an irreversible ashen tone – grew inexorably, and we took them to be the truth.

Because Moncha Insaurralde had locked herself in the basement of her house with some – but not enough – Seconal, with her wedding gown that she could use, in the veiled placidity of the sun of our Santa María autumn, as a real skin to wrap around her thin body, her harmonious bones. And she lay down to die, bored of breathing.

And it was then that the doctor could look, smell, prove that the world he was offered and that he continued accepting wasn't based on traps or sweetened lies. The game, at least, was a clean game and respected with dignity by both parties: God-Brausen and him.

Far away, there were still some fanatic Insaurraldes who wished to claim that the dead woman had had an unexpected heart attack. In any case, they won, there wouldn't be an autopsy. This is perhaps why the doctor hesitated between the obvious truth and the hypocrisy of posterity. He preferred, almost at once, to give himself over to absurd love, to inexplicable loyalty, to any form of loyalty capable of engendering misunderstandings. Choices are almost always made like that. He didn't want to open any windows; he finally accepted breathing in unearthly communion the same foul air, the same smell of rancid filth. And finally he wrote, after so many years, without needing to take time to think.

He trembled with humility and justice, with a strange incomprehensible pride when he could finally write the promised letter, the few words that said everything: the given and family names of the deceased: María Ramona Insaurralde Zamora. Place of death: Santa María, District Two. Sex: female. Race: white. Country of birth: Santa María. Age at death: twenty-nine. The death hereby certified occurred on the day the month the year at the hour and the minute. Cause of death: Brausen, Santa María, all of you, I myself.

1968

Matías the Telegraph Operator

When Jorge Michel, in María Rosa's house, once again told the story or incident of Atilio Matías and María Pupo in front of several witnesses, I suspected that the narrator had achieved a level of estimable perfection, undoubtedly threatened with decline and rot in predictable future repetitions.

This is why, without any higher purpose, I will attempt to transcribe the aforementioned version, if only to protect it from time, from future postprandial conversations.

The incident, which is not a tale and doesn't even brush against the literary, goes, more or less, as follows:

For me, as you know, the bare facts don't matter at all. What matters is what they contain or carry, and then to discover what lies beyond that, and then beyond that, till we get to the deepest depths, which we will never reach. If a historian were to address the journey of the telegraph operator, it would be enough for him to establish that, during the government of

Iriarte Borda, the packet boat *Anchorena* set sail from the port of Santa María with a shipment of wheat and wool on its way to the countries of Eastern Europe.

He would not be lying; but the best truth lies in what I am telling, even if my account has often been derided for supposed anachronisms.

The journey must have lasted about ninety days, and I might, with some effort, be able to specify the role of the crew; at the beginning I forgot his, the telegraph operator's, name, swept away as I was by superstitious hatred. I will baptize him Aguilera on this page for my convenience. The name of the woman, whom I never met, I will never forget: María Pupo, from Pujato, Department of Salto.

"What can I do. Her name is María Pupo," as the telegraph operator, Aguilera, would say.

We must navigate by the light of the stars, someone began to sing one morning while whitewashing a door, and immediately the infection spread, everybody crooning the same line, using the sentence as a greeting, a response, a joke, and a consolation. We must navigate by the light of the stars. Mysteriously, the tune managed to be stupider than the lyrics.

You, someone, when it's your time, which is always at dawn, clamber onto the landing dock with a necessarily blue bundle banging defiantly on your back, sleep-deprived, hungry but queasy, still a little drunk and keeping an eye on the sloshing of warm beer in your stomach, alert also to the slow disappearance of memories, face, hair, legs, the firm and maternal hand of the whore you ended up with under the corrugated tin roof. These are simply the rituals, a timid, swelling arrogance, a maritime tradition.

And you, someone, already filled with premonitions about the fate of the freighter and its soggy adventures, pull out your papers and humble greetings as you examine, almost without moving your eyes, the new faces, and you begin to evaluate what they can offer you as far as help, hindrance, or misfortune.

Gathered together, hypocritical and prone to patience, we listened as the captain spoke of the fatherland, sacrifice, and trust. A boring and discreet man, he lifted one arm, wished us a good journey, and requested, with a smile, that we do our utmost to let him also have a good journey.

We were so grateful that he hadn't mucked around for more than three minutes that we gave him a robust military salute on a merchant ship and bleated out a hurrah.

I ran to make sure that I got Vast, the gringo, as a cabin mate. But it was too late, the bunks had been assigned the previous day, and on the door to my vomitorium I found a card with two names on it: Jorge Michel – Atilio Matías.

Washed and refreshed, we inevitably found ourselves face to face at seven thirty, each one sitting on his bunk, each one with the heavy futility of a man's motionless hands between his knees. So Matías, the telegraph operator – *I have to go to my post soon* – coughed without phlegm and said:

(He was, and will forever be, ten years older than I; he had a long nose, restless eyes, the thin and twisted mouth of a thief, a trickster, a compulsive liar, skin protected from the sun since adolescence, fairness preserved in the shade of a wide-brimmed hat. But above all this, like a permanent coat, there floated sadness, misery, fierce bad luck. He was small, fragile, with a smooth, downturned mustache.)

"I have to start my shift," he repeated.

But there was still half an hour to go before his stupid task of receiving meaningless telegrams, and we in the meantime had a bottle of Puerto Rican rum.

My need to be in motion was the only reason for my first embarkation.

This third one was different: it was to flee for three months from La Banda, from Multi's implausible patronage, from the precise genuflections of people I used to respect and, in some cases, love.

In the dim light we had the rum, the glasses, the cigarettes, the blue anchor tattooed on my forearm.

Half an hour. So Aguilera, Matías the telegraph operator, spoke the beginning of the truth that he believed to be certain, without needing to be asked. Cautiously protected by the fantastical ill fortune that was bent on destroying him, he talked a little, confessed.

Twenty minutes before his shift began, the stench of rum was dribbling out as he spoke. It was not, he knew, something that could be categorized as a persecution complex, shoved aside so he could move on to something else. Because, listen, Matías more or less said, or I was seeing in his sad face – with his resolute expression of childish indignation – the words that were stuck in his throat and not being uttered. For example:

"You know Pujato," somewhere between asserting and asking. "You, you know Pujato, you have to be aware of the difference and the scam, between grey and green, at least. It was the Telecommunications Agency, and I can show you the documents, one after another, in chronological order, which for some reason I decided to save. The National or General Telecommunications Agency. First step: enter the lottery to apply for national job openings for radio-telegraph operators. I won't deny that I had a friend who knew Morse, who could receive and send as if it were nothing, without paying much attention, the way you breathe or walk or speak. My friend, also from Pujato, was also the telegraph operator at the railroad station for decades. Received commendations from the English at every inspection. Pujato, don't forget, almost without par, like Santa María itself.

And my friend wanted to retire and leave me his job, a legacy of our friendship. So as soon as he heard it first announced, here it is, he told me, the job is yours, and he started training me, and long before the deadline I would hear Morse and my fingers would move in Morse. It wasn't the piano, it didn't matter that I'd messed up my fingers working on the farm.

"It was all about a job as a telegraph operator at the railroad station in Pujato. It was all about Pujato, in peace and quiet till the end of my life. Pujato and getting married to María, whom I won't talk about because such things are sacred to a man. But about Pujato, yes, one word, that says it all. Point to whatever you want: one morning, one afternoon. Sometimes, who knows, even at dawn. Green and yellow Pujato, farmers loading wheat and corn onto trucks, which some dump in bulk into the silos near the station, where they then ask for a date, a shift, and wagons. And me, there, solving their problems with Morse, half bothered, half amused, never really bothered. Me, and you see how I saw myself, telegraph operator and master, married to María, who could live with me at the station itself or be waiting for me at a cottage down the road.

"You see, you can see us, Pujato, my wife, and I. Now look at the other document, the third one, and the fourth, where the scam is. On the third one, among more than two hundred applicants, I place as qualified. And in the fourth document, ten months later, they send me to work the telegraph on a ship, this one, far away from everything I told you about. Germany, Finland, Russia, so many names I'd had to learn, always thinking they had nothing to do with me, not in school or afterwards.

"What do you want from me?" Matías the telegraph operator asked defiantly. "You want me to be happy?"

I let him leave, the rum kept flowing, and I fell asleep fearing diseases.

At six in the morning they woke me up with those dead and vulgar words, the ones that are a dime a dozen; stoker or fireman, I descended into my hell without seeing Matías, almost forgotten.

Someone arranged things so that we'd take turns occupying the cabin for the next few days, and we barely saw each other at lunch, the long table intervening. Fate kept careful watch over Matías's existence and forced me to postpone my Christian and optimistic reply, my *Alborada del Gracioso* until a few hours before Hamburg, heat, small lapses of discipline, imprecise hatreds, spitballs for words.

I already said or thought that this was a story about seafaring folk, and that only they would be able to truly understand it. I add, unapologetically, that many times in ports or on real dry land I wanted to explain and argue that all of us, citizens, mountain dwellers, and peasants of the lowlands, we are all at sea. Often, and always failing.

This is said so that you will come closer to understanding why, from the moment the ship left Santa María, I began to feel the indifference, the avoidance, the poorly hidden scorn from the crew, from my friends from other journeys.

Maybe I'm exaggerating, because words are always like that, never exact, a little more or a little less. But yes, I'm certain, quick greetings, silences tolerated patiently, smiles without eyes, deflected conversations.

Because I, not guilty of anything more than living in the cabin they assigned to me, was the friend of Matías the telegraph operator, the partner of failure, the shadow of bad luck.

And it didn't do me any good to mock Matías in front of them and Matías himself. I had been infected by the illness, the hostile fate of the man from Pujato — that's what they believed or suspected — and they were prudent to subject me to a cordon sanitaire, a quarantine. Hence I had to feel the injustice of being connected to Atilio Matías and sail by his side through a sea of hostility and persecution. He, Matías the telegraph operator, from his beginning to his end; I, for a three-month-long journey.

"Look where they send us," he said to me at one of our inevitable encounters. "They send us to the cold, a deathly cold, so different from what we have, I suppose, during the winter in Pujato. Think about the little room of the wireless operator at the railroad station, with boiling maté and a stove and some friends with real subjects to talk about, who hopefully will have brought a bottle of grappa, even though I'm not much of a drinker."

And it was futile to exaggerate the number of times that I'd already taken this same route, through these same ports, during the same month of the year.

"Look, in Finland now, even in Hamburg, in Baku, people walk around in their shirtsleeves, and the women at beach resorts wait for the light of the moon to go skinny-dipping."

He simply didn't believe me; it was forbidden for him to accept the kindness of summer, and he shrugged his shoulders to shake off any possibility of optimism. He wouldn't even answer; I knew what he was thinking about: María Pupo, Pujato, or the other way around.

Up there, above the fire in the boilers, someone was scrupulously keeping track of the day, the hour, the daily entries in the logbook. For me it was different, as always happens in Hamburg.

When we got to port one morning in summer, a little before noon, I walked away energetically to look for a streetcar stop, and I heard the pursuing footsteps, the resolute voice:

"Hey, Michel. Where are you off to?"

"The other direction. I'm itching for St. Pauli. Women and something stronger than beer to forget that I'm shipped out, and that tomorrow night

I'm back with the boilers. But you, Matías, are going to the Kaiser Hotel, I heard you say so. You've got to cross the street, go in the other direction, take the other streetcar."

A smile of disagreement was hovering, even though he accepted his bad luck. It must be easy if you get used to it. Then he said, and no streetcar was coming:

"Do me a favor."

"No," I said, "I'm going to St. Pauli, I'm dying for St. Pauli, and if you want you can come."

It was useless, because he didn't hear me, because he, Matías, had spent years in the practice of unholy despair.

"You can do me a favor and then you can go and get drunk. I didn't tell you this the whole time on board, but today is María's birthday. With your help I can send her a telegram."

"I don't understand. Why don't you just send it from the ship? Why don't you go back and send it?"

He didn't even look at me. He smiled as he walked and spoke patiently, as if from a father to his son.

"Fourteen. Article fourteen prohibits all personal communication except under dire circumstances and even these must be approved in writing by the captain or station chief."

"Of course, forgive me," I translated.

From where we were, you couldn't see the city; just a few square towers sticking out in the sun. But I could smell it, I could taste it in my dry mouth, and I can swear or promise that St. Pauli was calling to me. But no; his misery, Matías the telegraph operator's misery, was more powerful than my appetite for smoke and whatever might come to pass around a a great big round table. Pujato and María Pupo were the victors.

"Telegraph?" I started, giving in and covering over the shame. "Yes, right here, there's one two blocks away."

"So, if you don't mind coming with me. It'll just take a minute. I don't speak the language, and you can get by."

So we walked toward the telegraph and post office, each step taking us farther away from St. Pauli.

Consider, if you will, that the *fraulein* at the telegraph and telephone counter had been born there forty or fifty years before, and that her glasses, her wrinkles, her mouth like a bitter half moon, even her voice, which sounded like the voice of a macho pederast, were, like her soul, the product of her miserable salary, her absurd love for her work and for efficiency, indestructible faith augmented by the mystery promised and denied by the letters T.T.

Hence, at a satisfactory speed, the message went from the Pujatoan dialect, passed through my sailor's English and into the perfect German of the *fraulein*, to be translated into something like "María Pupo, Pujato, Santa María. Happy Birthday from Matías."

She made three carbon copies, charged three or four marks, and gave us a copy and a receipt.

We found ourselves once again on the streets and it was time to be hungry for lunch, and all the streetcars started moving toward St. Pauli and its promises. Now the voice wasn't coming from Matías the telegraph operator but instead from my hunger, my weakness, my mollified nostalgia. The voice said:

"Hey, Michel. Do you know anything about graphology?"

"At one time I pretended to know something. But I never really did."

"But, of course you know or at least you are aware of it. Think about that woman's face."

"No."

"Yeah, she disgusts me, too. Three marks forty-one is more than a dollar. And she didn't even type out the telegram, she wrote it with a ballpoint pen and we have a copy. Take a look, even if you keep claiming you don't understand."

At an intersection, afraid that the evening would begin on an empty stomach, I wanted to punch him and I couldn't, I swore at him and grabbed him by the arm.

Everything, anything; but in Hamburg there would always be, even on the most unlikely corner, a delicatessen in waiting. Beer and Scandinavian dishes. There on the table, held open by Matías's thumbs, was the copy of the telegram to María Pupo, Pujato.

"Think about it calmly," Matías said. "First, the woman, a nasty piece of double-crossing work, which we agree on."

I took a sip of beer, I filled my mouth with seafood of name unknown, and I gave myself over to a sudden, irresistible admiration for Matías's subtle intelligence, revealed to me in exchange for forty-six days of burning my hands in the bowels of the ship, aware that inside the same hull, over the same wave, just barely separated from me by thin layers of wood and steel, traveled the inconsolable sadness of a radio man.

"For starters, the face," Matías continued, "and now we have the handwriting, and even if you pretend not to understand, the two things together are indisputable. Conclusion, and forgive me, but the gringa is out to get me. Even more obvious: she already did and has kept the money, which I don't care about because I have a lot, and she didn't send my telegram. Based on her face, her handwriting, and because I'm a certified telegraph operator and I understand a little about these things."

The English of sailors is a universal language, and I always suspected that something similar occurs with whisky, in every latitude and altitude, whether it be joy, misery, tiredness, boredom. Matías was crazy, and I had nobody nearby to share the astonishment and joy of this discovery. So I agreed, nodding, pushed aside the mug of beer, and ordered a whisky. This is how they served it: a bottle, a bucket with ice cubes, soda.

Nor did I have a friend I could whisper to about the glaring madness of Matías, who had decided to remain quiet for a while as he gulped down seafood and beer.

He was still the same as always: ten years older than me, long nose, restless eyes, the thin and twisted mouth of a thief, of a trickster, of an addicted liar, small, fragile, with a smooth and downturned mustache. But now he'd gone crazy and was shamelessly exhibiting an ancient and concealed madness.

It was already the afternoon when I decided to interrupt his repeated utterances about faces, intuitions, and accent marks.

"We must navigate by the light of the stars," I told him. "And since you, Matías, have so much money, the best, the only thing you can do, if you truly value your fiancée's birthday, the only thing you can do is walk back to the T.T. monster and request a telephone call to Pujato."

"From Hamburg?" he asked bitterly, with the graceless sarcasm of the persecuted.

"From Hamburg, and through T.T., I've done it thousands of times. You can hear better than when you call from Santa María itself."

His struggle was between hope and atavistic incredulity. In jest, he patted his roll of bills in his pants pocket and said, "Okay, let's go," as if he were daring a child.

We went, I, just a little drunk, and he, determined to prove, once and for all and to himself, that he had been denied all and any guise of happiness from the beginning of time and nothing could attenuate this, his very own curse, from which he derived enough pride and distinction to go on living.

The telephone office was in the same building as the telegraph office, as the old maid who'd cheated Matías out of approximately three marks forty, keeping for herself, out of revenge or avarice, the words of Happy Birthday meant for María Pupo, Pujato.

But the telephones were in a different wing, to the left; we dragged each other to the counter, to the thin young blond with a carefree smile. She was another T.T.

I said, I translated, I explained, and she looked at me sluggishly and without any real faith. I said it again, enunciating each syllable, proving my sincerity and enough patience to last till the end of the world.

She wavered, and finally accepted, her face blanching with her exaggerated and perhaps painful smile. It's true that she hesitated for yet another moment before believing it and said:

"One moment, please," then she nodded and yielded the counter to us, disappearing, she as well, young as she was, behind the doors and curtains, way behind the big T.T.

Then there appeared an older T.T. with round, thin, gold spectacles and asked us if what seemed impossible to him was true.

"This coincidence, gentlemen . . ."

I knew. I can't know what was going on inside Matías, how he was dealing with these delays to his preferred personal destiny. I was, as I said, a little drunk and brilliant. Tolerating more interrogations, more T.T.s, each one older than the last. And I repeated with candor, with certainty, the correct answers, because we were also finally given the privilege of pushing back curtains and walking through doors until we were face to face with the oldest T.T., the real and definitive one.

He was already standing behind a tiny black wood desk in the shape of a half horseshoe. With the help of the heat, the two-year-old whisky, Matías's recently arrived madness, I was able to believe for a moment that the man had been waiting for us ever since we left Santa María. He was tall and heavyset, a man who had been a champion in the field at the University of Greifswald and had stopped playing two or three years before.

Blond, ruddy, freckled, friendly, and revolting.

"Gentlemen," he said. I pretended to believe him. "They have told me that you would like to place a telephone call to South America."

"*Ja*," I said, and he asked us to have a seat.

"To South America," he repeated, smiling at the ceiling.

"Pujato, sir, in Santa María," I said, turning to look at Matías and ask him for help.

But nothing was forthcoming from that quarter. The telegraph operator's madness chose, out of cleverness or definitive rebellion, an absent expression, empty eyes, a silky mustache, droopy and foreign, blown by the breeze of the air conditioner. He, Matías, wasn't participating, he was merely an alert, waggish witness, certain of defeat, indifferent, remote.

The corpulent man surrounded by the half horseshoe of his table held forth. He was older than us, and the cheerful fraternity of his discourse very soon turned into decency and weariness.

By now he was surrounded by civil servants with happy expressions on their faces, and we were all drinking coffee while he explained that

Telefunken T.T., of which he was a simple cog in the gears, had just put in operation a new line of communication between Europe and South America, and that on this occasion, Matías's quivering longing should be celebrated, because the love call we were requesting was, in fact, the first that would be made, apart from, of course, the numerous tests carried out by the technicians.

When he leaned back and lifted one arm, we saw that the entire wall behind him was an enormous world map on which the rigors of decorative geometry had no respect for the whims of coastlines. And he smiled again as he told us that, because of the celebration, the call like the cups of coffee was gratis, no more than three minutes.

I nodded enthusiastically, spoke words of gratitude and congratulations, as I was thinking that all of this was normal, that inaugurations had always been free, as I looked at the telegraph operator's furtive face, his adversarial anticipation.

There was a pause, and the big man pushed one of the telephones toward Matías. It was white, it was black, and it was red.

Matías didn't move; and if a joke can be serious, there was a joke in his drained profile and in his voice.

"María doesn't have a telephone," he said. "You call, Michel. Call the store and ask them to find her, though I don't know what time it is there. Ask them because maybe it's very late and she's asleep."

He meant to say that Pujato is asleep. I spoke to the manager, we checked Greenwich, and we found out that the sun was just beginning to set in Santa María. Calves mooing around Pujato, the station barriers dropping lazily and creaking as they wait for the 18:15 train to the Capital.

Then, slowly, due to premonitions that acted upon me like arthritis, thinking about freedom and St. Pauli, I reached out my arm and pulled the telephone toward me till it touched my chest. Frozen, not looking at anything in the room, Matías spoke to my hands.

"It's 314 in Pujato. The general store. You'll ask them to get her."

After receiving specific instructions from the main German, I spoke to the operator. Through patience and repetition, the difficulties were easily overcome.

I don't know for how many seconds and how many minutes the woman said to me, "Please remain on the line; your call is being placed," or similar words. And then even Matías was forced to lift his eyes and appreciate the miracle spread out on the wall that was the world map. We saw the tiny red light go on, right there in Hamburg; we saw another light up in Cologne; we saw, successively, sometimes blinking, other new ones at a confident, unbelievable speed; Paris, Bordeaux, Alicante, Algiers, Canarias, Dakar, Pernambuco, Bahía, Río, Buenos Aires, Santa María. A stutter, a fluctuation, the voice of another woman: "Please remain on the line, calling Pujato, three one four."

Finally: "Villanueva Hermanos, Pujato." It was a thick, serene voice, full of indifference and the first glass of vermouth. I asked for María Pupo and the man said he'd get her. I waited, sweating, determined to ignore Matías till the end of the ceremony, looking at the world illuminated with points of fire behind the wide face, the happy smile of the manager surrounded to his right and left by the respectfully less important smiles of the robots of Telefunken T.T.

Until María Pupo was on the line and said, "This is María Pupo. Who is it?"

I am innocent. I spoke politely but not boldly, I explained that her fiancé,

Atilio Matías, wished to speak to her from Hamburg, Germany. A pause, and María Pupo's contralto voice, crossing the world and the flickering noise of its oceans: "Why don't you go fuck your mother, you shitfaced asshole?"

She hung up the phone, furious, and the little red lights quickly went out, in reverse order, until the world-map wall sank back into the shadows and three continents agreed in silence that Atilio Matías was right.

1970

The Twins

The twins were born half an hour apart, and they always argued in their slum dialect about who was older, who younger. I had chosen one, the skinniest, the least merciful. I don't even remember her name.

It would have frightened me, as I told my wife one night, fifteen years later, to consider what remained in me of the twins, or of my twin.

Or suddenly I ran out of momentum, out of love for the situation and its problems, out of the unquestionable joy I derived from being at the very center of that perfect misery that seemed, astonishingly, to have been invented for me and by me.

A time when everybody could be happy by simply deciding to be, and those who hadn't decided could, even in spite of themselves, achieve another kind of happiness, more complex and veiled, more profound and conscious.

The newspaper where I worked was on Plaza Libertad, and life surrounded the plaza with its bars and shops, its feeble and provincial but unfailing frenzy. You could hear it from press time at dawn until my return at eight at night; and there was always evidence that it had been buzzing during my absence, jubilant and tenacious, over and underneath the noise made by men and machines. Perhaps life vibrated there for everybody, and everybody could hear it and smile at it.

As for me, I had promised myself at least one surprise a day, and the pact was carried out with as much precision as the fortnightly arrival of my salary as proofreader. This was during the last war.

So the appearance of the Twin, the sole twin for the rest of my life, didn't excite me then as much as it would today. I first saw her at three in the morning, at the Metro Restaurant, engaged in an argument with the most senior waiter.

"No," she said, laughing, "I could never eat soup, not since I was little and no matter how much they beat me. I want potato salad with cold cuts."

"It's got to be vegetable soup. It's nourishing," Castro insisted. "You're too skinny, and with the life you lead . . ."

I'd taken a seat at the nearest table even though the dining room was empty, and I waited for the dialogue to end before asking Castro for a glass of caña, hoping that María Esther wouldn't show up as promised, that no friend of mine would show up, that nobody from the newspaper would think of sitting down at my table to talk about whether or not Roosevelt's speech was delaying the gringos' entry into the war. I fiddled with the freshly printed pages of the newspaper as I analyzed the surprise they would grant me at the beginning or the end of my day.

I looked at the woman's long thick hair, brunette, pulled back and loosely tied at the nape of her neck, framing a pale, childish face with a straight, very short, nose, and a large, sloppily painted mouth, which pierced the hungry hollows of her cheeks with every laugh.

I looked at her dirty hands, long and skinny, the humiliation of her summer dress, not made for her, opaque and sagging from too many washings, too broad for her small chest, with armholes too large for her skinny little-girl arms.

"My sister's paying. Don't you believe me? She's on her way. My sister always has money."

"Okay, if you eat your soup," Castro said, angrily.

He came over and slapped his napkin down on my rattan table, a little older than usual, more serious and more tired. I ordered caña in a loud voice and told him, without looking at the girl, that if the sister didn't come, I'd pay.

"If the sister doesn't come," Castro said, "I'll pay. Don't add to it. I'm already tired enough of this story. It's already sad and dirty enough without you getting involved. Believe me."

Castro was born in Granada, and he didn't need to wear those ridiculously tight black pants, nor his white hair greasy and plastered down over one temple to prove it. He must have died of a liver ailment, of low blood pressure, of Wilson's disease, or simply, of Spain.

At that time, when that night occurred, all the immigrants from Spain who hadn't become owners of shops or bars preferred to die of Spain. I'm talking about those who were in the city long before the civil war. Those recently arrived, according to the statistics, turned out to be immortal, though Spain hurts them a bit as well.

"Do me a favor and don't complicate things. Leave her alone, she's a pathetic creature. Fifteen years old, at most, and working as a prostitute, without knowing how, instead of playing with her dolls."

"Caña, ice and soda," I said.

I turned to look at the girl and smiled at her. She responded to all smiles, whether they came from men or things, from difficulties or short memories.

"I'm not a client, Castro. If she's hungry, I can pay for her meal tonight. Anyway she's too young, too skinny. I don't like them like that."

The truth is I'd started to like them like that. Not the lanky undernourished girl, not her small and innocent face, not even the guileless and defiant way she smoked cheap cigarettes from a crumpled pack. But she – I could imagine with great detail the exciting parting of her scrawny thighs over the chair's wicker, her scant fuzz dangling – she and her difference from the night streets, the guiles of prostitution, the techniques and haggling in forlorn furnished rooms.

I didn't lie in order to stop Castro from separating me from her, from my daily surprise; I lied to prevent him from distorting it by talking out loud about the FAI, about poor Blum, and about the incontrovertible filth of the world the three of us belonged to. I lied out of fear that they'd turn her for me into a woman, a person, a symptom of something or other.

She had her back to the open window and at the end of that summer night the wind made the scraps of paper and the dirt in the plaza swirl between the wheels of the large white buses, which had just arrived or were about to leave.

Before I took my glass and my newspaper to her table I was inventing for her, erroneously, a past and a future; I imagined the details of her body's thinness, the traces of recent and ancient weariness, my need to help her.

And even though all of this turned out to be true, even though I confirmed with superstition, pride, and fear – like when you bet on a number and the number turns up, and you feel like you've just established a precarious relationship with luck, a stuttering code for giving and receiving orders – that everything I had been sensing while watching her and the air of enchantment, failure, and injustice that surrounded her, while watching the thick edges that joined her to and separated her from the world, most noticeably at her temples, at the nape of her neck, and in her decidedly sunken shoulders; while I looked at her purposeless smile that she was showing me without realizing that it was, for starters, the most mine of the surprises that life was affording me; even though all of that turned out to be true in a servile and possibly excessive way, I never before heard assertions like the ones I was hearing from the second Twin, recently made up and sleepy, at four in the morning, in a slow and practical voice, as she persisted in moralizing, accepting and performing her pedagogical duties, under the restrained fury of Castro's head, as he kept bringing us caña until the first disappearance of night in the hollow of the plaza.

The second Twin – she was born, as I said, a few minutes before her sister – was a dubious replica of the other: shorter and wider, blondr and more composed, full of self-confidence, wise and protective, almost with breasts and hips. I was ten years older than them and I was watching them grow up, listening to their babbling as they tried to learn to use words and old assertions, as they tried to create the vulgarities and clichés they needed to populate, give shape and walls, to the unprecedented, worn, dirty world of impressions they were continually constructing, inevitably, for as long as they acted and agreed to breathe.

"Because no advice does any good with this one, and sometimes I've considered letting her work things out on her own," the second Twin said in response to the other's embarrassed, mocking smile. "You wouldn't believe me if I told you that there are nights she works harder than me, she has more luck, or they understand just by looking at her, and all the same, with my three to her five, I end up with thirty pesos in my purse and she's got nothing. And she's taller, skinner but prettier. And she knows that ever since we struck out on our own we have to work but we also have to charge."

"I work," the real Twin said, defiant and cross, and then smiled at me like a little boy, asking for support. "We both agreed to work, and I work, and you just said I sometimes work more than you."

"You see?" the second Twin said to me with resignation and pity. "Just like I said. Work and charge. Because the gentleman knows that you don't live off your work but off what you charge for your work. It's a business deal, you exchange one thing for another, and if someone did it for free, it really would be immoral."

"It's not my fault."

"The same thing happened to me, but only a couple of times, and only at first. But all I had to do was charge up front, and if I didn't get the ten pesos, nothing doing. Even at the door, I'd turn around and leave."

"It's not my fault. I work, and more than you, because they either bore me or disgust me so I don't stick around blabbing for hours when they sit me down at a café table. Sometimes I start laughing and can't stop; but I don't chit-chat. It's not my fault if they say 'later,' if they look at me as if I were the one trying to rip them off. And if later I get all worked up while they're getting dressed, they're the ones who laugh. I can't blame anybody, and I laugh, too. Is that my fault?"

Every day, for a moment of variable duration, the city goes backwards one hundred years, and the huddled air of a village descends upon it, it lets itself be strewn with faded colors. Behind all the noise can be perceived the echoes of the trees' leanings, of mooing and henhouses, of stones trodden with heavy steps during the siesta. On that day, that moment arrived at dawn and froze the view of the plaza behind the real Twin while I watched her sister's mouth in motion, the round and serene face that explained to us, patient and certain, how the world works, how we are condemned to being.

We, her sister and I, had already learned that the tough and wise law is the law of money, the law of honorable deals, and that whoever doesn't pay for what he takes, demeans; we'd started to listen to a sermon about the importance of dignity, about the duty to never compromise, about the unforeseeable consequences of an isolated act of concession and tolerance, when a face with a hat appeared and stopped a few meters from the window. The second Twin paused and smiled at the semidarkness of the plaza.

"I don't know if I'll get back in time to take the last bus," she said. "Maybe I'll take a taxi, maybe tomorrow."

So I was left alone with the real Twin, and she kept talking to me, giving me the same smiles she would use to beg everyone else not to make fun of her, of her love for Josesito, of her hatred for her stepfather, of how nice and fun it was for her to put on makeup and walk through the streets of the city center in high heels.

At that time, I remember, I didn't think about God, either as a possibility or as a challenge; I didn't know whom to thank for the daily surprise that kept getting drunk and laughing night after night until the last #141 entered the station and turned off its lights.

And at that moment, for the first time, we understood, the real Twin and I, that she couldn't return home, that we could have our last drink only at the politicians' club upstairs from Tupí Nambá, because a minor can't spend the night at a real hotel. We had our drink and went to sleep in a dirty rented room, in a huge room with ceilings of plaster relief, which imposed a kind of personal solitude, which rendered us defenseless and exposed, which proclaimed every attempt at confession and intimacy with prolonged porous echoes.

She was skinny and fat, like the photographs of malnourished indigenous children. I stroked her head until I sensed that she had fallen asleep, I heard her talk about Josesito, a neighbor, who was fifteen years old and loved her more than he loved his own mother. I insisted on shutting myself off from the world she represented, sleepy and stuttering, without purpose or pride.

A world, a skinny but tenacious migratory flow, a recurring story of old potato farmers and horse trainers who came from everywhere to the Capital. First to odd jobs and prostitution; later: we'll see. The Twin was in the first stage, she was naked, undernourished, and unused in the large bed with golden bars in the huge room of the ancient boarding house. She was asleep and drunk, contemplating her dreams with knitted brows, with drops of saliva at the corners of her large, thick lips. And before it was day and the Majorcan came to throw us out, she had time to wake up three times and throw her arms around me, shouting, "The cops, they're coming to get me. The cops."

I lifted her, half asleep, into my own wakefulness, struggling against the tide, against the flabby swelling of the absurd.

Three times a night, every night, pursued like insects through filth, shadows, the sordid ruckus of cheap rooms at the port, where they never asked for ID, she shouting "the cops" or mumbling tender words to an unknown Josesito, repeatedly killing my hopes, my need for sleep, until pity leads to resolve, almost unknown in endless insomnia, to cover her mouth, her face, the past, and the nevermore with the thickest pillow I would be able to find.

1973

Death and the Girl

for María Rosa Oliver

I

The doctor leaned back, banging the now useless prescription pad – dead from indolence, old age, and unsought wealth – with the end of his green pen.

For a moment he thought about himself; he thought while looking at the ascetic face of the unforeseen, unforeseeable visitor, the well-dressed and healthy sick man sitting stiffly in his chair after his confession.

It seems there's nothing to be done, he thought gently. *It seems this spawn of a goddamn bitch and seven classic spurts of semen from seven unknown dogs is stuffing all of us, one after the other and in even less of a hurry than a leap year, into his bag. He walks around listlessly telling everybody about*

*his future crime, murder, homicide, uxoricide (some of those words are for
when the police remember me, when they need a medical examiner); he strolls
around what's left of Santa María with a sign hanging around his neck and
lightly banging against his back, because his stride is malicious and slow, a
sign that announces in grey and red: I will kill. That's enough for him. He's
sincere, he can't be accused of coveting his neighbor's wife because that would
be a lie. His only neighbor is himself. And this is the way he is turning everybody into his witness for the prosecution and the defense: the bishop and Jesus
Christ, Galeno Galinei and I, all of Santa María. And it's possible that night after night, crying and on his knees, he prays to Father Brausen who art in Nada
to make him an accomplice, to tangle him into his plot, without really needing
to, out of an obscure desire for an artistic punch line.*

"That's it exactly, Doctor," the visitor said in a voice that was accustomed to resignation; then he added, "What can I do?" Díaz Grey dropped
his pen and stared in silence at the trap, the hypocrisy, the hidden harshness,
the congenital guile.

"What about her?" he asked, as if he believed he was gaining time, timeless and utterly useless time.

"I don't understand, Doctor," he said, sitting up tall, dressed in dark
and expensive clothes, his thin blond hair plastered down, still handsome
but aggressive and ignoble like his hard nose, which always looked like it
had just risen out of the open pages of one of those enormous yellowed
Bibles brought to La Colonia Suiza by the first immigrants.

"I mean . . . If she knows. If doctors told her, like they told you, that
another pregnancy would endanger her life."

"Yes, she knows. They told her here and in the Capital. They told her
in Europe, last year. But they didn't say it would endanger her life. They
guaranteed her that she would die."

Each time, with each sentence, better aimed and determined to convince. Scrambling his criminal confession, anticipating it almost with joy, in any case a fatalist, guilelessly inhabited by despair.

"One question," Díaz Grey asked. "The first child, the only child, I assume, when was he born? How old is he?"

"One year, thirteen months."

"Since then, since his birth and the postpartum quarantine . . ."

"Since then we've been suffering. We look at each other, we wring our hands, we pray, and we cry."

"But she," Díaz Grey said halfheartedly, as if he were talking to a teenager who was making fun of him, "she can help you. She can, as they say, take precautions, she can also say no."

His client shook his head, patient, misunderstood, exhausted by incomprehension.

"She knows, as I do, that any precaution would be a mortal sin. And," he lifted his head without pride, "she wouldn't say no. The conflict, I repeat, is mine alone. That's why I wanted to talk to you."

Not the only reason, you son of a bitch; there's terror behind it, there's calculation. He felt weaker than his visitor, he had started to sincerely hate him. With deliberate slowness and without any noticeable purpose, he started unbuttoning his threadbare, pointless coat, which he kept using out of habit and in homage.

"Okay," he said indifferently, as if he were speaking about aspirins or tonics, "it's about you, exclusively about you: that you love her and desire her and more and more each day, the more your love fills your heart and your semen your testes; you, who can't go to a prostitute because that would mean sinning against Brausen; who can't spill your seed in your sheet, who can't masturbate, who can't be saved, other than by killing her."

The well-dressed man's thin face seemed to be counting in silence and serenity while Díaz Grey spoke. Then he nodded in agreement.

His coat was open, the doctor slipped it off his shoulders.

"Like you, I'm not in favor of killing her. If there's no other way, destroy yourself and I'll try to help you. I'm not talking about total destruction because that, too, would be a mortal sin. And Brausen doesn't forgive desertions. I know that; it's something we agree on. It's a question, then, of prescribing you cold morning showers, bromide and camphor, two- or three-hour walks each day, Good Friday abstinence every day. The idea is to make you impotent many years before its natural onset. It's sad, I understand. To lie next to a beloved wife without any hope for immortal desire to be satisfied. But in this way desire will die before she does, and you will be freed from your demons and from remorse."

Now the well-groomed man barely smiled, little white teeth sunk in a riddle for which only he had the key.

"I agree," he said without emotion, "I will try everything you prescribe," and then he gently added, "Doctor."

Díaz Grey picked his coat up with two fingers and let it slip off the back of the chair and onto the rug decorated with large, trampled, withered flowers.

"No," he said. "Not a prescription; I don't want to write it down or give it to you. This is enough, I trust your memory. And, above all, I believe in your intelligence. I believe in it and I'm not happy about it. By the same token, your confessor priest doesn't write out certificates, either."

He was certain that his tone had been definitive, almost as definitive as if he had pushed the other man out of the room. But the tall, thin, blond man – pressed, polished – had also stood up, and in a measured tone, his eyes upturned, repeated:

"No, he doesn't, either. I'm not looking for documentation. It's enough to be listened to."

"Of course, I understand. The coadjutor bishop, or whatever he's called these days, already listened to you. I still call him Father Bergner. Now it's my turn. And, undoubtedly, at least all of the older inhabitants of La Colonia know the prologue you just recounted to me."

"Could be," his client said. "But I've spoken of this only with you and the bishop. With the bishop, it's true, I didn't make it a confession. But I've known him since childhood (mine, naturally), and I trust in his discretion, as I do in yours."

For the first time during the interview – though Díaz Grey could not swear, afterwards, that it really was the first time – the man let slip a cynical, almost bemused, smile. He said:

"Neither you nor Father Bergner. But it's not impossible that she, as desperate as I am, and a woman to boot, has spoken to friends and relatives. With women, it's different. As you know better than I, they, like people with chronic illnesses, believe that if they share their problems they will get help, or at least support, in exchange for each confidence. For now we've agreed on a deferment. We could call it a temporary solution. Perhaps the good Lord will help us. I'm planning a trip to the Capital and Chile for a few months, to teach a few courses. Alone, naturally."

Díaz Grey had no argument with that. He nodded, affirming his conviction to remain cornered, with his back to the wall, because of a scam, a quibble, an indefinable, gritty, and disgusting presentiment.

The man also nodded. And in spite of everything written, someone might have said that they parted politely and united.

II

Díaz Grey knew the condemned woman – Helga Hauser – and had examined her three times, twice the previous year in the silent presence of her husband, who overstated his desire not to know; the other time without warning and almost on the sly. That time, the doctor rattled off the diagnosis, the prevention. He palpated the woman spread-eagle on the table with rubber, distaste, and incomprehension.

"I don't understand. But they already told you in the Capital and in Europe. For me it's certain, undeniable, there's no margin of error. I don't understand why you are consulting a doctor like me, negligible, from Santa María, who isn't even a gynecologist."

"I don't know," she mumbled as she was getting dressed. "A hope. A preference to die here."

After paying she laughed for a moment and mocked herself.

"Maybe I want to complicate things. I don't know."

Love had departed from Díaz Grey's life, and sometimes, while playing solitaire or chess alone, he thought confusedly about whether he had ever really had any at all.

In spite of his absent daughter known only from bad snapshots, who was now, disastrously, stumbling through damned and dirty adolescence, and whose birth would require a prologue. Adolescence with mistakes and filth, always illuminated by a belief in the eternity of peak experiences, unconscious faith that the inevitable seasons would constantly erode.

Every Thursday at twilight, regardless of the moon, he had a woman on the squeaky bed or the inappropriately thick rug where dozens of indefinable odors fused, or at least the combination became indefinable.

The condemned woman had been there more than a year earlier. The proclaimed murderer, one day before that.

Women didn't really matter to him: they were people. He ate lunch, hungry, and lay down in bed in his clothes.

Based on the movement of the sun, Díaz Grey might have assumed he'd spent more than an hour immersed in the meditation that came to him instead of the missed siesta and the habitual dyspepsia. He didn't remember the murderer-visitor or the future that promised his impassive confession. He didn't remember for himself, or for anybody, not even for an impossible tramp who bummed around or slept on the nearby beach.

Indifferently, he harbored doubts about his own age. Brausen might have had me be born in Santa María with thirty or forty years of a forever inexplicable and unknown past. He is obliged, out of respect for the great traditions he wishes to imitate, to keep killing me, cell by cell, symptom by symptom.

But he also has to follow the monotonous example of the innumerable previous demiurges and sort out life and reproduction. Thereby came the vanished adolescents, their courtships and matings, the daunting births I had to attend; thereby came the girls, their adjectives, their shapes, their hair, their firm breasts and thighs. They came and they remain, always absent, cheerful or melancholic.

(That genuine moment when one of the lovers, almost never the woman because she knows herself to be, and it's true, immortal, jealously repeated from the beginning and toward eternity. That fleeting, quickly forgotten moment when one of the two manages to see, unintentionally, with a flimsy desire to ask for forgiveness, to apologize, underneath the skin of the other's face, polished by love or wine, to see straight through the skin on the beloved's face. When one of them comes up against, passes right through without meaning to, the woefully defenseless taut or soft skin on the other's face. And for a single second sees, imagines, and measures the hardness and audacity of the bones, the frankness of the cheekbones, the fragility or the uselessly greasy boldness of the chin. When one of the lovers suspects – a spark and then oblivion – the future skull, already placed in the world, in the life, of the other lover.)

Those women, always far away and untouchable, separated from me by a difference of thirty or forty years imposed on me by Juan María Brausen, damn his soul that hopefully will burn for a couple or two couples of eternities in the appropriate hell where he will soon be met with a Brausen, a little taller, a little more genuine.

III

Augusto Goerdel was conceived in La Colonia Suiza or was already in his mother's belly on the long journey in our wobbly *Mayflower*. In any case, he was born here, in La Colonia, recently founded, if you can call a capricious and asymmetrical cluster of tree trunks, green stakes marking out a plot, and a methodical search for dung and soil to make bricks a founding.

The land was easy, twenty meters from the coast; digging across and under the sand, they found reddish and damp soil that they spread out in the sun and the air after it was hauled to the mystery they had condemned to be colony and settlement. As for fertilizer, during the day they sent out brigades of children who knew how to carefully find their way, remaining alert to the neighing and the mooing. Later came the night robberies, huge sacks reeking of stable and shelter. And even later, on dedicated mornings, the separate bonfires, the slow cooking, fear of sudden rainstorms and fog, fear of crumbling and fragility.

If you can call daily suffering a founding, suffering that can't be measured in the hours spent stacking bricks, raising walls, making roofs out of branches, even the brute rest of the exhausted man who thinks he has a home and manages to have a peaceful and grateful Sunday, kneeling on the enormous, almost unmanageable Bible with a black cover in front of the trembling circle of Latin words spoken by a priest who came from somewhere, anywhere, because he was indispensable.

And then, for me and for Santa María, the bewilderment. Nobody knows, and it doesn't matter, how many months or Aryans passed – helped, pushed without mercy for themselves or anybody else – until the stern blond rats who disembarked with less hope than suicidal rage became fat and wealthy and took over the city founded by Our Lord Brausen without any need to show that they had. Maybe they were repelled by the evidence. They were oblique, they were indirect, they were modest.

It's demonstrably true that time doesn't exist on its own; it is the child of movement, and if it stopped moving we would have neither time nor erosion nor beginnings nor ends. In literature, Time is always written with a capital letter.

Nobody can deny that the visits of the then Father Bergner and the inevitable Dr. Díaz Grey to La Colonia Suiza probably coincided. One was implicating God in a baptism, in the marriage of fiancés who previously had stood stiffly for the tripod of Orloff, prince or grand duke, artistic photographer, or in a vagary of death, the result of an old sophistry accepted without a struggle, at times also already stiff, at others about to be; the other, Díaz Grey, setting a broken leg or draining dropsy.

I repeat, they could have coincided many times and one of those times, why ever not, they met at the house of the Goerdels.

I can see them greeting each other, briefly effusive, appropriate for enemies who would have preferred not to be, who have for each other the deep and cold respect of equals.

It doesn't matter what the doctor prescribed for the catarrh of Augusto Goerdel, who was eleven years old at the time of the supposed coincidence. This can be tracked, if it mattered, in the records kept by Barthé, druggist, alderman, and again druggist. What matters is to never know – and therein lies a kind of happiness – what Father Bergner said, what he knew, what he deduced from the possible visit, which, if we feel like it, was crepuscular, slow, and calm. Because, and this should never be forgotten, Bergner's parents also came on our *Mayflower* to the coast of Santa María, as Brausen wished. Linked to the Goerdels through the similarities of their histories, through language and, above all, through the style with which they made it colloquial.

Very important because the Father's visits became more frequent, and less than a year later Augusto Goerdel went to live in Santa María to continue his studies at the cathedral, with a very meager scholarship, the precise amount required for Bergner's plans.

Because the Father was pretending to be manufacturing a priest, even though he always knew that this was not Augusto Goerdel's destiny or usefulness; he was thinking longer term. Much longer term than the cathedral's Chapter of laymen and clerics that met and feigned resolve twice a month in the austerity of the deliberate penumbra in the elongated refectory.

Bergner wasn't a Jesuit; he distrusted and admired them. But he had heard them say, and more than once: Give us your son and we will return him to you with a degree in hand.

He studied his future false priest calmly. If the inspiration, the project, really came from Brausen and was not a trap laid by the devil, time didn't count. He knew that the boy was intelligent, that he had been born ruthless with ambition and the Germanic need to triumph, to exact revenge. Whatever his destiny was now, with or without Bergner, he would never return to the poverty of his house in La Colonia; he would no longer accept the predictable peasant future of animal husbandry and brute labor.

A decision that Bergner fortified, skillfully and inattentively. His task, AMDG, even if he violently rejected those initials, was the patient labor of refinement and corruption. Out of the coarse young man, out of the student and altar boy, would be born his instrument, his fanatic servant of the Church.

He knew that young Goerdel, now his to handle, was ambitious, subtle in his falsehoods and his cautious retractions, hard behind his childish smile, instinctively knowledgeable about those futures, useful probabilities, that he should praise without excess, detached, without the crassness that would make them unworthy of cultivation.

He also knew from the very beginning that the instrument and the fanatic would be his for as long as the Church allowed him to prosper and grow.

Wordlessly, at least until the advent of the hypocritical goodbye, Bergner also knew that he had not made a mistake, that his choice was the right one and couldn't have been better. He confirmed it day after day and year after year: among all the inhabitants of Santa María and La Colonia, Augusto

Goerdel was the man most suited for his purpose; and the Church's education and discipline were the best way for the patient and resolved will of the child, adolescent, adult to triumph. Bergner believed in divine inspiration; Goerdel believed in opportunity and good luck.

Bergner remained pleased until the separation, until his death. But long before that, a great mutual farce had become necessary.

Or, rather, the end of the farce that Bergner began ten years earlier and that was suspected and followed implicitly by the sick child on his cot in his room in the shack in La Colonia, who knew how to lie prone, cry in silence, discover in the wattle and daub ceiling the paralyzed spiders of fear and mystery.

During that first meeting the boy, alone or with the help of his mother, managed to wrap his hands around a rosary, to move his fingers with a delicate despair that skirted the unspoken plea with detachment and distress.

A few years later, in the wing of the church that had been baptized Seminary even though the only seminarian was Augusto Goerdel, Bergner smiled from the shadows upon a similar and perfected scene.

From the always poor room of the adolescent – where only holy cards of saints and virgins were there to enact the ritual of the prologue that would bring on sleep – stretched an always cold tiled corridor that led to a spiral staircase, which twisted down to the temple, Mass, confessions.

The second scene was contemplated by a cautious and concealed Bergner, awakened at dawn by the sound of a door opening and closing. A deliberate sound, he thought, fearless and curious. He left his bedroom, barefoot and slow, like a thief in the night.

Encrusted in the wall in the corridor, which always smelled of damp and absence, lit dimly by a greenish phosphorescent light, protected with the ambivalent help of a window, a bloody wax Jesus Christ was nailed to the cross. Under the light of fireflies could also be read a poem by an anonymous author. Four lines on an ochre and fluttering piece of paper:

> *To all who pass, look at me.*
> *Tell of my wounds if you can.*
> *My child, you never repay me*
> *for all the blood I shed.*

And there, in his shift and on his knees, pounding his chest in time with his cries, was Augusto Goerdel.

He must do that every day at dawn, Bergner thought, *sweating or cold, tenacious and punctual, betting on the law of probabilities, certain that at some point I'd have to see him, catch him in his act of valor and believe in him. My poor, hypocritical idiot, my brother.*

IV

Throughout the great foretold – but not final – mutual farce, both demonstrated unquestionable resolve and wordlessly acknowledged their own and the other's strength.

Inside the adolescent's small room, invaded without warning and almost completely filled with Bergner's enormous body, the conversation pivoted to time, basic theology, questions and answers printed in the catechism children used to read, until Bergner stepped away from the grey opacity of the window and asked, without raising his voice:

"God, Brausen. Do you believe in him?"

Goerdel looked at him, bewildered, and docilely told a lie:

"If I didn't believe in him, I wouldn't be here. I've been here, Father, for five or six years."

"Ah, yes," Bergner said, nodding. "I would have given the same answer if an imbecile had asked me that question." He paused, looked briefly at the condensation on the window. "But," he continued, "neither of us is an imbecile. Tell me slowly if you believe that the sins of thought and action, lamentable and lukewarm, that you have committed and accumulated in this filthy cell are enough for Brausen to send you, without a trial, to hell, to make your immortal soul burn forever. Supposed immortal soul, that you supposedly have or endure, or something similar."

The young man, wearing a black sweater, torn dirty blue jeans, now lowered his eyes to look at his sandaled feet. Other than at Mass, he always dressed like that, robust against winter, indifferent to sweating during the hot season. But now, at the end of that morning, of eleven o'clock Mass, weak and waiting for lunch, Goerdel's garments and Goerdel himself showed signs of tattered distress.

He responded in a surprised and timid voice, slowly, without hostility:

"You should know better than I, Father. You would have to know and judge, pass sentence without having to ask questions or ask for help. You are my confessor."

"That's true," the priest said, smiling. "For five years, the trap was always open. It was so simple. You coveted your neighbor's wife, but you didn't kill him. You took the name of the Lord in vain, but as a joke. You honored, with contempt, increasing contempt, your mother and your father. I ordered a punishment for every foolishness of yours, for every lie you whispered in the secrecy of confession. You knew how to stammer and blanch. For five years I urged you to tell all. To reveal to me the depth of your mind. Souls will always remain unknown. Sometimes you despaired on the other side of the curtain; at others, more anxiously, without warning, anywhere in the church, I'd allow myself to be cornered. You and I respected each other, solemn as we were. You and I enjoyed ourselves seriously, and we obeyed (we were gentlemen) the rules of the game, which might have lasted too long, which ends now," and he repeated slowly, "which ends now. At noon on the thirty-first of March, according to the Gregorian calendar."

"Forgive me, Father," the young man said, "but what ends? And why today, now? What did I do . . . ?"

Bergner lifted his calm hand and deferred his smile. In spite of hunger and the bad weather, there was no hostility between the young blond-haired man, uneasy and grim, and the mature, almost old man, though the wrinkles did not form on his face in order to show his age. Instead they showed, exhibited, a will that would now and always pierce straight through the necessary and secret skepticism built from experience. So many years of seeing and measuring.

He measured again and contemplated the youthful, expectant face; then he looked at the window blinded by the rain and, as if he were giving a sermon whose interpretation was impossible, said calmly:

"You studied, Augusto. A week ago the Curial gave you your degree, and as far as I remember, *cum laude*. Yesterday, the secular and reformist university ratified the degree. Obviously they didn't have *laude* to offer or bestow. As for theology, your grades are acceptable," he said, turning to look at the young man, faintly smiling with his eyes. "Then came the moment, which you pleaded for, sometimes kneeling and in tears, to continue in the Seminary, if we can call this that, to study, to make promises, to move through the inescapable lies, to don your robes and serve the Lord. I answered by patting you on the back, silently, maybe agreeing with a nod. That's what happened, isn't that right?"

"That's what happened, Father."

Bergner lifted his years out of the hard wooden chair, contemplated the marble cross – polished, dead, without nails or spears, without suffering; he let his fingers slip along the dark spines on the library shelf, took his time looking at the titles, and slowly sat back down with a pained expression on his face.

He sighed, exhausted, and crossed his fingers over his belly. The young man had not moved; with his belly pressed against the table, he let the blackness of his sweater rise slowly and tenaciously until it darkened his face.

Bergner waited the minutes that had been determined, minutes that were neither long nor short, but that had their life laid out for them. Then, more bored than exhausted, he said:

"You and I have been playing the same game for years. You and I respect each other, we've known how to pretend; each of us accepted the relationship, as if it were real, the deceitful and always selfish attitude of the other. In short, you and I agreed to lie, we've accepted the lie that protected the silence. But now . . ."

The young man lifted his head, his motionless face inserted into the corresponding evening.

"Agreed," he said, "I agree with everything. Here and now. I listen and I obey."

He didn't say it sarcastically. He was ready to listen and to speak. He waited until Bergner turned his eyes, uncertainly, to see his own soul, until the priest rose up, blaspheming:

"Damned be their souls. *Ora pro nobis*. Did you ever really believe that I believed in your farces? Didn't you know from the start that I was pretending to believe in them . . . and in my own words of encouragement and consolation? I knew you the first time I saw you and chose you. I needed four years of your life and four years of mine. Brausen gave them to me, blessed be his name. I now know you better than the mother who gave birth to you. The mother you are today ashamed of. And that's fine, because although you are commanded to respect your parents, your first duty is to love God above all else."

"That's what I do," the young man said, making a face of resignation full of weak, new-found cynicism.

Bergner took note of the ludicrousness of the prologue and his own fatigue. Then he surrendered to comedy and pathos. He jabbed his stiff index finger into the young man's chest.

"You weren't born to serve the Lord within the church. Nor did I groom you for that. I see you, I aspired for you to always be part of the world, Santa María and La Colonia, not representing Our Lord but rather introducing, strengthening faith in our Lord. Without the habit, indeed, because you never really wanted to wear it. But useful, with some kind of degree, to serve the church and with the church's support. I want you to be rich and triumphant in this terrestrial life; I want you to be hypocritical and subtle. I want you to serve us, and I offer to serve you. You will have to go to the Capital with a stipend that will just barely keep you from starving, and with other means of support that we'll talk about later. It will mean five or six years of absence and vigilance. If you fail, we will let you fall. In God's infinite wisdom, sparrows also freeze to death."

Bergner vaguely remembered the hundreds of times he'd said that last sentence. He settled back in his stiff chair like a laborer at the end of brutal day of work, accepted the young man's smile as unreserved agreement; then, slowly, looking at the black window, he spoke calmly about executors, mortgages and purchases, about the assets of the world, about inheritance and dazzling numbers. He said nothing about tithes because he considered the subject both hasty and inappropriate, and because they were waiting for him at the Club.

That's how the date of Augusto Goerdel's departure was set, as well as his destiny. And Father Bergner was the first to discover, after crossing himself under the streetlights in the plaza, that the face of the horseman in the statue of Juan María Brausen had begun to show traces of bovine features.

Nobody noticed, nobody told me that. Perhaps the old folks didn't see the change because they had the habit of looking at the head almost daily; the new folks, because they'd always seen it like that, without looking. Perhaps the patina, the poor light, the pigeons, my worn-out eyes, maybe a twisted joke of the devil. I'll look again tomorrow, in the sun.

The hardness of the bronze showed no sign at all of growing horns, only the placidity of a solitary and ruminant cow.

V

I heard the arrival of the horse at dawn and the whistle Jorge Malabia always used to announce his presence. I let him whistle and wait, I turned over in bed to pursue a happy, elusive dream. A while later another dream came, disjointed and melancholic, populated by the already forgotten dead.

It was probably between seven or eight in the morning when Díaz Grey accepted being awake, asked the servant to bring him a large cup of black coffee. Through the window he saw the colt furnished with all the silver imaginable, and Jorge Malabia sitting on the grass, drinking maté out of a thermos. He looked heavier, more patient and mature, maybe even fattened up by overwintering.

The horse had been guided there by an ancient custom that it shared with or that was imposed on it by Marcos Bergner (lost so many years ago in the fog).

A long time ago, the nationalists, the ranchers, strove to speak in rural slang, to wear hats with raised brims in the winter, and they favored ponchos over raincoats. It was the fatherland even if they trembled from the cold and had raincoats brought from Manchester or London at home.

In a different order, descending, Jorge was learning how to be an idiot. He now had two automobiles, but he insisted on using his part-Arab horse, and on openly carrying a gun when he had to communicate news that he considered important. Perhaps that way he felt more like a gaucho and a local.

The unwavering affection, the due respect of the old for the young, was now, from the window to the grass, invaded by resentment and distrust.

He watched him for a while until he emerged lucid from his dreams. He saw the colt and its silver furnishings, he saw Jorge constantly sipping maté, he saw his Canadian lumberjack shirt. The faded blond hair falling to his shoulders. That year, he remembered, long hair was the symbol, the shibboleth of machismo in Santa María, popular among the doubtful.

Two legacies, he thought, that will one day either unite us or separate us. Angélica Inés, his wife, was upstairs, asleep and drooling. Jorge was stretched out on the ground, bursting with the news that had propelled him to me, that forced him to wait for me, enter, place it forever in some corner of my office or the drawing room, inside me, in any case.

He, Jorge Malabia, had changed. He no longer suffered from suicidal sisters-in-law or impossible poems. He kept a fickle eye on *El Liberal*, bought land and houses, sold land and houses. He was now a man forsaken by metaphysical concerns, by the need to capture beauty in a poem or a book. Beauty as eternal and definitive as crushing a butterfly or a moth between his hands and observing for a brief moment the radiance that follows the blow and death.

His face and belly were fatter, and nobody could know to what end, what they would mean two or three years later. Nobody would make a sure bet about the almost immediate future of Jorge Malabia.

But I also felt changed. Not only aged by the years Brausen had imposed upon me and that can't be counted by the passage of three hundred and sixty-five days. I understood a long time ago that one of the aspects of his incomprehensible punishment was that he brought me into his world with an unchanging age somewhere between ambition, with limited time, and despair. Externally, always the same, with a few alterations of grey hairs, wrinkles, passing ailments, to conceal his purpose.

I, too, was different: my initial indifference had turned into false cordiality, on lips always ready to smile, a shameless and appeasing smile that meant: Brausen is in heaven, the world is perfect, you and I must be happy.

They believed me, when I could offer neither cures nor comfort. But the change in me had another aspect. I knew that it was easier and more powerful: I listened to secrets, always helping, absorbing, smiling. Then I would retreat, into a darkness I had prepared, to show my face that vacillated between worry and contemplation. I suffered the diseases of my sick patients. It wasn't an issue of my expertise as a doctor; there was a time when each one of my organs suffered the pain and distress of the patient's organ. (There were exceptions, of course, but nobody discovered them.)

Later, all of a sudden, I'd once again don my smile, my happiness, my understanding of the plenitude of light. Everything understood, everything cured. I would ask two or three questions, I would bare my teeth during each answer, and write out – in studied hieroglyphics – prescriptions for Barthé's pharmacy.

We were all happy, except my steel-trap vanity, which was shrouded from the moment I awoke until dawn, intermingled and distinctive in my dreams, never exposed, hidden until death by my sympathy and kindness.

I made him wait. The small horse below tilted its head, looking for real food in the grass. I shaved, bathed, dressed with care as if I didn't know who the visitor was. The sun was high in the sky. I told the monster on duty, dressed as a nurse, to bring Jorge into the office. There was more light there than in the drawing room.

I heard the sound of his boots on the stairs, and I begged silently for Angélica Inés not to wake up, for a few more hours to pass before the daily limbo and purgatory began, the first for her, the second for me.

Jorge entered, surprisingly like the man described on the previous page. The red and grey lumberjack shirt, the deliberately unkempt beard, the big boots, the ridiculous and large S&W moving on his hip, a deliberate tang of sweat that reached me not from his underarms but rather from the entirety of his defiant body, legs astride, imposing.

I looked at him calmly from my armchair. I knew that my empty eyes, my calm hands, resting and motionless, fingertip against fingertip, would make him explode. So we dispensed with the greetings.

"He killed her," Jorge shouted. "He killed her at midnight with a boy. She'd always thought it would be a girl. He killed her at midnight, and we looked for him to kill him but he'd already gone into hiding. We're going to find him, doctor, I swear we will."

And didn't he see – didn't he himself see – his grotesque dead Abel, resurrected by friends, acquaintances, in the village? Wasn't he thinking of God and Cain?

Because Cain was compelled to do it, he was compelled by a mandate that was not explicit but was inescapable.

He never wanted Abel's sheep, he rejected the tools of farming and became a hunter under the tireless gaze of God. Cain did it.

But Brausen carried out his forever inexplicable plan for us, acting like a political caudillo. He defended Cain before the examining magistrate, he warned the police that any punishment of the killer would lead to a seven-fold repetition of justice and revenge. And he hung on the killer a sign for prevention and immunity.

And in his cave, at the hour of the stag and sleep, he contemplated the green and triangular eye that peered at him unceasingly. Two or three weeks without words: *You had to know I would do it, because You yourself chose me, out of so many; You wanted me to do it and I did it. I don't know why You ordered me to do it. I don't care about the disquiet You promised me. I hunt and I eat because that's how You made man.*

You look at me, eye and triangle; You make me sleepy. Now the darkness is coming, now I am worn out and sated. I'm going to sleep. Tomorrow, perhaps, You will remove the eye, convinced it is useless. Tomorrow, perhaps, we will talk. You know me by heart; I want to see You.

He waited for weeks and months in the smoky cave. But Our Lord Brausen let centuries go by; the conversation became impossible because the ways of Brausen are unfathomable and because he wanted to establish murder in the race he had invented, or because he wanted to establish for-ever the certainty that for centuries the strongest would prevail against the weak and the peaceable.

For as long as it lasted, the green triangle defeated the insomnia of the fratricide, the hunter; it helped to eradicate his tiredness, his memory. He was happy, sprawled out and muscular, contemplating the soft light from the clear eye that was looking at him, now insignificant, never friendly but now listless, perhaps, he as well, sleepy.

VI

"Yes," said Díaz Grey. "It was inevitable. A few months ago, Goerdel himself came to me to announce the murder. A crime that had been initiated two hundred and seventy days earlier. And it was impossible to prevent it. It still hadn't happened, but it was impossible to stop it. Only by killing her, shooting a bullet into the victim's head."

"Words," said the young man, disguised and stiff, after incomprehension, anger, and silence. "The son of a bitch murdered Helga and knew what he was doing. We're going to look for him until we find him."

Díaz Grey held back. He held his stance as a well-dressed doctor at the opening of his office, clean-shaven, with a new tie, his long clean fingers clenched together to do damage to the terse jaw.

Then he yielded to his accumulated hatred of stupidity. He lifted his eyes to assess the figure, with its Alaskan shirt, high boots, a gun hanging off the wide belt. He also measured the faithless insolence.

And he said sweetly: "I've always hated those sons of bitches who now persecute Goerdel, Augusto, I think. I always hated, ever since I was a child, those half-starved sad sacks who (dressed in civilian clothes or in rags) salute a sergeant, an officer, or half a one. Both of them need it, the one for his hunger, his imagined children, his petty vices. The other wants a man who doesn't ask questions: not before shooting or after. During the exchange between the son of a bitch and the bastard there are no promises other than a weekly ration of crackers, the monthly barrel of maté. Moreover, of course, the miserable salary, the bloated uniform, worn out at the knees and the armpits."

"I'm not interested in your murder mystery. We're not interested in the police. We're going to find him today, wherever he's hiding, and then he'll figure things out in hell."

"Paradise will be a shared hell for all of us. Don't look for sins because the truth is, they don't exist. Brausen didn't even give us time to invent them."

Jorge Malabia had long ago passed the age of listening to sentences with biblical rumblings.

"Patricio," this was the name of the brother of the dead woman, "was far away, drunk all day and crying."

"And all of you, your circle of intimates, even if you're not crying, you are drunk out of a sense of solidarity."

"Also. We're Patricio's friends. And that Jew murderer tried to get into his wife's wake to show off a tear or two. And Patricio couldn't stand it anymore and tried to kill him."

"But you held him back, didn't you? Patricio came back from far away, but not from his drunkenness, to say goodbye to his sister and, while he was at it, exact his revenge. But his brother-in-law . . ."

"Fired a shot. That dirty Jew murderer."

"Goerdel is more Aryan, most likely, than you and I. There's probably not a single Jew from La Colonia. Aryans, Swiss, Catholics, Germans. But here, in Santa María, none of those words function as insults. As you were saying, Goerdel the Jew."

"The son-of-a-bitch murderer. And someone said he came here at dawn to hide. Is that true?"

Díaz Grey felt his hostility increase as Jorge paced, making the floor resound under his foreign and oversized boots. It was not, he thought, envy for the years that separated them, because the young man had time and he no longer did. It pained him that Jorge would offer his future to nothingness, to earning money without effort or purpose. It pained him that he would get fat, that he would mingle, so innocently, with the stupidity and filth of the future the city offered him.

"No," he said, "he didn't knock and ask me for help. But if he had, he would be here, with as much protection as I could offer him from idiotic and arrogant killers. Why didn't you kill him when he was being held at the wake? Because Patricio wasn't suffering enough, because he wasn't drunk enough or was too drunk. And all of you held Patricio back for reasons of decency and allowed the murdering Jew to escape."

Jorge had stopped in front of the desk and tried to meet the doctor's eyes.

"No," Díaz Grey continued, "you never had a love made real through melodrama. But you happily accepted the ease of denying yourself through farce. It's unfortunate; as Bergner, your family member, would say: May Brausen forgive you."

With an implacable smiling face, Malabia slowly and scornfully said:

"I think about my youth and I cry. Maybe, when I'm as old as you. Too bad we'll no longer be able to cry together. Unless you ask me to travel to where the cypresses grow. Even so, it will be a solitary cry."

"That's true," Díaz Grey said. "It will be impossible, I suppose. But still I can see the buffoonery. And if I do cry, I won't cry for myself. I don't have Goerdel here in this house. But I do have a lot of tall mirrors for you to see yourself in. One of Angélica Inés's whims, full-length mirrors. They all say she doesn't know anything about anything. But she understands, or understands herself. It doesn't matter; in every room you'll find a mirror that would work for your disguise. From the boots to the lock of hair. Not to mention the shirt and the comical gun. And if Patricio wanted to kill Goerdel, it wasn't with bullets, I'd wager. It would have been with a big knife for butchering deer. And now you'll chase down the murderer with wild dogs or with police dogs that they'll let you borrow from the garrison.

"But Goerdel didn't ask me for help," Díaz Grey continued. "The truth is, he called me from Colón at dawn. He said something about an airplane. I can imagine the journey. His voice. His voice wasn't cynical or afraid. He was just saying goodbye."

Malabia stopped and started to look at him, as if remembering, as if he could isolate each time he'd seen the doctor over the years. And those memories remained independent, united barely by name.

"A curiosity," Malabia said. "A very old curiosity. Now I feel like you've been prolonged, a cumulative effect, like the pharmaceutical prospectuses say. Who are you? Forgive me; I don't care, I don't need you because I can see you and judge. But I am interested in knowing your past, knowing who, what you were, Doctor, before you mingled with the inhabitants of Santa María. The ghosts that Juan María Brausen invented and imposed."

The question seemed funny and sad to Díaz Grey. At least the tension, the pursuit, the unavoidable idiocy of the people who populated his world faltered: the stupidity of the appeased, the stupidity of those who said they believed in universal – or Santa María – happiness, writing in underground newspapers or talking at tables in cafés along the coast.

Of course there were other young people, respectable young people, who let themselves die in the few remaining forests, of thirst, of unknown insects, of fevers that seemed to descend from remote tropical regions, from the green jungles of the Amazon and the Orinoco, determined and unmistakable. Sometimes, to their greater humiliation, they were killed by the machine guns of the Legion for Good Decorum that, supposedly, followed the orders of Juan María Brausen.

"My past?" Díaz Grey said slowly, brooding.

VII

Díaz Grey got up and brought two decks of playing cards and a thick envelope full of photographs and letters to his desk.

"There is a past," he said, almost with bewilderment, as if he didn't fully understand.

Jorge Malabia says or thinks: It's sweet or has for me the sweetness of mystery to still call the woman in the pictures the faceless woman. And since faceless woman was what Díaz Grey himself said that time, with a different intention, perhaps the first time that he agreed to talk about her, acknowledge to another her existence in a steady recitative voice, a voice that even for him reached the heights of mystery, it didn't refer to the past and its remote pain, nor to the present and its bewilderment, its perplexity. A rheumatic Díaz Grey, Malabia imagined in a falsified memory, wearing a bathrobe, boiled-wool slippers, a scarf and a beret, leaning his left shoulder on one or another Bach concerto, the bottle of rum, the lemon juice, the large steamy jug of hot water to his right.

Díaz Grey and the relentless survival of his sparkling eyes, of the almost totally disengaged testimonial expression on his thin, smooth, and eroded face. Díaz Grey, barely moving in the large armchair in the enormous and absurd sitting room of the house built by Jeremías Petrus, so many years before, so many times propped up, maintained in a farce of good repair by master builders and laborers, never distinct from the capricious, difficult, original plans laid out by Petrus himself with cold resolve and fury. The mansion resting on pillars that was now his through the rights of unsought conquest. Díaz Grey saying, telling me:

"I saw her last when she was three years old and I've held onto every photograph I've been able to obtain, almost from the time of her birth until that age. Then, very infrequently, I received other portraits, other faces that briskly scaled the years, nobody knows in what direction, but definitely moving father away from what I had seen and loved, from what was possible for me to remember. With Brausen's permission, naturally. And these, those new faces were for me, with each dull, slow mail delivery, with each year, more incomprehensible, much more, much more remote from something that undoubtedly mattered more than she or I: my love for the three-year-old girl. Yes. The new faces were divorced from me, from my love, or from my love for the memory and for the suffering of this memory. With cyclical regularity I would substitute the playing cards of my nocturnal solitaire; the solitaire games that slowly and without conviction accompanied me through the misfortune of insomnia and the familiar sounds of the dawn. Of course there were never as many of those photographs face-down as there were playing cards. It was, is, the only trick I allow myself. It was, is, always the gentle, irresistible summons of a debauched need. Later came the pills, sometimes the needle, sleeping till noon. But before that I had no choice but to give in, lean back in my chair, place my keys on the desk, and stroke them with my index finger until I touched the key to the desk drawer. I'd take out the envelope with the photos, pile them up, the playing cards of the new solitaire, and continue playing my game, a game that always died without letting me know if I had won or lost. Then I would scatter the photos, now face up, those that were mine and those that had sped up her escape. Though timeless, though knowing I was a slave to the dream of a paranoid wretch, I respected the chronology. Each portrait has on the back a tiny date, written in my myopic digits. I would spread them out on top of the desk, on top of the months, to the left, on top of the years at the end and to the right. From the baby in diapers a few months old to the most recently arrived. And then, Jorge Malabia, I played the big game of solitaire; I looked carefully and calmly at the faces in order to suffer better, so that the game would be worth playing: the face, the faces, evolution and change, small and vindictive transformations. I would light a cigarette, bring my eyes up close, then move them far away, I would understand the changes or try to understand. Sometimes for hours, always wasted. But solitaire with the photos had its own rules and I respected them. I ended by gathering up mine, those that didn't go past the age of three, and then I focused on those of the escape, carried out with violent leaps. Now appeared the doubtful similarities, the secret, the impotence, twelve or twenty faces of disgrace. Growing and challenging me, carefully placed in chronological order, the faces quickly started disappearing, almost without gradations, exhibiting the impudence of the changes, altering the ovals of the faces, the shapes of the lips and the meanings of the smiles, the shape of profiles, necks, and cheeks; selfishly and incessantly changing the shape of the eyes that, nevertheless, remained alert, large, and apart. Until I found out, that's how long the game lasted, that she was not she, that I was looking at another person with no relationship to the pile of photographs collected over the first three years, far away from here, in the other lost world.

"And one night, which will not be any sadder than the others, I will burn all the photos of ages past three years old. If I decided to think of her as a faceless woman, it wasn't because she wasn't turning into a different woman, year by year, one delayed mail delivery after another. I did it because I didn't have the strength to tolerate her being a person.

VIII

At first Goerdel used a buggy, a vehicle topped with a black hood that hailed from the hysterical whims of time, pulled by a fat unclipped bay. The vehicle fit with Father Bergner's plans and the dirt roads of La Colonia taking shape under the weight of carts, oxen, carriages, trucks, men and women who walked back and forth, demolishing the grass under their feet.

It is impossible to seriously calculate the duration of this first stage during which Goerdel sensed his own foolishness and the change of seasons from inside his black buggy and his required attire, also black. Testaments, mortgages, sales and purchases, loans with interest rates determined by Father Bergner, with money provided by Bergner or the mysterious Chapter, which met at the church on the second and fourth Monday of each month.

Much later it became known that Goerdel's favorite duty was settling disputes among neighbors in La Colonia: fences and walls built during the night, livestock grazing on someone else's land, narrow streams forced to seek different courses.

In those cases, Goerdel made do with his percentage. But he was much happier listening to complaints and depositions, investigating, wearing himself out writing certified reports, which always argued, to the judge, for the validation and innocence of the client who was paying him, a tax on chance.

For Goerdel the weariness, the convoluted discussions, the smiling diplomacy, the measured pats on the backs of his clients, the sighs that confirmed that an eviction could be converted into money, into thousands of reales astonishingly more numerous than those he could have aspired to during his first forays as a merchant or middle man. Starting with his very first earnings, he turned over his entire profit to Father Bergner, but he never renounced, never agreed to discuss, the unyielding five percent that he settled on before his first torturous journey to farms, ranches, and slums, which aspired to conduct business in bricks, adobe, and electric lights.

"It's better this way," Father Bergner had said, approving the rickety buggy and the small, hairy, and tireless horse. "For now, they don't trust the rich; when they get rich with their cows, their milk, their butter, wines, and cheeses, they'll start to not trust the poor."

Bergner also said: "I know La Colonia is Catholic. But you mustn't forget that each family brought its own Bible, and that's where they keep track of births, marriages, and deaths. You mustn't forget the physical, Teutonic weight of those tomes. And that they prefer the Old Testament to the Gospels. I don't worry about the atheists, because they'll return to us in their misfortunate, uncertainty, or old age. But I fear the incursions being made by the heretics of the Seventh Day, those twosomes of Jehovah's Witnesses, those Mormons, those colonels of the Salvation Army. That whole pack, tenacious and better paid than us. In the meantime I don't know if Jews have arrived. But I fear that the chosen land, La Colonia, could, by dint of patience, become fertile ground for those wretches. That's why I need you, more and more with each passing day."

Goerdel did his part by defending the One, Holy, Catholic, and Apostolic

Church, without any need for polemics, as confident and calm as if he were alluding to the distant places where the sun rose in the morning and set at the end of the day.

He believed disproportionately in Father Bergner's fears; he persisted tenaciously in his five percent, in his multiplication tables.

So Bergner came to think of him as a safe ally, as a young, strong, handsome blond man, who spent every day wandering along the roads of La Colonia, pursuing his five percent, swearing his faith in the true Church, in Saint Peter and his successors.

Then Bergner began to think differently, and he convinced himself that he had been charged with another duty.

He was intelligent and clever, his opinions continued to be sacred to many hundreds of the faithful, he knew how to identify the lies during confession without ever showing it, meting out punishment, without any scorn, with Our Fathers and Hail Marys, the number and speed adapting to the sins mumbled to him hesitantly, before the feigned doubts, before the always romantic, "Father, I know that I have sinned." And, moreover, age did not prevent him from valuing and intuiting the qualities of the women kneeling on the other side of the pretend curtain that separated God from the guilty, who reeled off their repentance on a daily basis.

On the other hand he knew, one could say, all of Santa María, all of La Colonia. And his conversations with Goerdel helped him learn of increased or eroded fortunes, of others who tolerated without difficulty the inheritance taxes, the taxes on the unconscious use of air, on the right to walk through the streets.

He managed figures, beauties, reputations; he could act slowly and surely, and he brought Goerdel close to the Hausers – a house in Santa

María, land and a house in La Colonia; he conspired, made definitive statements that could sound like fair observations, objective and weightless.

Once he was certain that he had won he didn't want to rush things; he kept talking and dropping comments, alluding for the sake of the Hausers to a bloodless but inexcusable holy war against vague and powerful enemies. He judged his surplice to be old and worn and ordered a new one from the Capital, spelling out his preferences, inserting a touch of heterodoxy to the cut and length.

Months later, the Friday before Christmas, he married Augusto Goerdel to Helga Hauser, nodding to every *I do* that he prompted and heard. Already then, Patricio Hauser, a witness at the wedding, hated Augusto Goerdel.

IX

We weren't allowed to age, only grow slightly deformed, but nobody prevented the years from passing, from being marked by celebrations, by the disgusting and joyous to-do of the large and noisy majority that was unaware – sometimes oblivion could be believed – that Brausen's bureaucrats had brought them into the world with a death sentence attached to every birth certificate.

Therefore, tearing pages off the calendars generously distributed by drug companies was never more than a habit, more or less symbolic, like tearing off sheets of toilet paper.

This should, this could, I'm attempting to explain persuasively why nobody in Santa María knew the precise year, month, the number that corresponded to Goerdel's return. Nor could we – nor can we now – believe in any convincing response to his short, unnecessary visit.

We'd forgotten about him; apathetically and routinely, we tore many pages off the calendars, persistently casting aside the days of Saint Sylvester and Saint Lucian. Suddenly – on Saint Maurilius Day – we found out he was among us, first at the Plaza, then in one of the houses he owned, next to the beach, in Villa Petrus. In a place that could have been mine.

He came: worn, pale, tall, and upright as always. Brausen's green light must have been due to a secret motive, to a plan that we wouldn't be able to understand until we had grandchildren. Not understand even once we were convinced. To us, Brausen always worked in mysterious ways.

Goerdel arrived and remained in seclusion for a week in the white-washed building the assistant archbishop called Church or Seminary. It depended on the listener. But it was always a church to us.

Then one rainy day Bergner requested a meeting with Díaz Grey and they spoke about other mysteries, comparable to the almost equally unavoidable and infinite one that was common to all holidays and usual misfortunes.

The priest was still tall and broad but he appeared to be slightly diminished and ill-tempered.

Bergner said:

"I neither believe nor have stopped believing, putting aside Goerdel's penances, his confessions and the number of hosts he continues to swallow. For a while now I've wanted to ask you if you've noticed that sometimes, in the afternoons, the head of the horse in the statue has features that are more bovine than equine."

"It's possible, I've never noticed," Díaz Grey said.

He looked out his office window; but from there he could make out only the damp haunches of the inferior beast.

"But the horseman. Yes, I've always suspected him of misunderstandings. As for the saddle, I think that on certain nights the horn seems to rise; I'm certain that with the help of a few hours of contemplation, I see spurs. But I don't think it's worth the effort. With all due respect, Father, I think we'll still be alive to enjoy the earthquake that will carry the old nag and the ambiguous horseman all the way to hell. Too bad Santa María is so far away from the Andes."

"But during the inauguration and the speeches," the doctor continued, "the horse was on the verge of looking like a docile cow, and the figure on top had the features of a foal, of an unbreakable beast. I didn't look carefully at them again. But the process must have continued. The docile cow and the mustachioed horseman. But don't forget: a cow gives milk but can also gore."

Díaz Grey opened the book on his desk and began to read out loud:

"And to return to the horseman, Father, I think it possible to make out the head of a horse, the snout of a stubborn donkey, the narrow forehead of a bulldog, the pug nose of a pig, the stupid profile of an ox. As you can see, last night I was reading Ibsen. To humor my insomnia."

"A lost soul, but great," the priest said absentmindedly.

Then the Father quickly made the sign of the cross and wanted to speak about more important, more immediate things; though he didn't want to appear rushed, whether he was or not. At least he was speaking as if deep in solitary meditations.

"Augusto Goerdel, Doctor. As you already know, for you live in a city where only good deeds transpire in secret, Goerdel, the accountant, returned to Santa María and spent a week or more in seclusion in my Seminary. He slept in the same room he occupied during his years as a student. One could almost say that, apart from liturgical rituals, we spent seven days face-to-face. He left, and he could have gone to find repose at the most luxurious hotel in Colón. Patricio Hauser disappeared a long time before, and Jorge Malabia has better things to think about and remember than that absurd vengeance. Besides, these people, the people of Santa María, are weak when it comes to holding on to their passions. Even curiosity fades after two or three months. On the other hand, Goerdel is rich, very rich. And in this world the rich suffer only brief preliminary scandals. Fireworks."

"Forgive me, Father. Goerdel had a mother. I saw her myself, years ago, in the poorest house in La Colonia. Planks and sheet metal and cardboard."

"Yes, Goerdel's son (we always think about the second one), both of Goerdel's sons are studying in Germany. Years ago Goerdel gave his mother a good house in La Colonia. She never stepped foot in Santa María. And she died two months after she moved."

"It must have been a long time ago. I don't remember signing the certificate. So our friend Augusto Goerdel has no heirs here. And other than you, no friends, either."

"He's not my friend," Bergner said curtly. "He is my son in God."

"I understand. I never knew you to lie."

During a tacit pause, during a silence that had become tacit through both of their wills, they continued to look at each other and look away. Finally Díaz Grey lost and said:

"Mr. Augusto Goerdel, notary public."

"Yes, we must return to our flock," the priest said, barely smiling; he didn't seem ill, rather confident as always. "Of course, I've consulted others. And our Lord every night. But I was interested in your opinion and not because you're a medical doctor."

Díaz Grey nodded in agreement. Bergner wanted to forestall an extended pause.

"You must know the Insauberrys. A couple of deadbeats more roughly hewn than a gaucho's boots; believers, irreproachable. If things worked through example, this city would ring in heaven, and I could lock up my confession booth."

"Yes," the doctor said. "Once in a while the Insauberrys called me about something going on in their lungs or liver. She or he. Or one of those childhood diseases. Fortunately, nothing serious. I think they also have millions here in La Colonia, in the Capital."

"Yes, untold acreage and many businesses. But they remain as humble and frugal as they were when they were poor, when I married them. They aren't rich; they are, materially, powerful. But they will pass, without any difficulty, I am certain, through the eye of a needle."

"News flash," Díaz Grey said. "There are no camels."

"Right; some poor, far-away creature read and wrote camel."

Then the priest lifted his pure and tortured countenance; his eyes reflected the afternoon light and Díaz Grey's pessimistic gaze.

"And in addition to all those assets, they have a twelve-year-old daughter, the youngest of six previous ones, all girls.

"Now let's talk," the priest continued, "about what matters, the reason for this visit. As you know, Augusto returned to the Seminary about ten days ago. For all that time, without me being able to swear if he was sincere or deceitful, August Goerdel was telling me a dream. He told it so many times, between tears and prayers, that now, for me, it is exactly as if I had dreamed it. I close my eyes and I see it, perhaps I embellish it, perhaps I mix it with the memory of a prayer card. For years, shortly after the death of Helga Hauser, Goerdel dreamed every night that his dead wife, dressed in white all the way to the ground, came to him holding the hand of an Insauberry girl and just barely pushed her so that she would move ahead and be recognized. He would say that in that dream – repeated, chronic – the dead woman's attitude was not one of ordering or offering. She was simply displaying the girl, she wanted the dreamer not to forget her."

"Okay," the doctor said, mocking him in his thoughts but respecting the priest, "now our friend Goerdel wants to adopt a twelve-year-old girl. It's understandable. He had only boys."

Bergner sighed, between offense and fury.

"Forgive me, Doctor. But your jokes don't amuse me. Brausen was right to have placed you in this world."

"Agreed, Father. Nor did he err with you. Santa María needs you. I would almost say that this city is inconceivable without you, nor you without this city. I would add, without much of a stretch, La Colonia."

The priest nodded and managed to adopt a meek and neutral voice.

"A bad joke. You sensed the truth at my first mention of the dream."

"Repetitive, persistent, and reliable. And I don't believe in Goerdel. Not in his dreams or his vigils. He's a bad apple, with all due respect for your opinion. But I don't know your opinion."

"Just a moment. If I didn't have doubts I wouldn't be here. I would know my path and reach the end without consulting anybody but God. But I have doubts. There are moments when Goerdel's desperation seems to me to be sincere. He makes me feel pity, compassion. I see him pursued by this dream, I feel he is a condemned man, I think Helga begs him, night after night, to accept the girl."

"Yes," the doctor crooned. "I take her as my wife, my lawfully wedded wife. When I was a child, I heard and repeated in unison the same song. I didn't understand it completely, it was impossible for me to understand the carnal meaning of the words. But they were funny and moving. I think Goerdel already knows about that. Not to mention the millions, of course. You, father, have doubts, and I have none. So I can help you. Trust Brausen. One day, to your surprise, he will enlighten him. Nothing about the millions, of course. Because *su madre es una rosa y su padre es un clavel*. Strange, isn't it? *C'est toujour la même chanson.* But anyway it's about a party or a childhood doubt. You said the child was twelve? And unable to foresee the horror that awaits her of blood in her panties as she's serving water tea and biscuits to her dolls."

Bergner got up and said goodbye with barely a nod of his head. He didn't slam any of the doors.

X

Two or three months of mellow and ochre autumn crawled through the leafless streets of Santa María.

The doctor, Díaz Grey, was walking from one end of the city to the other, writing identical prescriptions, saying flu to the youngest, influenza to the elderly. He didn't kill any of his patients, or nobody, in spite of their different ages, agreed to die. Miramonte and Grimm chewed on their disappointments; but they both continued to greet the doctor politely and with respect, trusting in a proximate and happy future.

For Díaz Grey, at least, it was no secret that Our Lord Brausen had agreed to bestow his light on Father Bergner. So many days and nights of entreaty and prayer, so many sweaty dawns with the dead woman pushing the girl forward, finally breaking her silence to dole out her instructions. Always dressed in white.

Perhaps Bergner needed a new roof on the Seminary; or he longed to bring an organ from the Capital, one that didn't reproduce with ungodly verve the wheezing of an old asthmatic or the caterwauling of ten cats in heat. Leaving Juan María Brausen aside, he did not act, I'm certain, out of personal desires.

Whatever the reason, every Thursday Bergner and Augusto Goerdel paid a visit of several hours to the Insauberry mansion. It always took place at five o'clock, tea-time; and while the adults conversed in the main sitting room about future harvests, the winds of fate, scandals (barely alluded to), and the quality of the cake, María Cristina, the intended, was playing with her dolls in her bedroom. It's possible that the four adults, bored, speechless, expected and believed they would bring on, through magic or desire, the happy, ignorant girl's first period, so they could speak unimpeded about money, a dowry, and a honeymoon that, by dint of silence, expanded its vistas, and thereby its chimera.

XI

"Crazy," Jorge Malabia said.

It's likely that by that time he had given up poems and was only writing editorials for *El Liberal*, dictated to him by his father from beyond the grave, timidly embellished with populist, almost demagogic turns of phrase.

"But," he continued, enraptured, "not the kind of crazy one might imagine. You must understand that, you must know. Not the threatening, incoherent kind of crazy that puts us on our guard. This is something else. Serene and proud, speaking about deals and pricing with the confidence of a travel agent. Unhurriedly broadening the offerings so that the newspaper will publish the ones he calls proof of an injustice that won't hurt anybody, not after all these years. Firmly, calmly, certain that the only problem is the price. Proof of his madness and his clever corruption. I said no to him seven times. I think I convinced him, and then hunger struck. It must have been three o'clock when he collected the copies and stood up. He was still talking about posthumous justice, even though he's still alive, both sad and carefree. He promised to see you, he doesn't want anything to do with my uncle Bergner, whether dying or healthy. It's easy to explain; I've kept the surprise for the end. He lives in Germany, true; but in the communist part. And he's a Catholic priest, a papist. He keeps having children. He's on his third, with his second wife, the Bock. Maybe a special bull, maybe he just dresses like a priest. He wears a cap of unknown origin, a cap, I'm certain, stolen off a corpse from the war. It's made of grey wool, with four leather straps. Over his prop, the cassock, he wears a lined overcoat, with a leather collar and lapels. He's no longer Goerdel. Out of humility, he lowered himself to Johannes Schmidt. He clicks his heels when he greets you and bows when he offers his hand. But he's still the same sleazy son of a bitch, and he shamelessly offers up the benevolent smile of a Catholic missionary or of a communist who's passing out slogans like medallions. He discovered, I have no idea how, the book of very bad poems I wrote and published when I was twenty. He also found an old and faltering Chilean edition of Ernesto Borges. Essays. He sent all of it to his patron in Berlin. Since he's a gentleman and mocks our, Latin America's, sentimentalism, he considered it his duty to leave me a copy of what he engendered, in a frenzy, on one of the typewriters at *El Liberal*. I brought it for you. I don't know why he talks about Juan María Brausen's conjugal exploits. Everybody knows he's still in the clouds, controlling us from heaven."

That's my memory, translated, of Malabia's excessive words. It was the middle of the afternoon, the drizzle and the distress were brushing against my windows, alcohol turned out to be useless.

Then I read the letter sent by Goerdel Schmidt to Berlin, too long to copy here but containing a few curious details:

Herr Director of the German State Library,
Berlin, Democratic Republic of Germany

Highly Esteemed Sir,
I haven't been able to send you books for a long time. I think one of the last books I was able to send you was a copy of Sokrates, signed by the author, Monseñor Romano Guardini. I am now sending you a book by Jorge Malabia, dedicated to your library by the author, as well as a work by Ernesto Borges.

As for Malabia's personality, allow me to inform you that he is sophisticated, skeptical, not at all amenable. He doesn't offer anybody so much as a glass of water. But, in spite of all this, I would say that he is almost the national prototype of the Santa María native, because I have spent many days in this place and can say honestly that in the forty-nine countries on four continents that I have visited since the Second World War, I know no country less hospitable than this one. People here are sullen. And I don't think that this is all due to the country's internal political situation. I believe this is "national character" already historically crystallized. Because it doesn't belong to only one social class. It belongs to all of them.

Hence, after getting to know Santa María personally, I do not shed as many tears for this country as I did before. If they want to be selfish and adopt the position that "we are better than you and everybody else in the entire world," then let them solve their own problems and not ask anybody else for anything. They state clearly the subjective motivation of the revolutionaries: sex and power, to destroy those who are in power because they are in power, because they are aesthetically ugly, unfair, rich, et cetera. But this obviously is not pure idealism, it's idealism that is not positive but rather destructive, negative. If they don't want to build a society based on love, what kind of society do they want to build? Obviously, all they want is power, in order to feel powerful. Pure vanity. Pure expression of "machismo," the sui generis disease of Latin America, all rooted in the sexual, and very primitive. At the level of the most primitive societies of the jungle.

The university students are disgusting. They envy the First Lady because she has eighteen children.

But to show off, they try to impress one with how important they are. The doctors say that they are so good they can easily go to other countries . . . everything from Santa María is superior to everything else. And they don't even exist in Latin America. They say they go to Australia and Canada and "they realize that, being from Santa María, they are culturally superior to their neighbors."

So I believe that this country, with all its presumption, doesn't need anybody's help. I'm leaving next week. I've done nothing. What can one do in a country where everybody is a genius?

Greetings to your entire staff. See you soon.
Johannes Schmidt, student

Nightfall, always slow and deceptive when the weather is bad, had begun. I had the lights turned on, I used the stethoscope with the solemn manipulations of a shaman, I wrote out prescriptions whose futures were uncertain, I returned to my chair and to my reflections on that small part of the world that I had been allowed to believe to be comprehensible.

My notes on History, when I was a student and ambitious, were always poor. Not for lack of intelligence or attention; I found that out much later, and without any need for analysis. The fault lay in my inability to correlate the dates of military or political battles with my vision of the history they were teaching me and that I tried to understand. For example: from Julius Cesar to Bolívar everything was, for me, a novel that was obvious though unachievable. Endless facts, sometimes contradictory, were offered to me in books and in class. But I was so free and awkward that I constructed a fable out of all this, never wholly believed, in which the heroes and events merged and separated capriciously. Napoleon in the Andes, St. Martin in Arcola.

I always felt the repetitiveness: heroes and peoples rose and fall. And the results that I was able to assert, I know now, were a hundred or a thousand Santa Marías, huge as far as population and territory, or small and provincial like the one I had happened upon. The dominant dominated, the dominated obeyed. Always awaiting the next revolution, which would always be the last.

It wasn't the best mood to be in to welcome Goerdel, in the exclusive Santa María night.

I think everything was proper; we shook hands, and nobody thinks in detail about what that outstretched hand has done in the past few hours.

At least, I believe, not either he or I. Hands always acted previously and in secret.

He must not be crazy, I thought; rather: obstinate, scornful, with a fixed idea. The man seemed determined to walk like a lunatic through all the walls built by the sane; to violate, lucidly, all the obstacles that we might construct as the heirs to the madness of well-being, to the unchanging self in passivity.

I felt the old fear of an encounter in the wasteland.

I offered him a seat and a drink. He chose to place his drizzled-on hat on the carpet.

To use words I don't like and serve no purpose, I will say that the man was serene, having run out of time, having been violently released from a doubt that had continued to grow until it cast him, once again, for the very last time, upon the coast of Santa María.

After meaningless greetings were spent and faded, Goerdel spread out on my table the six or ten photocopies he had used with Malabia.

There was no prologue, I didn't look at the shiny copies; I looked at him and I waited. I could never know if he was improvising woe or reciting a speech he'd learned by heart. Perhaps the same one that bombed at *El Liberal*, the same one he was willing to repeat in the ears of those people of Santa María who were eager for the latest scandal. And not to everybody, because Goerdel had worked out respectable and foolproof points of dissemination. I believe that the request to publish the letters in Malabia's newspaper never went past the bluffing stage.

I continued to wait, and he spoke. He was almost bald, his blond and white hair plastered down with grease. Taller and skinnier, I thought, more at ease and almost floating in his new clothes. I looked for diagnoses, syndromes, certain I wouldn't get it right. He looked older and in good health, unbridled and shy in turn, until the silence, my quietude, impelled him to speak. He only said, as if he were recurring to various omissions, patchy and calm:

"Here are the letters, doctor, at least the irrefutable photocopies of the letters that Helga received in the months when the entire city – her friends, relatives, those driven mad by a nonexistent truth – spurred each other on to accuse me of a crime. There was no crime, there couldn't have been, even though I was, even if I were, the one responsible."

The subdued voice hewed closely to the automatic speech he had brought, for me, as well, the voice that was complicit with the twilight that was beginning to devour the daily light Brausen, Juan María, almost Juntacadáveres for the atheists, repeatedly gave us.

"Read the letters, now or tomorrow. I was far away, in the Capital, and afterwards, attending Catholic workshops in Chile. Frei and Tómic. The letters, you will see, are disgusting. But the dates don't vary, they are precise. You are a doctor and understand. I wasn't in Santa María when my murderous daughter was conceived. Not even if she had been a well-formed seven-monther."

The most disconcerting part was that the man was speaking without irony, without smiles. No sadness, either. He remained upright and calm, turning the leather easy chair into the hard stool of a friar.

And afterwards I understood that he had returned not only to fight against injustice and slander. He wanted to talk about himself, he wanted to explain himself, he wanted to cover with disinterested cynicism a time in his past, the anecdote of a woman who'd died, years before, not because of him but because of a baby girl, the unfathomable will of Brausen. He didn't mention sin – the word, for me, had no meaning; perhaps it no longer did for him, either.

So he spoke about Goerdel, dispassionately, always in a recitative monotone.

"Ever since I was eleven or twelve I was determined to triumph. The start date is vague, I admit, but it should coincide, a month here or there, with the first contamination of my dreams. If you were as intelligent as I, you would understand that the will to triumph had nothing to do with what we call success, mediocre greed, profit, money. A lot of money in my case. What obsessed the young boy, me, was the need to escape from the poverty and the stench of cows in La Colonia, newly established. La Colonia was built according to a plan, a development plan, if I may, approved of by the adults. They had beards and conversed after work, food was scarce, almost always radish salad, I think, and then cocoa. Very thick; I don't know how they did it. Maybe they brought it on the ship or ships, maybe they bought it or stole it, precisely in this land where only a madman would think of planting cacao. But they were happy looking at the motionless teaspoon stuck in the heart of the cup. Always cups that were bigger than normal. We had arrived together, we had, all of us, come from the same place. But I listened to them without understanding them, I could only see half smiles and scowls that would last till tomorrow, an entire day. The noise dominated by voices. Silences came, but I didn't understand; I saw only dark mouths and teeth sunk in the fleece of the beards that scrambled over the blondness and stopped long before they reached the mustaches that blackened the distance and the sweetness of Santa María's weather. As you hear, Doctor, I'm using the same language that works for you when you lie. No offense intended. We all lie, even before words. For example: I tell you lies and you lie listening to them. But something always remains, invincible, from the first, the oldest memories, that are conserved in spite of every effort to forget them, unlikely also to be eroded by any of those deliberate attempts that we all make to remember, without meaning to, with varying frequency. And so it was, allow me to explain. All those imbeciles who walk around Santa María and La Colonia would like to know (sometimes, frankly, when they light their pipes and pretend to be interested in the colors of the sunset; others, smoking fake Cuban cigars at the Plaza or the Club). They all asked, directly or backhandedly, about my old memory, the first and last one, that I had brought from Europe. You see: I always lied. I talked about people fleeing down the highways, I tried to offer them burning villages, scents, columns of smoke. I also deceived Father Bergner. He merely listened and nodded with an approval that seemed incomprehensible, without asking me to pause so he could pray in Latin.

"But my real and, I know, eternal memory, has nothing to do with the brutality of the war. That one or any other.

"I returned to Santa María to defame and feel absolved. A whim, if you like. But sometimes what they call a whim is the result of years of shame, of silent suffering."

The visitor's voice continued in a monotone, without pits or peaks, without any indication that it could stop before finishing the memorized speech.

Díaz Grey listened, almost without moving, attempting out of habit to collect the symptoms and form an opinion in silence. He couldn't say that Goerdel was crazy, he couldn't accept such a perfect farce. He said:

"Excuse me. You live in Europe."

"Germany."

"You live in Germany and I think you'll die there. I don't understand why, after so many years (you must have a son who's a cadet in Prussia), after so many years you return to this parody of a city to spread your defamation and seek absolution for a fantastical crime."

"There is no longer a military academy in Prussia."

"Forgive me. But in one or the other Germany there must be academies where they teach the art of killing any girl older than fifteen years old."

"I understand. It's difficult, it seems strange to you. Maybe, a bit more than that; abnormal, absurd. But my response is: pride. Maybe I want revenge. But that's not worth much, that's not my motivation. I want only to prove that the child couldn't be mine. I didn't kill Helga. I had nothing to do with her pregnancy and the birth. It's the pride of proving, so many years later, that I am or was innocent. My pride is stronger than anything those poor fools can pull together. I want to prove it, I am proving it, with these photocopies of the letters. Compare the dates. A cold-blooded cuckold, very Nordic, thank God, and each day more so, if you wish, but never a murderer. Understand: it's a fantasy about the last name Goerdel that will soon be forgotten, and forever, by the louts who besmirch what they insist on calling a city but is merely a sixteenth-century town, and to those who continue to disembowel the land in La Colonia that is neither Swiss nor German. I'll be at the hotel for less than a week, and then oblivion, goodbye forever, which on the other hand is completely unimportant. But I ask you to read the letters and spread the word."

"The Plaza Hotel?"

"Possibly. But I won't receive any visitors, and I plan not to answer the phone."

Then he stood up quickly, unnecessarily smoothed out his garments, and before clicking his heels, his head held high, almost looking at the ceiling, thinning out each word, he said:

"I don't know his name, nor do I care. But all men should be saddened and angered because a vile act was committed in the town."

XII

Jorge Malabia was suddenly in a good mood. Mine remained the same, adult and serene, and changed only many months later when my daughter arrived in Santa María and I tried to bring them together without any specific purpose, only out of almost scientific curiosity, to watch them, as far as I could, react. Perhaps this is not a different story.

Malabia would arrive at nightfall and I'd give up my chess, my solitaire, and Bach. But I never gave up the ritual of going to Angélica Inés's bedroom to bring her a full-length mirror and listen to her giggle with happiness when she looked at her body, more skinny than naked. I had multiple ways of helping her. Sometimes I'd tell her enthusiastically that the world had never known a whore as whorish as she; others, I appeared saddened, not too much, because she looked lustful, lost in her impudence. She would probably never understand me. But she always pressed the bones in her arms into her ribs to make herself laugh or cry. She always ended up happy, sliding into one of her mysteriously tangled dreams that sometimes she remembered, or dreamed again as she held me, trembling, so that I would listen to her.

I repeat that thanks to the resurrected Jorge, sarcastic and almost happy, we spent many dawns with a bottle of J.B. and the inseparable good fortune of all fools' paradises.

So, little by little, with feigned impatience, we came to believe that all the photocopied letters had been written by a man; that the same man had written all eight of them;

that in six of the letters he referred to or insisted on the birth of a child;

that in one of the letters he had written, shamelessly, "the fruit of our love";

that the salutation went from "Dear Helga" to "My love or divine or adored";

that the dates matched, without irrefutable exactitude, the gestation and birth of the girl;

that all were signed with the letter *H* in capital letters;

that the person who had drawn the letters had chosen black or dark blue ink and had spilled it with a hand that though astonishing in its firmness maintained margins of unchanging width;

that, having no paper other than the too shiny kind used by photographers, it was impossible to determine the true age of the letters.

We also discovered – and this was perhaps the only poor pride left to us by dawn – that all the letters had been written in an identical style: they began crude and platonic, continued like that for two paragraphs, then descended, wallowing in a furious list of anatomical features and in the meticulous memory of the most curious forms of coupling. That was not only pornography copied from the little Catalan booklets that used to accompany us throughout the few solitary hours we managed to carve out during our pubescence: they reeked of deliberate crassness, hatred, the desire to offend.

Until, one night, after asking the newsroom at *El Liberal*, right before closing, if there had been any news about the Palestinians or the death of one of the Kennedys, Jorge Malabia opted to be obvious, one of the many ways to err offered to man.

"All this filth isn't equivalent to an absence. A single letter written by her. Even if it was just a note. A "love you your.""

"Indeed. As Goerdel would say, let the dead bury their dead. And let the sons of bitches remain faithful to their destinies. And it is also written, I think, that whoever kills condemns himself to defamation and lies."

It was already morning when we stopped playing chess. I stood up to open the window and silence Bach's andante.

1973

Dogs Will Have Their Day

for my maestro, Enrico Cicogna

The foreman, bareheaded out of deference, was handing pieces of bloody meat to the man in a top hat and frock coat. At the end of the day and in silence. The man in the frock coat traced a circle with his arms over the kennel, and the dark flash of the four Dobermans, gaunt, all bone and sinew, immediately appeared, along with the blind excitement of their snouts, their countless teeth.

The man in the frock coat stood there for a while, watching them eat, swallow, then ask for more meat.

"Okay," he said to the foreman, "as I ordered. All the water they want but no food. Today's Thursday. You release them on Saturday, right around sunset. And then everybody goes to sleep. Saturday, you're deaf even if you hear something from the warehouses."

"Boss," the foreman said, nodding.

Now the man in the frock coat handed him more bills the color of meat without hearing his words of gratitude. He pushed his grey top hat over his forehead and spoke as he looked at the dogs. The four Dobermans were separated by wire mesh; the four Dobermans were male.

"I'm going up to the house in half an hour. Have them get the car ready. I'm going to the Capital. Business. I don't know how many days I'll be there. And don't forget. Afterwards, you have to change all his clothes. Burn his documents. The money is yours, as well as anything else you want – rings, cufflinks, watch. But don't use any of it for a couple of months. I'll tell you when. The money's yours," he repeated. "You'll never lack for cigarettes. And the hands, don't forget the hands."

At the time he was short and strong, dressed in grey-embroidered garments, a wide and heavy silver belt, a dark poncho, and a black tie, a color imposed on him when he was thirteen – he'd long forgotten why or by whom. The silver *facón*, sometimes, to show off or as decoration, and the wide-brimmed hat pushed back on his head. His eyes, like his mustache, were the color of new wire and just as stiff.

He looked around without true hatred or sorrow, always the same to others, as if he were certain that life, his life, would continue to accumulate placid routines till the very end. But he was lying. Leaning against the fireplace, he lied as he looked around the room, at the silk and gold upholstered easy chairs he never consented to sit in, at the cabinets with their turned legs, their glass doors full of coffee, tea, and cocoa serving sets, which had probably never been used. The enormous birdcage with its fearsome racket, the curves of the trusted armchair, the small, low, fragile tables of unknown purpose. The thick wine-colored drapes extinguished the peaceful afternoon; only the suffocating bric-a-brac existed.

"I'm going to Buenos Aires," the man repeated, as he did every Friday, in a slow and serious voice. "The ferry leaves at ten. Business, they want to swindle me out of your land in the North."

He looked at the sweets, the slices of ham, the small triangular pieces of cheese, the woman holding the teapot: young, blond, always pale, currently mistaken about her immediate future.

He looked at the nervous and silent six-year-old boy, paler than his mother, always dressed by her in feminine garments, excessive amounts of velvet and lace. He said nothing because everything had been said a long time before. The woman's disgust, the man's increasing hatred, born on the same extravagant wedding night when the girl-boy was conceived, the one now leaning, mouth agape, on the mother's thigh while coiling around his restless fingers the thick yellow ringlets that fell to his neck, to the necklace of small holy medallions.

The cabriolet was black and glossy and glistened as if it had recently been varnished; it had two enormous lanterns that many years later the wealthy folks of Santa María would vie for to use as electric lights instead of candles on their front gates. It was pulled by a dappled horse the color of silver or tin. And Daglio hadn't made the carriage; it had been brought from England.

At times he calculated with envy and almost with hatred the strength, the blind youthfulness of the beast; at others, he imagined being infused with its health, its ignorance of the future.

But also on that Friday – less than ever on that Friday – he didn't go to Buenos Aires. He wasn't even, in fact, in Santa María; because when he arrived at the entrance to Enduro, he turned the young dappled horse pulling the cabriolet to the left, making clods of earth fly off the dry-mud road that led, through fields of burned grass and a few solitary and always far-off trees, to the dirty beach, which many years later, by then a summer resort full of chalets and shops, would carry his name, contributing in very small part to the fulfillment of his ambition.

Farther on, the horse trotted through a large field, flanked by the docility of the growing wheat, the farms that looked abandoned, timidly fading, sinking into the afternoon's rising heat.

He stopped the carriage in front of the largest shack in the village and, not responding to the greetings offered, handed ten bills to the dark-skinned man who had come out to meet him. He paid for the horse's fodder, its stay in the farmyard, the secret, the silence that both knew was a lie.

Then he walked to the newly built and whitewashed little house surrounded by weeds and almost leaning against a gigantic and erect pine tree, planted by nobody half a century before.

Imperious and rude as usual, he knocked on the flimsy door three times with the handle of the riding crop. This might also have been an implicit part of the ritual: the woman, silent, maybe distracted, taking her time. The man didn't knock again. He waited without moving, breathing heavily while imbibing this first dose of the weekly suffering that she, Josephine, obediently and generously served up to him.

The young woman opened the door submissively, hiding her weariness and disgust, which had once been pity, took off her robe, let it fall to the ground, and returned, naked, to the bed.

One Friday long before, restless because she feared another man, she had looked at her watch: that's how she knew that the whole process lasted two hours. He took off his jacket, put it together with his riding crop and his hat, and, already trembling, placed all of it over a chair. Then he approached and began, as always, at the young woman's feet, sobbing in his hoarse voice, begging forgiveness in incoherent babbling for an ancient and unremitting offense as he slobbered, wetting the red-painted toenails.

For most of the entire three days, the girl had him on his back, rolling cigarettes, silent, emptying without hurry or intoxication the bottles of gin, getting up to go to the bathroom or to approach, docile and rabid, the torture of the bed.

Carried aloft upon the capricious breeze by seeds shrouded in silky white threads, the news reached Santa María, Enduro, the small white house next to the coast. When the man received it – the dapple's keeper summoned the courage to rap on the door and communicate the news, averting his eyes, throttling his cap in his large dark hands – he understood, difficult as it was to believe, that the naked captive woman in the bed already knew.

Rising, going outside, leaning over the servile and declining murmurings, the owner of the platinum mustache, of the cabriolet, of the silver horse, of more than half the land in town, spoke slowly and spoke too much.

"Fruit poachers. That's why I have the best dogs, the most murderous dogs. They don't attack. They defend," he said, with neither a smile nor sadness as he glanced up at the impassive sky then pulled more bills out of his belt. "But, don't forget, I don't know anything. I'm in Buenos Aires."

It was noon on Sunday, but the man didn't leave the small house until Monday morning. Now the horse kept to a rhythmic trot, needing no guidance as it returned to its querencia with the air of a robotic beast, a wind-up toy at a fair.

A soldier, the man thought with indifference when he saw, leaning against the wall near the huge black-iron gate decorated with the ostentatious black intermingling of a *J* and a *P*, a young, bored policeman wearing a uniform that had once been blue and had once belonged to a heavier and taller man who'd since disappeared.

The first soldier, the man thought, almost smiling and slowly swelling with excitement, with the fun he was just beginning to have.

"Excuse me, sir," said the uniform, younger and shier as he approached, in the end almost a child. "Commissioner Medina would like to request that you drop by the station. At your convenience."

"Another soldier," the man mumbled, enveloped in the vapors and scents of the horse. "But it's not your fault. Tell Medina I'll be home. All day. If he wants to see me."

He shook the reins gently and the animal joyously carried him past the garden and the grove to the half-moon of dry ground where the stables stood.

Dejected and deft, none of the men who came up to him and unsaddled his horse mentioned either Saturday night or Sunday at dawn.

Petrus wasn't smiling because years before and perhaps forever he had unloaded his scorn onto his steel-wool mustache. He vaguely remembered the moment when he reached fifty; he knew everything he had yet to do or attempt to do in that strange part of the world, which still didn't show up on any map; he knew that he would never face a more stubborn or viscous obstacle than the stupidity and lack of understanding from others, from all the others with whom he would be forced to cross paths.

Then, in the afternoon, when the heat began to relent under the trees,

Medina, the police chief, arrived – eternal, heavy, and indolent, driving the first Model T that Henry Ford managed to sell in 1907.

The foreman greeted him by bowing his head too low and too slowly. Medina took his measure with a mocking smile and said, softly:

"I expect you at the station at seven, with or without Petrus. It's in your interest to come. I promise it won't be in your interest if I have to send for you."

The man let his arm drop and agreed with a nod. He wasn't intimidated.

"The boss said that he was home to you."

Medina trod over the parched ground and climbed the granite stairs, much too long and wide. *A palace; the gringo thinks he's living in a palace, here, in Santa María.*

All the doors were closed against the heat. Medina clapped his hands in warning and entered the large salon adorned with picture windows, fans, and flowers. Wearing a different suit than in the morning but just as well-groomed as if he were dressed to go out, hat on, smoking in the only seat that seemed capable of supporting a man's weight, Jeremías Petrus placed the book he was reading down on the rug and lifted his fingers in greeting and as welcome.

"Have a seat, Chief."

"Thank you. The last time we saw each other I was called Medina."

"But today I decided to promote you. I know what brings you here."

Medina looked suspiciously at the plethora of small golden chairs.

"Sit on any one of them," Petrus insisted. "If you break it, you'll be doing me a favor. And more importantly, what are we drinking? I've had it with gin."

"I didn't come here to drink."

"Nor to tell me that you don't drink when you're on duty. I haven't received any bottles from France in months. Some soldier must be drinking my Moët & Chandon while playing spoof. But I have a Campari, bitter, that seems just right for this time of day."

He rang a small bell, and a servant, who'd been listening from behind a curtain, appeared. Young, dark, his hair plastered down and greasy. Medina knew him as grist for the reform school mill, a messenger boy for illegal prostitutes – and what woman isn't? – and a careless thief. He remembered, as he sought but didn't find his eyes, the already classic and twisted sentence: *I see you, Mirabelles*. It was comical to see him in his white jacket and bow tie. He thought: *The old scoundrel brought with him from Europe his furniture, a wife, a whore, a carriage, and a foal. But he couldn't find an exportable servant; he had to find one in the garbage dumps of Santa María*.

Memories paraded past, of lost harvests, of remarkable harvests, of the rise and fall of livestock prices, remote winters and summers were mentioned, some spent and rendered unreal by time, when the bottle announced that there were only two shots left of the red liquid, as smooth as fresh water. Neither of the two men had changed, neither had revealed either scorn or dominance.

"The missus and the boy went to Santa María. Maybe they'll just keep going. You never know. I mean, you never know with women."

"Forgive me, I didn't ask after your wife's health," Medina said.

"It doesn't matter. You're not a doctor, you came here because my dogs ate a chicken thief."

"Yes, forgive me, Don Jeremías. I came to bother you about two things. We took away the dead man in disguise. Your peons had dirtied his face, his hands, they'd dressed him in the foreman's clothes and stolen his belongings. Rings: all you had to do was look at the marks on his fingers. All you had to do was clean him up to see that he had arrived washed and groomed. They forgot about the perfume, every bit as refined and feminine as the one your wife uses. A sloppy ruse carried out by your gang. That's all I need because I already know his name. It's very possible that you don't know who he was, and it's possible you'll be able to place him once I decide to tell you or when you see, if you want to bother, the file at the station. The dogs ate his throat, his hands, half his face. But the dead man didn't come to steal chickens. He came from Buenos Aires, and you didn't go to Buenos Aires on Friday."

They both chewed on the pause, a shared fear.

Petrus smelled danger but not dread. His workers had been sloppy as had he for trusting them and this grotesque farce.

"Medina or Chief. I went to Buenos Aires on Friday. I go almost every Friday. I paid a lot of money to make sure everybody would swear to it."

"And everybody did swear to it, Don Jeremías. Nobody swindled you, not even by one peso. They swore on their fear, the Bible, and the ashes of their accursed mothers. Though they weren't all orphans. Not to sing your praises, but it seemed as if they were swearing allegiance to something else, something more than money."

"Thank you," Petrus said, without moving his head, a scornful line pushing on his stiff mustache. "End of story, case closed, I was in Buenos Aires."

"Case closed because the dead man was inside your house, on your land, on sacred private property. And you didn't commit the murder. The dogs did. I proved that, Don Jeremías. But your dogs refuse to confess."

"Dobermans," Petrus said, nodding. "An intelligent breed. Very refined. They don't speak with police dogs."

"Thank you. Though perhaps not out of disdain. A simple matter of discretion. Again: case closed. But a few things need to be cleared up. You weren't around here on Saturday night. You weren't in Buenos Aires, either. You weren't anywhere, you weren't alive, you didn't exist, from Friday to Monday. Odd. A story about a vanishing ghost. Nobody ever wrote that one, and nobody ever told it to me."

At that point Jeremías Petrus stood up and remained standing, stock still, staring at Medina's face, the useless whip hanging off his forearm.

"I've been very patient," he said slowly, as if talking to himself, as if muttering in front of the magnifying mirror he used every morning to shave. "This whole thing bores me, gets in my way, wastes my time. I want . . . I have more to do than will fit into the life of a man. Because to carry out that task, I stand alone," he continued, then stopped for a few moments in that large sitting room crowded with things, things that rose and were imposed by and for the never defeated female story, and his voice sounded ever so slightly like a prayer and a confession. Now it turned cold, circling back to the quotidian stupidity of asking, without curiosity or affront: "How much?"

Medina smiled gently, coordinated his pathetic happiness to the room full of unbearable glass cabinets, japaneries, fans, gildings, dead and captive butterflies.

"Money? Nothing for me. If you want to pay off the mortgage, that's your business. I live and sleep in the house, but it won't matter to me. It belongs to others, Don Jeremías. To the bank or to nobody. There's always the cot at the station."

"Done," Petrus said.

"As you wish. In return I want to tell you something that might bother you at first, from now till tomorrow, let's say . . ."

"You never liked to waste time. Me neither. Maybe that's why I've tolerated you for so many years. Maybe that's why I'm listening to you now. Speak."

"You're the boss. I thought a bit of preamble, between two gentlemen whose hands are clean . . . The thing is that Mamoasell Josefina didn't want to say or hear a word. Forgive me, she did say, a single time, something like 'se petígarsón.' She cried a little. Then she poured some pounds sterling out on the bed. They're still at the station, along with the brief, waiting for the judge who went to the horse races and might stop by here on his way back."

"That's fair," Petrus said. "It doesn't matter that they heard her. The pounds, a bit less than a hundred and thirty-seven, they also don't matter and have no connection to this matter."

"Forgive me, again," Medina said, trying to sweeten his voice, "less than half of one hundred."

"I understand, there are always expenses."

"Indeed. Especially traveling expenses. Because Mamoasell was talking from the phone at the train station. You know poor Masiota and you know how poor Masiota treats all women, other than his own, of course, as we all know, all you have to do is look at her left eye on Monday after his Saturday conjugal binge. All women except the one he puts up with and who had the good luck of finding him half-asleep on Monday morning at the station when you reappeared. All he needed was a coin, a smile, a 'mesié le chef' for him to offer her all the telephones, all the cars filled with cargo and cows that were waiting on the sidetracks, all the infinite rails that go who knows where, those on the left and those on the right."

"So what?" Petrus said, interrupting him and urging him to hurry up with a flick of the crop against his boots.

"I took my time because I was speaking about gentlemen. Forgive me. I know, we don't like to waste time. Here goes: Mamoasell must have used all her energy of our stationmaster. But in one or two hours, she got what she wanted. Train, hotel, boat to Europe. I found out a few minutes ago, there's always some drunkard or bum on a bench at the station."

Petrus had been chewing on the silver of the whip handle, meditatively, devoid of the desire to strike, while Medina, never trusting even by accident, slid his thumb along the trigger on his belt. Without previous agreement, his teeth and his thumb slowly prolonged the pause, for so long that it wasn't useful for this story. Finally, Petrus spoke; he used a sluggish and hoarse voice, the voice of a woman undergoing menopause. He had enough pride not to ask.

"Josephine knew the name. She knew the name of the chicken thief and, I'm certain, a lot more. I don't see any other reason for her to leave."

"Could be, Don Jeremías," Median enunciated, aware of the crop's verticality. "Why would she leave?"

It had been so long since Petrus had laughed that his open and black mouth began with a long moo and flickered out like a lost calf.

"Why explain, Chief? All women are whores. They're worse than us. Better said: mares. And not even real whores. I've known a very few I thought it appropriate for me to remove my hat for. They were ladies, *señoras*. But these days they're nothing more than sluts, pathetic little sluts."

"True, Don Jeremías," he said, retreating in the face of the remote memory of Madame Petrus serving him tea and cakes in that very room. "Almost all. Poor things, they weren't born to do anything else. You fight for your shipyard. Against the whole world. I fight on Saturdays to get the drunkards to sleep, sometimes to find out who was the owner of stolen sheep. I also need time to paint. To paint the river, to paint all of you."

"I bought two paintings from you," Petrus said. "Two or three."

"You did, Don Jeremías, and you paid well for them. But they aren't here. They're in the workers' quarters. It doesn't matter. You were right about what you were saying. Women don't have the brains to be anything other than what you said."

The whip fell between his legs, then onto the ground, and Petrus, sitting down, asked:

"Shall we have one more, Chief?"

When Medina left, he saw that one of the dogs was taking a long nap, protected from the sun.

1976

Presencia

for Luis Rosales

I'd already spent days with the dirty money I received through the forced sale of the newspaper. For me, there no longer was and never would be a reconstructed Santa María or *El Liberal*. Everything about the river, about nothing, was dead, incinerated, and lost. I ate with my friends, got drunk with them, spent days shut away in my apartment. The dirty money always in my pocket, without it ever shrinking, without me ever spending a single dirty peseta of it. Sometimes I'd go hungry or couldn't be bothered to make any effort to eat; sometimes I'd let hours pass, from the senseless bustle of daybreak till night, stretched out in bed, repeating my own name, syllable by syllable, looking at the picture of María José that regularly traveled from a pocket to the nightstand then returned in the morning. Only during my insomnia did I allow myself to know that I wasn't happy and was pining away. On my world map there were twenty centimeters between Santa María and Madrid.

Sometimes I received *Presencia*, a copy printed on a poorly inked mimeograph machine. It would be sent to me from the most illogical places in the world, and I would imagine the unknown group of people from Santa María taking turns writing and distributing it. Always bad news. General Cot's tyranny was brutal and you needed to have a martyr's calling to carry out that task. And I was compelled to spend the money from the expropriation on María José, and on her alone.

The man isn't small but was made small by life, which still respects his large skull, the oily sheen across his forehead, the fixed glint of anxiety in his bleary eyes. Something arachnoid in the hairy hands that he places on his desk as if they were things, that he clenches into fists to feign resolve, to let me know that he is still alive, in spite of the past torments I imagine he has suffered, in spite of hope's constant setbacks. He asks then reflects, without much conviction piercing through the cunning, the deceit, and the ancient habit of mendacity and embellishment. He doesn't smile; he leans forward, looks at me, and turns his eyes away. Then he says, testing the waters:

"I can manage it for five thousand. Things like this are always difficult. The right agent happens to be available now. But I can't keep him hanging, on hold. I'll need five thousand cash. Then we'll see."

I thought: here's exactly the partner in madness, in a gamble, that I'd hoped for. I looked again at the ad I'd clipped from the newspaper and brought with me: *Private Detective – A. Tubor – 30 Castilla Vieja, – Madrid and España – By Appointment Only.*

I counted out the banknotes while showing him my smile of faith, of meager enthusiasm. He let the money fall onto the wood and withdrew his hands as he wrinkled his brow. We were both suspicious. Then he said, in a threatening voice:

"I have to give you a receipt."

When he went over to the filing cabinet – and there was nothing in the cold room of early spring but the vertical cabinet, the desk, and the two chairs – I discovered that I was right, that the man's legs were very short and weak. He returned with an orange folder and sat down, scrounging around in his pocket to find his last pen. He wrote the date on an index card and, leaning forward, asked:

"Name?"

"Mine or hers?"

"We always use the name of the client on the receipts and the files. You're the client."

"Malabia, Jorge Malabia," I told him.

I added my address, my telephone number; I invented a house for María José: 37 Sancho Dávila.

"What do you want?"

"Everything. I want you to follow her, tell me what she does, whom she meets. She also works. In a public library. On Fernández de Oviedo. I don't remember the number. But it's the only one on that street. It'll be in the directory."

"If you can describe her. And a picture."

I handed him the photograph without any sadness, with an absurd and partial feeling of liberation.

"She comes up to my mouth," I said and stood up. "Her hair's not really blond, more light brown. Her eyes, I don't know, maybe they're green. But not always. When you have something, call me on."

When I left, the bills were still on the table. I had said to him: María José Lemos, and the name still seemed so right, so her, like a part of her body, like her skin. The name surrounded her and betrayed her.

The man, who went by Tubor, Private Detective, went down to the bar on the corner and ordered a bottle of Rioja wine. The man behind the counter didn't look at him or seem to see him. Tubor hesitated, then placed one thousand pesetas in the dirty dampness between them.

"This'll cover everything I owe," he said.

Sitting down at a table, he started to drink, the first glass for anxiety, the rest for pleasure, thereby initiating a three-day drinking binge. When he managed to fall asleep and wake up in his own little room, he wet his face and neck in the large flowery washbasin. Then he looked through his pockets and went out, walking in the fresh morning air to the church of San Blas. He bought a thick candle from the religious store across the street owned by the priest and walked through the atrium into the darkness, then straight to the left, toward the virgin who'd never yet failed him.

She was a very small virgin, carved sloppily out of wood, with big eyes; so poor, so squalid, that she had to perform miracles to make amends, and Tubor took advantage of this. On his knees, he said many Hail Marys, trying to stay focused, trying to boost his faith. So many times he'd said: I don't believe in God, but I do believe in the Holy Virgin.

Cooler now and bored, he waited in the shadows at the small dirty window, in front of a bottle of wine. He now had half a dozen in his filing cabinet. He waited for night and silence to come to the building. Then he went down two flights of stairs and through the hallway, looking for the night guard of Westinghouse.

"The typewriter," he said.

The other stroked his scraggy face and said: "Five duros. Now it's five duros. I've been thinking about it, and it's a situation that could end up costing me a lot."

"Five," the man said, and handed him the coins.

Now he had an electric typewriter, latest model according to the newspaper ads.

REPORT 3/2/78–859:
AFTER MANY ATTEMPTS I MANAGED TO FIND AND IDENTIFY M.J.L.,
WHO APPEARS TO LEAD A NORMAL LIFE BETWEEN HER HOUSE, HER
WORK, AND A FEW WOMEN FRIENDS, WHOSE NAMES I HAVE YET TO
VERIFY AND, IN MY OPINION, THIS DETAIL, WHICH I ADD ONLY
FOR GREATER CLARITY, HAS NO RELEVANCE. SHE RIDES BUS #12 TO
CRISTO REY. . .

Thus, for a thousand pesetas a day, I had María José out of the prison in Santa María; I could see her walking through the streets with her friends, down to the promenade – in fog and withered sunshine, wearing rubber boots, the flimsiest ones from the rowing club – not totally happy, because she wasn't with me, because she was wondering what prevented me from writing to her, or imagining my last letter of measured optimism that once again slipped the promise of seeing each other in between the lines.

I saw her, nimble and teasing, rejuvenated, almost like a little girl, all as a result of the tenacious lies I wrote to her. I saw her free, her fleeting profile traversing the landscapes that we had walked together, the dark resting places we sought out wordlessly, where we could kiss and touch. And I also saw her walking on her long legs and with drops of drizzle on her face as she went, unawares, to the corner where we met for the first time.

This reiterative happiness lasted twenty days. Tubor called me on the phone and we made a date in a cafeteria two blocks away from his office. He was sitting in front of a glass of wine, and I didn't want anything to drink. I noticed he was nervous, excited at the prospect of the coming revelation, his squalid eyes looking at me with a disgusting mixture of affection and fear.

"This wasn't something I could mail to you. You hired me for a mission, and I always deliver. Without any personal gain, I can tell you. The agent and the expenses almost cost me more than what I'm charging you. But my word is my word."

He emptied the glass and ordered another one with a gesture. I waited for his story as if for a gift, making room to receive it and wring it dry. He took a sip and lit a cigarette.

"Montera and Bécquer," he said. "Does that mean anything to you?"

"No. I rarely go to that part of Madrid."

"Well. You'd be the only one. There, on the Bécquer side, there's a love hotel. The best and most expensive one in the neighborhood. Don't get upset, but they saw her enter on Monday the seventh, at 17:15 in the afternoon. And, needless to say, she wasn't alone."

Bewildered, stunned, I mumbled:

"But she works at the library till six."

"Please. Women. They'll always find an excuse. Sorry, but that's what they were born to do. Invent excuses, I mean."

"Could they see the man?" I asked.

"Not the first time. It happened in a flash. But later, yes. He waits for her every afternoon as she leaves the library. In a green Seat, 4022M. He's tall, older than you, with some grey hair. Very well dressed, that's for sure."

I asked for them to find out where they were going now, if the man had an apartment he took her to, and I paid him in advance for another week.

That was the first day of a believable spring. And that's when the nightmare began. I bought a bottle of whisky and went up to my place, returning the doorman's smile, pressing the wrong buttons in the elevator. I closed all the windows, undressed without looking at my genitals, and lay down in bed: I disconnected the doorbell and the telephone. There, drinking and smoking, I effortlessly watched María José leave the library in Santa María and get into the car. They didn't kiss, they barely exchanged a turbid smile in order to prolong the imminent scenarios in the small chalet in Villa Petrus that the man – faceless, strong, indefatigable – had rented or perhaps he owned it. It was a Swiss-style chalet with a red tile roof, as secluded from the world as was my bedroom at that very moment. They might have caressed each other in order to prolong their anticipation of the large bed. They might have immediately turned to each other and embraced. In any case, María José didn't let him undress her. Just as she had done with me, she was the one who stood up, who took off her own clothes, offering the man a twisted smile, measuring and enjoying his arousal, his impatience. The little house was near the noisy river, and the windows allowed in streaks of the setting sun. I knew the window faced west because the chalet where they were was now identical to the one where I used to meet her. Then suddenly began a series of images, everything that can be done within four walls, everything we had done, the touching, the exploring, the pursuit, that we thought we were doing to invent the other's happiness. But what had been clean and sacred was now grotesque and brutal. And they discovered impossible unions, nonsensical copulations: the grey-haired man increasingly voracious; she, María José, more and more animalistic and open, her enormous haunches – out of proportion to her girlish body – almost exposing her entrails, requesting, pleading, coarsening the words of love that she had shouted at me so often. In the past; never again.

After I finished vomiting I was able to end the night walking clumsily through the nearly empty streets, where every car, every stoplight, every pedestrian, distracted me, gave me a fleeting hint of amusement and oblivion.

That's how April passed, and I, as if ashamed when I sensed that my sadness, losing the sharpness of its edge from the chafing of the days, was diminishing. After the fair in Seville, where I grew bored and tired, where I felt I had been betrayed by friends and announcements, I returned to Madrid and called Tubor so many times that I learned his number by heart. When, a week later, the telephone didn't even ring, I went to his office on Castilla Vieja and it was empty. Nobody could give me any leads about the private detective's new address. I didn't calculate how many pesetas the charade had cost me, and I returned to my life of sloth and sleepwalking.

But at the beginning of May, Tubor called me and said:

"I've been going crazy trying to call you and could never get through. Now I've got something big, really really big. I moved into a different office because that one was a dump. It embarrassed me to receive clients and friends there. I'm rushing around like mad. I'll wait for you at international arrivals at Barajas tomorrow at five. In the afternoon, yes, in the cafeteria. But you've got to bring another five thousand, I've already spent almost everything. It's been a long time since I've had such a difficult case. Don't forget; if you stand me up, everything's over."

It was pretty hard for me to find him, pick him out of the crowd, the unpleasant stream of those arriving after passing through customs and my vague affection for those awaiting their fate, the voice over the stuttering megaphones. It was the same repugnant and long-suffering head, shaved and clean. The clothes had nothing to do with Tubor: they were new, too new; his black and silver tie stood out against his very white shirt. He'd failed to attend to his shoes, too little shine, a bit bent out of shape. On the table was a small, brown, square briefcase with gold lettering. It looked like a cash box.

We shook hands in silence and I passed him the roll of bills. We barely spoke because his airplane was about to take off. He didn't tell me where he was going and I didn't care. I remember only a few sentences and the to-ing and fro-ing of the man's hairy hands.

"You're going to think it's impossible, but it's true. Proven. The most difficult job I've ever taken on. She vanished, bolted. Didn't return to the library; at her house they've had no word from her. As they say: swallowed up by the earth."

"The photograph," I said quietly.

"Of course," he said, and took out a snazzy new wallet, looked through it, and carefully placed the photo, now wrapped in cellophane, on the table.

The man looked around, as if his airplane might be somewhere around there and he would be able to escape. I got up without saying goodbye and went out to find a taxi.

Soon thereafter, summer fell on Madrid with a vengeance. Three months of hell, as people repeatedly called it. One day, in the afternoon mail delivery, an issue of *Presencia* arrived with stamps from Switzerland. I looked at it indifferently, unfolded it, and saw in a box of text:

María José Lemos, student, in custody on Isla Latorre since the military coup, was arrested by members of the Guardia Nacional on April 5, the same day she left prison and regained her freedom. Since then she has been reported missing, disappeared, and nobody in the military or the police has taken responsibility for her whereabouts.

1978

Friends

From the moment he saw her leave the cathedral with her mother, he disappeared from the Friday meetings at Tupi-Nambá. When we asked his neighbor, she said that he wasn't ill, she'd heard him moving around in the basement where he lived, and now that the weather was improving he went out after the siesta with his easel and that dirty box of paints to look for unknown alleyways in the Barrio Sur.

Twice before the last time, I visited the basement. That's all it was, with a toilet in one corner and bars resting on the sidewalk, a window with a hole made by a rock in one pane of glass, and a curtain made out of a burlap sack dyed dark red, so lopsided that it made me think of a hearty, almost impossible horizontal vomit of red wine; the sagging mattress, a large trunk used as a table, a dirty and bare light bulb hanging from the ceiling. The rest was all his: the dust already converted into hard filth by the rain that entered through the hole in the glass, the painted or raw pieces of cardboard, warped by summers, the old and dirty clothes strewn over the floor tiles, which had once been red. And, above all, what was really his, what neither the National Gallery nor the Municipal Gallery could cheat him out of, the sour odor, the odor of an old and sickly body, the disgusting odor that builds up in superimposed layers under unwashed sweat, a combination of armpits and tired feet.

That's how and where Simón lived. Until one day I was commissioned by the pseudo-artists who met with me at the café to defy the neighbor's motto, *He doesn't want to see anybody, not even me*, and confront him in his cubicle to demand an explanation for his absences.

The night the decision was made, in order to humor the painter's misogyny, the long-haired poets who had nowhere to publish their sonnets, elegies, and free-verse poems, the Picassos without galleries, decided that it was imperative to collect funds and imitate Zeus with Danaë. The most generous were the authors of *plaquetas*, broadsides, which were read with raptures and kisses by relatives, girlfriends, and those sitting around our café table. I among them.

We spoke with the midnight manager and arranged to have all our bills turned into silver fifty-cent coins. Before the arrival of the rude and tormenting rabble, that's what coins were, I swear: fifty-cent silver coins. Today coins of the same size are worth five million, small change, as grey with lead as a rainy afternoon on a Monday in winter.

Five of us fit in my car, and the rest left earlier and walked. Gonzalo Ramírez, between Médanos and Ejido. Cafiani, I remember, was protectively carrying the paper bag with the kilos of *argent*. We waited until we'd all gathered; there was a candle lit below. Simón would be reading or had forgotten to blow it out. The broken window was open, and hands, fists full of silver, could fit through the rough black bars.

When Hernández whispered *now*, we all stuck our fists through the bars and opened them. We were frightened by the clattering noise as much, or almost as much, as it must have frightened Simón, reader or sleeper that he was. We then ran toward Ejido, as if we'd just stolen something. After all, who knows.

Who knows, because when two nights later the Tupí court decided that the moment had arrived to demand explanations for Simón's absence, I had to go, respond to an insult from the *He doesn't want to see anybody* woman, and descend, pushing through the stench with my shoulders until I reached the cubicle where Simón was reading a book by the light of a kerosene lamp made of thick dented tin. I brought him a bottle of grappa, but he had another one, almost full, on the ground, next to his stiffened arm.

And now, once again, he had for himself the beauty of dreaming with his eyes open, the present and future of his incredible story, born out of sclerosis and the defunct bottles that created a cordon around the room.

The story, which he told from the well-preserved filth of his bed, with his grey locks grown stiff from their antipathy to soap spilling over a torn pillowcase, as he clumsily lifted the bottle from time to time, seemed like a roller coaster that started with an image of him limping down the promenade, past the deserted ruins of the gas factory and the heavy outline of the "English Temple," the Cathedral of the Most Holy Trinity. He himself, dragging his permanently bad leg, his easel, the wooden box, the restless and sometimes scornful curiosity of the multicolored children who lived in misery in the Barrio Sur. That's how I saw him many times and it's the way I prefer to remember him.

"I," he said, slurring his words, "I stopped drinking with you guys in the Tupí because getting drunk in a café was too expensive for me, and I needed to save the miserable eighty peso pension Bellas Artes gives me, as if out of the mercy of their hearts, after all the years they owe me, years of teaching drawing and painting to spoiled brats who will never know how, because those that matter don't need teachers to discover what they're like and what they want to do. Yes, of course, I was born in Italy, and I saw plenty before coming to America. I needed to save money, and it costs me much less to buy bottles and drink alone in the basement so I can afford the bouquets of flowers I send her at the end of every month when I collect my pension. Love. Nobody, not even you who flits from one to another, can understand. It creeps up on you from behind, like some deaths. And then there's nothing you can do, not kick and scream, not want to destroy. Because you can't know if it's something that struck you from outside or if you've been carrying it around inside like it was asleep, and sometimes you thought it was dead for good. So, what happens then. You've been carrying it around inside and without any warning it suddenly leaps out and spills over your entire body and you have to accept it and even worse, you have to feed it and make it stronger every day, force it to make you suffer more and more. And it doesn't pay any attention when you say that it's impossible because she tells you just maybe but you're bound to not get rid of that sorrow and to keep hoping, and even more when you realize that hope is futile. And that's how it goes and over and over when you're *sborniato*, you cry and it's like bending over the bed in a show of compassion for your own self, so old and sick and poor. And then you feel ashamed. I saw her at the cathedral. But before that she'd been at an exhibition of my paintings and she chose one that her parents didn't let her buy, even though they have millions they could give away so that God would forgive them for having spawned that silhouette, that hair, that body. But she had to leave me her name and address and so I tracked her down and found her. And I thank you for the money that you threw like strong hail because now I can keep it for the wedding."

I thought about his paintings, about his geometry of subtle tones like memory and those little dilapidated houses in battling colors, which only remained standing through the willpower of oils and palette knives.

"Until, one day, she came out of church without her mother and through the drizzle I said to her: 'The flowers'; and she kept walking without hearing me and then turned around and asked, without looking at me or looking at me with disgust: 'How do you know?' And all I could say to her was: 'I, and maybe you understood,' and since then it's like we were friends."

Cafiani had seen him on many nights, clear or rainy, rigid, half in the shadows, facing the lights of the girl's house. His face, twisted and motionless, always as if silvery from the water or the moon, and he'd tell us in the café: "Like the zinc statue of his disgrace." Cafiani wrote poems.

1979

Soap

The figure made no sign for Saad to stop the car, standing still and patient, perhaps bored, by the side of the road, under a tree where spring was starting to emerge, in tiny spears of a still indecisive green.

Saad stopped the car in front of the tree and saw the large black suitcase, saw that the person who was smiling at him had the head of a woman, young, extraordinarily beautiful, and a red sweater over a chest with no hint of breasts; the flat chest of a man; black trousers showing no trace of a bulge. Man, woman, ephebus, hermaphrodite – Saad suddenly had a powerful and throbbing need for that. He needed that to get in the car, needed that with dread, began to believe that he had been waiting for that since he was a child, and almost began to believe that he would need the presence or nearness of X – the cut of the hair was masculine and there was no makeup on the face – for the rest of his life.

Upon entering, X said, "Thanks" and Saad thought that the voice revealed nothing. It belonged to someone, man or woman, who had drunk and smoked a lot the night before.

"Where do you want to go?" Saad asked as he turned his head and examined the skin on the cheek of his passenger; no trace of a beard but the chest remained hostile and flat.

"A ways. I'll let you know. Straight ahead. What were your plans?"

Nor was there an Adam's apple in the white throat. *Were*, Saad thought, as if X was determined to change the itinerary. As if this was possible, desired, as if he, she was confident of being able to impose his, her own plans without the use of force. The large suitcase resting on the back seat suggested a move, a desired displacement. And inside the suitcase was the key to the sex, if X had one. Because there were no signs of the adulterated femininity of a male invert; nothing of the buried virility of a lesbian. If only he could dig around in the suitcase . . .

"No set plans for me. I have a month vacation of, God willing, not doing anything I don't want to do. I thought about stopping in San Sebastián for lunch. Then continuing on to Pau, where I rented a little house I don't know if I'll be able find. If you want you can have lunch with me and wander among the huge pine trees looking for the place. I know only that it's called *Pourquoi Pas* and is near the Jabalí stop."

No answer; reclining in the seat, the face again lit up with a smile, and the neck resting against the back like someone preparing for a long journey.

A few days later, Saad's desire continued to grow, and he had moments of silence and hidden pain beside the other's beloved, placid presence. Because that adored creature offered him – or merely insinuated – its double face, its two bodies, and very soon the man felt the agonizing impulse to advance and conquer, indifferent to whether his imaginary embraces would envelop the body of a man or a woman.

But he wanted to know. And while X was carrying the basket of groceries and strolling down the winding path that had been cut through the large expanse of green grass by the insistence of so many lost steps, he entered like a thief into the bedroom of the longed-for monster and examined the bed, the two tables, the small vials of medicine. None of which helped him at all, none of which revealed the secret. The large black suitcase always under the bed, locked.

And when he lay in the sun, shirtless and in shorts, X curled up, black pants and red sweater, in the shade of the eaves of the small house or under the large trees, and smiled serenely at the beauty of the white buildings spread haphazardly along the small, gently sloping hills.

He had the absurd hope, which he believed in for a while, that he would resolve his doubts by entering the bathroom when X had finished showering. But sniffing around he found the pine-scented soap that had made suds all over the body, the chest, and between the legs wherein lay the mystery, always alone and sealed off from him.

Until, almost from one day to the next, Saad began to accept, to desire, more than physical possession, the permanence of the secret, of the doubt. And now he jealously watched over X, afraid that one reckless move, one sentence, would reveal the truth, the ignorance of which he now enjoyed continuing to suffer.

He watched X clambering down the path, agile and quick, the body leaning slightly to one side from the weight of the basket. He felt cold and old, and he went into the little house thinking vaguely about what X had bought for dinner.

1979

The Cat

Many unpleasant things can be said or imagined about John. But I never suspected him of lying; he had too much disdain for others to invent a fable that would put him in a favorable light.

So when he cheerfully told me the story over dry martinis — for my sake, above all — of one of his failed weddings, I didn't doubt it. It felt, or was, like watching and listening to a movie without any chance of starting over or any concern about its believability. Nor was there any room left over for a smile.

I had arrived a week earlier from Paris and was hoping to update, confirm, and dispose of the rumors that had reached me about friends, whom we more or less shared, during my absence.

John was a gregarious Englishman, and he knew how to mock everything with detachment, sometimes pity, never malevolence.

We drank and there was a long silence; John seemed to be undecided as he mulled something over, his brow furrowed.

He placed his glass on the table and, with his legs still crossed and his demeanor still resolute, he said:

"She was French and you know her. Maybe you already heard, because we were practically married. All we needed was the priest, the judge, and the delivery of expensive antique furniture that she hadn't wanted to get rid of. Great-grandparents and grandparents and parents, almost the entire history of France. She, Marie, was all I cared about. You can search through all the Maries you can remember. I was madly in love, and sometimes I thought that it was sexual madness. All I had to do was see her, smell a handkerchief she left lying around, enter the bathroom after she'd been there, that's all I had to do. We saw each other every week, here or in Paris. Two or three days at a time. We came and went. And each time my desire increased, and I gave into it, wallowed in it; I wanted more and more. And every more was like a stair that pushed me to climb down another, always descending, because I knew I was doing damage to my health and to my mind."

Without turning away from me, he gestured to Jeeves and two glasses arrived: a dry martini for him and a gin and tonic for me. He lit his pipe (he knew very well that smoking would speed up my death) and sat thinking for a while, almost smiling, with lips that did not sweeten his cheer. As always happens with these kinds of stories, I remained silent, waiting; I was rewarded. Without looking at me, Johnny said:

"I named the cat Edgar. And not because it was a black cat with white symbols of horror on its chest."

"It happened one night when Marie, as planned, arrived at the airport. I went to pick her up, we had cocktails, happy as usual. We toasted to our marital happiness. This isn't funny, but it is comical. We went to eat dinner and then to my apartment. I haven't told you, because I wasn't sure of it, and maybe I don't care, that the concierge and part-landlady had a crush on me, or she simply hated me unstintingly. Something like that.

"We entered and turned on the light. She'd never been there. She looked around with a smile that showed approval before it even emerged. And she saw, we saw, in the middle of that large bed with a virginal white bedcover, a large, fat, black cat. A cat that I was seeing for the first time and that seemed used to purring right in that spot. With its feet curled up under its chest, it looked at us with curious eyes, then closed them. To this day, I don't know how it got in. I have my suspicions. I stepped forward to caress its back and throat, and she exploded, saying that I should throw out that filthy cat, that it was going to fill the bed with fleas. Shouting and stamping her feet on the floor. I lit a cigarette and opened the door. I told her that it had made me happy to unexpectedly find somebody welcoming us. She called me stupid and clapped her hands until the cat ran to the front door and out into the darkness of the hallway. Well, let's have another drink, that'll do as a preamble. What happened next is simple and laborious for me to explain. At that moment I decided that I could never marry that woman, that it would impossible for me to live with her, be happy with her. I didn't tell her at that moment, and we spent the rest of the night, until the exhaustion of the dawn, as we expected and desired."

He gulped down his drink, relit his pipe, and smiled happily and defiantly. Then he turned to look me in the eyes and said:

"Which explains, for any intelligent man, why I've only had affairs since then, and I've made sure they never last very long."

1980

The Marketplace

Due to an excess of festivities Martha woke up in the middle of the night, tossed and turned, but didn't want to cry as she usually did so that Helena would fuss over her. She tried to recover her dream of happiness and failed. Now she did start to cry but with her sorrowful face pressed into the pillow, so alone and unhappy in the black night.

But Helena knew, she sensed without hearing, and came in from the other bedroom. Patiently, she listened to the tragedy.

"Because they stole half a happy dream about a beach and the sea with its chalk horses."

The other girl, Judith, joined the dismay.

"I had a weird good dream but when you woke me up it was gone, I lost it, and I don't remember anything."

So, in the morning, Helena got the girls dressed, and they went to the marketplace.

The entryway was wide but a bit farther on they encountered thick marble columns that were streaked with intense colors like in the mosque in Cordoba and that forced them, as they continued, to walk in single file and press their shoulders together and make their way down twisting paths until they reached the large tiled courtyard with its continuous fountain of water. Near the ceiling, winged and sleepy marmots circled slowly. One of them landed and, without looking at Helena, gently nibbled on the girls' heads and led them through a new forest of columns until they reached a small altar where a seraph welcomed them with a smile and didn't need to ask questions to know what they wanted.

Helena, still at the door, maybe forgotten and impeded by the rising columns, tall and thick mottled cylinders, growing with each step, arranging themselves in such a way as to force her to take a circuitous path, which turned into an imperious labyrinth and then opened up, leading her without force to the door without leaves, to the sidewalk where the girls were already waiting for her with the familiar petals of poppies that provide sleep and its sacrosanct absurdity.

1982

The Piggy

The woman always wore black and smiled as she dragged her rheumatism from the bedroom to the living room. There were no other rooms, but there was a window that opened onto a small dun-colored garden. She looked at the timepiece that hung around her neck and thought that the boys would arrive in a little more than an hour. They weren't hers. Sometimes two, sometimes three arrived from the run-down houses past the small plaza, across the wooden bridge over the gully, now dry, which rushed with water during the winter rains.

Even though school had started, the boys always managed to escape from their houses or their classrooms at the calm and lazy hour of the siesta. All of them, all two or three of them, were dirty, hungry, and physically distinct. But the old woman always managed to find in them some feature of her lost grandson; sometimes Juan had his eyes or the frankness of his eyes and his smile; at other times she found these things in Emilio or Guido. But no afternoon passed without her finding some gesture, some expression of her grandson's.

She went slowly into the kitchen to prepare the three cups of café con leche and the crepes filled with quince jelly.

That afternoon, the children knocked on the glass of the front door rather than ringing the bell on the street. Some time passed before the old woman heard the knocks, which continued insistently and with the same intensity. Finally, because she had gone into the living room to set the table, the old woman heard the noise and made out the three silhouettes that had climbed the stairs.

Sitting around the table, stuffing their jowls with the sweetness of the jam, the children repeated their habitual banter, accusing each other of failures and betrayals. The old woman didn't understand them but watched them eat with a frozen smile; that afternoon, after observing closely so as not to make any mistake, she decided that Emilio was reminding her of her grandson much more than the other two. Especially the way he moved his hands.

While she was washing the dishes in the kitchen, she heard a chorus of laughter, then the whispering of secrets being shared, then silence. Some furtive steps, and she couldn't hear the dull thud of the iron on her head. Then she no longer heard anything, her body swayed then lay still on the kitchen floor.

They rummaged through all the drawers in the bedroom and looked under the mattress. They split up bills and coins and Juan suggested to Emilio:

"Hit her again. Just in case."

They walked slowly in the sunlight and when they reached the plank that stretched across the ditch, each returned separately to his impoverished neighborhood. Each one to his shack, and Guido, when he got to his, which was empty as usual in the afternoon, picked up clothes, scraps, junk from the box he had next to his cot and pulled out the filthy white piggy bank where he kept his money; a plaster piggy bank shaped like a pig with a frog on its back.

1982

Full Moon

Her name was Carmencita and she must have been fifty years old, at most. In bed, she completed her third toss and turn, pulled the sheet off her face, and realized that she wasn't going to fall back to sleep. The sounds of Saturday night in Buenos Aires were still reaching her ears.

She caressed her tired breasts and spent a while thinking about her last period, definitely her last. The young man who visited her almost every Saturday because it didn't cost him anything or pose threats of complications didn't know about that ending. It was an ending for her, exclusively, and nobody would suspect it because she was still thin and knew how to make herself up.

Defeated, she turned on the light and lit a cigarette. Then she grabbed the curtain over the window and almost believed that her forehead was striking the round yellow moon that hung like a drumhead in the blackness of the sky. She remembered:

The yellowing of autumn's parchment
like the old drum of a pilgrim.

She thought several, many times of the words of that poem, lost like so many things that used to be. Also:

I had, I had, I used to have
and now I have no longer.

Her tongue moved around inside her mouth, repeating the lines. Always in silence. She remembered her fright at age thirteen, the first time. Then, in brief snippets, faces and bodies, movements, gestures, and almost the voices of the men, not all of them, who had mingled their skins with hers. But only one stayed around, the most idiotic one, a good provider, as she found out when they married. For two and a half years the man read with an approving smile the poems and the stories she wrote. But it wasn't all that serious, and every reading ended with a pat on her head, on her curly hair. Two and a half years, sixty months, and she moved to a small and light-filled apartment on Ayacucho Street, the same one where she was now smoking, sad and enraged and seeing other bygone things, the first book she paid to have published, her other books, praised by friends, the prizes with which they paid her back for favors rendered. And she, always knowing that everything she'd written could disappear without anybody realizing it, knowing that everything was mediocre and pretentious. Knowing and hating the men she used and who used her. So many years.

She started to search, as if finding it were possible, for the moment, the line that separated youth from old age. In any case too much time had passed since the beginning of the body's wretchedness. Because even if she permanently remembered the ring of wrinkles around her neck – always hidden under silk scarves, bright with adolescent and raging colors – she still felt young and healthy, and her mind, she was certain, had not gone the way of the wretchedness of her body, its horrifying, willful, unstoppable, undeniable tendency toward decadence, shrinkage, and death.

She'd also managed – and she lived off this font of revenge – to get a newspaper that almost nobody read to give her a column for her literary criticism. And since all, almost all, of the men who had come and gone belonged to the intellectual fauna and published books from time to time, she was able to use it to unload her bile and her derisive laughter, so broken now, a far cry from chimes and tinkles.

She heard a police siren driving away from the Barrio Norte and the slam of a car door. Someone returning from a bed, she thought without sorrow. She remembered her conversation with Mario, last summer in the sand on a hidden, almost private beach in Mar del Plata. She was the one talking while Mario's hand played with the sand. She was the one talking about how unfair it was for God or nature to make a fifty-year-old woman involved with a twenty-year-old man seem ridiculous and for the opposite to appear to everyone as perfectly normal.

When dawn broke she snubbed out her last cigarette and searched through the drawers of her nightstand until she found her birth control pills and the bottle of sleeping pills. She lifted the blinds and threw out into the soft morning light the pills that had been so unnecessary for such a long time. She swallowed the sleeping pills with the help of sherry guzzled straight from the bottle.

What remained of the night: the blackness surrounding her, trying to convince her of the need to rest, a slow and unimpeded sinking. She rebelled listlessly and managed to see herself at a town fair, where golden wine brought only joy and nobody was drunk and the circle of dancers spun in and out of songs, wrapping themselves in them, her circle, where she was dancing in a flowered dress, moving tirelessly, happy and without forebodings of wrinkles or mild pain in her joints, so clean, so smooth, the skin on her face now pink from happy tiredness, and a carnation in her hair, a carnation on her chest, a carnation between her lips. So happy, so afraid of no longer being happy, that she groped around in the darkness to grab more sleeping pills, more sherry; and then the joy of the unending dance refused to return under the light of the lanterns, the candles wrapped in folded cylinders of colored paper, one blue, one green, one red; and the suction of the bed redoubled wisely and gently and master and slave of the blackness she agreed to sink breathing in for the last time the faded scent of lavender of the sheet that covered her chin.

1983

Tomorrow Will Be Another Day

The rain had nearly emptied Las Ramblas and the only people still there were gathered in the glass-enclosed café, where, for months now, they had not allowed her to enter.

Sonia, standing in the doorway of the empty house, watched as the rain sluggishly turned into tame drizzle, watched it stop as the cold of the wind increased, and thought that it was a sign of good luck. A little farther on, from the other side of the broad promenade, the lights of the city started to come on. Night was beginning and Sonia, breathing in the sad scent of her wet coat, thought that now was also the beginning of hope. She smiled, without really believing, like a little girl listening to an implausible story she'd already heard.

Again she touched the blond wavy wig, and with great care – her fingernails were very long – she pulled on her wet stockings held up with a garter belt.

Again she felt hungry and remembered that she had a ham sandwich in her pocket. But she couldn't spoil the mouth she had painted with *rouge* and so much care. She also remembered that she was on probation until the end of the month, and she forced herself to keep walking, approach the edge of sidewalks, smile at the cars, move her hips, and then stop, pretending to look for something in her enormous purse. But nothing, nobody, and no money to try her luck in the bars where they still let her enter.

It was night and then it was dawn in the shabby district of the big city. And Sonia, no longer hungry, almost without hope, kept walking on the pain of her spike heels.

The brief exchanges with the men she passed repeated themselves.

"Hey there. Want to come with me?"

"Up yours."

"That's what I want. I can also go up yours if you want to see how it feels."

Men and more men and her disgust for them. The clean light threatened to arrive from the port, and the other lights were going out. She climbed the stairs, treading on her expensive silk stockings. She opened the soiled door and turned on the overhead light. The young man, who sat down on the bed, asked apprehensively:

"How'd it go?"

"Like shit, girl. I'm starving. I think we have a can of sardines and there's bread left over from breakfast."

The young man, dark and skinny, got up from the bed and rummaged around in the cupboard; in a voice both whiny and spoiled, he said:

"You still haven't given me a kiss."

"In a sec."

Facing the mirror, Sonia took off her wig and caressed her cheeks.

"Again bearded woman."

Then she undressed and stood looking at her breasts puffed up with paraffin and her sex that would hang there useless and tremulous until after the sardines.

1985

The Tree

On that morning of happy skies, when the young woman, violin in hand, knocked at the door of the little garden house of the Fides family, a man in civilian clothes, a little mulatto, pulled it open and forced her inside.

"Hands against the wall."

As she obeyed, she had time to glance at the face of the Fides's maid, which was ashen; she was moving her hands over her belly, sandwiched between two other apes who took turns plying her with questions or mixing their interrogations with the old techniques they'd learned so well, had used so often. The three men were in their shirtsleeves and sweating, feigning urgency and importance.

The doorman frisked the girl, his hands lingering with congenital insolence on her breasts and ass.

"Clean," he said. "Open the violin."

"The case."

"Yes, Doctor. The violin case."

She had hidden the little blue pieces of paper, which Fides's wife had given her last night between a B flat and a *pizzicato*. But they finally appeared.

It was a list of names of people sentenced to death who perhaps were still alive.

"And this?" the first one asked smugly, trying to insert into the tenuous light of the morning an expression of intelligent threat.

The Fides's maid repeated:

"No, I already told you. He brought him to the house yesterday. I don't know where he is. I already told you. He didn't call and I didn't see him. I already told you. I don't know where he is. I already told you."

"Now you're going to go to the garden with the boy," the man told her. "And no funny business, we haven't even gotten started."

So she opened the glass door and in the small garden she smelled the damp earth and the scent of summer that gathered around the large solitary tree. Bob was sprawled out on the highest branches.

"Go get the ball, it's there in the back," Bob said.

The ball was two meters away, up against the grey garden wall. It was rubber, large, and seemed to be painted in stripes of every color.

The girl threw the ball to the boy and the boy to her and thus they carried on, both of them laughing. Now they could hear the Fides's maid; sometimes she was screaming, sometimes crying. The heavy voices of the men mixed together, rose, and faded into the distance.

"I don't know. I already told you. I don't know anything."

The impact of a blow and a curse. The boy remained ignorant and laughing; she smiled, looking at him. Facing him, the ball came and went, rolling, shining, and happy over the ground dotted with a few clumps of grass. They played, and the girl was sure that she wasn't there, that she was dreaming the bouncing of the ball. There were no men inside the house assaulting the Fides's maid; the threat of captivity, interrogation, torture didn't exist. She looked at the damp wall surrounding the garden, she thought of the possibility of jumping over it, of fleeing from the dream, of fracturing the nightmare.

There was nothing in the world besides the squalid garden, the bouncing of the ball, the happiness of the child whose parents were being killed in some other remote unimaginable place, country, continent, planet.

It was necessary to continue to play with the boy, feel the ball hit her in the belly, throw it back again.

The boy, such a small child, so close to the house and the horror; the boy, the only thing remaining of his parents at that moment, and she had to be mother and father for as long as all this lasted: the infinite nightmare, the vulgar voices in the house, the nervous laughter of the boy in the tree.

Because, if the monotonous game continued without pause, they would both remain apart from time, never chafed by the filth of the world.

1986

Montaigne

We had all received the same message, the same unbelievable offer. And we were there, the six of us, and he was there, of course, because the gathering was at his apartment. Charlie's invitations, epistolary or by telephone, consisted of informing us that on Friday, at seven in the evening – I don't want to ruin your Sunday – I will start to kill myself. Whoever fails me will be cursed because he won't have the opportunity to make amends. There will be abundant food and drink.

There were six of us in attendance at what we believed would be an exhibitionist prank. I heard that some of the other invitees had laughed at the joke. The weather was sunny and humid, and they had decided to escape the city.

I arrived a little late, minutes, and greeted everyone with a nod and some with a smile. I might have kissed one of Marta's cheeks because she was the prettiest and I had always calmly desired her. Moreover, the scent, the perfume that her neckline divulged was a provocation she is quite conscious of and amused by.

Charlie was sitting on the sofa, a woman on either side of him. He greeted me with a smile, lifting his hand. Behind him, hanging on the wall, was a large mirror.

The guests, four women and two men, Brausen and I, took our seats, two women on the sofa and the other two on strange white garden chairs. He had furnished the apartment in accordance with his disconcerting tastes. I distinguished them by their names but also by their colors. My task and role were difficult and painful.

Not one of them was older than thirty. The one in the short green dress forged an almost convincing giggle and said:

"Charlie, what's with this madness? Always the charlatan."

"A week ago," he answered, "you weren't calling me Charlie or a charlatan. Though sometimes, it's true, a clown. It was Saturday, right? That's when you were giving me other nicknames. Maybe the same ones the other three used, in happier times. Nicknames that I won't repeat so as not to make you blush."

The girl blushed. María del Carmen, the one in the sky-blue dress, stood up, picked up the bag she had placed on the floor, slowly walked out of the room, quietly closed the door behind her.

Three women now remained. Enriqueta, the blushing one. Isabel, tobacco-colored pantsuit and tie. I always had my suspicions. Aurora, wearing dungarees, a leather jacket, and her hair laboriously mussed. Aurora, or her father, had many millions, but they were never flaunted, not even shown. Gentry.

We had all been friends since our excursion to and prolonged stay at a house Aurora owned at the beach. Interchangeable friends, but, I write with sadness, nobody fell in love with anybody, though Charlie married Natalia, who had refused to witness the slow suicide he promised.

For a moment, Charlie held his smile. He was counting us. Sometimes he had a mustache, which he would shave off and then let grow back, and the change altered, though not too much, the expression on this face.

"So," he said in a resigned voice, "Natalí didn't make it. Always willing to fulfill her conjugal obligations. But not this final and different one, not this."

He pronounced her name with a strong emphasis on the last letter. Next to me, standing, Brausen opened a small package of mints and placed one in his mouth. With a slight stammer, he asked:

"Did you suddenly accept the fact that you're extraneous in this world? Or are you, quite simply, escaping? Suicide is advisable in certain situations, but I'd like to know what bullet you're dodging. Whether it's an illness or the eyes of some cruel and perverse woman. In any case, you're rushing things. It'll come all on its own within a few years. And then you might kick and scream in protest."

"Yeah, Brau," Charlie said. "You with your good sense and bad jokes. But if I explain it to you, this time will pass. And it's mine and, if you think about it, it's the only thing I have and can manage. It's also true that in a hundred years we'll all be bald. Forgive me the speech. I love, or loved, all of you, to different degrees, of course."

Isabel feigned a yawn and patted her pockets. She was looking for, showing that she was looking for, a pack of cigarettes. I lit one of my own and placed it between her lips.

"Thanks," she said, more ungracious than I.

"No problem. Sorry it's not your brand."

"But Charlie, dearest," Isabel insisted, "why the spectacle? Why not blow your brains out all on your own? It occurs to me that maybe you're hoping that this audience of lovers and a man and a half will stop you from killing yourself. I know you."

Charlie pulled a handkerchief out of his chest pocket and positioned it for a sneeze. I observed, without envy, that he was dressed very well for the ceremony. A white shirt under an astonishing thousand-colored vest with four large pockets. Hand-painted tie. Shoes that were much too shiny. As for the suit, English cashmere, I think.

We'd always seen him dressed as an artist: old trousers, a heavy flannel shirt, lumberjack-style, a pipe hanging from his teeth, rarely lit. In winter he'd wear a velvet jacket, never a coat, and a flashy scarf instead of a tie. His head was always bare; he never wore a beret because he knew it would be too *bohème*. He didn't show his paintings. "Not yet," he'd say evasively. On the easel, always a blank canvas; the painted canvases facing the wall.

Charlie said:

"I have the flu. But that doesn't count. I won't allow it to interfere with my time, this short time I've chosen that is totally mine. But I don't want to be selfish. You will also be able to claim your time this afternoon." He looked at his wristwatch. "As you all know, I'm so rich that I have two rooms, a kitchen, and a bathroom. In the other room there is a buffet and good things to drink. I ask you, as my last and second-to-last favor, to go, eat, drink, party. I promise I'll wait. For obvious reasons I can't eat. I haven't eaten for a long time."

Sighing, he stretched his long legs out on the sofa and closed his eyes. He was pale, insolently handsome as always.

We started moving toward the other room, almost in single file. But one of the women lingered, and I could hear an already classic elegy that rang for the first time and to no avail in the already dead ears of F. Scott Fitzgerald:

"Poor son-of-a-bitch."

I also heard the final period, the spit.

As opposed to the anecdote, however, Charlie was still alive.

We found a long table, the kind large families use, covered with a very white sheet as a tablecloth, bottles of white wine and rosé, fifteen-year-old scotch, and a variety of edible delicacies, enough to feed us for a week.

We ate, we drank, we exchanged bad jokes that held on to their charm for barely a second, because we tacitly agreed that we were living a prank, that Charlie was immortal and it was good to have nearly the whole gang together. All of us who'd come were huddled together and having fun, offering toasts.

We had been so promiscuous, and with such unusual variations, that the women were already old friends and spoke without venom or jabs. Brausen seemed to me a bit uncomfortable, moving his head and eyes to furtively scrutinize faces and expressions.

Every once in a while a head would pop in to check on Charlie, and all it would see was his hand moving strangely from vest to bottle. Then he would seem to be calm and would leaf through his book. Nobody asked.

But our time also passed and, during a brief silence, we heard the bells of San Cristobalón Desnudo, an enormous church almost in ruins that towered over that part of the city.

When we returned, with our stomachs full of food and drink but twitchy, we tried to avoid both the sofa and the mirror. A wordless pause until we really looked at Charlie. Now he was sitting and had switched on the lamp on the small table, where we could see another bottle of fifteen-year-old scotch. He was pretending to read a book while slowly sipping from a glass that was undeniably crystal. He also pretended, for a while, not to notice the small commotion caused by our return.

Charlie placed the book on the sofa and showed us his white smile, his eyes too wide open, as blue as María del Carmen's dress. I'd known that look for years.

"Please forgive me," he said. "I forgot to hire a waiter. I don't know how much they are. Cost, I mean to say. It turned out to be vulgar self-service. But I see you're happy, aren't you? Though somewhat disconcerted in the face of destiny."

I knew Charlie's face and remembered it showing ill humor, serenity, and that gift of his for the sarcastic comment, always tossed off carelessly, creator of enemies. But now I saw a subtly different countenance. His eyes, guileless, were looking at something he'd never seen and that was invisible to us. Suddenly I understood; I saw him move his hand to one of the four pockets of his flowered vest and bring it back to his mouth to take a swig of whisky. Drugs, undoubtedly.

Someone else, perhaps more or less quickly than I, understood. That someone, with a confused chorus behind him, almost shouted, pleading and in a rage:

"But Charlie! You're crazy!"

The now doubtless lesbian was now controlling with caresses the shoulders of the known nymphomaniac. That moment might have been the beginning of a friendship as intimate as it was strange.

"All of you, crazy," Charlie said, stumbling lightly over the consonants. "You're forgetting about my friend, Rubén, about the awaiting grave with its funeral boughs. Not for me, I'm going to be burned. But for the girls, such good friends, I think they once recited it, I mean she recited that sonnet at the Villa Mongo Cultural Club. Never mind. I'm lying," another pill, another swig. "Not one of you girls. But you do believe that I couldn't hire a waiter. You're all crazy and you all forget that funeral boughs are waiting for you. More and more tired but I've still got energy. I could afford many waiters, one for each of you. Now that I'm leaving is when I got rich."

Pity and disgust drifted around the group and caused pain. Sometimes, the two together; sometimes, at odds.

Another pill, and swig, and Charlie, now after much delay, said:

"Rich and dying. Because I invited you to watch me die. But rich people like me shouldn't commit suicide. But you, who sometimes shared my joy. Correction: joys, because the other, the real one, there's no such thing," sip and pill and I wait. "Because finally I sold my father's land in the south. I'm rich and it's all Natalí's, no will," pill, sip, and he fell on the sofa forever with his big eyes – blue, surprised, looking, and seeing. "Not out of love or the ashes of love," he said, now mumbling, groping around to find each word, one by one. "Because she respected me and she accompanied me through the bad moments that can now never be repeated. Understand?" he asked, indifferent and weak.

Awkwardly moving his arms as if they belonged to someone else, he grabbed a handful of pills out of his ostentatious vest and finished off the bottle. He stretched out to his full length on the sofa, closed his eyes, and began to breathe audibly until he began to snore, his mouth open. A line of saliva stretched slowly down the right side of his face, which was fading, the face that had kissed and been kissed so many times on that very sofa, his animal fury and his slow caresses strengthened by the added images of the mirror.

I approached him to observe the process. My back separated me from the group, and I heard shouts, the inevitable and predictable words: ambulance, doctor, police, stomach pump, maybe.

I took our Charlie's pulse. Very weak, very slow.

"My dear friends," I told them, "this heart will stop beating in two minutes. Must be the last dose of pills. It was massive. As for myself, I'm leaving. The maid doesn't arrive till Monday. If we stay, we'll be meeting up again at the police station, having to answer stupid questions till who knows when."

"But, what, are we going to leave him like this?"

"He's already gone," I said. "Farewell. Do whatever you like. I just ask you to forget that I was also here."

I went down in the same elevator that María del Carmen had used. The building where Charlie had lived was in the Barrio Sur, which was beginning to come back to life, fortunately while also preserving its large mansions and their Andalusian patios. The café was comfortable, no flourescent lights, and from my table I could spy on them and count them calmly as they left or fled. Brausen was the last to leave and it looked to me like he was waving his hand to hail a taxi.

I waited through a disgusting whisky, domestic, and two cigarettes smoked slowly, long ashes. I paid the waiter and left. I had the two keys, so I went up in the shaky elevator and entered the apartment. Charlie was getting cold, and his mouth, without a good woman to fit him with a chin strap, was open and grotesque.

Nor was there a good man. In bed during the siesta that afternoon, Natalia had told me that Charlie was leaving the money from the sale of the family land for her inside the second volume of Montaigne's *Essais*, somewhere in the library. It was a large and heavy envelope full of bills, also large, and it was hard to fit in my pocket.

By the time I left, I was no longer curious at all about the dead man. But I did bend down to flip over one of the canvases leaning against the wall. It was, to my taste, a very bad painting, with violent colors that seemed to be fighting among each other. It's likely that Charlie had seen it the same way.

1987

Ki no Tsurayuki

I met and spent time with the Andrades a few years ago, for a few years. Today I will recount the most interesting part of their lives, and whatever I don't know I will imagine with confidence.

Like every day at noon, by the time Andrade woke up Marisol was no longer in bed. The room smelled slightly of sweat tempered by cosmetics and the aroma of fresh coffee that wafted into the bedroom from the kitchen.

He drank down the rest of the whisky, now luke warm, left over from the night before, and lit a cigarette. The smoke rose in a spiral of the same grey color as the light through the slits of the Venetian blinds. He thought sadly that spring still hadn't arrived and that nobody knew why.

Marisol ran the social page of her newspaper, always the most important section under every government that ever was or would be, civilian or military, the fierce little Bible of the oligarchy and the Church.

After the bathroom – clean, shaved, and wrapped in a luxuriant robe

– he was in the small dining room, sitting across from Marisol and enjoying a substantial breakfast. He opened the newspaper so that she would forget that he'd looked at her reproachfully. Her sparkling eyes, the tiny white specks along the edges of her nose. Her pleasant nervous joy. And yes, on top of the world.

How many times had he heard her swear: Never again, I swear. Or a variation: If I don't go to parties, I'll perish and I'm out of a job. And when I go, I can't say no to a line, like some kind of country hick. And without the newspaper or meetings, I can't help you.

"Is there anything?" Andrade asked.

"No time or energy to look."

Andrade turned the pages until he found the well-nourished obituary page. He looked at the woman, heard her stab her spoon into the middle of the grapefruit. There was another moment of calm and then she offered him more coffee in a large mug. He accepted in silence, moved the newspaper aside, and watched her laugh silently.

"Don't be mad or pretend to be. Why do you look at the page if you don't know how to interpret it? I have the key and I'll tell you later, as always. But first an apology and a chuckle for mommy."

Now, through the large window of the living room/dining room, spring appeared for a few minutes, only to retreat as if in regret, rejected by clouds and wind.

She said:

"Okay, so I have to get ready for my luncheon in the *campagne*. Don't waste your time looking through the newspaper because you don't know anything about widows. I'm keeping an eye on two very promising dying men. I wish you good luck. And you have my blessing. Don't forget to look at your calendar. You missed the Camarosa one."

She made a face of affectionate mockery then went into the bedroom to get dressed, to smarten up.

Marisol, educated at a university in the States, had established a dietary regime in her apartment that took Andrade a while to get used to: a big breakfast, a silly little snack for lunch, and they frequently ate dinner out.

In the afternoon he did a little work on the calendars, one for this year and one for the next, because not everybody dies before July first. September tenth, blank page. He kept paging through and confirmed that no visits were planned through the middle of October.

Andrade lived a carefree existence thanks to a grandfather or great-grandfather who, in the previous century, built a fence around some unclaimed land. Through successive and complicated legacies, that vast expanse of grass, now shrunken, adorned with bovines and equines, was his by law. The steward cheated him punctually with every remittance and report. But what did reach Andrade generously covered his needs. Marisol, from a family that had come down in the world but had a patrician surname – at least one that continued to be an object of envy – and with the salary from the newspaper and the perks obtained by including the name of the dressmaker who had made the bridal gown or the girl's coming-out party dress, earned the couple enough money to nearly complement Andrade's income. To all this, in addition to companionship and bed, could be added that both were generous, carefree, and unpredictable.

Moreover, for years Andrade had been writing a novel. Nobody had ever seen a page of it, maybe not even he. The only trace of literary creativity could be detected in an old sign nailed up on the wall above his desk. It said: "A literature that would make everything written till now seem, in comparison, like the simple prose of a schoolchild."

Andrade was lying when he told Marisol that her phone call had caught him just as he was beginning the very difficult fourth chapter of his interminable novel. It's well-nigh certain that he was napping with the help of the last glass of cognac and a bit of soda. I assume Marisol said:

"Time to get moving, my love. This morning Ramón Estévez died in the hospital where he went for two operations. An emergency, his heart. He was your friend and there are no children and he was obsessed with skydiving, out there at the Morón Shooting Range. Not mourning clothes, silly, just dark, careful with the tie, and your face, of course, crushed."

Within a few hours, Andrade had embellished his friendship with Estévez, puffing up small memories, convincing himself that there had existed between them frequent interactions that approached intimacy. School, military service, bold leaps when they both jumped from airplanes and floated through the air dangling from their parachutes, landing gloriously and with stomachaches in often hostile terrain. Deep friendship over drinks and shared secrets.

It was no longer important for him to know or guess what his old friend Dr. Estévez looked like physically, the face he'd never seen. Death levels out faces and imprints itself on them (imprints itself on us) or constructs a single expression that asks, with indifference and sarcasm: Why me? I've faithfully carried out my part of the deal.

At dawn he put on a dark blue suit with very thin white pinstripes. He walked a few blocks to the Barrio Norte, very close to where they lived. After signing the visitor book in a neat and open handwriting that could be read easily, he entered the room filled with whisperings, and avoided, without appearing rude, the black, gold-trimmed coffin. Many people stood around the young widow, protecting and consoling her, and, by doing so, identifying her. She sat perfectly still and without tears in her eyes, and she was very beautiful with her black hair parted down the middle. Such a desirable promise for half a year from now.

This widow: a face as pale as a newly whitewashed wall, impassive, suffering without full awareness such a brutal, unexpected blow, which had come to sunder her life in two, destroy her happiness that will from now on be merely a collection of memories, every day more ambiguous, less painful.

He had prepared a few stupid words, but he exchanged them, whispering, for other similar ones:

"Hard to believe. Ramón was such a good friend. May he rest in peace."

Then he retreated, as if to be forgotten, as if hiding, and went to sit in a corner where he turned down the coffee and port that a servant offered him. After an hour of laments, mourners, friends, and renewed tears, he could discreetly slip out and return to his apartment to write – a lie – the interminable novel, which, though it never existed, he had the respect not to call brilliant. The truth must have been that he drank more cognac, smoked a pipe, and read detective novels, the kind without names or titles or memory, waiting for Marisol to return.

It is true that after his brief visit to Estévez's funeral, Andrade got to work. He pulled out his calendar and, since that day was September twenty-first, he counted six months and wrote: "On March 20 of next year: Mrs. Estévez. Today, give or take."

He found he felt like working and, after fortifying that feeling with cognac, he did a quick review of the very satisfactory results of his twelve so-called semi-annual and sometimes furtive visits, which had resulted in only two failures. Either he had arrived late or his coveted spot had already been taken for more than a year, since before his first mourning visit.

And all of this, which was somehow anti-poetic, like bureaucrats punching time cards when they get to work, in the context of the grand poetry that happy results created.

And this entire task, none of it very demanding, had begun a few years earlier because of a story-poem written by the Japanese poet Ki no Tsurayuki, published in 905 and translated into the barbarian languages in the twentieth century.

The poet lied about having visited a cemetery where he saw a small beautiful woman kneeling, tirelessly waving a large fan over the dirt covering a grave. Driven by curiosity, the mother of knowledge and poetry, Ki approached the young woman and, after making the requisite three bows, he made bold to question her, perhaps without any need for words, with only the quizzical expression on his face. The girl – all beautiful women remain adolescents for years – stopped moving her wrist and lifted her eyes, offering a doubtful and rigid Japanese smile. Then she said sadly: "My husband, on his death bed, made me swear that I would remain faithful to him for as long as the dirt over his coffin remained wet. And this has been a very rainy autumn."

After this beauty, which made such a deep impression on him, Andrade eagerly remembered bits of gossip and some experiences he'd had. He made calculations and decided that six months of widowed solitude established a vulnerable psychological state inside the carapace of a forsaken woman and that it was then feasible to lean into longings and toss out memories. I don't know – I was traveling on business – how much time passed, or how precise Andrade's calculations, always assisted by Marisol's complicit wisdom, ended up being. I suspect that his lover guided him with confidence so that the basic requirement would be met: the targets death afforded him would be young, beautiful, and with an indefinable quality that they, and I, would call class.

When I finally settled back down in the most beloved city in the world, not one of your Romes, Viennas, or Parises, as a Mexican poet once said, and after having given an account of myself a bit in the style of a great sea captain to whomever was minister at the time, I started to learn, without meaning to, about a series of unfortunate events. I leave aside the ones we all know and recall Marisol's death and Andrade's prior automobile accident. I learned that he had gotten married, madly in love, to one of his biannual widows. Her name was, and is, Hortensia. Stronger than he in erotic dalliances, more persuasive in bedlinens, beautiful and *allumeuse* from birth, she led him gently and peacefully to judges and priests.

She wrote the preamble with linguistic mastery, with slit skirts that hinted, in summer, at white and powerful thighs; and in winter she wore pants so tight they made it possible to see, guess, and desire, the blue buttocks they offered to view.

All this was whispered, sometimes spoken in different words, by close girlfriends who added pasts and presents, some possibly slanderous.

None of it mattered to him because, even if true, the following day a sexual romp is forgotten and never took place.

After their honeymoon, they returned to the city. The highway is dangerous, and it was there that Andrade, taking a trip on his own to look for beaches and sun, hit a truck and almost died, saved in a sanatorium but left impotent and with unusable legs.

Now, waking up from one of his daily slumbers, Andrade would try once again to conquer the world, the room, sitting uncomfortably in his wheelchair, which he had almost learned to use competently.

Now he'd hear Hortensia's voice as it reassured the whisperings of a masculine voice, and said: "Don't worry, he won't wake up till night." And the silences, crueler than any word, would pay a visit, prolonged, to his room for the disabled, the incurable.

Without any need for a calendar, Andrade calculated that six months had passed since the almost fatal accident, which had removed him from the living, the healthy, and the eager.

1987

The Shotgun

It was not yet the dead of night when I stretched out my arm to switch on the table lamp. I had to finish my article before the early morning hours and run to put it in the mail then wait and wait, curled up, for the postman to return in the fog that the dawn was punishing with a whip the exact color of fresh and shiny blood. I returned all fat and sassy carrying my monthly check, and I had to hurry, it was just a matter of turning on the light and hearing the sounds of someone trying to force the lock and all around me the solitude of the deserted town, paralyzed by the vertical moon smack in the geometric center of the immense world filled with so many millions of beds where diverse and slumbering subjects babbled in their dreams, each with a line of spit running down their cheek and spreading strange draw-ings across the whiteness of the pillows. Then I jumped up and stood on one side to the door, asking over and over, in a steady rhythm, who's there, what do you want, what are you after. And silence and the scuffling sounds surrounded the small house and kept working at one of the windows, I don't remember which, pushing me toward two successive actions, almost without stopping, to shield the light on the table with the palm of my hand and open the wardrobe, take out the shotgun, and then walk from one window to another and from a window to the door, according to the changes in the sounds made by the thief, always asking, until I grew hoarse, what do you want, turning the shotgun here and there, as the sinister smell of fear and doom rose from my chest and armpits.

After a pause and a small rustle of paper, the man in the white robe spoke into the nape of my neck. His voice was muted:

"This is an easy one. An elementary dream. Even a child could interpret it. I am the thief who is trying to know, to enter your ego. Why are you so afraid?"

1993

She

When She died after long weeks of death throes and morphine, of hope, of sad news forcefully denied, the Barrio Norte closed its doors and windows, imposing silence on the joy it celebrates with champagne. The most intelligent among them ventured: "What do you want me to say. To me, and I'm not usually wrong, this feels like the beginning of the end."

All the many things, poor millionaires, She had made them swallow. And the sad part was that She had been infinitely more beautiful than those fat ladies, their wives, who still smelled of manure, as an Argentinean once said. Now also they could swallow the polite smiles with which they had greeted the orders and humiliations. Because everyone felt, with no proof besides the speeches delivered in the Plaza Mayor, that She was, in this incredible reality, more dangerous than the shady political and economic oscillations of Him, the commanding commander, He who commanded us all.

When She finally died, killing off hopes and desires, it was the end of July, a time of year filled with cruelties, cold, wind, downpours. From skies blackened with clouds and night fell a slow, implacable rain, in needles that threatened to last forever. They ignored coats and human skin only to soak bones and marrows without delay.

The humidity increased the sour smell of the threadbare garments of makeshift mourning: almost motionless, wordless, because only one person was to blame for their misfortune and he could not be named even though he was the master of the cold, the rain, the wind, and the misfortune.

According to the tale, so often closer to the truth than History written and published with a capital H, five doctors surrounded the bed of the dying woman. And all five agreed that science had its limitations.

Downstairs there was another man, impatient, pacing, on the telephone answering questions from generous or friendly journalists, perhaps also a doctor, though this doesn't matter in the least.

He was Catalan, a well-known professional embalmer summoned by Him a month ago to prevent the sick woman's body from undergoing the fate of all flesh.

And there was a silent but dogged struggle among the five men upstairs and the one man below. Because if this one believed to a point of distraction only in the Virgin of Montserrat, those upstairs were divided among the Virgins of Luján, La Rioja, las Siete Llagas, and between the Virgins of San Telmo and Socorro. But they agreed on the basics, on the One Holy Catholic and Apostolic Church. And they believed in the Sunday belches of priests.

In order to carry out his agreement with Him, the Catalan embalmer needed to give the corpse its first injection half an hour before it was declared as such. The unyielding believers upstairs wholly opposed the embalming, even though said Catalan had shared generous and indisputable evidence of his talent. I remember the photo in a brochure of a child who died at twelve years old sitting peacefully in a chair dressed in an impeccable sailor suit. They displayed the mummy every time he would have had a birthday – he was scornful, time didn't exist, his cheeks were still rosy and his glass eyes shone with malice – and, inexorably, on the anniversaries of his death. Twice a year he held the place of honor, and the relatives who remained – time did exist – sat around him drinking tea with cake and maybe a shot of anisette.

They opposed the first and indispensable injection. Because the Holy Faith that united them distributed souls so they would listen forever to the music of angels who would never change their musical staff – or maybe their confused little heads had memorized them – or so they would relish tortures never conceived of by terrestrial policemen.

So, when those liters of morphine stopped breathing, they looked at each other and nodded and looked at their watches. It was precisely 20:00. One lit a cigarette, others yielded their exhaustion to chairs.

Now they were waiting for decomposition to commence, for a green fly, in spite of the season, to land on Her open lips. Because the Holy Church ordered them to breathe in cadaverine, the almost immediate stench, and imagine the exhausting task of seven generations of worms. All this in keeping with God's wishes, which they respected and feared. The minutes pass quickly when a qualified man safeguards his faith.

Emilio, the most obedient one to the unquestionable manifestations of the deity, said:

"Hey, turn up the heat."

Later, they decided to go downstairs to deliver the news, sad and expected.

He was eating dinner and nodded. He then expressed gratitude for the services rendered and asked that their honorariums be paid. Then He pointed randomly at one of the men in uniform and ordered the radio stations, priority given to His own, to be instructed to report the news.

The Catalan doctor climbed the stairs two at a time, carrying his small suitcase. He prepared the injection and was dismayed when he felt how cold the corpse was.

The doors remained shut, and the crowd began to squabble and shift. The police stopped offering little cups of cold coffee and immediately there appeared vendors of chorizo, pastries, hot drinks, peanuts, dried fruit, chocolates. Few made any money because the first contingent began to arrive at nine at night from the neighborhoods unknown to the inhabitants of the Great City, from the slums, from shacks made of tin, automobile crates, caves, from the earth itself, now mud. They soiled the silent and uninhibited city, lit candles in any concavity the walls along the avenue offered, on the marble statues on the way up to the locked gates. The rain and the wind respected some of the flames; others not. People hung up cards and clippings from magazines and newspapers that unfaithfully reproduced the extraordinary beauty of the dead woman, now gone forever.

At ten in the morning they were allowed to proceed, two meters every half hour, allowed to pass through the doors of the ministry in groups of five, pushed and beaten; the blows preferred by the military were knees to the ovaries, a blessed cure for hysteria.

At noon word spread from block to block, along meters and meters of the slow-moving line: "Her forehead is green. They're closing so they can paint Her."

And this was the most accepted rumor because, although untrue, it was perfectly apt for the thousands and thousands of necrophiliacs, muttering and grief-stricken.

The Araucaria

Father Larsen descended from his mule when it refused to climb the steep street of the shantytown. He was wearing a cassock that had once been black and now tended decidedly toward bottle-green, the consequence of years and indifference. He continued on foot, stopping every half block to breathe through his mouth and telling himself that he should quit smoking. Carrying the small black bag that contained everything he needed to save souls that were about to leave bodies, escape from suffering and the surrounding poverty. He was not preceded by an altar boy with a bell, nobody was swinging a cruet, nobody was praying, except he himself every time he stopped.

The small house painted a dirty white was flanked by two others, almost the same, and the three houses opened onto the packed dirt street through inhospitable and narrow doors.

It was opened by a man of uncertain age wearing white alpargatas and bombachas. He crossed himself and said: "This way, Father."

Larsen felt the coolness of the whitewashed room and almost forgot the aggressive sun of the shoddy streets.

Now he was in a poorly furnished room; in a double bed a woman was twisting and turning, swinging from cries to defiant laughter. Then came her words, incomprehensible sentences that pierced the silence, the momentary serenity of the sun that was trying to reach into the approaching shadows.

A silence, a foul stubborn smell, and suddenly the suffering woman tried to lift her head; she was crying and laughing. She calmed down and said:

"I want to know if you are a priest."

Larsen moved his hands down his cassock to show her, to confirm for himself that he was still wrapped in it. He showed the air – because her eyes were wide open and she was staring only at the white wall opposing her death – the engravings of sharp though faded colors, small lead medallions, shrunken with age, some serene, others tragic, with oversized naked hearts pushing through open chests.

Suddenly the woman shouted out the beginning of her soul-saving confession. Father Larsen remembers it like this:

"With my brother, since I was thirteen, he was older, we fucked every afternoon in spring and summer next to the stream under the araucaria, and only God knows who started it or if we were both inspired at the same time. And we fucked and fucked because, even though he looks like a saint, he finishes and starts up again and never tires, and you tell me, what more could I want."

The brother stepped away from the wall, shook his head no and reached his hand out toward his sister's mouth, but the priest stopped him and whispered:

"Let her keep lying, let her unburden herself. God listens and judges."

Her words added very little to his collection. He already had several cases of incest, unavoidable in this dump despoiled of men through war or poverty; but perhaps no other so persistent and repetitive, almost matrimonial. He wanted to know more and whispered compellingly:

"My child, that's life, the world, the flesh."

Now she opened her eyes wide once more, losing herself in the protective pause of the whitewashed wall. Again she laughed and cried without tears, as if the cries and laughter were the sounds of words and grave secrets. Larsen understood that she was neither dying nor pretending to. She was crazy, and her brother, if he was her brother, watched over her madness, his face as rigid as a plank of wood.

Confused, he ordered Our Fathers and Hail Marys and, as in the past, he hesitated briefly in ancient disgust before bending to bless the head covered in wet and tangled hair; he couldn't and didn't want to kiss her forehead.

He heard, as he was leaving, guided by the emotionless brother:

"Next time I'm about to die, I'll call you and tell you about the horse and the little milking stool. He helped me, but that's all."

On the street, under the sun's stubborn whiteness, the mule rubbed its nose against the stones, looking in vain for something to nibble on.

On their way back to the corral, the animal trotted tamely and in some hurry while Father Larsen, without opening his red sunshade, weighed what he had obtained and looked forward, with hope, to the woman's second dying moments.

Father Larsen looked but he didn't find an araucaria.

At Three in the Morning

With the last kick, he was smashed into the grey cell wall. He hit his head and maybe had time, one second, to be grateful for passing out: unconsciousness, oblivion from the torments.

The soldier closed the door, held the machine gun upright in his left hand while with the other he looked for a handkerchief to dry his face. He was young and until they forbade it, he would sport a small mustache that refused to grow.

In the cell there was only a cot with a plank as a mattress, a bucket already reeking from old urine and excrement and, very high up, an oblong opening covered by bars.

Whenever he thought he woke up, night or morning, cold or sweating, he didn't know who he was. He settled into the personality that made him happy, that was happy and detached not only from any past but also from time.

He was the other, with an indifferent past and destiny, with vices, with pain, with memories and expectations. He was freed from life, freed from so many thousands of shitty men hell-bent on making life into filth and thorns. He was free and lucid, stripped of everything, like a newborn.

It was three in the morning, though he knew nothing of schedules. Three in the morning was the time when they bring to Headquarters the black truck full of prostitutes, of shouting, laughter, and cussing that crash into the low ceilings and tumble headlong without meaning or destiny, without wounding, without even brushing against anybody. Words so old they're dead, words on a short and slow flight. Nothing more than words, nothingness.

It was three in the morning and it was possible to feel and believe in the invisible presence of the other by his side, not moving and maybe with a memory of choking in a vat full of shit, of ineffable electric currents from his penis to his nose or vice versa, alternating or permanent. With no memory of the blows of the first beating, the forgotten caresses.

He understood without interest that at the Big House there was a plethora of monsters in human shape. But he wished to hold onto, with the fingernails he had left, the sputtering happiness and the nothingness that never had beginning or end. It was there. It didn't matter that the other one, by his side because of sadness, his lost half, would write an immortal poem erroneously attributed to Pavese, so far removed from his style and his concerns.

The Imposter

I was tired of waiting but the man arrived on time, and I watched him smile shyly at me as he told me his first name. He told me he was He and repeated in a whisper, as if sketching or sculpting the pile of circumstances that had kept us apart. I wanted to believe him, but he wasn't He. Twins, I had to think. But Jesús never had brothers, not my Jesús.

He kissed me affectionately and without coercion, and his arm around my back made me believe for a moment. I took a chance:

"How did things go in London?"

"Good; at least I think so. With something like that you can never be sure," he said, looking at me and smiling.

"More important," I said, "is to know if you remember the goodbye party. The epilogue, I mean."

He looked at me sardonically and said:

"Is that a question? As you know, and will find out again tonight, I couldn't forget. I remember your dirty and marvelous words. I could re-peat them, but . . ."

"God, no," I almost shouted, and my face turned bright red.

"I'm not that crude. It was a joke, an affectionate threat."

Looking at the two bottles, he smiled teasingly. One was red wine, the other white.

"At this time of day, and as usual, a glass of white."

That's what He preferred; He would have used the same words.

We drank and then we walked around the house. This He walked slowly, scarcely looking around, and stopped at the door to the bedroom.

He looked at the bed, smiled, placed an arm around my shoulder, pressed the nape of my neck, and as usual, I got hot and wet.

Between the sheets, seeing him naked, feeling what I felt, I knew that he wasn't He, wasn't Jesús. In bed, no man can deceive a woman. But after the panting and the cigarette, he said:

"Okay, let's go look at the Van Gogh. I still think it's a fake, that you made a bad buy for the gallery."

Jesús had said the same, the very same words, before his trip to London. And only He and I knew about the clandestine purchase of the Van Gogh.

Kisses

He had known and missed his mother's. He had kissed every woman he was introduced to on both cheeks or a hand; he had abided by the prostibulary tradition that prohibits the joining of lips; girlfriends, women, had kissed him with their tongues shoved down his throat and had lingered, wise and scrupulous, to kiss his member. Saliva, heat, and indiscretions, just as it should be.

Then, the surprising entrance of the woman, a stranger, passing through the circle of mourners, wife and children, tearfully sighing friends.

She approached, undaunted, the cheeky whore, to kiss his cold forehead over the edge of the coffin, leaving between the horizontality of the three wrinkles a small crimson smudge.

Her Hand

A few days after starting at the factory, she heard some coworkers whispering as she passed by them on her way to the bathroom, and out of the whispers she took the scornful: "The leper."

All because of her gloved hand, which for many years before the glove she had been able to hide behind her back or in her skirt or around the neck of her dancing partner.

She wasn't a leper, no finger had fallen off, and the intermittent itching quickly vanished with the prescribed ointment. But it was her sick hand, sometimes red, sometimes with white scales, it was her hand and she was already used to loving it and pampering it like a weak, crippled child, one who required a surfeit of affection.

Dermatitis, the doctor at the clinic had said. He was a calm man, wearing spectacles with very thick lenses.

"They'll tell you many things and prescribe strange names. But nobody knows enough about it to cure it. As far as I'm concerned, it's not contagious. I'd even say it's psychological."

And she thought that the old man was right because, though she wasn't a dwarf, her height didn't correspond to her age; and her face didn't quite reach ugly, stopping at the common, squat, round; eyes so small their faded color could not even be detected.

So, for the end-of-year dance that the factory owner held so the wage earners would forget briefly about their wages, she bought herself a pair of white gloves that hid her hand and went all the way up to her elbows.

But out of fear or lack of interest nobody invited her to dance, and she spent the night sitting and watching.

In the early hours of the morning, back home, she threw the gloves into a corner and got undressed, washed her sick hand again and again, and in bed, before turning off the light, she smiled at it and kissed it. And it's possible she whispered the tender words and affectionate nicknames she was thinking.

She settled in for sleep, and her hand, obedient and grateful, slid down her belly, caressed her mound, and then two fingers proceeded to shoo away the disgrace and accompany and elicit the joy they were giving her.

Back and Forth

He was alone in the waiting room and started to look through the newspaper he was carrying under his arm. His hands were trembling slightly. He took out a cigarette and, before lighting it, stroked the smooth mustache whose growth he'd been keeping a close eye on for weeks. He had never been able to tolerate tobacco smoke, and he coughed with tears; but he had to keep smoking like a man until the moment came to get up. He could not remember, in order to imitate it, the expression of a cynical man, a man who had reached a certain age and had returned.

There were three doors in front of him and he looked from one to the other as he felt his heart pounding. The middle door opened precisely when he was looking at it, and a large blond woman appeared: at ease, calm, and fat; an open robe hung from her shoulders and she smiled at him from a great distance, friendly and cheerful as if she might have recognized him.

"Come on in, my *negrito*," she said. He had brown hair.

He got up from the stool and walked forward without any sign of disgust, without the ability to respond to the lifted and motionless smile. The room had a large bed, covered with a crumpled sheet, and a chest of drawers on top of which was a large green pitcher with embossed leaves in a cracked basin. There was some perfume lost in the unforgettable smell of a kerosene heater.

The woman, now without her robe, smiling from the bed, began to look more and more enormous to him as he took off his clothes. He approached the heat of the flickering flame to finish getting undressed. Then the fat woman took charge with expert patience, maternal and kind.

Until he could, triumphantly, begin his journey back and forth through the invisible tunnel, moist and dark, back and forth until he managed to see the face of God for the first time in his life.

Once outside, he thought that what he had bought could not substitute for the word love either in his dreams or his intuitions. But he couldn't be wrong, it was in the cards that one day in the not-too-distant future his body and soul would fuse together in the blessed and anticipated truth.

Tu me dai la cosa me, io te do la cosa te

The brick walls of endless passageways and of a small and well-tended Jewish cemetery was the only Paris that the window's stingy view allowed them.

An apathetic sun around noon and then the cold, weak, blurry drizzle and the wind filling eyes with tears.

Norberto Coriani, the People's Canary, strummed his guitar on his narrow bed. Machine Gun Kid, a gratuitous nickname, was pacing back and forth, door to window, up and down the corridor formed by the other bed.

"So, are we leaving? Starving, repatriated in a hold the size of a nutshell."

"Who started it?" Norberto asked or said to his guitar, now pissed off at the E string, never satisfied with the hoarse vibration it repeated, it rectified, never wholly satisfied like all artists.

The Kid, too offended for a futile face-to-face encounter, kept moving while he repeated the worn-out arguments of the last few days.

"I was right and I was sure of it when I talked you into it. Gardel at the

L'Olympia, Arolas filling his coffers. I got you two concerts in El Garrón and you crapped out on me."

"My voice crapped out, brother. The cold, my nerves. You know, when I'm in top form, it's goodbye Gardel."

"If I were you I'd send him a letter of apology. Then I'd go to Notre Dame to pray for forgiveness."

"Bullshit, I tell you. I didn't crap out on you, my voice crapped out."

"Yeah, but I had to deal with everything because in the end, I'm the impresario. Was the impresario, I mean."

"Okay, cut it. We fucked up and it's over. The piles of francs, the chicks you dreamed of, or were you just playing me?"

"Gardel had all the chicks he wanted. Everyone's a whore here, and they know how to do it. But, of course: with Gardel. Not with just anyone. Not with a tone-deaf stutterer."

"I told you, cut it out. I'm not going to say it again."

Norberto put the guitar down on the bed and wrapped himself in the blanket as if it were a poncho.

"You got any smokes?"

The Kid stopped and offered him a Gauloise that was sticking out of the pack. They smoked for a while in silence, letting the smoke cushion the failure, the poverty, the implacable cruelty of Paris.

Then, from inside the cloud of smoke, the Kid started worrying again.

"I mean, it can't be. Two months and not a single woman. Now we can't even pay for it. I, who used to get them with a snap of my fingers."

"Forgive me," Norberto said, managing a smile. "That's true but it's different. You always were one to go for those women of the night. You were friends with Larsen. I, on the other hand, couldn't keep up with my fans."

The color of the window turned quickly from grey to black, and the Kid could see, somewhere unknown, the distant lights of streets or windows.

Now the guitar, invisible, as if embedded in the bed or the wall, repeated a sharp, insistent B, just barely metallic, that echoed as it hit the wood.

The Kid tolerated it in silence. Finally, he raised his voice:

"Two months in Paris and not a single chick. Can you imagine, to return without having fucked. Not even once."

The guitar continued insistently, not calling, stubborn and confident. There was not a single insolent word, and nobody feigned a glimmer of affection. The Kid flipped a silver-plated five-franc coin high into the air, which had enough strength to shine in the darkness and determine the sequence of the humiliating but victorious – the only – orgy in Paris.

Cursed Springtime

That morning, very early, Aránzuru opened the large window onto the scents of the garden, and a gentle and capricious breeze touched his face and tussled his hair.

As he shaved, half sick with exhaustion from having slept so little, he stopped to stare at himself in the mirror. His face was wrinkle-free but there was loose flesh under his chin; greying, badly cut hair on his temples; his dull eyes, where curiosity was dying; his still-red lips ending abruptly in bitter downturns. He found no trace of the alcohol from the night before.

He stood under the warm, then cold, shower, soaping himself with maniacal force.

Over the phone Helga had promised to come in the morning, come before noon and prepare lunch. He had seen her for the first time when she was sixteen years old and he was pushing forty. They'd been intermittent lovers for two years. Then they took her out of the country and now she'd returned, five years after saying goodbye.

He didn't know if Helga, who was now a grown woman, had called him in order to tell him that the parenthesis was closed. He didn't want to know why that voice had sounded recognizable though different from the one he remembers as happy, slow, confident.

During a downpour, after the groaning and semi-faints in bed, she insisted on making lunch and went into the kitchen wearing one of Aránzuru's old robes. He always cooked in the middle of the day and didn't eat anything at night.

Smoking in bed, he heard the sound of eggs frying and inhaled along with the cigarette smoke a faint scent of something burning. Then, abruptly, and without any definable motive, he began to have doubts. And these doubts stretched into the past as he felt the mild burns of the ashes on his chest hairs. His doubts moved backwards until they reached the preamble with Helga, all the way to the happiness and the faith of their first clandestine nights, when Helga told her family that she was going to spend the night with her best friend. They also covered an afterward, when she didn't have to get anybody's permission, and he, possibly exclusively, was the recipient of the lies. Until the doubts reached his legs — after slipping without response over his masculine trio, now withered, crumpled up in its request for respite — and forced him to leap naked out of bed and stick his head out the open window, to see and breathe in the spring and think of an anonymous verse, an imprecation: *Why have you returned, cursed spring.*

During the drab meal, Aránzuru looked at the sunlight and drizzle on the window and listened to her chew. Then he knew that he wasn't wrong. A quick lovemaking session on the edge of the bed, a series of repetitive and deliberate caresses on the forehead and chin. Then the gaze, the helpless eyes before the humid plea:

"I want to go to Ibiza, I have to go. And I don't have any money. Oh, my love, if only you could help me."

"Ibiza?" he asked, knowing he was cheating. "Ibiza. Let's go together."

"It's just that I . . . Truth is, I have a commitment."

Aránzuru got out of bed, so much wasted semen, and went to sit down at his desk.

Both of them naked, almost ridiculous. She started to get dressed.

"You always were a whore and I was crazy about you, because I'd never come across a whore quite so whorish. Tell me how much you want or your new stud wants. I'll write you the check."

Now the sky was clear, the sun intense, and outside, the plants again raised their flowering stalks.

Beachcomber

She must have been five or six when I first learned of her existence. Until then she was the first daughter of the Torres family, a child so beautiful that she seemed made by the hands of an artist, but not in the usual way. An irritating little thing who was learning to speak and listened to conversations without understanding them, eyes glued on the grownups' speaking faces.

Of course, my nocturnal visits to the Torres's, with drinks limited only by the protests of my liver and stomach, always or almost always reduced to literary topics, discussed almost without disagreement with Rodrigo's admirable intelligence and infallible poetic intuition and some visiting writer passing through with his partner, were repeated over the course of several years. Alicia knitted the hours, indefatigably, with multicolored yarns.

Soon the girl reached her first half-dozen years and a subtle and memorable change of atmosphere came about again and again at the break of dawn. Her name was Beatriz, they called her Bea, I called her — and still do – Beachcomber. Poorly dressed comber of beaches, resigned to a paltry daily harvest.

A change came about. Every once in a while Alicia would stop working to pronounce, head bent, a short and venomous phrase that fit gently and skillfully into the conversation and was often meant for me. Her smile was merely a distraction; it never accompanied the petty malevolence of her words.

As I was telling you, a ritual had been established. It was as if one night she had suddenly stopped wetting her bed, and we all looked at her in surprise, certain that the years had passed only for her, two or three, and she would intrude on our interminable conversations, perhaps the same one we had bored her with while she was fleetingly a babbling babe.

So, one night when I was the only guest who continued to talk about books and gossip, when I was left alone with her parents, she, Beachcomber, showed up in one of her mother's negligees, embroidered along the edges with violet-tinted marabou flowers, dragging it across the rug; she pretended to yawn and stretch, she walked around the table drinking all the forgotten dregs in our glasses. Then she approached, her mouth pouting and frowning, her eyes shining with laughter, and settled down in front of us on the large, now empty, sofa, and played with the decorations on the negligee. Her hair was long and blond. She smiled at us, at the angels, at the little devils, her friends. Every once in a while a futile question, a fake bit of curiosity uttered in a whining voice, which didn't require an answer.

And so on, night after night and every night I visited. She was too young for me to look at with any eyes other than those of a man with a daughter of almost the same age, who lives in another city and was taught to hate me. But no feeling of nostalgia prevented me from looking at my

Beachcomber and thinking sadly that by the time she was fifteen I would be irremediably old.

Later, without any visible warning, as these things tend to occur, Grace descended upon Alicia, and she had herself baptized and confessed and was filled with dread, and as if the girl were ill, decided to baptize her without a moment to lose.

Beachcomber had a millionaire uncle who lived on a yacht and at the time was sailing through Canadian waters. Catholic, only fitting for a wealthy Latino, he eagerly accepted the invitation to be her godfather and wired the date on which, by wind and engines, he could be in Montevideo.

But by then Bea's heart was mine, granted without my having asked for it. It was all she could give me; but she had already done so in silence and nothing had been remedied.

And nobody could change her veto of the golden godfather. Not sermons, not reasoning, not persistent repetitions. I would be her godfather or there would be no baptism. She couldn't have made a worse choice.

And then the morning arrived when I entered the church or chapel with my hangover, tolerated the priest's Latin, watched them anoint Bea's forehead with holy oil, place salt on her tongue, and I followed Rodrigo into the sacristy to pay for the fabrication of an angel. Bea, dressed up as an impossible bride; only the Lord could have her in his bed.

Out on the street I watched my eyeglasses cloud up; I was confounding my absent daughter with my only goddaughter. And I remembered that both would grow up and lose forever the paradise of childhood.

The Visit

I remember that the very tall woman was wearing a grey tailored suit and carrying a closed umbrella; on her head, a two-cornered hat, possibly rubber, in a reddish color.

She made no noise as she walked toward my bed. I was awake and hadn't yet begun my journey. In the other bed slept X. She leaned over slightly to kiss my forehead and whispered two words in an unknown language. She was smiling and her entire vulgar face was shining affectionately.

When she moved away from me and toward the door and the foot of X's bed, her head was a skull covered with strips of green, rotting flesh; one strip hung dangerously in the suffocating air of the room.

She pointed to X's sleeping eyes with her umbrella, which seemed to me to never have been opened, and smiled effortlessly, showing her lipless teeth.

Saint Joseph

He was a good carpenter and known to his friends as Joseph. When he went to the tavern on Friday nights, he drank only one glass of wine and never took part in malicious or bitter conversations, or the frenzied topics of Romans, consuls, or Caesars. He also never played darts.

He was so good that one day his friend Francisco asked him to accompany him into the deepest part of the forest, and there, with infinite patience and a permanently sweet smile in his eyes, he explained to him the soon-to-be easy secret of how to talk to animals. Joseph was grateful for the extraordinary gift, though he didn't understand how it could help him. He owned only one donkey and a few stray cats and dogs that visited him for food then disappeared again into the curves of the dry earth.

He exchanged few words with these beasts, guttural sounds that required no answer.

Joseph had married young, without wanting to, on the advice of his parents and rabbis. Her name was Miriam, and she had also been urged on by relatives and fanatics.

They lived in peace and were happy because her joy was her spinning wheel and Joseph's was to build and finish furniture. They worked together in the large nave on top of the same red and hardened dust; not even in the big bed blessed by the Lord did they have any desire for closeness. They ignored each other.

During the day he worked, at night he dined on the invariable red soup, listened to the summary or the exaggeration of the tiny secrets of the day recited in the sweet, frank voice of his wife, then he lay down so that sleep would cleanse him of fatigue.

While he sanded and polished, he frequently heard the reflections of the donkey, a donkey who worried about the following day, the meaning of the weeds, the movements of the sun, and the purpose of all things.

He listened to the braying, sometimes in rebuke, other times with an even temper. But he didn't answer. He pretended not to hear or understand all that nonsense and kept at his work. He exchanged greetings of joy and farewell only with the birds in the sky, always busier than he was.

One afternoon he heard the cooing of a pigeon and had to turn his eyes and head to find it. It was small, a damp and dirty grey.

"Listen to me," the bird stammered. "The Lord has ordered you to build a dovecote three meters high and at least two meters wide. And he demands that it be completed before sunrise."

"That can't be," Joseph said. "I'll have to work all night."

"You must," said the dirty pigeon and flew off. He turned to shout hoarsely: "Command from the Lord."

Joseph was left saddened and dutiful. He ate his blood-colored concoction and conveyed his sadness and resignation to his wife.

Unavoidable. He worked all night without any conversation other than the affectionate ones offered by the crickets and an old, skeptical, and scaly frog.

Dawn arrived and the enormous dovecote was built. Joseph dragged himself from his workshop to his house and slept exactly sixteen hours. He woke up at night, ate a couple of spoonfuls of cold soup, and went back to bed to find sleep.

"Did you do it?" she asked.

"Command from the Lord," he responded, and gave himself over to the stubbornness of his fatigue.

And one evening with a red and yellow sun, while he was hammering the soles onto a pair of pilgrim's sandals, he saw rise from his house, out of the hole that served as a window in his workshop, majestic and confident as it departed, barely flapping its wings, astonishing in its holiness and beauty, the silver dove of the Holy Spirit.

Text set in HTF Requiem
Italics set in Mercury Text G1 Italic
❧ Ornaments in Adobe Wood Type ❧